CADY FLETCHER

The Bone Riders

First published by Wildflower Coyote Publishing 2026

First edition

ISBN: 979-8-9936570-1-1

Editing by Christina Walker

This book was professionally typeset on Reedsy.
Find out more at reedsy.com

Contents

1

Chapter 1

Horses are big animals. They don't fit easily into suburban life like your average house pet, sleeping at the foot of your bed and chewing their toys on the living room rug. It takes a big space commitment to keep a horse. A standard stall is 12' x 12', and they need at least two acres of pasture per horse for grazing. Even with all that pasture you have to fence and maintain, you still need a place to exercise them too, to replicate the constant movement they would get in the wild, or they start chewing the fence.

They took up a lot of space dead too, I realized as I stood knee-deep in the hole I had dug in the back pasture of a local riding school. "What do you do with a dead horse?" is probably not something most people ponder. Fido and Fluffy get buried in the backyard or have their ashes preserved in little boxes on the mantle. Sending a faithful mount to his final resting place was not quite so simple. I'd done a lot of research into the morbid subject over the last few months. All my best Nancy Drew skills had informed me that Hillside Riding School had a few old school horses buried on the property.

I hoped that was true, because I really needed to dig one of them up.

The hole that had been dug to bury this horse would have been made with an excavator. As renting large equipment was not conducive to stealth, I was armed with only my trusty shovel, and I was beginning to comprehend the ludicrousness of what I was trying to do. It wasn't that I didn't have the stick-with-it-ness to dig up the entire horse. It was that I had to finish my weird animal grave robbing before it got light outside and someone saw me, and I could already tell I wasn't digging fast enough.

The moon was only half-full, but the flatness of the pasture made every tree and fence post stand out against the stark landscape. Some of the horses left turned out overnight had gathered to watch me exhume their dearly departed friend but had gone back to twitching their tails sleepily when I didn't prove entertaining.

"You have an exceptional ability for choosing the hardest possible way to approach any task."

I narrowly avoided hitting my own foot with the shovel when I jumped. I had been worried someone would see me silhouetted against the flat terrain, but I hadn't seen another human shape approaching over that same ground. The figure solidified out of the shadows into a woman with dark red hair and a cloak worn incongruously over one of those mock neck shirts made out of hi-tech athletic fabric.

"Hi, Fiona," I said, trying to play off as though I wasn't embarrassed at having been startled. How did she know I was out here? "Is there any chance you've come to help me dig?"

"None," she replied succinctly. She began to walk a slow circle around the hole I was digging. When she finished, her disapproval was clear. "What exactly is your plan, Andrea?"

I liked Fiona, but her presence always had a way of making me feel like I was about fourteen and trying to explain myself to a teacher instead of a twenty-six-year-old woman with a job and an apartment and permission to set my own bedtime. She just radiated maturity and competence, like car mechanics would never try to lie to her about the state of her brake pads and police officers would apologize for pulling her over. It didn't help that I could never tell what she thought of me. She was perfectly civil to me, but she never really warmed up to me either. I don't think she *disliked* me; she was just old enough to have seen a lot of people come and go, and she waited to see if they were going to last before she bothered liking them.

"The plan is to dig up this horse, take the bones, and fill the hole back in before anyone comes out here to catch me." I renewed my digging with confident gusto she probably wasn't going to fall for. "It would be a more successful plan if I had some help," I suggested when she didn't say anything. Nothing ventured, nothing gained. Maybe she'd take pity.

"The flawed logistics of that aside, are you certain you are digging over a skeletonized horse?" she asked. The live horses had started to gather around her like iron filings aligning to a magnet.

I leaned on the shovel for a moment to catch my breath. "Yes, I know they buried some of their school horses out here, and this is a grave-sized depression in the ground."

"You don't know which horse this is or how long it's been buried."

I started digging again. "It doesn't matter. I'll take whatever it is. I don't know how else I'm going to find a horse."

She held out her hands to the horses that now fanned out around her. Even in the dim light she looked like some sort of Renaissance painting of a pagan goddess taming wild horse spirits, and something indecipherable hinted to the part of the brain responsible for knowing brightly-colored insects had a poisonous bite that she was a lot older than the forty-odd years she looked. "You could go to the fields where the mustang herds graze and find a skeleton there. You could try an animal rendering facility. You could ask someone whose horse has recently died if you could purchase the body." She pondered that a moment. "That is the best way, as you have the most control over what you get."

"I can't imagine how awkward that conversation would be. 'Hey, I know your beloved horse just died, but can I buy his dead body from you?' Where would I even find them to ask? And I can't afford to go all the way to Nevada or wherever and find a skeleton."

"You could ask a vet to tell you when someone is euthanizing their horse," Fiona suggested. "People are often shocked at the cost of disposing of dead livestock and would be happy to be paid instead of paying."

"That's true," I admitted grudgingly. "But what would I do with the body?"

Her tone was practical. "Remove the meat and clean the bones."

I gagged, mostly to let her know my opinion of that. I could be pretty clinical about some things, but defleshing a horse skeleton was beyond me, even if Fiona had a point. But it wasn't really the ick factor or the money that was limiting my options. I also just didn't want anyone to know what I was doing. Wanting a horse skeleton was weird. Every part of me wanted to limit the knowledge of how weird my life had become to just me, as if that would contain it to a level my mind could deal with. Talking to vets and horse owners and rendering facilities meant drawing the attention of other people to the weird, which might force me to acknowledge the weird was real and here to stay.

Fiona studied me as if she knew what I was thinking. She'd known a lot of new Riders, so maybe she did. "Perhaps you should wait a while longer before trying to make your own horse."

Not a chance. "I don't want to be stuck riding Charon forever. If I'm going to do this, I don't want to be confined to the kiddie pool." As far as I was concerned, the horses were the only good part of being a Rider, and being saddled with the work but not the perk of my own horse chafed.

Fiona's disapproval intensified. She might have been about to speak, but she turned her head to look at something in the distance, and I looked too. There was a pinpoint of light outside the barn, a flashlight by the way it bobbed. I cast a wider glance around at the surrounding pastures. Not only were all the horse in this one gathered around Fiona like she was a new salt lick, every other horse was standing at the fence line of their own pasture as close as they could get to her. For all I knew, the horses in the barn were all staring in this direction too. Now someone was coming to check out what all the horses were focused on.

"We should leave," Fiona said crisply, then strode away to do just that.

Pointing out that the ruination of my master plan was her fault seemed imprudent and unhelpful in this situation, so I did as she suggested and hightailed it for the fence close to the treeline. I kept moving as quickly as I could, wincing at the noise I was making. Slow down and be quieter? No, I decided. It wouldn't matter if someone heard me as long as I was gone before they reached me. They probably thought the horses were looking at a coyote or something and wouldn't be trying to chase it down. I reached my elderly truck where I'd left it parked off a back road without incident and hauled off so fast I almost slid into the drainage ditch. I really needed to get new tires.

* * *

"Magic has always been a part of our world," the green-haired woman on the TV screen explained, her sincerity almost palpable. The banner beneath her earnest image identified her as Alice "Moonstone" Phillips, member of a local coven. "But now its presence is growing stronger. Something is changing, and we all need to be ready for it."

I kept one hand on the coffee maker as I loitered in the office break room to watch the little TV in the corner, hoping I would look busy to anyone walking by. Opposite Alice on the screen, the reporter made a stark contrast with her expertly made-up features schooled into an expression of interest so deep it was almost mocking. I wasn't sure which woman to think was pitifully naive.

"The ghosts have been more active lately," Alice continued unabashedly. "Wildlife has been gathering in certain places and avoiding others. Plants grow overnight only to wither the next day. Something is about to happen. It's time the world woke up to the truth." She looked into the camera on the last sentence as though beseeching the audience to heed her warning.

The clicking of high heels alerted me to someone approaching, but it was only Kara, who was probably avoiding work herself and wouldn't snitch. She spared a glance at the TV before starting to pick through the off-brand coffee pods for something decent. "They always pick the wackiest people possible to interview when they pretend to investigate this stuff. It's like the interviewee doesn't realize they got picked to be made fun of, not because someone is taking them seriously."

We both looked at the screen, where the coiffed reporter and her office counterpart were now discussing the strange happenings local citizens had reported lately with a gravitas that would have befitted a war report. Kara was probably right about why they'd picked Alice "Moonstone" Phillips with her green hair, but I didn't think the warning would have been taken any more seriously had it been delivered by a professor in a suit and wire-rimmed glasses who could back it up with facts and charts. People wouldn't believe anything mystical was at risk of affecting their daily lives if you shoved it in their faces.

"There are a lot of weird things going on lately," I said, leaning back against the counter. "Maybe it's weather patterns or bad ground water."

"Maybe, but I think it's just that phenomenon where everyone is talking about the same thing at the same time so it seems like there's more to it than there is," Kara decided. "Like shark attacks."

"Maybe," I agreed.

I wasn't about to tell her that magic existed and that Alice was right that it had always been there. I kept the normal and the crazy parts of my life separate like I was living a double life. I was confident it wouldn't have mattered anyway. People like Alice had been saying things like what Alice had been saying since always, and it didn't matter any more now than it usually did. Sometimes the observant noticed strange things, but it was the nature of humankind to resist drastic changes to their worldview.

"So, do you want to go out tonight?" Kara asked hopefully.

I took the cup of coffee I'd half-forgotten about out of the coffee maker and started adding sugar. "I can't tonight."

Kara arched one perfectly-plucked eyebrow at me. "Yeah, because you have plans? You never have plans."

"Next week?" I suggested. Kara was about the only thing I liked at my current job, a little bright spot in a cerulean blazer and matching heels against a field of gray cubicle walls. I tried not to turn her down too much, though she was right that I didn't exactly have a hopping social life. My friend circle during vet school had dwindled down to fellow students who had their noses to the same grindstone as mine, and they had all drifted awkwardly away.

"I'm holding you to it, Drew. No wiggling out of it this time. Not Friday, though. I have a hair appointment," she added, leaning to examine her hair critically in the cheap mirror someone had stuck to the fridge and smoothing imaginary flyaways.

There was a grunt from the break room door, and we turned to see Glen Tanner, paper-shuffler and micromanager extraordinaire, eyeing us suspiciously. If Kara was my favorite person at Stevens and

McKinley, Tanner was my least. Unfortunately, he was also my boss. "Ladies. The work isn't going to do itself."

"Just getting coffee," I said like the little gray rock I pretended to be at work. He'd probably been counting the seconds since I'd left my desk. God forbid I wasn't wiggling the mouse constantly.

Tanner grunted again and left.

"Ass," Kara whispered. "I guess we'd better go sit at our desks and pretend we have something to do so management can feel like they have a reason for existing."

"I guess so." I had never expected to be working in corporate America, and the vagaries of office dynamics were still inscrutable to me.

Before I left, I glanced at the TV again, where the reporters had moved on to the weather forecast, the mysterious events of the city left behind and probably already out of the minds of the local populace. At least I wouldn't have rain while I worked tonight.

2

Chapter 2

As the newest and greenest member of the Bone Riders, I got the crap jobs no one else wanted, usually accompanied by my temporary loaner steed, Charon. I do not know who thought it was the peak of humor to name a Welsh pony "Charon," but I hope their coffee is always cold. In the usual way of ponies who are so cute and fluffy no one has the nerve to discipline them, Charon was a terror on pint-sized hooves. Tonight he and I were on roadkill duty.

Death and what happens after we meet its cold embrace have been one of life's most-discussed mysteries since, well, always. Religion, psychics, scientists, and philosophers have tried to understand and explain it, but the truth is, we can't really know the truth because the dead don't come back to tell us. I got an unexpected peek behind that curtain when I died last winter.

I don't remember much about the car crash, which the doctors say is normal. I do remember standing in the road after it happened, staring nonplussed at my own body still in the passenger seat of the car, watching Cole shake me by the shoulder (which is not something you should do to someone who's been in an accident, by the way).

There had been a faint line of golden light between the me standing in the road and the me still in the car, flexible but intangible.

I was studying the car lights and crushed metal and broken glass with all the indifference of a TV show on mute when a sort of darkness opened behind me. I had turned to look at it, a void dark like a storm cloud about to spit out a tornado, drawing something toward it with the persuasive power of a riptide. What little of me was left had decided the "something" it was trying to draw was *me*, and that had frightened enough emotion out of me to make me mentally grab that golden line and jump right back into my body again.

That was the end of my memory of the accident because my body was in no shape to be conscious. I woke up later in the hospital and assumed what I had experienced was just a typical Near Death Experience. People always talk about a light or a tunnel or out-of-body-experiences. I didn't think much about it beyond that. I didn't even tell anyone; my family was already upset about the crash, emphasizing that I might have been a bit dead for a minute there would just distress them more.

It wasn't until I was woken the first night back in my own apartment by a bunch of strangers who had let themselves in without knocking that I learned my experience hadn't been quite so typical.

Death doesn't always happen as it should. Most of the time, people (and animals) die and go on to wherever the dead go without trouble. But sometimes a little bit of that life gets stuck on its way out. That was where the Riders stepped in to help, freeing that spark of life trapped to a dead body. Things were not supposed to be able to snap themselves back into their bodies and continue living. It was at this point in the explanation that I concluded they were there to kill me because I wasn't supposed to be alive, and I had opened my mouth to scream for help.

Some bruises and one bitten hand later, Fiona had informed me from where I was smooshed into the carpet with August and Kevin pinning me down that no one was going to kill me. The fact that I had the power to pull myself back into my body meant I had the same power over death as they did, and they would like me to join them. When I issued a decline to Fiona's shoes, all I could see of her from the floor, she told me that was all right, but they would be watching me anyway in case I accidentally revived something else. I was welcome to come talk to them after I'd had some time to think about it.

I immediately decided to go the ostrich route for this problem because I didn't want to be involved with loonies who thought they had power over death. But then I started getting paranoid about people watching me. And I also started noticing things dying.

The first time I saw an opossum on the side of the road connected to another opossum by the same golden thread that had connected me to myself after the car wreck, I had braked so hard I'd left rubber. The ghostly opossum wouldn't do anything but stare blankly at me, and I'd sat on the side of the road weeping until a pair of hooves like marble appeared in front of me. I'd looked up at the horse with a coat of dark velvet and a mane that rippled with silver.

"You've got to stop doing that before someone sees you and thinks you're crazy," Luis told me gently.

I'd let him talk to me for a while, then agreed to go to a meeting with the others. At least if you have to be crazy, it's better to not be crazy alone. I was pretty half-hearted about this whole "magic" thing; it was the horses that drew me in.

So now I was honing my death-rectifying on roadkill duty, assisting with the departure of the animals run over on our county's roadways. Unlike me, the little opossums and squirrels didn't have the ability to snap back into their own bodies, and they needed help to be on their way to the great hereafter. The first time August had taken me out to do this, I'd thrown up and threatened to go home. I don't like dead things, and I like run-over, rotting dead things even less. I still thought it was disgusting, but I was coping.

I saw the sad body of a raccoon on the shoulder, a shimmering, gray facsimile of itself sitting next to it, watching me. The two raccoons were connected by a familiar golden thread. The life left attached to the body wasn't a soul or consciousness; it didn't contain any personality or emotion. It was just the energy that had powered the body, a little spark of life that needed to be returned to the ecosystem of the universe instead of tethered to a dead thing.

"Hey," I said softly to the raccoon, pulling Charon up next to it.

The raccoon looked at me curiously. They sometimes seemed able to hear me, which was unnerving. I had been crushed by the thought of the little animals trapped with their bodies, suffering and afraid, but August insisted they didn't feel anything. I was suspicious he had made that up to comfort me, but they really didn't seem to have much reaction to being dead. What would happen if I put the life back into the body and then treated the critter's injuries? I had asked Fiona when I'd first started.

"An abomination," she'd replied with her usual disinterest in explanation.

That was hardly ever an option with roadkill since their bodies were no longer inhabitable, and I wasn't sure I could do it anyway. I didn't know how I'd done it to myself. I knelt next to the mirage-raccoon and used my knife to cut through the tether. The gray image of the raccoon disappeared, leaving only the battered remains of decaying flesh behind. I wrinkled my nose at the smell.

Charon heard the hoof beats on the pavement before I did, his fluffy ears pointed toward the muffled sound. A tall horse materialized out of the darkness, his coat an unnaturally shiny dark red and strands of metallic silver streaking through his mane and tail. August had crafted him from one of those vinyl wraps used on fancy cars, butter-soft leather, liquid chrome, and a rubber tire, which accounted for the quietness of his hooves. It was the most car-geek concoction of ingredients imaginable, but there was no denying the results. Spyder was a gorgeous creature, and I was sure my complexion turned faintly green every time I saw him.

August had a lazy way of riding, the reins in one hand and the other arm swinging free, the horse's movement rolling up through his back without resistance. He was actually a good rider when the situation called for it, but his equitation would make any instructor gnash their teeth. August drew Spyder up next to Charon, and we eyed each other for a moment. He was probably my age, though perhaps not of my generation, and he wore his Nordic-blond hair pulled back in a messy half-ponytail.

"Hey, Drew," he said conversationally.

"Hey."

August reminded me of the terminally laid-back frat guys I'd met during my undergrad, the kind that bummed their way through life with the situational awareness of a goldfish and a pure-hearted confidence that everything would turn out okay somehow, but he'd grown on me over the last few months. He was a little vacant sometimes, but he never seemed annoyed when I got frustrated trying to come to terms with the dead stuff. I thought Fiona might have paired him with me because he was the definition of unflappable.

"Do you need help?"

I shook my head. "There's only two more over that way."

I started off leading Charon down the two-lane road, and August rode next to me.

"Why are you walking?"

"No point in getting on and off again." I wasn't too heavy to ride Charon so I wasn't in danger of hurting him, but I was too tall, and I looked a little foolish on his back. The magic he carried helped shield me from people who might want to know why I was poking roadkill, so I had to have him with me. Fortunately, Charon was savvy to the fact that the faster we finished, the faster he got to return to the barn, so he was being cooperative tonight. Somewhat less fortunately, he was trying to encourage haste by pushing me with his head when I moved too slowly.

"Fiona told me you're hoping to get your own horse soon," August said as he followed. "That's a big step."

I shot Spyder another envious look. "Yes, I think it's time." No point in complaining that Fiona had ruined my most recent attempt. No, screw that. I was complaining. "Did she also tell you that she sabotaged my attempt to get a skeleton? She showed up while I was digging, and all the horses started staring at her until someone came out to check. She did it on purpose."

August wasn't about to get involved in that. "I'm sure she didn't mean anything by it." He pointed. "There's one."

I spent a moment miming petting the squirrel's tiny head even though it wasn't really tangible enough to touch, not caring that August was watching me with interest, then separated it from its ruined body.

"You don't have to pet them," he said. "They don't know."

"Maybe the petting is for me." There had been a time when I'd intended to spend my life making animals well, not interacting with their dead bodies.

Headlights rounded the corner of the county road, and we both stepped off into the razed cornfield next to it, squinting at the sudden brightness. The car passed by without seeing us, and I waited for my night vision to return before I moved on.

"Were you working tonight?" I asked him, wondering why he'd chosen to join me.

"Yes. I got done and came to check on you." He looked uncharacteristically troubled for someone who would probably finish his beer before going to the hospital to get a finger reattached after a fireworks accident.

I felt a little bad at that. I hated roadkill duty, but at least no one asked me to take care of people who had gotten stuck. It took me a while to learn not to cry over the opossums; what if the tethered life were a child's? Maybe he'd had a rough night tonight. He was never a talkative guy, so it was hard to tell if something was wrong or if he'd just slipped into a zen state.

I wasn't going to say anything else, but he spoke again. "How many have you had tonight?"

I thought. "Six."

"How many animals have you passed that were just regular dead?"

"I don't know. Two or three?"

"So more not-right deaths than right deaths?"

"Oh," I said. "Is that not normal?" I had mostly been thinking about how sad it was that man's progress had impinged upon the habitats of the wildlife until so many of them were struck by cars.

He shrugged. "Could be a whole lot of nothing. Let's get the last one."

The last one turned out to be a deer, and I felt unexpectedly sad. Every time I thought I'd gotten used to this, there was something new. I knelt next to the gray shimmer that was lying with its legs tucked beneath it and reached to stroke its head.

A very real and solid hoof kicked feebly by my knee, and I flung myself backward onto the gravel shoulder with a squeal. The allegedly dead deer half-opened one brown eye.

"August! It's not dead."

He scrunched his nose. "Cut it loose, and it will be."

"But then I'll be killing it," I protested.

"It isn't going to live anyway. It's almost dead now. Set it free."

"But then *I'll* be killing it," I repeated more aggressively.

August eyed the deer with clinical interest, its plight not tugging at any emotion inside him. "How is this different from what you usually do?"

"The difference is this deer isn't dead, and you're asking me to kill it!" That was certainly what was going to happen if I cut its tether. The other animals were already dead when I cut theirs.

August swung down from Spyder's back. "It's okay. I'll do it. Turn around." He wasn't annoyed that he had to do it for me, but his expression said he sure didn't understand why I had such a problem with it. When you're about as deep as a reflecting pond, not much troubles you.

Maybe I was just supposed to buck up and say I'd do it myself, but I didn't. I put my face in Charon's mane and let August kill the deer for me.

* * *

The Riders aren't so organized that we have regularly-scheduled meetings, so the short notice of Bennett's request for us to gather Friday night meant something unusual was up. Then again, Bennett was a pedantic over-planner who would have gotten along well with Tanner, so it might be nothing.

I dashed through the drive-thru of a burger joint when I left work and was still scarfing fries when I reached Bennett's house. The driveway was already full of cars, and I speculated on what his neighbors in this prim neighborhood thought he was doing when he had people over—Dungeons and Dragons? Bible study group? I parked on the street and let myself in the side door without knocking.

The Riders had no official leader and were technically a democracy, but more practically, someone had to make the decisions, and the more experienced Riders usually handled monitoring what needed watching and divvying up the workload. Bennett was retired and had a large house with space for meetings, and he had appointed himself our unofficial logistics manager. Fiona was the most experienced of the Riders by far, but she seemed to have no desire to take the helm. Some people seek the crown, others have it thrust upon them, and the rare few take the offered crown and hand it right back to go on with their lives. I don't think it was a lack of devotion; she was more of a zealot about being a Rider than anyone else. She just wasn't interested in managing the rest of us.

Valerie made room on the shorter couch for me, and I plopped down next to her. Valerie was twenty and looked about sixteen, with a bleach-blonde bob and baby blue eyes. She was petite and pretty, and the viewer could be easily fooled into thinking she was a vapid cheerleader in a Lilly Pulitzer miniskirt. She actually played field hockey, and I'm pretty sure if you pitted her against a bodybuilder, the bodybuilder would leave crying. She was mean.

"Ah, Drew. Welcome," Bennett said, settling into an armchair that would have been at home in an Edwardian mansion. Part of me always thought he leaned so hard into the "esteemed professor" persona with his neatly-cut graying hair and tweed jackets that it couldn't quite be real. The den with its shelves of leather-bound books and green patterned wallpaper could have been a movie set background for his erudite persona.

I glanced around, nodding hellos. Almost everyone looked like they'd come straight from work and was eager to be home. There were nine of us that lived here in the city, not including Della and Sean Cantrell, who lived a few hours north and mostly worked with each other. Helen was squeezed between Trish and Luis on the overstuffed couch, while Kevin claimed the remaining armchair. True to habit, August had eschewed a chair in favor of slumping on the marble fireplace. Fiona leaned against the wall at the back of the room where she could see everyone. I was sure I could feel her gaze on the back of my head.

"I have rush planning at my sorority," Valerie said pointedly.

"We'll be quick," Bennett assured her graciously. "I think this is important though." He settled back so he could gaze at everyone over his spectacles. "From reports we've received from all of you and some observations in general, we're noticing an uptick in incomplete deaths."

There was a murmur and an exchange of glances.

"As for what could be causing it, it could just be that the rift is experiencing a surge of some sort. It has happened before, though it is rare."

The rifts were what we called the anomalies in the world's fabric that the Riders believed caused the failure of some lives to pass on after the death of their bodies. There were theories that these rifts were openings to death itself or to the afterlife, which was why death had the occasional hiccup around them, but other sorts of magic tended to flourish around rifts too, which made that theory questionable. The exact location of the rifts was uncertain, but there was one in the nebulous location of Asterville. Whatever they were, Riders were drawn to them. Or perhaps made by them. The memory of the drawing darkness the night of the car crash made me shiver involuntarily, and Valerie side-eyed me.

"For now, we will be hypervigilant in our work, which means extra hours," Bennett continued. "Luis and I have started a compilation of locations and numbers to chart this potential surge, and we've reached out to contacts around the world to see if anyone else is experiencing this as well."

"So what happened the last time a rift had a surge?" Kevin wanted to know. Kevin was in his early thirties and had been a Rider for a few years, so he had far more practical experience than relative novices like me and Valerie, but more complex, nuanced things were still new to him too.

Bennett shrugged. "Surges seem to eventually subside on their own accord. We have never really understood the rift or what it is. We just seem to be the select few that can sense it and what happens around it."

I'd always found that odd, personally, that the legacy of the Riders extended so far back into history but no one had ever managed to crack the mystery of the rifts. But maybe it was a case of over-familiarity. Humanity had been interacting, however inadvertently, with the rifts for their entire history too. They were responsible for magical powers that ended in witch hunts and strange artifacts that engendered plagues that devastated villages only to disappear again without a trace. They were just an odd and random danger of the world we lived in, like a sun flare or a cave filled with poisonous gas. We didn't particularly need to understand them to continue living with them. And truthfully, they weren't that strong or that easy to find. Most people just didn't have the ability to see magic or its effects; of all the people in Asterville and its surroundings, there were less than a dozen in this room who had any idea of the rifts' existence.

Still, the science major in me wanted to see that data Bennett was collecting.

"Do the other strange things happening in the news have anything to do with the rift surge too?" I asked, thinking of Alice "Moonstone."

Bennett shrugged like he was going to politely discount this theory, but Fiona cut in with a terse, "Yes."

I, and everyone else, craned my neck to look back at her. She was still leaning against the wall, her arms crossed over her chest.

"I don't believe any of the local 'coven' are actual magic users," Bennett said, ever polite.

"But they are still observant," Fiona replied. "Even if they don't know what is happening, they know to look for signs. Fake magic imitates the real magic it is a shadow of."

Fiona knew a lot about magic, but I was privy to none of her secrets. The fact that I had slingshot myself back into my body after dying and that I could see the golden thread connecting life to a body meant I could likely use magic of other sorts too, but no one had trained me yet, and I hadn't shown any inclinations independently. I hadn't really pushed for instruction on the subject because, frankly, I was still getting used to comprehending the very possibility of magic. Harry Potter would have been waving a wand by now, but the disruption of my worldview was a little more tough to chew as an adult.

"Quite possible," Bennett agreed. "But even if the rift is responsible for any odd happenings in the area, it won't change the things the Riders need to do. If everyone could fill out their availability for the next week on the sheet, I'll make the schedule and email it out."

Fiona didn't argue with him, but she didn't need to. She wasn't the kind to bother making her point more than once; you listened, or you didn't. I could tell by the way she frowned that Bennett was wrong about something, and I wondered what it was.

3

Chapter 3

Saturday found me snoozing late into the morning as I tried to catch up on the sleep I'd sacrificed for my recent nighttime escapades. I woke up to a voicemail from my mom complaining that I was ignoring her and reminding me that I was supposed to have dinner at my parents' house Sunday night. My relationship with my parents had soured after I'd put vet school on hold. They thought it was because of my Near Death Experience, but that oddly didn't make them any more sympathetic. There wasn't exactly any way I could tell them the whole magic thing had made it difficult to continue.

I also had a text from Cole asking if he'd left his earbuds at my place. We both knew he hadn't, so he was just making up excuses to talk to me. He had broken up with me after the car crash because he couldn't get over his guilt about it, and he'd thought not having to see or think about me anymore would fix that. I hadn't been angry with him about the crash, but I was certainly angry about the breakup. And because 'out of sight, out of mind' didn't actually do anything for the guilt he felt like he thought it would, he still found excuses to talk to me that were actually attempts to check on me.

I texted my mom that I would be there Sunday, mostly because the contents of my fridge were looking a little lackluster, and I told Cole that I'd thrown his nonexistent earbuds in the trash weeks ago. Problems successfully avoided for the time being, I left for my usual Saturday activity.

I didn't care much about the magic of being a Bone Rider, but the gig came with a massive perk I couldn't resist: Fiona's barn.

I grew up riding horses and was your stereotypical "horse girl" straight into high school. I probably drained my parents' bank accounts dry with all those riding lessons, equipment costs, and out-of-town competitions in exchange for a banner of ribbons over my bedroom mirror. I couldn't afford to do the whole horse thing as an adult, but the itch never really went away. Getting a horse of my own again had become important enough I'd tried to dig up a dead one. Fiona was a horse trainer, and most of the Rider horses lived on her property where she had a stable set-up that would rival a professional show barn and acres of pasture for them. I had taken to spending most of my weekends there, pretending I was trading stall-cleaning for saddle-time. It might have been Fiona's way of bribing me into liking Rider life, but I was one of the few Riders who was a horse enthusiast pre-magic, so she might have just appreciated having someone around who shared her interest in them.

Most of the horses were turned out to graze, but a few heads popped over the stall doors when I walked in, and I did the reception line of petting noses and rubbing ears. The creation of their horses was what first drew the Bone Riders together as a group, uniting a few people who had some capacity for magic and a desire to do something about some of the strange things they saw. They had made the first horses from the bones of real horses mixed with other arcane elements in a spelled cauldron the size of a hot tub. The horses that stepped out were creatures of magic and dreams and terror. The power of the horses and the shared purpose were credited with the longevity and cohesion of the Riders while other groups formed covens, sects, and societies that lasted only a generation. I think the fact that the horses were just so damn cool was probably the biggest factor.

The cauldron currently lived in Fiona's garden buried beneath a cover that was masquerading as a deck covered in potted plants. The horses created in modern times were still made from horse skeletons, now mixed with items influenced by the Rider's personality and taste, like August throwing in car vinyl and tires when he made Spyder. It was a big deal what you selected because it influenced both the horse's appearance and personality. Whoever had decided to create a horse out of a Welsh pony's bones when they made Charon had used baby blue felt and boucle yarn in a variety of pastels. I'm sure that contributed to his horrible temperament, achieving consciousness to find himself ridiculous. Valerie's Arabian looked like a mermaid horse, with a softly shimmering golden coat flecked in places with pink and green sequins like scales and delicate hooves that looked like they'd been dipped in glitter. I think she'd bought thousands of tiny bottles of Sicilian Sunset Shimmer nail polish and drained them into gallon jugs to pour into the cauldron, which was the sort of single-minded determination I expected from her. I'd been hoarding things for my own horse since I'd first learned about them.

"Andrea."

Fiona stood at the other end of the barn, wearing jodhpurs, paddock boots, and the content expression she wore here in the center of her meticulously cultivated universe. I imagined that if the world had changed so much around me from the time I was born, I would have a hard time dealing with it, but I never got the impression Fiona struggled to keep up with modern times until I saw her here. Even then, it was less like the world was moving too fast for her and more like she'd learned to be fluent in a second language but wished for the ease of speaking in her native tongue again.

"Help me finish up in the barn," she told me, "and you can take Kai out for some exercise."

Some horse owners think of "barn chores" as the necessary dues to pay for getting to ride, but I enjoyed most of them. The work had a soothing, satisfying quality to it I didn't get from my office job. We had the horses turned out, the stalls cleaned, and the feed bins refilled in less than an hour, working in companionable quiet. We got along well in situations like this. I hosed out buckets, and Fiona swept the center aisle. When we'd finished, I saddled Kai, Trish's sea glass-colored Paint, and took him out to the dirt-floored arena.

The Riders' horses may have looked like fantasy creatures, but they mostly acted like real horses. I had been told they generally looked like regular horses to the average person who was expecting to see a horse, such as if someone were driving by and spotted them in the pasture. In places where they weren't expected or didn't want to be seen, they weren't exactly invisible, just unnoticed. I wanted to know if the strength of that magic was up to taking the horses out for competitions, but my idea had been rudely nixed. Kai wasn't much for jumping, so I practiced lead changes and half-pirouettes for a while before taking him back to the barn.

Fiona was sitting on the cut log she used for a mounting block when I came back out, waiting for me, a frosty bottle of Coke in one hand. The glass bottle seemed like her. She had brought one for me too, and I took a seat on an overturned bucket and held the bottle still while she popped the top off with a bottle opener. We sipped companionably for a bit, enjoying the peaceful green of the pastures and the satisfaction that comes with being slightly tired from useful work.

"You were right to question if the other strange events being reported are related to the uptick in incomplete deaths," she said at last. "The rifts are the source of all magics. If there is a surge, it will affect all things that possess magic."

"Why does Bennett think otherwise?" I asked. Fiona had been around a long time and knew a lot about magic. What I really wanted to ask was why he didn't believe her opinion on something she was better informed about.

"Bennett is a scholar by training." Her tone implied no criticism, just a statement of fact. "It is in his nature to specialize deeply rather than widely. He narrows the focus of his study to the skill we all have in common, not the breadth of what is possible."

"Most of us can't do any other kind of magic," I said. "I can't."

"You haven't tried yet."

"I don't think I could even do the death thing until I resuscitated myself." I realized with some irritation that she had lured me into a discussion about using my magic through camaraderie and sugary soda. I was about to pay the piper for the riding with a lecture. "I think it was the exposure to the rift when it happened that gave me that ability, so maybe that's all I've got."

"You did that because you were scared," Fiona replied. "And your current disassociated state removed any inhibitions you may have had about knowing why it shouldn't work. A capacity for logic or uncertainty at that moment would have stopped you. Your magic woke up because that was the first time you really needed it."

I only half-believed her, but I didn't argue because I wasn't brave enough to argue with Fiona. I did believe that my temporary death had brought about the abilities, but I still thought that was the moment I'd received the abilities, not just activated them. I was pretty sure I'd dipped into the rift, or at least stared into its face for a moment. The exposure had brought something back with me.

"Most of the others don't have any other kind of magic either," I pointed out. It was mostly the older Riders who had other magical talents, not the younger crowd like me, August, and Valerie. "Maybe not all of us do."

"Most of our current members ended up with the Riders instead of some coven either because death was the first magic for which they showed an affinity, or because the Riders were the first people to recognize their potential and invite them," she replied. "There aren't many legitimate magic groups here anymore. The Riders have mostly taken up that spot in our local ecosystem. And most of our members have chosen to be content with Rider magic, where they feel comfortable. Which is what you've done," she added.

I ground the toe of my boot into the dirt instead of looking at her. Fiona didn't usually chat with me about idle subjects, with the notable exception of horses, so she must have a specific point to this conversation. Knowing her, she was probably going to wait for me to figure it out on my own. "What *should* I do then?"

"The original Bone Riders weren't founded to be just grim reapers on horses," she said, not answering my question. "We've just become specialized over the years as we did a job no one else was doing and we recruited everyone who seemed to have suitable abilities. There became so many magical groups that we all settled into our respective niches." She turned her cobalt blue gaze on me, and all the heat left my body. "Magic doesn't work that way, Andrea. There's no reason you can't learn to do more if you want to."

I didn't want to, but I didn't bother saying so. Fiona seemed finished with her cryptic lesson of the day though. She stood, took my Coke bottle (which I had not finished drinking), and disappeared into the barn. I listened to the glass clink into the recycling bin. She should really stick to teaching horses.

* * *

"You should just go to the dean of the school and explain to him nicely that you're ready to be re-enrolled," my mother said, settling the casserole dish of potatoes onto the wicker potholder so it wouldn't mar the shiny surface of the dining room table. Sunday dinners required the full complement of matching dishes and lit candles, even just for the three of us. I usually ate on my couch at home. My parents weren't aware I was such a heathen. "I'm sure he'll understand. You nearly died, Andrea. That would shake anyone up."

"It's too late now," I said, mostly to make word-sounding noises. No one was listening to me. I had been granted academic leave after the accident, and I was supposed to restart my third year of vet school this fall. In a fit of decision paralysis and frustration, I hadn't done it, and the opportunity had passed. Truthfully, if I'd gone to the school administration sometime that summer and requested an extension of my leave, they would have given it to me, but I thought my chances were slim now.

"That job you've got is a dead end," my father continued with his part of the script in the regularly-scheduled "criticize Drew's life choices" meatloaf and green beans dinner revue. His knife scraped against the porcelain plate, making my mom wince. "If you're going to work instead of finish school, you should find a better job than the one you've got."

"Ditto," I agreed. Much as they'd quit listening to what I had to say a long time ago, I'd quit caring what they thought around the same. "May I have the bread, please?"

My mom passed me the basket of bread sticks nestled in a checkered towel that matched the place mats. "Did you do anything interesting this week, Andrea?"

"I went to Fiona's and rode for a while yesterday." As far as my parents knew, Fiona was a nice middle-aged lady who let me exercise her horses in exchange for cleaning stalls and scrubbing buckets.

"Fiona is such a dear to let you ride her horses," my mom said, making me wonder how Fiona would have reacted to being called a "dear."

My father spied another opportunity. "You could have your own horses if you got a decent job. Vets make good money."

This was not worth the free food.

A text message appeared briefly across my watch screen. *New situation. Meet barn.*

Thank god. I stood and went to scrape my plate into the trash. "I've got to go. Kara locked herself out, and I've got to take her her spare key."

"That Kara." My mom shook her head. "Take her a piece of cake."

I took the cake, fully intending to eat it myself, and high-tailed it toward the barn. My parents' house was a half hour away, and there were several other cars parked angled off the drive to the barn when I arrived. It looked like just about everyone was here.

I grabbed the duffel bag with my riding clothes out of the backseat and hustled toward the barn. I had never been summoned for a "situation" before. I guessed this was that increase in duties Bennett had been talking about. I'd mostly expected that to affect me by meaning I had to work roadkill duty extra nights to free everyone else up to do other things. Maybe I was getting included in the real work now. I wasn't sure how I felt about that. Maybe I was just along to observe and learn.

Trish was already on her horse's back, waiting outside the barn. "Hi, Drew. Glad you could make it. We're all hands on deck tonight."

"Hi, Trish. What's happening?" I dropped onto the mounting block outside the barn to change my shoes.

Trish was probably pushing fifty-five, but she had the soul of a teenager. She kept her gray hair long and flowing and wore bell-bottoms and crocheted shawls over band t-shirts. I studied her hippie vibe pretty closely, as I planned to emulate her one day. "There's a lot of activity at a morgue tonight," she told me. "Bennett and Fiona are already on their way. The rest of us are supposed to follow."

"Sounds exciting. Thanks for letting me ride Kai this weekend."

She smiled, but her gaze was drawn by Luis exiting the barn with his horse in tow before she could speak.

"Drew—good, you're here. Saddle up," he told me. "Time for you to get some real experience."

August and Valerie were both trailing after him, and they went to join Trish while I ran into the barn to get Charon, who was still munching his dinner, bits of hay stuck in his fluffy forelock.

"Looks like it's you and me again, buddy," I told him.

Charon sensed he was about to be made to work and promptly laid down. By the time I got him to stand up again, August had come to hurry me up, and I was in the embarrassing position of slowing everyone else down. He helped me wrestle Charon into his tack, and I hauled him outside to join the others.

I'd been on rides with the group before, and we usually rode at night for the cover it offered, but seeing the horses shimmering with otherworldly colors under the moonlight, hooves of marble or abalone dancing across the grass, made me feel like I was joining the Wild Hunt. There was magic snapping in the air that wasn't usually there when I was riding by myself. Luis waved an arm in a "follow me" motion, and I fell in line behind Valerie as we rode down the path leading away from the barn. After a few steps, the air began to cool and thin, a tinge of something sharp brushing across my skin and making my eyes water. The group broke into a run, and then the magic of the Riders rushed us away.

There was no way Charon, on his short little legs, could keep up with full-sized horses, but there was no way any horse could move as fast as we were going. I'd only hit Rider speed a few times before since I couldn't do it by myself. I usually couldn't see worth crap when we did this either, but this time I settled back in the saddle after a few minutes and managed to watch the world go by. I had been on a high speed train once, traveling a mind-numbing 254 KPH. That sounded ridiculously fast, and it probably looked that way to someone standing right next to the tracks when the train went by, but it felt no faster than a car ride from inside the train. Fast-riding was like that too once you got the hang of it. The city was visible; the ground was a blur.

We were going car speed over a non-car route, and I was glad I wasn't the one navigating. We shot across a parking lot, and then across a busy street, headlights like supernovas barreling toward us. Maybe the drivers saw a herd of deer streaking across the road. I hoped they didn't attempt to swerve. I didn't know what part of town we were in until we pulled up outside the city morgue.

I walked Charon around to cool him down while I studied the building. The sign outside said it was Asterville Regional Forensic Center, much nicer sounding than a "morgue." The staid, brick building was the practical kind usually built for government purposes, and I expected it would be all linoleum floors and florescent lighting inside, but there was nothing of the creepy, rundown quality TV shows assigned to these places. The forensic center was quiet and nondescript in the darkness, no sign of catastrophe. But as I neared it, I could feel that same sick tug of wrongness that I had learned to sense when I was searching for roadkill. I didn't have much experience with that feeling around people, but I was sure that's what this was.

Fiona materialized from the shadow of the building, her horse a darker gold than Valerie's, the hard shine coming from the real thing and not nail polish, and the mare's eyes shining like a pair of amethysts.

"How many?" Luis asked as we reached her.

"There are six. The signatures are strong. Bennett has moved to the funeral home on 8th Street." Her expression was inscrutable in the darkness, and I couldn't get a measure of how normal this situation might be. "I'm going to check the one on Baker if you have this here."

"We've got it," Luis said grimly. He began to ride around the outside of the building as if planning how to lay siege to it.

No one else followed, so I stayed put. "How does this usually work?" I asked August. I felt really ridiculous perched on Charon's back so far below him. It was like bring your kid to work day. "Do we sneak inside?"

"If we have to." August didn't seem concerned, which was no more a measure of the situation than Fiona looking indifferent. "Sometimes you can catch them from the outside."

There were still a few cars in the parking lot and lights on inside, so I was guessing the place was never unoccupied. I wondered if we had to *Oceans Eleven* our way inside via an air duct or something.

Luis returned. "I've been here before, and I suspect we most likely need access to the refrigerated storage room. It will be easier if we get everyone else out of the building first rather than try to dodge them."

"How are we going to do that?" August asked.

Luis absently tried to finger-comb his pomaded black hair back into the style the wind had ruined. "I was thinking I'd just pull the fire alarm."

"Cool," August said, pleased.

"We'll have to be quick before the fire department shows up," Trish warned.

Luis nodded. "We don't know which doors they'll exit, but they'll probably congregate in the front parking lot. Valerie, you keep watch on the employees and for the fire department."

I glanced at Valerie in time to see her nod. She'd been very quiet tonight, and she looked stone-faced now under the brim of her pink helmet. I saw her often at meetings, but I realized now that I never actually worked with her, and I had no idea how she felt about this whole thing. I usually assumed I was the only one struggling with the strangeness. Valerie caught me looking at her and shot me a glare that made my gaze skitter away from her again.

"Trish, can you guard the back with the horses?" Luis continued. "That will provide us some extra coverage at the door, and Valerie can communicate with you so you can pass on her warning. Once I've pulled the alarm, and the building empties, Drew and August will join me. Drew, bring Charon with you."

My eyebrows went up. "Bring Charon inside?"

Luis shrugged. "I have enough magic to hide myself a little bit, but I can't hide the two of you, and Charon will help with that."

"Do we have keys to this place?" Trish asked.

He shook his head. "No. We'll have to override the lock."

"Why would we have keys to the forensic center?" I asked.

"We've managed to obtain keys to many of the funeral homes and morgues we often have to visit," Luis explained. "Of course, now everyone has alarm systems too, so it doesn't help as much as it used to. If there's an 'open door' button on the inside, I might be able to press it to release the lock without sounding an alarm. If not, I'll try the push bar, but it might be too heavy for me."

I was really curious about how he was going to press the button from the outside, but I didn't think we had time for him to explain it to me. Luis was one of the experienced Riders who could do a little magic beyond Rider magic, which was why Fiona had left him in charge.

"Stay back until the building is empty," Luis warned.

"Security cameras?" I asked. I didn't need my mugshot on the evening news.

"You'll be really blurry," he assured me. "They only have cameras pointed at the doors, not the interior."

We moved to our assigned places, and Luis approached the back door, his head and face covered by a broad-brimmed hat. He looked to be staring fixedly at the door for a long minute, not moving. Then he caught the door handle quickly with one gloved hand and eased it open. He disappeared inside.

As Luis had predicted, when the fire alarm began to wail, the building's inhabitants streamed out the doors on the first floor. No one was lagging, but no one looked particularly concerned either. The lab workers in their plastic aprons and shower caps joined an elderly receptionist in a lavender twinset and a security guard in a rent-a-cop uniform in the front parking lot so they could all stand around with their arms crossed and chat while they waited for the all-clear from the fire department. They knew the building wasn't really on fire, but scientists are excellent at following procedures. Hell, maybe they enjoyed the break as much as I used to when someone would pull the fire alarm at school.

When it looked like no one else was coming out, August and I jogged to the back door, and he opened it first to check the hallway. The fire protocol must have turned off the electric locks. When he gestured for me to follow, I led Charon inside, praying Luis was right about the security cameras because I didn't have a hat. Charon was completely all right about walking into the building, having probably been many strange places before, right up until he smelled the interior of the forensic center. To be fair, if the antiseptic smell was this harsh on my nose, it was probably burning his. He planted his little hooves on the linoleum.

"Charon," I pleaded. "Please move." I tugged his bridle. He did his best cartoon donkey impersonation.

August crinkled something plastic in his jacket pocket, and Charon's ears pricked up. He pulled out a bag of M&Ms and waved it at the pony. "Treats?"

Charon decided food trumped fear, and he took a few steps forward to accept the candy from August's hand.

"Can undead ponies eat chocolate?" I asked.

"Charon could probably eat a tin can," August replied.

"You two, come on!" Luis stage-whispered from the end of the hallway. "We've only got a few minutes."

We followed him down the sterile hallway, August continuing to crinkle the candy wrapper alluringly any time Charon showed hesitation. The alarm had mercifully subsided to a low, repetitive tone at this point. Luis led us through the air-locked doors into an anteroom, then to the refrigerated room where the bodies were stored.

The adrenaline of breaking into a building and Charon's stubbornness had kept me from focusing on the "dead people" aspect of what we were doing, but there was no avoiding it now. The bodies were enshrouded in black body bags and laid out on human-sized shelves that looked like triple bunk beds. And in a terrifying little twist, there were what looked like five ghostly-pale people also standing in the dimly-lit room, staring at us. The people, three men and two women, were all watching us with polite interest. It took me a moment to tear my gaze from their faces to find the golden threads that connected them to the bodies in the bags.

"Fiona said she thought there were six," Luis said. "I'm going to check the autopsy room upstairs while you two take care of these. Don't wait for me when you're finished. Rejoin Trish."

He left, and I stood propping the door open so I could hold onto Charon's bridle. "Now what?"

"You take left, I'll take right," August replied, pulling a fishing knife out of his pocket.

I decided Charon couldn't go far anyway and let him go. I dropped the doorstop on the heavy metal door so it wouldn't shut behind me and nervously approached the first woman on the left side of the room.

"Hi," I told her.

She was middle-aged, maybe in her fifties, but the translucent quality of the life energy made it hard to tell. I don't know what she was wearing in her body bag, so maybe the floral dress was a reflection of how she saw herself. Her colorless eyes moved back and forth across my face, but there was no indication that she'd heard me.

"Drew, we don't have time to chat with people," August warned.

I very, very carefully did not look at what August was doing.

"You've gotten stuck," I explained to the woman, "but I'm going to set you free. Okay?"

She nodded slightly, expression unchanged.

I slid the antler-handled knife Fiona had given me through the golden thread as gently as I could, and the gray image of the woman winked out. "Goodbye," I told her softly.

I stepped to the next person, narrowly beating August, who was moving much more quickly than I was. I realized at some point my desire to not have to do this had been eclipsed by my desire to not let August shove everybody off like he was pulling weeds.

My second victim was a younger man with buzzed-short hair and an oversized basketball jersey. He looked a little more attentive than the woman had and a little more solid.

"Hi," I began again, ignoring August's grunt of impatience. "It's time to go now. I'm going to untether you from your body."

"Okay," the man replied agreeably.

I froze. Never once had the tethered life energy of a body *spoken* to me. In fairness, my subjects were usually animals. But I don't think I'd ever even heard of someone speaking. I wasn't even sure if I'd heard the word aloud or in my head.

When I stood there, shocked and indecisive, August grabbed my arm to pull me out of the way and brought his stupid camouflage fishing knife down through the tether. The man disappeared.

"Drew, we've got to go." August almost shoved me through the door and kicked the doorstop up. "I can hear the firetruck."

I had thought Charon couldn't go far because the doors to the room outside the refrigerator were shut, but I hadn't really anticipated that he could cause havoc anyway. He must have caught part of his tack against an office chair, because it now lay on its side at the end of a trail of destruction. He was trying to eat a box of nitrile gloves.

"Charon, no!" I grabbed his bridle and tugged him toward the door. "What do we do about all this?"

"Nothing," August said grimly. "Come on."

When we were out in the hallway again, I looked quickly left and right for approaching firemen. No one had entered the building yet, but I could see the lights from the truck reflecting from somewhere. I could also see the reception desk, a straight shot down the center hallway, in the opposite direction of the back door.

"Take Charon," I told August quickly, then darted toward the front of the building before he could stop me.

"Drew!" he hissed, but didn't follow me.

I leaned against the wall at the corner and held my breath so I could listen, then peered around the corner into the lobby. The reception desk was one of those office behemoths from yesteryear, solid to the floor and so tall the little lady in the twinset had her seat raised so high she needed a stool for her feet. Her keys were still lying under the hutch part of the desk.

There was activity in the parking lot but no one coming inside yet. I dashed for the desk and slid under it like a softball player. I clawed blindly at the surface of the desk while still sitting underneath it until my hand closed around the purple pompom attached to her keys. Like receptionists everywhere, she was the punctilious sort and had labeled each key in crisp handwriting. I unhooked "back door" from the ring, grateful her arthritis-afflicted fingers had chosen a keychain that opened and closed instead of a split ring, and tossed the pompom back into its approximate spot. Hopefully she wouldn't notice it was gone right away.

I was preparing to make a dash for the hallway when I had another thought. I pulled her top left-hand drawer out, then the bottom drawer. Score—a packet of keycards. They might not be activated, but it was worth a try. I started to get up again and heard the front door open. Crap—out of time. I crawled into the footwell of the desk instead, trying to muffle the suddenly obnoxiously loud sound of my breathing. They weren't looking for intruders, I reminded myself. They were just looking for fire. They weren't going to check for a fire under the desk.

The door jangled shut, and unhurried footsteps crossed the lobby, then proceeded down the center hallway. The smart thing to do would be to stay here until he left. Instead, I waited until the footsteps sounded further away, then crawled out from behind the desk, scrambling toward the hallway on the side of the building as quietly as I could. That hallway led straight to the back too, but I'd have to cross to the center aisle to go back out the back door. If the fireman turned left at the back, he'd be walking toward me. We could continue to chase each other around the building like rats in a maze. I peered around the corner again, feeling like the world's lowest-budget spy, and waited to see which way he'd go.

The firefighter, attired in the usual gear but with his helmet tucked under his arm, had reached the back of the building and was speaking into his radio. He must have stopped to open doors and check rooms as he went because it took him a lot longer to reach the back than it had me. Someone answered him in a riff of gargled static he must have understood because he laughed. Then he turned right, walking away from me.

I waited until he rounded the corner, then shot for the back door. The sound of my boots squeaking was louder than the fire alarm had been, but it was too late for stealth now. I slammed the push bar on the back door and stumbled out into the parking lot.

The rest of the Rider crew, including August and Charon, were gathered under a broken streetlight. I charted course for them, wondering if we were going to ride away at speed. I heard the back door open again about the time Luis caught my shoulders to stop me. He held his finger to his lips, and I put my hand over my mouth to try to quiet my noisy breathing as I turned to look behind me.

The fireman was leaning out the doorway, staring out perplexedly at what hopefully looked like an empty parking lot. Now that I wasn't in a panic anymore, I could feel the icy haze of Rider magic making us unseen. They'd gathered all five horses together to concentrate it to conceal my exit. Usually if we didn't do anything to draw attention, the magic would be enough, but the man was really *looking* in a way most people casually passing by didn't. After a long moment, he seemed to decide that even if he had seen someone, they were long gone, and he went back inside, the door thudding behind him.

There was a collective sigh.

Luis had about as much temper as a daffodil, but he was having a hard time keeping his tone even. "Drew, maybe we need to have a little talk about following directions. Where did you go?"

I held up the key and the keycards, all of which I'd somehow held onto during all the running. "I got the keys." My life had been devoid of adrenaline for so long, I had forgotten how much I enjoyed it.

"They'll probably just change the locks anyway," he warned, but he took the keys.

"This is a government building—they don't have the money." I must have needed to take the peppiness down a few more notches, because even kind and patient Trish was looking at me funny.

"Let's check in with Fiona to see where we're needed," Luis sighed. "And you stick with Trish for the rest of the night."

CHAPTER 3

* * *

Everyone gathered at Bennett's house Friday night looked about as tired as I felt. There were enough of us that we usually split the duties so we all only worked once a week or so; going out this often didn't fit well into anyone's regular schedule. I hadn't done anything but roadkill duty since the trip to the forensic center, possibly as a result of my going off-script, but I'd been out every night, and each trip took hours. I was grabbing fast food when I left work every day to make it to the barn and get started in hopes of getting home by a decent hour. I went to trivia night at the bar with Kara on Tuesday because I'd promised, and I spent the whole evening worrying about how late I was going to have to be out instead of enjoying myself. I could tell she wasn't finding me an enthusiastic teammate either, so now I had that guilt too.

The map Bennett and Luis had been using to chart incidents was tacked to one of those giant boards on wheels they used in old police procedurals, probably because they were both old enough to desire something more tactile than a computer screen. There were color-coded pins dotted over a long gash stretching across the upper half of Missouri and concentrated around the city of Asterville, but the colors formed no noticeable pattern. Luis, Bennett, and Helen were all standing around the board, murmuring their observations.

Helen, much younger and technologically aware, was probably wishing she could plug their data into some twenty-first century software. If there was a pattern to the uptick, she could display it in three different kinds of easy-to-comprehend graphs and charts. Bennett valued Helen's opinions, so the fact that he and Luis didn't accommodate her at something she was much better at than they was probably a result of his fear that he wouldn't be able to understand the technology and be left out. I thought that was a normal and valid fear for someone his age, but it was still kind of selfish.

"What we really need to know," Bennett mulled, "is how this compares to the last surge, and we just don't have adequate records."

The rest of us had been watching them cogitate somewhat listlessly, more intent on putting a dent in Bennett's tea supply than offering input.

"Surely there's a precedent for how long it's going to last," Kevin reasoned. He was looking at his giant, fancy watch like the expiration date of the surge might manifest there.

"The records are sporadic, but what little we have suggests a variance that doesn't allow for a prediction," Helen explained, trying to twist strands of her honey brown back into her scrunchie while holding her tablet with her other hand. I noted she had swapped whatever shoes she'd worn to work for red Chucks, somehow cute instead of incongruous with her plain sheath dress. "Why are the Riders so bad at recordkeeping?"

"Does it really matter?" August said philosophically from where he slouched on an ottoman with a dainty teacup on one knee. "We have to ride it out no matter how long it lasts, and there's nothing else we can do about it. Even if it's the strongest surge to ever happen, we still do what we do."

Luis rubbed the dark stubble that shadowed his chin. He was a fashionable guy who liked brightly-colored shirts and his hair combed just right, so the slightly less than perfect grooming gave away how stressful he was finding the last week. "It matters because we want to know if there's an end-date for this work level or if we need to form a longer-term battle plan."

"The increase in deaths we need to attend not only means more work, but means greater risk to everyone involved," Trish added. "Each time we have to break into a building and pull a fire alarm, we increase our chances of getting caught. Most of us have day-jobs that won't appreciate us having a brush with the law."

"Yes, and repeated disturbances at a funeral home or hospital morgue will cause a tightening of security everywhere," Luis agreed. "We'll have to start waiting for the funerals if it comes to that."

I didn't particularly see what was so bad about that, except that the dead would have to wait a few days more. We were always so urgent about attending incomplete separations, and I'd mostly put that down to keeping the workload from piling up, but maybe there was another reason.

"We'll have an easier time getting into the forensic center next time, at least," August remarked. "Since Drew stole the keys." He had decided my impulse-driven heist was amusing. "Those keycards were programmed, so we can at least get inside faster next time."

"*Not* a very wise thing to do," Bennett said sternly, his furrowed brows making it clear he could not approve of recklessness, however successful.

"I heard about that," Helen said, finally tearing her gaze from the tablet to smile at me. "How did you enjoy going out with the team, Drew?"

I shrugged. "It was okay. Exciting, I guess, except for that guy talking to me. That was weird." Acting like it had been the highlight of my month would probably not get me taken out to do anything again any time soon.

Luis left off looking at the board to stare at me. "What guy?"

"One of the bodies in the refrigerator," I said uncomfortably, having belatedly realized there must have been something out of the ordinary about that. "Well, not the body of course; the life energy, I guess."

"He spoke to you?" Bennett demanded. There was an intensity in his gaze that seemed out of character for him.

"I mean, he just said, 'okay' when I told him what I was doing."

Fiona had turned her attention toward me to listen, but she didn't interrupt.

"Drew, life energy can't talk," Luis said gently. "Getting used to interacting with the dead is stressful, and it was a hectic night. You probably just imaged it as your brain's way of coping with what was going on."

I don't consider myself an especially bold person, but I'm not easily cowed when I know I'm right. "He did speak. It wasn't loud, but it was definitely audible. He was responding to what I said to him. August was right there." I turned to look at August.

By his reluctant expression, I could tell he was going to insist he'd heard nothing whether he had or not. "I know you like to talk to the dead things, Drew," he said slowly, eyes focused somewhere past my head, "but they can't hear you or talk to you."

I was surprised by how traitorous that felt. August had been the one beside me for most of my Rider journey, and I'd sort of thought we were allies. "That was the first one to speak to me," I argued, "but even the other woman I spoke to that night nodded at me. You don't think they can listen because you chop them down like you're dead-heading roses."

He spread his hands out and looked at them instead of me. "Look, I just figured you like to talk to things because it's how you cope with all this, and I get that. But now you're straight up imagining things."

"Hush," Fiona said sharply to August. "Andrea, have you seen anything else unusual besides the man who spoke?"

I thought. "There was that deer that had a tethered life energy even though it wasn't quite dead yet. And you *did* see that one, so don't pretend otherwise," I spat at August.

He ignored me placidly, but he couldn't ignore Fiona.

"August." Her tone could have peeled wood varnish, though she didn't raise her voice.

August didn't exactly squirm, but only just. "It was fading in and out," he reasoned. "Its heart had probably stopped and started again."

"Was the energy fading in and out too?" Bennett wanted to know.

"No, it was steady," I answered before August could make something else up.

"How very interesting." Bennett's gaze was fixed far off in the distance for a moment. "Could it be the surge?" he asked Fiona.

"It must be," she replied. "The magic is increasing not only in frequency but in strength. Were they difficult to separate?"

"August did both of them," I said.

"No," August ground out.

"I'm not yet sure what this means for us," Fiona said, "but we may be facing new challenges. If anyone else experiences something like this, I want to be called to the scene if the timing allows."

"Maybe it just means Drew has an overactive imagination," August grumbled.

Something large and burgundy smashed into his face, making his arms flail outward and muffling his grunt of surprise.

Valerie raised the pillow she had smacked him with like she was considering going for another shot.

"Valerie," Bennett pleaded, "not the throw pillows."

Valerie returned the cushion to its place, completely straight-faced.

4

Chapter 4

Instead of making my usual Saturday trip to the barn the next morning, I dragged my laptop into the bed with me and opened the picture I'd taken of Luis and Bennett's map. We didn't know what rifts "looked" like, assuming there was anything to look at, or what form they took. They might have moved or shifted, but it didn't seem like they drifted very far because their effects were usually felt within a range that was adopted as the territory of groups of Riders. The rift under Asterville was thought to be especially large or active compared to others around the world based on the number of deaths that were incomplete here. There were other small groups of Riders who lived near their own rifts, and a few rifts that were managed by traveling teams or other magical groups who had taken the responsibility for them. Right now, Gideon from our Rider group had been dispatched on a year-long trip to South America to concentrate on that area like a traveling missionary. Our group was the biggest, and we had the added clout of keeping the cauldron from which the horses were born.

If I had hoped to learn about the whereabouts of the rift from the colored pins, I was disappointed. The area encompassed was no more detailed than the areas we usually patrolled. I wondered briefly if there was a way to get a similar map from some of the other groups, but I reminded myself that wouldn't help us understand what was happening in our own backyard. What we really needed was a similar map from another surge in the same area, or even just a map from normal levels to establish as a baseline. I was starting to empathize with Helen bemoaning the Riders' poor recordkeeping.

I grabbed my phone off the nightstand and called her.

"Hey, Drew," she answered, upbeat like she'd been awake for hours. "What's up?"

"Hey, Helen," I said, burrowing down into the comforter. "I was thinking about something you said at the meeting."

"Yeah? Shoot."

"The Riders keeping records, or I guess not keeping records—who is responsible for that?"

"Hmm." I could hear her keyboard clacking as she talked. "To all appearances, no one. But really though, the original Bone Riders were founded as a clandestine magical sect, and they wouldn't have wanted their secrets written down. They added new members so rarely, they had plenty of time to pass on their oral history. They didn't expect there to be future generations after them that wouldn't have the direct benefit of their knowledge."

"Were they not expecting the Riders to continue after them?" I wanted to know.

"I don't think they expected there to be an 'after them' situation," she replied. "They were all magic-workers who devoted their lives to the subject. It's impossible to get any real proof, but it sounds like many of them were quite...long-lived."

"Like Fiona," I said, feeling guilty like I was revealing a secret. Fiona's age seemed to be something we all sort of knew but never spoke about.

"Like Fiona," Helen agreed in the same hesitant tone. "They weren't immortal, but Rider magic seems to create longevity for some people, and they lived long enough that they expected the membership of the group to change very slowly. From what I can tell, we've only been adding so many new members in fairly recent generations. You, August, and Valerie are close in age and have all joined us recently. Kevin and I weren't long before the three of you."

That left seven Asterville Riders with any real longevity to speak of, a little over half. "If the old Riders didn't keep records, how do we know about their origins?"

"The stories of the first Riders were the most persistently passed down, and eventually later generations did actually record them in writing, which I appreciate greatly. It's the intervening years where things get foggy. The group was growing and turnover was higher, but no one had set up any kind of government for the group. Honestly, it's the failure of most recent generations to keep records that's appalling. Statistics have been a thing for a *while* now."

I bit back a grin at her exasperation even though she couldn't see me. "Would any of the other Rider groups have kept better records maybe? Something we could use as a comparison?"

There was silence as Helen pondered that for a moment. "The others are just a few people here and there, not a group coordinating together like we are. They are more like knights-errant devoting their lives to the work." She paused again. "I think some of them are also very old. I doubt they have records, but they might have long memories."

We both considered that possibility.

"So shouldn't Fiona remember all this stuff if she's that old?" I asked tentatively.

I could practically hear Helen's incredulous expression through the phone. "Why don't you go ask her?" she suggested brightly.

"Because I don't want to die," I grumbled. She laughed, and I was about to let the subject go, but I hesitated. "Is Fiona one of the original

Bone Riders?"

"I don't know, Drew," Helen said seriously. "I don't know if there are any of them left living, but I'd guess she was from somewhere early in their history."

"Even if we don't know how old she is, surely she's lived through enough rift surges to know what we're expecting here," I reasoned.

"I think if she knew, she'd tell us, but she's acting like something unusual is happening, and that concerns me."

It concerned me too. I thanked Helen and hung up, thinking hard. Okay, there wasn't any more data to be had from the Riders, but the rifts were the source of all magic, and there were other potentially magic-related oddities taking place. I pulled up every news story I could find reporting on the weird things Alice "Moonstone" and her like had noticed. Those weren't really highly sought stories for the news beyond local color pieces, so I found myself scrolling through an increasingly ludicrous rabbit hole of conspiracy theories and outlandish tales in chat rooms and social media web pages. Plagues of frogs, extremely isolated rain, a forest someone swore had grown overnight, a dead raccoon walking.

I'd taken care of the raccoon already, having had to watch it crawl around while I waited for Fiona to arrive and study it. It had been fading in and out as August had claimed the deer had. We couldn't tell if it was trying to reboot itself Drew-style, but we'd ultimately decided its body was too ruined to allow it to continue. The frogs I suspected had more to do with the notorious chemical waste in that wet area, and I wasn't sure studying the rain would be worthwhile unless I could catch it happening. The insta-forest it was, then.

It was nearly lunchtime by then, but I made myself some coffee and took it into the shower with me. Half an hour later I was dressed and eating an egg sandwich on my way out the door. As I turned around after locking the door, I nearly collided with someone who had walked up behind me.

"Oh, hey, Drew."

I stared into the man's gray eyes for a second, surprised enough to forget to chew. People don't pay much attention to gray eyes, but his were surprisingly bright, more silver than blue. They were eyes well-suited for his dreamy, sensitive face, the kind you expected a tortured poet to have.

"Hey, Cole," I said grudgingly.

"You look nice, Drew," he said. "Where are you off to?"

The olive green t-shirt I wore with my usual uniform of jeans and boots did match my eyes nicely, but I had forgone the hair dryer for the sake of time, so my brown hair still hung in wet tendrils down my back. I did not look nice. He did though, all temptation and promise like a shiny new car with terrible gas mileage and a tendency to roll if you took a corner too fast.

"Out," I told him. "Do you need something?"

"Yeah, I think I left my watch here. Do you mind if I look?" He finger-combed his dark hair back and gave me a shy, sweet look.

"Your watch isn't here," I told him, stoic. "It's a one-bedroom apartment; it would have shown up by now. I've got to go." I started to move past him.

"Drew," he persisted as he followed me to the parking lot, taking the sad tactic now because he knew I'd be tempted to fall for it. Worse, he probably really was sad. "Can't we talk for a while?"

"We don't have anything to talk about, Cole. You decided that when you broke up with me, remember?" I unlocked my truck and climbed into the seat. He stood on the sidewalk looking disconsolate. I was about to leave when I remembered something else. I rolled the window down and leaned out. "And stop driving by my parents' house, you weirdo. Move on." I hit the window button with one hand and steered with the other as I backed out. "And let me," I added to myself as I hit the street.

* * *

I would have discounted the forest as an exaggeration, but it had overtaken a playground in a middle-class neighborhood. The yellow paint on the slides and climbing equipment was still bright so it was unlikely the place had been abandoned even if it wasn't popular with the local kids. These HOA-types would never let an eyesore like that develop in their manicured neighborhood.

The neighborhood's developers had left a strip of land uncleared behind the subdivision, a narrow wooded area meant to muffle traffic noises and prevent the landscape from looking too barren. It looked like that leftover bit of forest had had an unexpected growth spurt and mounted an attack to take back some of its old land for itself. The trees that now grew up to the playground were only a few inches in diameter so they weren't old, but they had punched through the gravel footing of the playground. I knelt and tried to dig around the bottom of one of the trees. They were small enough to have been carried in; maybe this was just an elaborate prank and they'd all been planted. If they had been, someone had done a good job, and I couldn't do much besides break my fingernails trying to dig barehanded.

I was wiping my hands on my jeans when I heard voices approaching. That tightly-held instinct that I was supposed to keep magic a secret made me duck quickly into the little pretend submarine underneath the raised part of the playground before I remembered no one was going to suspect this anomaly was related to magic, and they wouldn't think I had anything to do with it if they did. It would be weirder to just pop back out now, so I peered out the sub's little porthole.

Approaching were two men in khakis, button-down shirts, and hardhats, the unofficial uniform of foremen and project leaders actually dragged to the job site. One of them even had a clipboard. They studied the trees like I'd been doing a few minutes ago. One leaned all his weight against a sapling and tried to drag it over, probably testing if it had roots.

"This is weird," the man in the white hardhat observed. "Do you sense any magic?"

My eyebrows shot up at that. Were they magic practitioners posing as city workers?

"Sort of," the clipboard man replied. "Not like active magic but sort of—an aftertaste."

"Like magic someone's worked recently?"

Clipboard man tried to scratch his head and belatedly remembered he was wearing a hardhat. "Would you believe me if I said it feels *raw* somehow?"

"Interesting," white hardhat reflected. "Is there anything we can take a sample of?"

"Let's cut one of the trees down," his companion suggested. "Maybe we can trace the spell used later. It's probably some sort of rapid-growth working someone was practicing."

"That would be useful for gardening," the man in the white hardhat reasoned. "And if someone's dug up an old spell that can do this, someone needs to find out what else they're doing."

"Yeah, if someone did do this on purpose, it was very indiscreet," clipboard man agreed. "Whether this was a magical working or a freak happening of nature, I'm sure it hasn't gone unnoticed. The government is going to sweep this under the rug so fast the broom will catch fire."

"They're probably going to have us destroy it, but we'd better get our sample now in case someone else beats us to it. I'll get the handsaw."

I would have crept from my little submarine hiding place then, but only one of the men left, and I didn't think I could sneak past the other.

Were they really magic-workers, or were they Alice "Moonstone" types who just fancied themselves witches? They hadn't done any magic, only claimed to feel it, and I couldn't feel anything, so I couldn't discern if they could or not.

The man who had gone to fetch the saw returned, and they cut down one of the smallest trees with it. They had a brief debate over how much of the tree they could reasonably be seen carrying around versus how big a sample was required for testing, then cut the trunk down to a foot in length and chopped off a few leafy branches to carry separately.

After they had left with their samples, I crawled out of my hiding place and tiptoed after them, hoping to see what they had driven up in. I made it to the road just in time to see a white truck like the kind city workers drive leaving the street, but I couldn't read the emblem on the door to tell if it was real or not.

I went back to the forest and examined the tree they'd cut down. Nothing about the growth rings suggested anything abnormally fast. I sniffed the cut edge of the trunk; just sawdust and—maybe ozone? I really couldn't tell. I took a few pictures with my phone, then decided that was about the extent of my sleuthing abilities.

I went home and studied the incidences map again. I wasn't sure how to quantify what I'd seen at the playground forest on the map except that I knew it was real and had been caused by magic. I dropped a pin in a new color where it had taken place; one wild news story confirmed. I couldn't fathom yet how the other weird happenings might be relevant to the work of the Riders, but I did know it was proof of magic stirring in the rift. If this one had turned out to be real; some of the others would too.

5

Chapter 5

My attempts to investigate the other strange incidents in our city didn't make much headway. I tried hunting for a flock of pink ducks someone had seen out by the county line on Sunday, but I'd been neglecting the rest of my life in favor of my Rider duties all week, and I had to do the old grocery shopping/laundry/house cleaning routine if I didn't want to be going to work in dirty clothes with a lunch bag full of saltines. And frankly I needed to sleep too because I wasn't getting a whole lot of that these days.

I showed up at the barn on Sunday night expecting to take Charon out for roadkill duty and found Fiona, Bennett, Luis, and Helen still there, congregating around with their saddled horses.

"You're coming with us, Drew," Luis told me. He was holding Charon's reins, and he handed them over to me. "We've got another incident that's going to take a lot of us."

"Another morgue?" I asked, checking the saddle girth before I mounted. Maybe I'd been forgiven for my little stunt with the keycards.

"A cemetery," Fiona said darkly. She moved out without another word, and everyone fell in line behind her in silence, readying their horses for a fast-run.

I figured in the hectic pace of the last week, that there had been bodies no one could get to until they were buried. That wasn't the preferable way of things, but at this point, it seemed like it made more sense to just wait until the bodies had reached the cemetery to untether their life energies. Cemeteries were a lot easier to access than morgues and hospitals, and most people were buried within a week anyway. Fiona hadn't seemed pleased by the circumstances, but there wasn't time to ask followup questions before we were galloping across the city.

I had romantic notions about cemeteries in general. I liked to read the names on the headstones and imagine what the people had been like when they were alive, and I liked to see the flowers and little tokens people left on their graves. Cemeteries were our way of saying we hadn't forgotten the dead, that their lives had left an imprint on the world. Being a Bone Rider was trying to ruin that for me.

We approached from the trees opposite the parking lot, spreading out to cover the vast expanse of the manicured commercial funeral park. The funeral home was on the far side, and a few paved roads allowed visitors to drive close to their loved one's grave. It looked completely normal from a distance, but I could already feel the wrongness.

It wasn't until I was much closer that I could see it too, as faint as it was in the darkness. Nearly the entire cemetery was lit up with golden tethers, all moving gently like strands of seaweed floating in a current. They were each connected at one end to a gray, vaguely human-shaped cloud and at the other to a grave. It was like the death of half the people here had been incomplete, but that didn't make sense because most of these people had been dead for years, decades even. Surely if they had been that way while in our territory, someone would have noticed.

"This is strange," Fiona ruminated from nearby. "I don't understand it."

I exchanged worried glanced with Helen. Fiona wasn't one to ruminate, and there was very little she didn't understand.

I nudged Charon closer to one of the graves. The gray mirage attached to it was so blurry the features were unrecognizable, like looking at a statue that had had its features weathered away. The date of death was 1923. Maybe the life energy deteriorated when it was stuck trapped to a dead body for a long time. But that would mean it had been trapped here for that long, and it couldn't have been.

"Has the energy reformed to its previous shape?" Fiona pondered to herself. She was still analyzing, trying to solve the puzzle. Which meant she'd never seen this before. Crap.

"Why don't we normally visit cemeteries to fix tethered life energies?" I asked Luis. "It seems easier than breaking into morgues." There were an unexpected number of them, but they were just floating there like balloons on a string.

"Because there's always a good chance they'll appear underground next to their bodies," he explained. "Sneaking into a morgue is hard, but digging into a grave without being seen has its own risks, especially with the concrete vaults. And it takes an experienced Rider to feel them underground until they've aged quite a bit, so we try to avoid it. In places with fewer Riders, they tend to be more used to dealing with that sort of thing."

So maybe these untethered hadn't been taken care of in our usual timely manner and had lurked underground until they had aged enough to rise to the surface. I didn't completely understand the aging mechanics, but Luis had ridden away before I could ask him.

I rode a little further away, trying to see how many graves were affected. It wasn't all of them, but it was certainly close. I was nearing the right side of the cemetery and about to circle back when I heard the crunch of a footstep behind me. I hadn't seen any of the other Riders come this direction, but the sound didn't immediately raise any alarms because I didn't expect to be alone. I turned to look just as a man stepped out of the trees from the far right of where we'd come. I held Charon still as the "don't see me" instinct took over. Was a mourner or ground staff here this late at night? Maybe the man was just taking a shortcut through the cemetery.

The man took a few more steps, then looked up at me and froze. His eyes met mine, and I knew that he could see me. Hopefully, he just saw a woman on a Welsh pony. We had a stare-down for a moment.

I glanced toward Fiona, whose attention was still fixed on a headstone. "Um, Fiona."

Fiona began riding a circle around one of the graves and chanting to herself.

"Who *are* you?" the man asked, incredulous. "And *what* are you?"

"Fiona," I repeated more urgently.

She looked up, and I nodded toward the man. "He can see us." I made awkward eye contact with the man again. I couldn't see him that well in the darkness, but he had dark hair and was wearing a dark long-sleeved shirt. His face was too shadowy for me to guess his age, but his posture suggested he was either young or athletic. There was nothing immediately noticeable to me that would explain why he could see me like he did.

He grimaced. "Of course I can see you. Your invisibility booster must be faulty, Ron."

I wasn't sure what "taken aback" looked like, but I was pretty sure I was personifying it just then.

There were more sounds of sticks snapping underfoot and leaves rustling, and I dragged my gaze away from the dark-haired man to see more people trekking their way through the trees toward the cemetery. One of the women who had just stepped out onto the grass turned to look at me and stopped short, just as stunned as the man. She could see me too. Maybe there was something wrong with the "unnoticeable" magic Charon was supposed to be giving off.

Fiona guided her horse a little closer as she coolly surveyed the people who were gathering behind the woman, some of them looking at us and some of them just looking confused. "It's all right, Drew. They don't really see *us*."

She was reminding me that even though the people were looking at us, Rider magic and their own expectations would color what they saw. The woman was watching us both very carefully, so it wasn't just Charon. Then she made up her mind and strode over, her companions trailing after her in confusion.

"Who are you, and what are you doing here?" she demanded. She was short and plump and wore her hair twisted back in a clip, the golf ball-sized stone in her necklace the only thing unusual about her appearance. It was glinting in a way that might not have been just the moonlight.

"We were just out riding and lost sight of our dog," Fiona said calmly, a gentle pulse of magic that didn't feel like Rider magic building around us. "What brings you to a cemetery so late at night?"

The woman raised her hands in front of her like she was cradling a bowling ball, and Fiona's magical persuasion collapsed with a sharpness I felt in my teeth. "Cut the crap. I can see you all, and I know you aren't just a couple of Joe Blows out for a ride at night. You're in a cemetery, and you're riding a horse with purple eyes. Who are you?"

Fiona surveyed the woman and her crew, who were all exchanging worried murmurs now. "You are magic-workers."

"Yes, as are you," the woman shot back. She looked like a librarian in a cardigan and twill pants, but she had the attitude of someone used to being obeyed.

Fiona nodded slowly. That skin-crawling feeling I got sometimes when my visceral brain recognized that there was something too old, too powerful about her for the body she inhabited made the hair on the back of my neck stand up. "Yes. So you've come for the same reason we have—you sense the disruption of the dead in this place."

The woman had stiffened under Fiona's gaze, probably catching a whiff of the same feeling I did, but she relaxed slightly as Fiona confirmed we were all experiencing the same thing. "We do," she agreed. "We've come to lay the ghosts here. We are the Hazelwood Coven."

Green-haired Alice "Moonstone" was probably the public's basis for a coven member, but the seven members of the Hazelwood Coven just looked like normal people. They had dressed in dark colors to avoid being seen in the darkness and worn practical shoes for walking through the grass.

Fiona's dreamy gaze turned to take in the cemetery again. "Is ghosts what you see here?" she asked pleasantly.

"Yes," the coven leader said. "Who are you?"

"We are the Bone Riders," Fiona said, turning to look at the woman again. "We will banish the dead in this cemetery. Your powers may be needed elsewhere, where the ghosts are restrained by no body. This is our work here." The words were politely said, but it was pacification, a suggestion the coven should run along and play with their toys because the grown-ups were working here. She wasn't even trying all that hard to hide it.

The other Riders had stayed distant, trying not to give strangers more to look at that would help their confused brains decide there was something unnatural going on, but they began to gather toward me and Fiona.

"Bone Riders?" the woman echoed, frowning. "I haven't heard of your coven. Do you operate in this area?"

Bennett drew Persephone up behind Fiona and slightly to her right. "We aren't a coven. We are not witches."

Fiona made a noncommittal noise.

"We assist the dead when dying does not happen according to its natural course," he continued with no sign he'd heard her.

The dark-haired man had been studying Charon in silence while the woman talked, and I'd almost forgotten about him. "Are you necromancers?" he broke in abruptly. "Your horses are—dead."

"They are not dead," I said hotly. "They are magic." The fact that of all the words a person could have used to describe the beautiful Rider horses, he'd picked "dead" showed a distinct lack of taste.

"They have bone inside them," he pointed out, and I wondered how he knew that. "You said you were the Bone Riders. You're riding bone."

"Bone is used as a raw material in many magical workings," Fiona said. "The original horses that inhabited these bones were not resurrected." I doubted Fiona would care if they had. "Our horses help carry the magic that allows us to attend to our work."

"And your work needs a clown pony?" he asked, eyeing Charon critically.

"The clown pony could leave some hoofprints on your forehead," I suggested. I really needed to get my own horse.

The woman was studying Fiona very carefully now, deciding her next move. "We will handle the departure of these ghosts," she said firmly. "This is within our territory."

Fiona's smile had an icy edge. "The territory a coven claims is meaningless to us. You may rest assured it will be taken care of."

The woman put her hands on her hips. "Taken care of. We don't know what code you follow or what you intend to do with these ghosts. We would prefer to handle it ourselves."

"Ah," Fiona said, smiling for real now, "you worry what intentions a group of necromancers may have toward the dead. Our code is far beyond yours, Witch. Our duty to the dead cannot be stopped. We will sever the ties that trap life's energy to the body so that it may return to the universe from which it came."

"You want to banish these ghosts without discussion, without trying to determine what they need?" the woman demanded. She was frightened of Fiona because she wasn't an idiot, but she was holding her ground. "Most spirits will move on by themselves if their needs are addressed. Very few require banishment."

"These are no ghosts," Fiona replied flatly. "I don't know what has caused you to sense them when normally you would not have, save for their unusual number, but this is far beyond your abilities. This is the charge of the Riders." She spun Orlaith around, indicating that the conversation was over and the witch and her coven deserved no more of her attention.

The other coven members, excepting the man who had insulted Charon, huddled together to discuss this rebuttal in a flurry of hissing noises and waving arms. I briefly met the man's eye to see why he wasn't joining them and found something bordering on mirth in his expression. If he thought Fiona's dramatics were amusing, he was a foolish man. The other Riders had followed Fiona's example and were to all appearances returning to work, so I did the same. I moved out of earshot of the coven members before I approached my first target. As I leaned to examine the hazy gray shape, I caught sight of movement out of the corner of my eye. The dark-haired man was following me to see what I did.

I didn't get a chance to challenge him because the head witch had attempted to stomp after Fiona and continue her protest. In a move that would have done a reining competitor proud, Fiona spun her horse back on her haunches and threw up a hand in a gesture that was part impatience, part force. The woman collided with something invisible and fell on her rump. The coven at her back winced in collective shock. The witch, properly angry now, was on her feet at once, and she hurled something vaguely glowing at Fiona, which Fiona batted away with another gesture.

Now that the first shots had been fired, patience and prudence were temporarily suspended, and everyone rushed into the melee.

I had no real experience with magic beyond Rider magic, but it turned out that when it was actively happening around me, I could feel it. It sizzled through the air like invisible, isolated heat waves as the coven members launched magic through the air at Fiona and at the other Riders as they joined her. I wasn't really sure what it was meant to do, if they were throwing spells to stun or kill or cause gingivitis. Whatever it was, Fiona was striking the magic out of the air like she was shooting skeet. She was nearly alone in her efforts because most of the rest of us couldn't work magic, but Luis was stirring up some Rider magic that I had a feeling was making us blink out of sight or confusing the coven members because some of them kept alternating between looking determined and like they'd just woken up from anesthesia. I had no magic to offer at all yet, so I wasn't sure if I should just wade in and make a target of myself.

"Ignore them," the dark-haired man suggested. He was closer now, and I could see that he was probably in his late twenties or early thirties and his eyes were brown. "Keep doing what you were doing."

"Why, so you can watch?"

"Yes," he agreed. "This entire fight could probably have been avoided if we just watched you work for a minute, and you proved you weren't raising the dead to do your will."

I rolled my eyes. "We don't raise the dead. We just help the ones who are stuck."

He continued to look at me expectantly.

I glanced at Fiona, who seemed to be enjoying herself. Her long hair was streaming behind her like a comet's tail, Orlaith's golden coat shimmering with a haze of magic in the darkness. She probably could have wiped the whole coven out without breaking a sweat, but she was letting them give it their best shot. Bennett and Luis were providing the frightening distraction of horses galloping around pedestrians. Helen was nowhere in sight.

"I didn't show you anything. You just happened to be following me while I worked."

He nodded solemnly.

I leaned toward the gray facsimile of a person. It was so blurry I couldn't even make out any features, much less tell if he was looking at me. I glanced down at the headstone. "Carl, you are dead, but you've gotten stuck to your body. I don't know how it happened, but I'm going to set you free so you can go on." Carl didn't show any sign of having heard me.

"Do they ever respond?" the man asked curiously.

I shot him a glare to remind him that we had agreed this wasn't an informational session.

He held up both hands in apology. "Perhaps you could pontificate about it aloud to yourself."

I turned back to Carl. "They don't usually respond, and Carl here is much, much older than our usual subjects. We usually find them very promptly." I pulled my knife and cut through the golden tether. I sneaked a look at the man to see if he could tell what I was doing as I did it, but he merely looked intrigued. The faded simulacrum of Carl disappeared. "Is your ghost gone?" I asked.

The man tore his gaze from the space above the headstone and flashed me a white-toothed grin that didn't match the worry in his eyes. "Nope. I enjoyed that, but you aren't even standing anywhere close to it."

Shit.

* * *

It took me galloping Charon up to Fiona to get her attention as she was now forced to protect me from enemy fire.

"Andrea!" she chastised.

"They aren't seeing what we're seeing," I told her, cringing as something like a Fourth of July sparkler without a stick bounced off an invisible barrier in front of us to sizzle in the grass. "They are definitely seeing ghosts."

"Oh, very well," she complained.

Fiona reluctantly stopped playing with the coven, because apparently she had been, and shoved her invisible wall back until the entire coven was standing in a bewildered huddle.

The dark-haired man gave us an incredulous look over his shoulder as he jogged to his team. He definitely wasn't afraid of Fiona, but his expression held more curiosity than dislike.

The coven members were disheveled and exhausted, but the magic targeted toward them had been largely defensive in nature, so they weren't really hurt. Fiona was still in high spirits, but she managed to feign some dignity for the sake of the discussion. She was enjoying talking to the lead witch from her superior position on horseback. Luis made apologetic faces behind her back.

The witches looked a little disgusted at Fiona's charitable permission to do what they'd come to do anyway, but they didn't have a lot of recourse since she'd trounced them almost single-handed, and they'd lost nothing but some dignity. I eyed Fiona for some evidence of why she'd bothered to fight with them in the first place. Maybe it was a territorial pissing match. She wasn't above minor pettiness when the mood struck her. Or maybe she wanted them to show their cards about what they could really do. I'd ask Luis later. He was good at interpreting her.

The witches set up some kind of circle made of braided vines with candles and little bowls filled with mysterious substances dotted around it. It looked like TV witchery, which made me more doubtful about their abilities than I had been before, but I didn't know anything about magic outside of ours, so maybe the TV shows had it right. Fiona had said fake magic imitates the real magic it wanted to be. They looked like they were running speed dating for ghosts over there.

Fiona directed us back to the rows upon rows of tethered life energies, and I was soon too tired to spy on the witches much. I could see the exhaustion and impatience growing on the other Riders' faces. Helen tried to count the life energies with her tally counter, but we didn't have time for her to collect the depth of information she really wanted. It was nearing dawn when we began our trek back to the barn. Nobody felt like fast-riding just yet, so we trailed slowly after Fiona at a walk.

"Have you ever seen anything like this before?" Bennett asked Fiona. He normally looked spry for his age, but tonight he looked worn.

"This is very unusual," she answered. "It appears life energies that were never trapped have returned to their bodies."

"Perhaps all life energies are attached thusly, and only some are visible," Bennett suggested. "Perhaps the surge is causing not an increase in attachments, but an increase in visibility."

"If that's so," Luis said from behind him, "then we shouldn't be cutting the ties as that would be the natural state of the body after death."

"It isn't," Fiona said simply. "It feels wrong."

"Why did they see ghosts?" Helen asked. "Are ghosts real, or are they nuts?"

"I suspect ghosts are some expression of the dead's personality and memory," Bennett pondered. "Whereas the life energy we sever is merely the electricity that powers the body. A soul, if you will, would proceed to whatever lies in the hereafter. The spark of life, I believe, returns to the universe. Wherever either of them go, they would normally be contained within the body while the person is alive."

"Could that be why I heard one of the dead speak at the forensic center?" I asked. "Maybe there was a ghost there too?"

"An interesting theory, Andrea," Bennett agreed. "If the surge is causing an increase in magic to the dead, perhaps the yin side is experiencing just as much an influx as the yang. I'm not sure how the two interact, but I would certainly be interested in learning."

Of course Bennett found this more fascinating than disturbing. "So could there have been ghosts present with bodies all along and just none of us can see them? Should we have been doing something about it?"

"No," Fiona said. "Ghosts are rare and generally harmless." She spoke as if she were certain they were real. "The surge appears to be affecting them as well if the coven is to be believed, but I am not aware if an extra influx of magic can cause a ghost to become dangerous. As none of us can see them, there isn't much else we can do unless someone wants to expand their magical abilities in that direction."

"You don't know how to do it?" I asked, more to find out if it was something learned or something innate.

"I never tried," Fiona replied. "Once you start seeing ghosts, you never stop. You should think about that before you choose to see them."

6

Chapter 6

If I'd hoped for a break from the deluge in the upcoming week so I could get some sleep, I was destined for disappointment. Fiona, Bennett, and Luis could work during the day because their jobs allowed it and they possessed sufficient skills to keep themselves hidden, but the rest of us were going out after our work days ended. I'd called in to work Monday morning because I'd been awake all night, and I'd decided to go ahead and stretch out my fake flu a few days since I wasn't likely to get any sleep in the upcoming nights either.

My ability to recognize the feeling of "off-ness" that tethered life energy radiated from a distance and navigate toward it was improving more rapidly than it had in the previous months I'd been a Rider since I was exercising it so much, but Fiona usually still paired me with one of the more experienced Riders. I wasn't sure if she suspected danger or just thought I needed supervision.

Usually she dumped the responsibility of teaching me on Luis or Trish, but Wednesday night Fiona took me with her to a graveyard on the farthest edge of the city, one old enough that it hadn't been used in decades. It had some of the oldest graves from the city's founding, and she wanted to know if the age of the deceased affected its susceptibility to whatever was going on. The gravestones were so worn and covered in lichen that the names on most weren't readable. The little church that had once stood adjacent was a pile of rubble being consumed by the grass, the mound resembling a recently-filled grave itself. It was so quiet I could hear the faint trickle of water in the nearby creek.

"Have you ever been out here?" I asked Fiona.

She didn't answer right away. "Not in a very long time."

Yep, not since these people had died two centuries ago. Right.

"We have always handled the incomplete deaths quickly," she said, staring out over the graveyard.

"What happens if we don't?" I asked quietly. "Or if we don't do it at all? No one has ever really said."

She turned her electric blue gaze on me. "Hmm. Why do you think, Drew?"

"Because we can see it and feel it, and it feels unnatural." I shrugged. "There's an urge to right the wrong. That can't be all of it," I persisted. "There has to be a reason it *matters* what we do."

"Have you not asked that question before, Andrea?" she asked, sounding only curious, not judgmental.

"Sort of, but it just seemed like we were the Riders, and that's what we do," I admitted. "I developed the ability to do something most people can't and became part of the group that does that thing, so I did it. I can't make the ability go away, and I can't ignore it, because I've tried. I want to know why things are the way they are, but honestly, on some level it hasn't mattered all that urgently because I have to do it no matter what the answer is. And these last few months I've mostly just been getting used to being what I am, which was hard enough. I kind of expected someone would just teach me that when it was time for me to know without me having to ask."

Fiona listened to this speech with her full attention. "You are right that someone should have taught you, and it's partly my fault that no one has. At my age I have a tendency to interpret time rather poorly." That was one of the only references to her age I'd heard her make herself, and she gave a wry little grimace. "A few months just drifts by for me. And like you, I was trying to give you time to adjust to waking up to find your life so different. You still hoped to finish vet school at first, and I didn't want to stop you." She shrugged. "You're still young, and before this surge happened, it still seemed like you had a life you should be allowed to live outside of the Riders."

"A life with a really weird hobby," I said, grinning weakly.

She had the decency to smile. "Yes. I still hope you have years to spend living a normal life, Drew, when this subsides again. Valerie too. She needs to be allowed to concentrate on finishing college."

Valerie had a busy schedule of school, sorority, and field hockey, and under normal circumstances she wasn't expected to participate in many Rider duties. I'm sure the surge was interfering with her regular twenty-year-old life, but I never heard her complain about it. She was surprisingly inscrutable.

Fiona and I surveyed the very, very faint life energies in the crumbling graveyard. There were only a few of them here, so perhaps age did help.

"Let's see what happens when we don't attend to the death quickly," she said, nudging her horse toward a gravestone.

I dismounted to scrape at the lichen on the stone, hoping to discern a name. "Asa?" I guessed.

Fiona turned her gaze on whatever shadow of Asa remained. "Drew," she said calmly, "did you feel the incomplete deaths in this graveyard on our way here?"

I thought. "No, not until we were inside it. My sensing abilities are getting better, but they're nowhere near yours." I had assumed she had felt them from far enough away that she'd known to bring us here, but I hadn't felt anything even as we drew closer. I'd chalked that up to how faint the connections were.

"I didn't feel anything either until we crossed where the fence to this graveyard once lay." She was speaking very conversationally still, like she was telling me about a new horse she was training, but I was starting to get an ominous feeling. "I thought to check this place because of the recent activity in the cemeteries, but even as we neared it, I didn't feel anything, and I should have."

"Is it because the dead are so long-departed?" I asked.

"No." She didn't raise her voice, but she was looking all around us now, her brow furrowed and her eyes searching. "No, it is because this place has been warded by someone so no trace of magic can be felt outside it."

I looked around too like I might see the ward. "Can you tell who did it? I mean, does that sort of magic leave like a signature of the caster?"

"Sometimes, if you encounter enough magic worked by the same person you can get a feel for their fingerprint on something, but it is unlikely."

"Did they put it here for us?" I asked quietly.

"Maybe," she sighed after a long pause. "Or perhaps the ward is very old and was put there to contain something else in this graveyard. One of our local covens may have attempted to do something here, though if this ward is theirs, there are magic-workers in this city that are more powerful than the coven we encountered. Let's look for it." She turned Orlaith toward the outer edge of the graveyard and began studying the ground.

"What are we looking for exactly?"

"Something that forms an unbroken line." She dismounted and started patting gently at the ground where she estimated the former boundary of the graveyard to be.

I did the same. No one tended to this place anymore, and the grass had grown high and tangled with the weeds. I spied something white and reached for it only to find I'd grabbed the rib bone of some animal. Ugh. I let it go again before I even had it off the ground. Just my luck to stick my hand in something dead. I pawed around a little more carefully and saw more bones. Trying to avoid them, I moved a little to the left, then a little further, but the bones continued. Had someone dumped an ossuary out here? Dumped a dead body in a graveyard to hide it?

"Fiona? There's a lot of bones over here, and they sort of form a line."

She came to look. "That has potential. You track it left; I'll go right."

A few yards later, we had a confirmed border of bones laid haphazardly end to end that probably went all the way around the graveyard.

"This is it," Fiona said, dusting off her hands. "The ward is tied to these bones. I suspect there's a layer underground too for it to be as strong as it is. Bone to tie death is especially fitting."

"Do we break it?" I asked.

She shook her head. "No, not until we know why it's there. Let's be cautious."

"I kind of accidentally picked up one of the bones," I admitted.

"It's fine," she assured me. "I can still feel the ward. If it were that delicate, the wind and small animals would break it quickly. Let's go back to Asa."

We reconvened in front of the headstone and eyed the cloud that was Asa.

"Cut him free," Fiona said.

I took my antler-handled knife out and gently sliced through the golden thread. Except it wouldn't cut. I tried again with a bit more force, then tried sawing at it, which felt like an indignity to Asa, if he were paying attention.

I looked at Fiona for help.

"This is what happens when they aren't tended to quickly," she said. "Let me try." She took my place and severed the thread with her wickedly-sharp golden dagger. The blade went through, but the effort clearly took force.

Instead of vanishing, Asa shot upward like a released balloon until he hit some invisible ceiling. Unable to go higher, the gray blob began to float around the expanse of the graveyard like it was covered in a glass dome.

"So if we wait too long to separate them, they get really hard to cut?" I asked as we both stared upward.

"Yes, that's one thing that can happen," she said. "I don't know if this ward was put in place to hide the dead from us, but even if it was placed for some other purpose, it still had that result. None of us were able to feel this place, and I wouldn't have thought to check on it if it were not for the effect the surge is having on the cemeteries."

"Should we remove the ward now to release the life energy?"

"No, I want to examine it further before we do that. I'll come back tomorrow and perform some tests." She started back toward Orlaith, who was waiting with practiced patience.

"What about the other dead?" I asked, glancing around at the few others in the graveyard.

"We will leave them until tomorrow too. I don't want to risk doing more harm to them until we know what we are doing." She swung into the saddle. "Come. We will return tomorrow night."

* * *

Before we could return to the warded graveyard, I had to drag myself to work the next day since I wouldn't be able to provide a doctor's note for my alleged flu. I was careful to let myself look like death warmed over, which, given my sleep schedule for the week, didn't exactly require Oscar-level acting. I threw in some fake nose-blowing and coughing to go with the dark circles under my eyes and figured I'd set myself up for calling in sick again tomorrow if I needed to. I caught a quick nap in my truck outside the barn while I waited for Fiona, oddly excited to finish what we'd started the previous evening.

Charon was not in the mood for another trip after all the exercise he'd gotten that week, and he wasn't shy about showing his feelings. He refused to fast-ride for more than a few miles, so we ended up trotting listlessly down back roads. This time Fiona had brought what I guessed were testing implements with her, magical paraphernalia that was mysterious to me. We left the horses tied to trees outside the graveyard and went to stand at its edge.

"So what first?" I asked.

Fiona took what looked like a tuning fork out of her bag and gave it a sharp strike. The note was high-pitched enough to startle the horses, and it lasted much longer than it should have. A faint orange haze appeared around the graveyard, giving form to that overturned glass bowl I had imagined the night before. I'm not sure we would have been able to see it even with the tuning fork if it wasn't glowing in the darkness. It lasted until the piercing noise faded, then became invisible again.

"The ward is still in place," Fiona observed. "Let's look inside."

We stepped over the bone barrier we had uncovered. I immediately looked upward to where I expected the helium balloon version of Asa to be. No gray blob floated near the top of the ward. He hadn't returned to his headstone either.

"Where is the life we untethered last night? Did it make it through the ward?"

"No," Fiona said. "Someone else has been here. Look at the other stones."

I did. "Where are the other lives? They didn't separate by themselves because of their age, did they?"

"No, I think they had help," Fiona said grimly.

"Did we get our wires crossed with some of the other Riders, and they came to check on this graveyard?" Even as I asked, I already knew that wasn't going to be it.

"No. Bennett and Luis are the only ones I told about this graveyard. I was going to tell Helen after we had the numbers to record."

I wrapped my arms around myself, wishing I'd brought a heavier jacket. It was getting colder at night. "So what now?"

"I'm still going to do the tests I planned," Fiona said. "I want to know if this ward is holding in something that needs to stay hidden, or if it was only meant to block the life energies from being felt. You can watch, but I need you to stand outside the ward. My tests will pick you up as magical."

"I wish more people saw me as magical," I attempted to quip. The ominous feeling was growing, and I didn't know why. I would have put it down to surge-related weirdness if it weren't for the shadowy specter of an unknown person. In theory as a magic-worker, I knew it was possible for there to be others who could work magic too, but the Riders never crossed their paths. The realization that they may have been working circles around us like we worked hidden from the non-magical people made me feel like I was being watched from somewhere in the darkness. There was never a time where I knew there were strange things lurking in the dark before I *was* the strange thing lurking in the dark, and finding myself back on the other side with my eyes now opened was unnerving.

I tried to focus my attention on what Fiona was doing instead of letting my imagination invent secret enemies. She used her tuning fork again from inside the ward, then appeared to be looking over her shoulder with a mirror. She filled a bowl from a water bottle and tossed something powdered into it. It wasn't all that different from what the coven had been doing. I couldn't see anything happening after each test, and I hoped that was a good thing.

The feeling of being watched was still growing. Orlaith raised her head suddenly, pricking her ears at something in the direction of the former church. I looked, but I didn't have a horse's night vision. It was probably just wildlife. I looked back at Fiona. She must have been doing something to the ward because I was starting to get that familiar feeling of wrongness that signaled a death gone awry. But that couldn't be it—there hadn't been any life energies left in the graveyard, unless they were just so faint with age I couldn't see them. Fiona would have said if they were still there though, right? Maybe that was the magic she was working now.

I rotated my head a few times like I was a radar antenna. The feeling was getting stronger, and it was coming from the direction both horses were now staring. Maybe there was a body outside the graveyard. That wasn't unusual; sometimes the boundaries got confused with time, or someone who couldn't afford a proper burial sneaked their loved one as close as they could to hallowed ground. Graveyards were also a great place to discreetly dispose of a body, right where a dead person was expected to be. I left Fiona to her tests and went to investigate, moving quietly toward the feeling and the old church as if I were afraid to sneak up on the dead.

The church had been built of wood, so there wasn't much of it left other than the heap of composting plant matter where it had once been. Still, it formed a sizable mound, and between it and the sloping ground, I was surprised by how quickly I was almost out of sight from the horses. The ground around the church had probably been cleared further back during its years of use, but the trees had grown up almost to it again. I was so close to the wrong feeling now that I thought I should be able to see it, so it must be hidden by the trees. I turned on the flashlight on my cell phone and took a few steps closer.

"Andrea?" Fiona's voice was surprisingly faint. She was only a few yards away from me.

"Here!" I shouted back. I turned back to face the trees again.

Something gray and shimmering appeared before me, only maybe ten feet away. I had just a brief half-second to think, *oh, there it is,* before that thought was immediately overridden by confusion. The gray, shimmering thing was rushing toward me, and it looked surprisingly solid for a life energy. It felt solid too as it hit me hard enough to knock me down, which shouldn't have been possible. It brushed on past me and made a circle like it was coming back. I scrambled to my feet.

Fiona appeared out of the darkness, a golden sword in one hand. She darted at the gray thing, more to drive it away from me than to hurt it, I think. I put my back to a tree and pulled my knife while Fiona positioned herself between me and the thing. It paused a few yards away to study its new opponent, and I studied it. It did look very much like the gray facsimiles of the dead, clear and distinct like those who had died only recently. But it was far too solid. It wasn't quite opaque because I could see the shadows of tree trunks through it, but it was present enough that I could make out the worn knuckles on the man's hands and the little patch on the knee of the trousers he wore held up by suspenders. He was very old, but he could have been mistaken for a real person in the darkness until you got close.

"Asa," I said, trying to keep the tremble out of my voice. "You are dead. Something has happened, and—"

Asa opened his ghostly mouth to reveal the poor quality of the dental care of his time period and hissed at me like a fucking cat. I decided I was done with the dead-soothing. He darted toward me, and Fiona drove him back again with a swing of her sword.

"This is the other thing that can happen if the life energy is left to linger," Fiona said, attention rapt. "It has drawn enough magic to gain form and strength. The phenomenon is rare and is the source for many tales of ghosts and ghouls throughout history."

"I take it they don't come back with their minds," I said.

"No true intelligence or motivation, just instinct and reaction," she confirmed. "They are a lot harder to dispatch this way." She paused to let out a piercing whistle, never taking her attention from Asa. "Try to stay where you are, Drew, so I don't lose track of you. It will be easier for me to protect you if you stay close."

She didn't wait for any followup questions before she lunged gracefully at the gray thing, her sword burning a golden arc through the air. Asa managed to dodge somehow and streaked away into the woods, blurring and disintegrating as he went. Fiona cursed and went after him.

Now I wasn't sure if I was supposed to obey the "stay where you are" or "stay close" part of her instructions. While I was deliberating, something large and pale in the moonlight pounded through the trees toward me. Orlaith galloped by in the direction Fiona had gone. Charon's indignant neigh followed; he was still tied up. I took a few tentative steps after the horse. I had made up my mind to follow Fiona when the crashing began to come back in my direction.

Asa, or what used to be him, roared back toward me with alarming speed. He wasn't running, just sort of floating above the ground like the memory of how to use his legs hadn't survived. He had probably just been fleeing blindly from Fiona, but when he saw me, he changed his course toward me. I swung my knife in a semi-circle, hoping to keep him backed away until Fiona arrived. It worked to stop him, but the knife was a lot shorter than Fiona's sword, and he was quick enough to dodge my little pokes. Worse, he seemed to be learning, and he would probably figure out I wasn't fast enough to block him every time.

I tried not to look as I heard the low thunder of approaching hooves, but I saw her anyway as the sword arced down. Fiona and Orlaith were both wrapped in a soft, golden glow, Fiona's face lit with the determination and righteous fury of an archangel descending. There was too much grace, too much power for a mere human to possess. The blade sliced through the dead man in a strike so fast and clean, I imagined it made a musical note just out of the range of the human ear.

Instead of slicing in half, Asa disintegrated almost as abruptly as the life energy usually did. The galloping horse continued on by, and I leaned against the tree trunk again, trying to catch my breath while I stared at the place where Asa used to be. Trying very, very hard not to look at Fiona.

I heard her return, Orlaith's hooves soft on the ground now. "Are you all right, Drew?"

I risked looking up. She was still glowing a little, so faint it would have been lost in the sunlight. "Yes, I'm fine. Are you?"

"Yes. We've got to get you a sword." She leaned to look down at the ground where Asa had stood.

"A sword would be sweet. Where exactly were you hiding yours?" She definitely hadn't brought that with her. It was longer than her bag.

She sat up so she could hold the sword upright in front of her again. She gave it a little shake, and it shrank back down to the golden knife she always carried with her. She put the knife back on her belt and dismounted.

"Ah, travel-sized for convenience." I nodded sagely. "What is that?"

Fiona let whatever she'd just scooped up trail back out of her hand. "Ash. He was corporeal enough to have left behind a little." She took a specimen jar from her saddlebag and began to fill it.

"That's so gross," I said faintly. "Can he come back again?"

"I don't think so," she said thoughtfully. "I can't think of anything that's ever come back from ash, though the world is a wide and mysterious place."

I found that less comforting than she had probably intended. Charon let out another horsey-scream of fury to let us know he did not like being left alone, and we started to walk back toward him.

"Drew," Fiona said as we reached the graveyard again, "I think whoever set that ward came and cut through the energy that was attached to the bodies. They couldn't get Asa because we'd already freed him, and he was inadvertently set loose. That means they were doing something intentional with the others. Maybe they just thought he wasn't useful for their purpose anymore and released him, not realizing he wouldn't just disperse to the universe like he was supposed to."

I put my cold face into Charon's warm neck for a moment. "Something intentional? What can you do with the life energy of the long-dead? Does that fall under necromancy?"

"I don't know." She sounded a little worried now, tired. Her eyes were still scanning around us for danger as I cuddled a Welsh pony, trying to hide from the things in the dark instead of facing them like she did. "Logic tells me the life energy that runs through us all is powerful. If someone has found something to do with that energy—it can only be sorcery of an evil nature."

Calling something "evil" seemed like fairy tale levels of dramatic, but I knew in my heart she was right.

"Whatever it is," she continued, "they need to harvest energy from the bodies, and they have the ability to create wards that can stop us from feeling lives they've trapped while the surge fills them with more and more magic."

She didn't need to tell me how hard this was going to make our jobs. "How are we going to fight back?"

"I'm going to start by laying a trap for anyone else who comes here," she answered. "I don't know if they will be back if they have realized we've been here, but it is worth a try." Her smile was faint like she knew something she wasn't going to say. "Come—you may help if you like."

After a second's hesitation, I followed her back into the graveyard, feeling somehow I might be agreeing to more than just watching her lay a trap.

7

Chapter 7

If there were other magical things going bump in the night, I wanted to know more about the other players who were sharing the supernatural landscape with us. Either we'd root out a likely culprit, or we'd rule out some innocent parties. I believed in Rider magic because I'd experienced it. Real witches had remained vague figures that lived in the past. But if there were witches here who could really do magic, maybe they had some resources we didn't.

I didn't tell anyone about my plan since I wasn't sure anyone would agree with me, but I decided to try to talk to someone from the one coven I did know existed. I tried looking for them on the internet, but unlike some of the other groups I found, they didn't seem to have a social media presence or a website. I had a feeling the groups with the hippie jargon selling incense and crystals were probably the fakes. It made sense that a real group would want to keep a lower profile.

I would have to track them down in person. If they were patrolling cemeteries like we were, perhaps our paths would cross again there. Fiona had decided to set traps around different cemeteries, and asking to accompany her would probably have gotten me the widest exposure, but it would mean Fiona would be there while I tried to talk to the witches, and I had a feeling they wouldn't be all that pleased to see her again.

My chance came when Fiona took Bennett with her to give him a lesson on setting magical alarms, and I volunteered to take half his territory for the night. I could tell Fiona wasn't sold about my being out on my own, especially since she had a bullshit meter that would rival a veteran teacher's, but she marked out the newest, most centrally-located cemeteries where I would be least likely to encounter anything unusual and let me go. I might not be a match for another Asa, but nobody but the most experienced few of us were. Everyone had been instructed to turn tail and go for help should that happen again.

I set out hunting for the coven, making Charon fast-run until he communicated his feelings by trying to scrape me off against a tree. I got lucky though, and there were people at the third place I tried. I hovered around the treed edge of the cemetery, trying to identify them in the darkness. It would be a bit unfortunate if I rode up on a group of mourners visiting granny's grave in the middle of the night. Or if I ran up on some grave robbers. Or with my luck it would be the wrong coven, and I'd have some awkward explaining to do about my blue undead pony.

The shadowy figures were standing in a loose circle, watching one of their members who was seated to do something too distant for me to see. The figure closest to me turned his head toward me, and I stilled Charon so he wouldn't draw attention. The person continued to look in my direction for a long moment, then returned his attention to the circle. I continued to circle around the edge of the cemetery, aiming for the parking lot. They didn't ride here like I did; they must have cars. Maybe they all had Hazelwood Coven bumper stickers.

I was skulking around a beige sedan when someone eased out of the shadows nearby. It was good sneaking; I wouldn't have heard him if Charon hadn't looked.

"Hey, were you looking for me?"

It was the dark-haired man who had made fun of Charon. It had been him that had been staring at me a few minutes ago.

"Yes, actually," I said, almost relieved it was him who had come. I could see him better here at the edge of the streetlight than I had in the darkness of the cemetery. He was one of those almost-good-looking guys that were in their own way kind of hotter than traditionally handsome men—roman nose, eyes so dark they were nearly black, and stubble that probably made his jaw look a little more square than it really was. He was wearing a brown leather jacket with the collar flipped up against his neck.

He smiled at me suddenly like he knew I was looking him over, teeth a flash of white against the stubble. "That connection we felt the other night—you just couldn't stay away?"

Flummoxed replaced relieved, and I stared at him for a beat. "No, sorry. This is business."

"Maybe personal can be later then?" he suggested. Fortunately he didn't wait for me to come up with a witty response. "Why are you here?"

"I think a little exchange of information between groups might help us both figure out what's going on around here," I said.

He raised his eyebrows. "And whose idea was that? Yours? If this was an official olive branch, your people wouldn't have sent you by yourself."

"What makes you think that?"

"You're clearly the baby of the group," he pointed out. "You're young, and you're riding the pony."

Yeah, he thought I was young because he hadn't seen Valerie, who would look like a grown-up sometime after she hit forty. And despite the number of times I'd wished for my own horse so I could stop riding Charon, I was getting pretty offended on his behalf. "Charon is perfectly good at his job," I told the man. "And I am perfectly good at mine. Do you want to swap info or what?"

"Yeah, but I'm not supposed to be talking to you either." He shuffled through a pocket for his phone. "We can meet somewhere else to talk later if you want. What's your phone number?"

I hadn't really planned on organizing secret liaisons, but he was right. That made more sense than trying to have an in-depth discussion in a cemetery parking lot. Or he was just going to tattle to his superiors on me. Nothing ventured, nothing gained, I guessed. I told him the number. "What's your name, anyway?"

"Case."

"What did you just put me in your phone as?" He hadn't asked *my* name.

"Weird pony girl," Case replied with a grin that said he was delighted I'd asked.

I took a deep breath and let Charon's reins go slack. He was a smart pony, he'd been around a long time, and he knew an opportunity when he saw one. He lunged forward and knocked his head right into Case's chest, knocking him down.

"You deserved that," I informed him with dignity. "And it's Drew."

I nudged Charon into a fast-run, which he did willingly for once, and left that bastard sitting on his ass.

* * *

I was afraid after I let Charon assault him that Case wouldn't call me to arrange our meeting, but he texted me the next morning asking if I could meet at the park at 3 pm. I was getting used to sleeping half the day, and readjusting to my regular work schedule was going to be a nightmare when this was all over.

CHAPTER 7

He was waiting when I got there, sitting on a picnic table bench with his back to the table, studying the park-goers through dark aviators. He looked so normal, sitting there in jeans and a gray henley with the sleeves scrunched up, not like someone who was part of a coven or talked to ghosts. I missed normal, but I was becoming more and more aware that it was just a facade. He didn't see me right away, and I stood watching him for a moment, starting to second-guess myself. Maybe I was about to be squeezed for information without receiving any in return.

Case looked up as I approached and pushed his sunglasses up onto his head. "Hey, I was beginning to think you were going to stand in the parking lot all afternoon."

"Just thinking," I said, dropping onto the other side of the picnic table.

He turned around so he was sitting facing me now, his forearms on the table. Without the jacket, he had square shoulders and biceps that suggested either a physical job or time in the gym, though he didn't have that bulky bodybuilder physique some gym rats pursued. "Will you get in trouble for talking to me?" he asked seriously.

I shrugged. "For telling you things, maybe. Not for talking to you. You've obviously been told not to talk to me."

"My mom always told me not to talk to strange girls," he agreed, but his heart wasn't in the joke. "What is it you think our groups can coordinate on? The mean redhead didn't look like she wanted any inter-group cooperation." His expression was skeptical.

Admitting Fiona thought they weren't worth her notice would probably not promote a friendly attitude. I propped my elbows on the table. "I thought maybe we could share data. We have our map of sites affected, and I'm sure you do too. It might be helpful to see where they overlap."

He looked blank.

Not off to a stellar start. "You don't keep track of anything?"

Case shrugged. "Keep track of what? Why? There have been a lot more ghosts than usual lately, but we aren't recording statistics on them. What would we need them for?"

"Aren't you trying to figure out where they're coming from?"

He eyed me cautiously. "No. We don't really have a higher calling or duty like your boss was shouting about. We aren't ghostbusters. We're just a group of people with a shared interest in the study of magic. We handle a few odd disturbances here and there, but we were mostly at the cemetery out of curiosity, not on a mission. We have no idea what's causing all these ghosts to suddenly appear." He leaned forward. "You do, don't you?"

I hesitated, hoping I wasn't about to reveal information that was supposed to be secret. "It's the rift that runs under this city."

"Rift? Rift in what?"

I shrugged. "I don't know, the world? It's where magic comes from."

The blank look was back with a vengeance. "Where magic comes from," he echoed. "What do you mean where magic *comes* from?"

"You're all magic users, aren't you?" I asked. "How do you not know where your magic comes from?"

He shrugged. "Magic just exists as part of our natural world, just as light and water do. Some people are capable of learning to experience and manipulate it. Using it is a skill that requires a combination of natural talent and training, just like playing the violin."

"Well, I guess we're in agreement that far," I told him, "except we believed it has a specific place it enters the world. The rifts are the source of all magic, like the atmosphere is our source of oxygen."

"I think trees are our source of oxygen," he pointed out, but the response felt like an automatic impulse to make a joke. He was staring past my head now, trying to compare what I'd just told him with whatever he had been taught to believe.

"Nitrogen then. Whatever. And probably beside the point. The point is, magic comes from the rift, and right now the rift is having a surge."

"So what does a surge mean?"

"Magic overload," I told him. "Weird things happening. Apparently for you, that's ghosts."

His distant gaze snapped back to my face. "How long is it going to last?"

"We don't know. Our records show a lot of variance. That's part of why I was hoping you had some records, so we could compare notes," I explained.

Case was looking a little disturbed now. "We have records of spells and magical workings and things like that we've collected over the years, but we don't really have historic records."

"Why? How old is your coven?" No wonder Fiona hadn't bothered with these people. Even if they technically could do magic, it didn't look like they were organized or knowledgeable enough to handle the supernatural turmoil that was happening right now. The Riders didn't have a great track record of recordkeeping, but we at least had a history.

"About twenty years, though some of us have been practicing a lot longer. I'm guessing if none of us remember one of these surge things, that they happen more than a few decades apart." There was a certain dread in his dark eyes now. "So how old are the Bone Riders that you have records of multiple surges?"

"Centuries," I told him almost absently.

"Centuries," Case repeated very softly.

If I hadn't sounded like a weirdo before, I certainly did now. I looked out across the park at the kids throwing peas to the geese from the pier and the chatty senior citizens doing laps around the walking track with their jackets tied around their waists to give him time to think.

"Well," he said after a long pause, "I don't think I'm being very helpful to you, Barrymore, but I've certainly enjoyed the magical history lesson."

"Barrymore?"

"What other Drew is there?"

"It's short for Andrea, Suitcase."

"It's Casey," he admitted sheepishly. He drummed his fingers on the table for a moment. "Some of us have gotten stronger magic in the last few weeks," he said quietly. "And some of the coven who couldn't do magic at all can now. I take it that's the surge?"

"Probably." I shrugged. "Why do you have people in your coven who can't do magic?"

"Because they wanted to learn to," he replied. "We don't always know if people can or not yet when they join us. We've always treated it as a skill issue, but I guess that's in question."

"What happens to the people in the coven who never learn?" Riders recruited talent-first, training later.

"They usually just slowly stop coming. A few of them have stuck around for the social aspect, and I guess it's paid off for them." He looked glum. "Are they going to lose it again when the surge is over?"

"I'm not sure, sorry," I told him honestly. "You were kind of right about me being the baby of the group. I'm probably the least qualified to give you a magic lesson."

He had the decency to smile at that. "Well, you taught me more than I taught you. Sorry I wasn't more helpful."

"It was worth a try. That doesn't mean we can't still compare notes about recent sightings. I did want to ask if you'd been out to a couple of cemeteries we've been to lately." I hoped I sounded sufficiently casual. I thought given his coven's low level of magical prowess, it was unlikely one of them was responsible for the ward and its nefarious use, but I was risking accidentally tipping off the perpetrator by asking.

I don't think Fiona would forgive me for that.

"Yeah? There's four or five in town we've been working. It's not usually like that though. Ghosts don't exactly like to hang out where they're buried; they like to imitate their habits in life."

"Have you been to any of the older graveyards?" I asked, hoping that was enough information without directly mentioning the warded one. "We want to know if there's a connection between the age of the dead and how the magic affects them."

He shook his head. "No, I haven't been out to any old graveyards. Maybe Rina has, but I don't think we've seen many old ghosts."

I exhaled the tension I'd been holding. "That's good news. Thanks."

"I'll try to write down some of the places we've been working, but I think they are just some of the same places you have probably already been, so I'm not sure that'll help," he apologized.

"That would be great." I wasn't sure it would help either. "Why did you agree to meet with me?" I asked him. He hadn't been concerned about an escalating problem like I was or trying to find the source of the odd happenings. He had come because I'd asked to compare notes, but he clearly hadn't been searching for information.

He shrugged. "I was curious. You have interesting magic I've never seen before. We had no idea the lot of you existed, which is impressive in itself. Those horses are cool."

"They are," I agreed fervently.

A slow smile spread across Casey's face. "Are the horses the reason you became a Bone Rider?"

Explaining how wrong incomplete deaths felt to me and how it was easier to join the Riders than to live having to pretend I didn't notice it was too personal and complex to explain. "Pretty much. Why did you join your coven?" He deeply didn't strike me as the "coven" type of person, though my views of that type were ever-evolving lately.

His expression wasn't quite derisive, but it wasn't enthusiastic either.

"When I figured out I could do magic, I needed someone to teach me. They were the people I could find who knew magic and had resources. They aren't the most talented or knowledgeable group, but there are a few like Rina who take things seriously. She'd probably build a solid coven if she could get enough people involved."

Yeah, I guess we both ended up with the teams that were available to us. It's not like we could shop around for the best fit like applying to colleges.

I stood. "If you see anything really strange while you're out chasing ghosts, will you text me?"

Casey's dark eyes had gone unreadable now. "Sure thing, Drew. Good luck."

Uh huh. Something told me my little bridge-building effort had mostly just served to educate Casey, and probably his coven by proxy, about what was going on. I wasn't going to get anything back for it. I hoped Fiona didn't hang me by my toes when she found out.

* * *

Monday I got to the barn a little earlier than I usually did, hoping to catch Fiona before the others started trooping in. She usually came back for a few hours around this time of day to eat and take care of the horses before she went out again with us. I wasn't sure when she slept, if she did, but I knew she'd been making long trips out to the farthest reaches of the rift's usual territory while Luis and Bennett managed the city itself. I found her cutting open bags of feed to refill the bins.

"I know you're busy right now," I told her, carrying a bag of oats to the appropriate bin, "but when things settle down, could you start teaching me some of the stuff you were doing the other night at the graveyard?"

"Magic," Fiona said.

"Yes, I guess so." Maybe she thought I meant her sword-wielding skills.

"Why?" When I paused too long, she glanced up at me and actually smiled. "Don't look so disconcerted. I'm just curious about what brought about this decision. Were you scared by what happened with the being at the graveyard?"

"I can't say I wasn't," I admitted. "But mostly it just seems like we're fighting a different fight than we were before, and it might be useful to have the right tools."

"And you want to wait until things 'settle down?'" she inquired.

Now I knew she was messing with me. After the surge subsided, there probably wouldn't be another one for decades. "You enjoy picking on me," I accused.

"I don't," she insisted, tightening the lids on the bins. "I just want you to actually say what you want, Drew. Don't equivocate."

"Fine. I want you to teach me to do magic. I also realize you are very busy with more pressing things right now, so I understand if you don't have the time or energy to do that until this is all over."

"All over," Fiona repeated as if there were something ironic about those words. "There's no point in waiting. You will only be able to learn a little at a time anyway. Ten minutes is enough for a first lesson. Come outside."

I stuffed the feed bags into the trash and followed her.

She stood in front of the barn, squinting at the autumn sunset, and didn't say anything.

"So do we start with theory?" I inquired. "Is there reading I need to do first?"

She looked at me and smiled for the second time. Two smiles from Fiona in one day—the world might really be ending. "I can't believe you and Bennett don't get along better. You're both absolutely pedantic. I could probably find you some reading if you're really curious, but that's not really how I learn things."

"Is it because there were no books outside monasteries when you were a child?"

"Keep on, Drew. We'll do the 'Labors of Hercules' style teaching. The manure pile needs rotating." I pretended to sober. "I thought we'd just start with the most basic thing," she continued. "Feeling magic."

"Okay, I can feel magic when you're doing it in front of me, like when you were fighting at the cemetery. What am I feeling magic in now?"

"Start with yourself," she suggested. "You use magic all the time. You should know what using magic feels like, so try to recall that feeling." She stepped around me and started walking back toward the barn.

"Wait, that's it? How do I even do that?"

She paused to look back at me. "You know when you free a tethered life energy that it isn't the knife doing it—it's you. You already do magic all the time, Drew. Call up the feeling." And she left me there to stand around confused about what I should be doing.

I stared after her for a while, still suspicious this was a joke, then set about trying to "feel" my magic. I didn't normally notice any kind of sensation when I did magic, at least not within myself. There was the feeling of wrongness that accompanied an incomplete death; that sensation just vanished when the life energy was severed. I tried thinking about my actions when I freed a life energy. It was just intent, right? So if I intended to do something, it should happen. I thought about Rider magic instead—that I could feel when I was with the group. It was icy, silvery somehow, like cold, thin night air on a mountainside. I called up the memory of how that felt and tried to feel it now.

A car door slamming made me jump, and I realized I'd been standing outside the barn staring at nothing, probably looking very deranged.

I tried to adopt a more casual demeanor as Bennett approached.

"Good evening, Andrea," he said kindly. "What are you doing?"

"Just lost in thought," I chirped. "I guess we'd better get going."

"Anything?" Fiona asked as I passed her on my way to Charon.

"I can feel Rider magic, I guess, but not anything explicitly from me." I still wasn't sure she wasn't just messing with me.

"That's a start," she said, leading Orlaith outside. "Try again tomorrow."

If this was magic learning, we'd be dealing with the surge a century in the future before I got the hang of it.

8

Chapter 8

"I'm never sure if it's easier or tougher for you all these days," Fiona pondered as we rode out to a cemetery at the edge of the county, trotting lightly through a field paralleling the road where the moonlight gave us long shadows. "Being a Rider takes up less of your daily lives than once it would have, but there is more stress on your livelihoods and routines now when something like this happens. A surge is rare though," she decided.

The surge may have been rare, but it was kicking our butts. Those of us with day jobs were swapping out every other night now so we could get some rest. Valerie had been told to take at least the week off so she could catch up on her studies. I was dragging myself to work every day because I couldn't take any more time off without either proving I was sick or getting fired.

The mysterious malefactor stealing life energy for enigmatic purposes continued to linger in our consciousness like a shadow but never became anything more. The traps Fiona and Bennett had set around the cemeteries weren't proving to be a fruitful endeavor. The rolling expanses of the purpose-built cemeteries were too huge to encircle with any significant magic, and there were too many false alarms from maintenance staff, mourners, or coven members looking for ghosts, though the wards only alerted at night. August, the most tech-savvy of us, was trying to wire cameras around some of the cemeteries, but it was slow going to try to do that clandestinely. Fiona's current plan was simply for us to keep working until there were no life energies left for the miscreant to use. We would chase him down slowly and surely until his path was forced to overlap ours.

"What did it used to be like?" I asked.

Fiona tilted her head briefly in a contemplative gesture. "Things have changed many times over the centuries. There was a time when Riders did little besides Rider work. It was their profession, not a secret side job."

She was unusually chatty tonight. "Was that back when Rider magic used to make people live a really long time?"

"What makes you think it doesn't now?"

I wondered how many centuries of practice it had taken Fiona to learn to punk people with that straight a face. "Because yourself aside, no one in the Asterville Riders is that old."

She deigned to curl one corner of her mouth up, probably laughing at me. "The two things are related, but it is just a matter of exposure to the magic. Then, there were fewer Riders spending most of their time doing Rider work. They were magical devotees. Now there are more of us here doing less work individually because you have jobs and children and lives outside of being a Rider. Some Riders work for a time and then retire. You aren't interacting with the magic all day, every day anymore."

She let me think on that for a while before she spoke again. "And while no one is as old as I am"—there was that quirk of a smile again—"not everyone is as young as you think."

"I know Bennett and Luis are a little older than they look. I don't really know about Della and Sean. But everyone else is pretty young,"

I pointed out.

"Depends on how you quantify a little," she mused. "Luis has grandchildren. Bennett is still living in the era of his youth as if the world hasn't moved on. It's hard to not age without someone noticing in these days of birth certificates and social security numbers."

I wondered, not for the first time, how Fiona had any of those identifications that let her buy her house and pay her electricity bill.

"Is that going to happen to me too?"

"Would you like it too?"

I wasn't sure I would. Being alive a long time seemed like it would come with a lot of burdens: watching your loved ones die before you, the world changing drastically around you, having to start over again and again. I didn't particularly want to say any of that to Fiona though because she had likely been through it all.

"It's okay, Drew," she said when I was quiet as if she knew what I was thinking, yet again.

"So did all these years of magic exposure give you mind-reading powers?"

She snorted. "I can imagine few things worse than being subjected to other people's innermost thoughts."

"Would you rather go back to the days when the Riders just did Rider work?"

"'Going back' isn't a meaningful consideration," she said philosophically. "We must change as the world changes around us. I could handle the entirety of the Rider duties in this area all myself if I had to. But it is better to have others trained to help. If something were to happen to me, there would be no one to take over the work. And I like having time to train horses."

Fiona drew Orlaith to an unexpected halt and fished what looked like a rudimentary map imprinted on a piece of cloth out of her jacket pocket. "One of the wards was breached." I assumed the map had something to do with how she knew when one of her traps had been triggered, and I knew she could sense them better the closer she was to them.

"Should we ride over there?" I felt the first tingles of excitement. Our mysterious villain at last?

"I don't want to ride all the way out there just to have to ride back here," she said. "It's Luis's territory, and whoever is setting off the ward will likely be gone before we get there. I'll let him know." She found her phone and held it to her ear, presumably calling Luis. I could hear the mechanical voice tell her to leave a message.

"I can take care of Thompson by myself," I told her.

She frowned. "I don't want to leave you here by yourself."

"We're a mile from the cemetery," I pointed out. "I'll get it done and meet you at Mount Olive." That would put us back on schedule without Fiona having to backtrack too much.

She still wasn't sold, but she didn't want to miss an opportunity to catch whoever might be sneaking around the graveyards. "All right," she agreed. "But call me if anything looks unusual."

"I will," I promised.

Orlaith galloped away almost too quickly for my eyes to follow, and I turned Charon on toward the old Thompson family cemetery. It didn't have a fence, and I approached it from the back to avoid the street on the odd chance someone was driving by at this time of night. I was about to enter when Charon froze, his ears pricked toward something in the cemetery ahead. I trusted his instincts, so if he heard something, there was probably something there, and I dismounted to creep closer on foot to check. Sometimes the homeless picked quiet cemeteries for their campsites, or the Hazelwood Coven might be visiting. I crouched in the brush at the edge of the trees.

Instead of a hobo with a fire or a witch with a salt circle, there was a dark shadow standing next to the grave, as tall as a human but so amorphous in shape it took me a minute to realize the shapeless darkness was a cloak with the hood pulled up. I'd never seen anyone outside a historical drama wear a cloak except Fiona. The shadow extended an arm toward a tethered life energy, trying to catch hold of it with gloved fingers. It wasn't material enough to grasp, but it wavered slightly as if feeling the touch. It wasn't really the knife that cut through life threads when we freed them, it was our intention, so in theory you could separate a tether with just your hand, but I didn't think that was what this person was trying to achieve.

I realized I'd been crouching there staring since I'd frozen at the sight of the person in the cemetery. I was hidden only by the fact that he, if it was a man, had his back to me and I hadn't left the tree line. I eased back behind a tree to keep watching.

The man had something like a small net in one hand now and was trying to toss it over the shimmering cloud. The net hung for a second longer than gravity should have allowed, tiny sparks like static electricity on a fleece blanket snapping along it, before it fell empty.

I wiggled my phone out of my pocket and texted Fiona: *Someone at cemetery. Doing something to energy.*

There was a long pause as I continued to watch the cloaked figure dousing the life energy with something from a glass bottle.

She texted me back: *Leave.*

Yes, always succinct, Fiona.

But the light from my cell phone or maybe the vibration had drawn the man's attention. He took a few cautious steps toward me as if searching the woods for the source. I'd already pocketing the phone, and I stayed statue-still, hoping he couldn't pick me out in the dark. He stood frozen as well for a long moment, then turned on a heel and darted back to the headstone to pick up the bag he'd left there.

I should have just stayed still, but the same burst of adrenaline that had spiked through me when I snatched the keycards from the forensic center flooded through me again, and I bolted after him. If this was the person who we'd been looking for, we might not get lucky enough to find him twice. I had to stop him from leaving until Fiona or one of the others got there. His running had the labored cadence of the unathletic, and stopping to gather his things slowed him down enough that I caught up with him. He raised a forearm to push me away right as I reached for him, and we collided awkwardly. If I hadn't thought through chasing him, I definitely hadn't made a plan to hold him. I held onto the arm he'd thrown up for dear life and felt my heels drag against the soft ground. I felt a little thrill that I was winning; he couldn't break my grip.

The man twisted away from me, but when I wouldn't let go of his arm, he turned back, right hand extending to shove me away. A white-hot line of fire seared across my upper arm, and I realized with distant shock he hadn't been trying to push me, but to *stab* me. My determination not to let go redoubled, not to hold him captive but out of self-preservation; I didn't want to fall on my ass with him standing over me with a knife. I grappled for the arm holding the knife and got a fist-full of sleeve. I couldn't catch his arm, but I was keeping him too unbalanced to aim another swing. I could hear him muttering to himself but couldn't make out what he was saying.

Then it was like someone hit me over the head with a mallet and pulled a bag over my face at the same time. My hands let go of his arms, and I had no control over my body anymore. I felt myself hit the ground but couldn't even brace for the impact. I heard the distant sound of running footsteps fading, then the soft whinny of a horse.

* * *

I had some vague perception of Fiona's face leaning over me and a sound like someone talking underwater that didn't match up with her mouth. Someone picked me up, and I was bobbing along like a balloon having its string jerked around by a child. The bobbing resolved into the familiar rhythm of a horse walking, and I relaxed. I raised my head again a few seconds later to realize I was sitting in a car seat, buckled in snugly. There was a rubber duck in a field hockey uniform on the dashboard in front of me. I looked left to see Valerie.

"I'm taking you to the emergency room," she told me, eyes fixed on the road, hands white-knuckled at ten-and-two. "Your arm needs stitches."

My arm did really hurt, now that I thought about it. It was more of a dull ache than a sharp one though. It matched the pain my head. "I don't remember getting in this car," I told her, not particularly concerned.

"Luis put you in the car," she told me. "You've been drifting in and out a few times. Fiona said someone magicked you to sleep very crudely, but you'll be fine when it wears off."

"Okay," I said. I watched the white lines going by in the headlights and thought about going back to sleep. "So why are you driving me?"

"Because I'm the least suspicious person to take an injured girl to the ER," she replied. "And everyone else is trying to hunt down whoever hit you. Do you remember what happened?"

I thought. "There was someone at the cemetery when I got there, a man in a cloak. He was doing—" I tried to rub my forehead and remembered my arm hurt. "I don't know. He saw me, and I tried to stop him from leaving."

"How did you cut your arm?"

"I think we were fighting," I said vaguely. A burst of fear shot through my nervous system for a second, a flashback to the adrenaline of the moment. I was starting to remember what had happened, but the memories weren't forming a cohesive whole yet. "He had a knife."

"Drew, we have to lie when we get to the emergency room, okay?"

Valerie told me. "You can't tell them you got into a knife fight with a man in a cloak."

"Why not? That's basically getting mugged by a batman-wannabe."

"Because it will require a police report. We need a boring accident."

I pressed my forehead against the cool window glass. "You make it up then, Valerie. I'll say whatever you want."

After she'd parked the Jeep, Valerie marched me inside, guided me into a plastic chair of questionable cleanliness, and went to check me in at the front desk. She brought back a clipboard and helped me fill out the paperwork with clenched-jaw efficiency. I think I got shuffled back to a bed in a curtained pseudo-room pretty quickly because my injury looked relatively quick to treat, but unfortunately while Valerie was explaining to the perky ER doctor with her crinkly red hair corralled by a scrunchie that I had tripped and fallen into the dishwasher onto a knife in the silverware basket (the most embarrassing way to get hurt Valerie could possibly have invented), I got dizzy and almost toppled over.

"It's just the blood loss," I insisted, trying not to slur. "It just made me queasy, that's all. Reliving the moment it happened and everything. It was so scary."

The perky doctor was not convinced and decided she needed to run some tests to figure out why I'd fallen in the first place. So I was stuck under an observation protocol while they tried to make sure I didn't have anemia or the flu or a brain aneurysm. The medical staff got even more vigilant when they pulled up my recent medical records and became concerned my current health problems were somehow connected to my previous injuries. I could hardly tell them someone had hit me with a magical whammy.

Two hours later, we were still sitting there, and I was getting pretty irritated. They hadn't given me any painkillers, and my arm had gone from dull pain to fires of hell. My bloody shirt was tacky against my skin because I'd refused to put on the hospital gown while sitting in a semi-public area. I was starting to consider just making a break for it. My arm would heal without the stitches.

"You never should have brought me here," I told Valerie resentfully.

"Fiona told me to, and you looked half dead," she hissed. She was amazing at talking *sotto voce* without moving her mouth. "If you'd just held it together for a few minutes, we'd be out already."

"It's not my fault someone hit me with a magical proverbial frying pan," I hissed back. We both seethed for a bit.

"What did you see anyway?" Valerie asked me quietly after a while.

The ER was loud with squeaking tennis shoes, beeping machines, and arguing patients, so it was unlikely anyone would overhear us. "I told you, it was a man in a cloak. He was doing *something* in the cemetery when I rode up. He saw me, and when he tried to run away, I chased him down."

"What was he doing in the cemetery?"

"Something with the lives," I told her. "I don't know what is was, but it felt sort of *wrong*."

Valerie understood the gut-feeling of *wrong*ness at least, so I didn't have to explain. "Could he have been another magic-worker who knew something was happening in the cemetery but just didn't know what he was doing? The coven seems able to feel the magic, but they don't have much practical training."

"Could be," I agreed. But the action had felt malicious somehow, not amateurish.

We didn't get a chance to continue discussing it because the curtain slid back on its track as a slender, dark-haired man shouldered his way past it.

"Drew!"

I groaned. "What are you doing here, Cole?"

Valerie's attention quickly fixed on Cole like a fox spying a rabbit, very still, ready to pounce.

"I heard you were hurt and came to check on you. Are you okay?" He took a few steps closer to the bed, anxiety in every line of his face. He was practically pasty under his tan, I observed. Cole really was upset, which made me slightly more sympathetic. He'd had to see me in a hospital bed before under much worse circumstances.

"I'm fine," I told him grudgingly. "I just cut my arm, and I'm waiting for the stitches. How did you know I was here?"

"Someone told me," he said vaguely. He glanced at Valerie as if wondering who she was and looked rightfully unnerved by her stare.

"That sounds like a pretty big invasion of my medical privacy," I remarked. There was no guessing who'd told him, but I wasn't surprised someone had. His friends knew who I was.

"What happened to you?" he asked, not apologizing. He picked up the chart from the foot of the bed like he had every right to my medical records.

"I told you, I just need stitches. I'm just having to wait because stitches aren't really a priority. I appreciate you stopping to check on me," I said very civilly, "but I don't need anything. You should go."

"*How* did you cut your arm?" he persisted. "It's the middle of the night, Drew. And why are they running all these tests for a cut?"

"Not your business, Cole," I told him firmly. "I understand the whole coming to check on me thing because I know the car accident gave you anxiety, but you don't have a right to information about my life anymore."

Cole dropped his eyes, looking devastated by my cruelty.

Valerie, bless her, had the intuition to realize I was on the verge of caving. "I'll call security and have him thrown out." I was expecting the viciousness, and it still surprised me. It certainly surprised Cole.

I sighed. I would love to see Valerie demand Cole be thrown out of the hospital. Hell, she could probably throw him out herself. "That wouldn't do much good since he works here, Valerie."

She wrinkled her nose. "Your ex-boyfriend is a doctor?"

"He's an intern," I corrected.

"I can at least stitch your arm up for you, Drew," Cole sighed. "Let me get a suture kit."

Now I was really torn. I didn't want any kind of help from Cole, but I also didn't want to spend the rest of the damn night at the ER. "Do you have the authority to get me out of here afterward?"

The curtain twitched aside again as the perky Dr. Smithers returned. "No, he does not. I didn't think you were on the schedule today, Dr. McBride." Her tone was pleasant, yet somehow suggested a warning loomed for any potential nonsense.

"I'm not." He looked a little sheepish. "I just came to check on Drew."

Dr. Smithers looked back and forth between me and Cole, realization dawning. "Ah. Andrea Harlow is *that* Drew. I see."

"How much do you talk about me at work, Cole? Seriously?" I demanded, irritated. Often enough for someone to have told him I was there.

"We dated for a long time, Drew. It's safe to say I talked about you at some point."

"Well, stop," I retorted cleverly. I leaned back in the bed and closed my eyes so I didn't have to look at Cole. "Dr. Smithers, please make Cole leave."

There was a long silence, then quiet footsteps. I peeked to see if he was gone.

"Let's stitch up your arm, Andrea," Dr. Smithers said.

"Look," I told the doctor very seriously when she'd finished with the sutures, "I think I must have been sleepwalking when I fell. I've been having a lot of trouble sleeping lately, and it's really been wearing me down. I think I fell asleep on the couch, and when I got up to move to the bedroom, I just wasn't as awake as I thought I was, and I got confused and tripped."

She studied me skeptically for a long minute. "Well, we don't have your blood work back yet, but you don't have a concussion, and you definitely aren't inebriated. We can send you home if you have someone to take you." She glanced at Valerie, who nodded.

"Great. Thank you. Could you write me a note for work tomorrow? It's three in the morning, and I don't think I can go to work like this."

Her face softened. "Of course. Why don't I write you a note recommending you don't use your arm for a few days."

"That would be great," I said meekly.

"You need to see your GP about that inability to sleep, Drew," she admonished.

"Yes," I agreed, rubbing my face with my good hand. "I know. I do. I'm just having trouble getting time off work."

"See if they can fit you in tomorrow," she suggested firmly, handing me my note. She looked down for a moment, and her sudden silence made me tense. "That's an interesting choice of shoes to wear to the emergency room in the middle of the night."

I looked at my shoes without thinking. I was wearing paddock boots that laced at the ankle, probably the last shoes a person with an injured arm would grab to put on their feet. "They were just by the door, and I picked them up on my way out. I didn't think about shoes at all until Valerie pointed out I was in my socks."

"I'm almost positive those are the only shoes she owns," Valerie grumbled.

Dr. Smithers didn't believe me, but if I was refusing to admit how I'd gotten hurt, there wasn't much she could do about it. "All right. Go check out at the desk. And follow your care instructions to the letter," she added sternly.

I liked her better when she was perky.

"I'll make her," Valerie stated like it was a threat.

When we hauled ourselves back into the Jeep, I told Valerie, "Thanks for taking me to the ER."

"It's no problem," she said reluctantly. "Cole seems like a dick."

I could barely keep my eyes open at this point. "He's actually pretty nice, which is what makes constantly having to rebuff him so exhausting. It's like kicking a puppy." I realized Valerie had turned right instead of left. "Hey, my truck is at Fiona's."

"It's at your apartment," she said. "The keys are under the floor mat."

Great—I could avoid Fiona for a few more hours. "How mad did Fiona look when you saw her?"

"I didn't see her before she left, but I'm going to imagine you will be seeing the Riders' work at a cemetery from an entirely different side soon."

"Not funny, Valerie," I told her grumpily.

9

Chapter 9

I intended to use the official parole from work I'd secured with the doctor's note to catch up on sleep, but lying around in bed imagining the villainous characters of the universe was making me agitated. No one from the Riders had called me to update me on their success in tracking down the person who had stabbed me, and I didn't call any of them because I was sure that would just be inviting a lecture about my irresponsibility I wasn't in the mood to hear.

After some debating, I worked up the nerve to call Casey instead.

"Hey," he answered on the third ring.

"Hey," I replied, awkwardness growing. "Are you busy today? Or this evening?" I amended, remembering he would probably be at work.

"I'm not on shift today," he said easily. "What's up?"

"Just wondering if you wanted to collab on weird magic stuff with me," I mumbled. God, I should have thought this through better.

Thankfully he didn't seem to find this stupid. "Like what?"

"I've been going around to a few of the places where weird things were reported to see if they were caused by magic," I explained. "I can't reliably feel magic that isn't Rider magic though, so I thought maybe you'd want to come since you can?"

I expected further questions about the point of this endeavor or a gentle turndown, but he seemed on board right away.

"Sure. Where do you want me to meet you?"

We negotiated the details, and after I hung up I did my best to make myself presentable. I didn't really care what Casey thought about the way I looked, but the long night at the ER hadn't done me any favors. One of the Riders was going to mistake me for the walking dead.

Cole texted me for about the fifth time while I was trying to breathe through the pain of braiding my own hair with an injured arm, this time threatening to make my parents check on me if I didn't answer him. I confirmed I was alive and told him to leave me alone. I tossed in a suggestion that I might pursue investigating which of his colleagues had summoned him to the ER if he kept bothering me. He knew I wouldn't do it, but at least he knew I could play the threat game too if I had to.

When Casey pulled into the empty ball field parking lot in a blue Chevelle, I was leaning on the truck and sucking iced coffee through a straw like it was a lifeline. We eyed each other's vehicles for a moment.

"Nice car," I offered.

"Thanks." He stroked the car's hood gently like it was a cat. "Yours actually is too. It will be an antique in a few more years. You should take better care of it."

I looked at my ancient truck with the paint peeling off the hood as if something new might be in the parking space behind me. I'd been really adamant that I needed a truck when I'd bought it back in college, citing my future as a large-animal vet, though it was probably more to fit the image of myself I saw in the future than out of practicality. I can't say I cared about cars all that much or viewed them as expressions of personality like August did, but in rare moments of reflection it did seem like the truck was a vestige of an old life that was out of place for the drab, boring office worker I'd become.

"It gets me where I need to be," I told Casey before I got lost in more introspection. "Do you want to go check out this spring?"

"Sure." We started in the direction of the spring that had erupted from the ground behind the city's baseball field. "You didn't have to work today either?"

I shook my head. "I called in sick."

He looked askance. "You called in sick to go magic hunting?" I couldn't tell if he was amused or judging me.

"No, I had to get stitches on a cut last night, so I got the doctor to write me a note."

"Shit. What happened?"

I was about to tell him it was a freak accident, now not sure why I'd told him about the stitches at all, but it occurred to me that Casey, and maybe the coven by extension, might need to know there was something nefarious going down at the cemeteries. "I kind of got attacked by someone with a knife," I admitted.

Casey grabbed my arm to stop me at that, successfully picking the arm where the mentioned stitches lay, then snatched his hand back when I shrieked in pain.

"Ow! Found it on the first try, Casey."

He grimaced in apology. "Sorry! Are you hurt?"

I lifted the shoulder of my shirt to peer down at my upper arm. There wasn't any blood seeping through the bandage or anything. "It's fine. It's just sore."

"I'm sorry, Drew," he repeated. "Who attacked you? Does he still need his ass kicked?"

"I was at a cemetery last night," I explained, "and I came up on someone trying to work some sort of magic with the life energy."

"Life energy?" he interrupted.

"Later. Anyway, when he saw me, he tried to run away, and I chased him down."

"And when you caught him, he, what, stabbed you?" Casey's tone was disapproving. "Why did you do that?"

"Well, I didn't know he had a knife," I said defensively. "I was just trying to keep him from leaving until someone else got there. And it was an impulse thing anyway. He hit my arm with the knife while he was trying to get free, then he knocked me out with a spell or something."

"A spell? Are you sure he didn't hit you in the head?"

"I like to think I'd know if someone hit me in the head," I said with dignity. "But anyway, Fiona said it was a poorly-worked knockout spell, and I guess she'd know." I looked at him sideways. "Do you know how those work?"

"I could do sleep, in theory," he replied. "Sleep is pretty natural to the body, so it's not hard, except you would have been fighting it. I wonder if that's what he was trying to do, and he just used massively too much force."

So Casey and possibly others in his coven could have knocked me out like that. I considered if there was a delicate way to ask if they were all accounted for that night. Probably not. "I guess you should tell everyone to be careful if they're in the cemeteries at night."

"I will. Maybe you shouldn't be going to them alone."

"I usually don't," I demurred. Hopefully if someone in his coven was involved, that would get back to them. "I think this is it."

The spring was perfectly round and the size of a kiddie pool, and it had already captured the attention of the locals. People had left flowers, trinkets, and polished stones as little offerings around its edge. It had also captured the attention of the city, because yellow "keep out" tape had been stretched around the trees surrounding the spring. Casey and I ducked the tape to peer into its depths. The water was crystal clear, which made it obvious how ridiculously deep it must be. The bottom was lost in shadow.

"Well, that's impressive," Casey remarked. "What did the city say about it?"

I knelt to dangle my fingers in the water. "I think officially it's a sinkhole. That doesn't seem impossible. What do you think?"

"I don't think it's impossible either if there's always been water under the ground out here. That's where springs come from. This is an unusually picture-perfect one though." He joined me to touch the water himself.

"Feel anything?" I asked.

"Yeah, it feels like it's full of something fizzy, like carbonated water."

It just felt like cold water to me. The breeze stirred the wind chimes and bells visitors had hung on the surrounding branches, and I looked up. The air was very still, despite the wind, as if the pool were the eye of a storm. I could see the little scraps of fabric tied to the trees flapping gently, but I couldn't feel anything. The hair on the back of my neck stood up as if something were looming nearby, something watching me.

"Hey." Casey's hand touched mine in the water.

For a few seconds, I could feel what he had been talking about as the water tingled like it had been put through a giant soda machine. I jumped.

"Do you feel the magic now?"

I moved my hand through the water again, but now that I wasn't touching him, I couldn't feel the tingle or the creepy stillness. "I did for a second."

Casey stood. "It's definitely at least magically-induced, if not entirely caused by magic." He offered his hand, and I let him pull me to my feet.

"The difference?"

"Well, someone could have known there was water under the earth here and used magic to create a hole down to it. I'm not sure how this formation compares with naturally formed springs, though I'm betting they aren't symmetrical holes straight down that deep."

"Could be an old well someone uncovered," I suggested.

"Seems more likely than a deep, narrow sinkhole," he agreed. "The other option is that whatever weird magical surge comes out of this rift you're talking about just made a deep pool of water out of nowhere. How does this compare to any of the other places you've checked?"

I told him about the forest in the children's playground and described the men who had come to inspect it.

"They don't sound like anyone I know, but I can ask around," Casey said thoughtfully. "Think there's any point in going over there to look?"

I shook my head. "I bet they've already cut it down."

"Probably," he conceded. "Let's go to the cemetery where you got into the knife fight."

"Why? Do you think you can pick up something there?"

He shrugged. "It hasn't even been a full day. Worth a try." We started walking back toward our cars.

"Okay, it's the little one on Thompson Road," I told him.

"We can just take my car," he suggested when I went to unlock the door to my truck.

I surveyed the Chevelle. It was gorgeous—shiny, sleek, powerful. August would be drooling all over it. "If I ride with you, you'd have to drive me back to my truck. We can just meet there."

"I don't mind bringing you back. It's not out of the way." When I didn't relent, he shrugged. "Suit yourself."

I cranked the truck and followed him as he roared out of the parking lot. He beat me to the cemetery because he drove like he was auditioning for NASCAR and because his vehicle didn't take half a minute to reach cruising speed.

"Where to?" Casey asked after I'd pulled in next to him on the narrow strip of grass that functioned as the tiny cemetery's only parking.

I led him to the side of the cemetery where I'd approached with Charon and tried to pinpoint the exact grave I'd seen the man standing next to. "This one, I think? Yes, it was the one with the dark stone."

We both looked in silence. There were scuff marks in the grass that had probably been made by our shoes digging into the ground while we fought. There was blood too, on the grass and a few drops splashed onto the stone. Mine. I felt a little green now thinking back to it. He could have killed me while I was unconscious. I wondered what it meant that he hadn't.

Casey held out his hand over the stone, his expression thoughtful. He tried the ground in front of it next. He wasn't speaking or tossing around magical implements, so I had no idea what he was doing. He could have been bluffing me like crazy, except I was pretty sure he'd touched my hand back at the spring to make me feel the magic he was feeling.

"Anything?"

He rubbed a hand over the day-old stubble he was growing. "This feels different. There's a trace of something like what I felt at the spring, magic like I felt the night everyone went all Hatfields and McCoys, but the rest of it feels like worked magic. Like the aftertaste of a spell."

"So there's magic that's naturally existing, and magic the man was working?"

He shrugged one shoulder. "That's my best interpretation. I wonder if you feel like magic too." He held out the searching hand toward me.

I stared down at his hand like I was expecting it to do something. "Do I?"

"Eh. I feel magic, but I'm not sure if it's native to you or just magic you've worked or that's been worked around you recently. It's strange magic though," he said thoughtfully. "I haven't felt anything like it before." He continued to stare somewhere in the region of my stomach, lost in contemplation, while I tried not to get squirmy.

My phone rang, and I pulled it from my pocket. Fiona. I answered, trying to feign casualness. "Hey, Fiona."

"Drew," she said, not sounding casual at all, "what are you doing back at the cemetery, and who are you with?"

* * *

"So you sought out one of the coven members and told him everything we were doing?" Bennett demanded in his very calm, college professor voice. His graying eyebrows were drawn together in stern disappointment. Apparently August had managed to install a camera in the little cemetery after my unpleasant encounter, and Casey and I had tripped all kinds of alarms that let someone know to check the feed.

"No, of course not," I replied. "I told him about stuff *I* was doing. I didn't tell him about the wards or someone trying to steal life energies or any Rider business."

"Yes," Fiona said. She had positioned her fancy camping chair, complete with footrest, in the sun just outside the barn so she could survey her domain while she reclined at leisure, queen of the barn and all that surrounded it. I had expected her to be the one angry with me, but she mostly looked resigned. "About the stuff *you* are doing. What exactly are you doing, Drew?"

"I've been looking into some of the other strange things happening in the city that might be caused by the surge," I admitted.

"Such as?" Fiona inquired, still staring out over the pastures. She took a sip from the straw of her giant travel mug.

"That forest that grew up overnight. A spring coming out of the ground. Stuff like that."

"Andrea, that has nothing to do with the Riders' work," Bennett pointed out.

"Exactly," I replied. "So why do you care that I'm doing it? Sounds like my business."

Bennett, who like many older men was not used to anyone under the age of forty daring to disrespect his opinion, stared at me over the gold rims of his glasses.

Fiona disguised a chuckle by taking another noisy pull from her straw. "Why did you ask the coven man to join you?" she asked before he could summon a response.

"I was hoping he'd share information about sites the coven had been visiting so I could plot them on our map to see where they overlapped," I explained. "They don't really keep records like that, but I guess my asking made him curious. I can't see or test for magical workings, but Casey can, so I took him with me."

"So you invited him straight into what we were doing," Bennett said. "Of course he came with you. You're feeding him information about our activities."

"You just said the magical happenings around the city are not Rider business," I pointed out stubbornly.

"What happened at the cemetery certainly was, and you took him there!"

"They visit those cemeteries too, so they should probably know if someone dangerous is there. And I wanted to see what Casey's reaction to hearing about it was anyway."

"He'll tell his coven what you told him," Bennett said. "One of them could easily be the man who attacked you. They are the only other magic-workers we know about in this city."

"Good." I shrugged. "If it's someone in the coven, I've set him on the trail to be suspicious of them."

"What if it was Casey himself?" Fiona asked neutrally.

"I don't think it was." When she frowned at me, I shook my head. "And it's not just because I like Casey and think he's above suspicion. He's too big to be the man from the cemetery, and honestly, I think if it had been him I was fighting with, I wouldn't have stood a chance. He could have overpowered me a lot faster. The entire coven could be colluding on whatever this is together, but I still don't think it matters if that's true. They'll know we're looking for them, but they would know that anyway because of course we would be after one of them stabbed me."

"Hmm." Fiona shook the ice in her cup thoughtfully. "Drew is right about that at least. If the miscreant is one of the coven, perhaps the rest of the coven will flush him out for internal discipline. If the entire coven is behind it, it matters not that they know we know."

"Exactly," I said, relieved that at least she agreed with me.

"It matters because Andrea is feeding information to a man she now thinks she's friends with," Bennett countered.

"Bennett, I'm really not so stupid to go around spilling all the measures we're taking to find this person to someone I just met," I sighed. "I thought the few other people in this city that are capable of noticing magic the way we are might know something we don't. If we had some kind of relationship with them, maybe they'll tell us if they know something." I paused for a moment. "Why don't we ever speak to them at all?"

"There usually isn't a reason to," Fiona said simply. "It's been a long time since this city had a competent coven or sect to even consider talking to. I must admit, I was taken by surprise that any of them could even work a significant amount of magic. Perhaps someone with some talent moved into the area and began to teach the others. That woman with the ugly rock around her neck, I guess."

Casey had said Rina was one of the few who really took the magic seriously, so probably so.

"Could any of the other covens in the area be capable of real magic too? You didn't know the Hazelwood Coven was."

"I generally find the more likely they are to advertise themselves as a coven, the more likely they are to be dabblers who don't even know they aren't doing anything," she said dismissively. "They just draw circles on the ground and chant nonsense and believe they fixed problems they only imagined existed."

"You said fake magic imitates the real magic it's trying to be. If they do all the right steps and say the right words, won't magic happen?"

"If you gave a pen and paper to a two-year-old, they could scribble trying to imitate having watched your write," she said. "But they wouldn't be writing. They would never learn until you taught them. You can give a person a spell book and a bag of dried herbs, and they'd just make potpourri until you actually taught them. Magic requires a force, an energy that has to come from inside you to work. Otherwise anyone could inadvertently read a spell and cause a lighting storm. It takes intent."

I thought if the coven really *intended* to do what they were doing, there was a chance they could succeed. "So it's either this coven or a third party we don't know about."

"Must be." Her expression was indifferent. "Whoever it is, we'll catch them. So did you actually learn anything from this Casey?"

I kicked over one of the buckets left out to dry in the sun so I could sit on it. "Not much that was helpful to us, just some interest in the sites. He said he could feel magic at the site we went to today and at the cemetery that didn't feel like worked magic, just magic there I guess."

"That would confirm those oddities are being caused by magic from the rift then," Fiona replied. "I'm not sure what else you could extrapolate from that information. Did Casey recognize the magic worked at the cemetery?"

I shook my head. "He didn't act like he did. Were you able to find anything? Valerie said you were looking."

"No," she said. "Just one unconscious girl who went chasing after an unknown, dangerous assailant after she was told not to." There was the lecture I'd been waiting for. "Valerie told me what you told her at the ER. Do you remember anything in more detail now?"

I described the events of the previous night as thoroughly as I could.

"So you didn't see his face?" Bennett asked, subdued.

"No, his hood was shadowing it for the few seconds he was facing me, and it was dark. When we were fighting, I was pretty focused on watching the hand with the knife."

"Hmm. Well, no more going out alone after that," he said firmly. "Do you need the night off? How is your arm?"

"It hurts, but I'll be fine."

The ground gave a sudden shudder like someone had dropped something very heavy nearby. It only lasted a few seconds, but the horses started, and I could hear the ice rattle in Fiona's tumbler.

I looked up, expecting to see a plane passing overheard. "What was that? An explosion?"

"Minor earthquake," Fiona said as though this were of mild interest.

"Do we even get those here?"

"You can get low-level earthquakes anywhere," Bennett confirmed, though he looked more uneasy than Fiona. "That wasn't enough to knock a lawn chair over."

"So, Drew," Fiona said, the conversational shift fooling no one, "since you aren't working today, why don't you come with me to check some of the furthest graveyards. I want to keep you where I can see you tonight."

"Sure," I mumbled.

"And until then, you can do some work around here. Why don't you take that sorrel four-year-old I'm training out for some exercise? He gets wild if he goes too long without riding, and I didn't have time today."

Yeah, that was really what my arm needed, being pulled on by a young, sassy horse. If I'd thought I was getting away without punishment from Fiona, I'd been fooled by her calm demeanor. Bennett might be the kind to scold and yell, but Fiona was going to grind me into the dirt without saying a word. I went to get a halter to catch the sorrel and accept my fate.

* * *

"The ward that was crossed last night was a false alarm," Fiona said as I followed her through the darkness to wherever we were working that night. I hadn't asked, preferring to be led off a clifftop or into the desert over reminding her I existed. She had been reasonable about the whole Casey thing when we discussed it with Bennett, but I had cleaned enough saddles this afternoon to know she was still angry I'd attempted to confront the man in the cloak.

"Just a random person in the cemetery?" I ventured.

"No, there was no one there but Luis. The ward accidentally responded to him when it should not have. He called me before I reached him, but at that point I wanted to find out what was wrong with the ward to cause it to misfire so I didn't turn back." There was an undercurrent of frustration to her voice as though she was angry at herself for the poor calculation. "Bennett set that one, and it appears he hasn't entirely mastered the finer points."

"Are we going to fix it?" I asked.

"Yes. That and all the others he made."

The whole ward thing had been a wash. The only thing they'd caught were me and Casey, but I guessed we weren't giving up on it. "Erm, does Bennett know?"

"No."

"Is it a secret?"

"No."

So she wasn't going to bother to tell him he was making the wards incorrectly, which meant she wasn't expecting him to do a better job in the future. That seemed odd. Fiona wasn't exactly the type to tiptoe around your feelings.

We reached the cemetery where the ward had alerted to Luis's presence, a smaller one that was no longer in use tucked in among the neighborhoods that had grown up around it. Fiona drew up a few yards from the edge and surveyed the moonlit headstones in silence. There were a few graves with tethered life energies wafting in the breeze.

"Ride inside, Drew," Fiona said. "I want to see if it reacts to you."

I nudged Charon forward until we entered the cemetery. "Anything?" Nothing happened that I could see.

"Yes." She looked troubled. "Perhaps he mistakenly keyed them only to himself. Go see if you can feel the ward. It will be good practice for you. You shouldn't need Casey to sense magic for you."

I left Charon and went to do as she said, approaching where I thought the edge might be and holding my palms out like I was feeling for a physical wall. I glanced at Fiona to see if she was watching me, but she was intent on her own business on the other side of the cemetery so I was free to look as stupid as I wanted unobserved. I focused on trying to find the ward, resorting to feeling around on the ground. The hastily-made wards set up as alarms were not meant to last a long time, so they were only anchored by chalk dust that had been sprinkled at the corners of the property.

There was a warmth around the perimeter of the cemetery, like a pipe channeling hot water had been laid just underground. I followed it, losing it sometimes to find it a few feet later. Was the inconsistency me or Bennett's ward-laying?

"Find it?" Fiona appeared next to me with preternatural silence.

"Yes. It feels weird right here."

She examined where I indicated without moving. "That might have been where he stopped and started the ward. Go back out for a minute."

She had already moved Charon and Orlaith outside the cemetery, so I went to stand with them while she walked around chanting under her breath. I concentrated on trying to follow what she was doing and managed to see a few glimmers of magic shimmering around the cemetery. It was like trying to catch something moving out of the corner of your eye, but I was getting better at it.

Fiona rejoined me and climbed back into the saddle without a word. We trotted off toward the next cemetery, wending through streets instead of trees this time. It was already dark because it was late in the year, but the city hadn't put itself to bed yet. There were cars rumbling quietly through the streets on their way home from gymnastics practice and algebra tutors and the odd person walking a dog or taking out the trash, but we moved in our little sphere. Fiona didn't seem concerned, so I wasn't either.

In the graveyard of a little clapboard Methodist church, she had me repeat the same routine, but this time after she'd finished fixing the ward, she sent me to examine it again.

"Do you feel the difference?"

I considered carefully. "I do. Is that because the ward is complete, or because it's your magic and not Bennett's?"

"The spell is just a different configuration than it was before. It will take you a long time to learn to parse the difference, but I want you to try to remember what this one feels like when we go to the next."

"Does magic have colors?" I asked her. The wards had kind of a yellowish-orange glow to me at times now that I was starting to see them. Rider magic was always silvery-blue.

She raised her eyebrows. "Does it have colors for you? You don't really perceive magic with your usual senses," she continued before I had a chance to be grouchy about her question-dodging. "But your mind needs a way to classify information, so if different kinds of magic have different colors for you, that is your brain giving them labels it can comprehend."

"So it could be a sensation or a sound instead?"

"Yes. I guess it could be a smell or a taste too if you wanted. But you might get annoyed at magic tasting like mint or peanut butter."

As soon as she said it, the ward magic took on a minty tang. I wrinkled my face up, but it didn't go away.

Fiona laughed. "Stop thinking about it. You'll just make it worse."

"I can't!"

"Well, come away from it then. We've got a few more to do."

"Why can't Bennett feel the difference?" I asked her quietly on the way to cemetery number three. "I mean, I get that *making* the ward must be very difficult, but you're teaching me to at least feel the difference between the correct and incorrect ward. If he can actually make one, why can't he tell that he made it wrong?"

"I don't know," she said neutrally. "Bennett sometimes has difficulty learning from me. We have dissimilar styles, and admitting he's struggling with something goes against his nature."

Yeah, he was a prideful old man who didn't want to admit to Fiona he needed her help.

"And wards are an art form that takes considerable time to master," she continued. "It is much harder to tell *what* is wrong with a spell than to note something is slightly different from something else. Making an exception to the alarm seems to be the only element he's struggling with."

I asked the second question that had been on my mind. "Why are you teaching this to me?"

"I wanted you with me tonight to keep you out of trouble," Fiona replied. "I might as well teach you while you're here. You wanted to learn magic."

I did, though I wasn't really sure where these lessons were leading. I doubted Fiona had much of an established curriculum, which was probably why she and Bennett struggled to work together. I guess I was still working on that "learning to feel magic" step.

"Did anyone else ever ask you to teach them to do magic?" I asked her.

"No," Fiona said simply.

"Why?"

She looked back at me. "Drew, a few weeks ago, you weren't interested either. You were still coming to terms with even knowing magic existed and that you could do it. You were still learning Rider magic. Now you have joined us in regular duties and you can even fast-ride by yourself. You picked that up all rather quickly once you wanted to. It's up to individual people to decide what they want to learn."

She was right, I realized. I hadn't disliked being a Rider before, but I wasn't all that excited about it either. I had abandoned school for a job I hated, and I had come to some weird conclusion that adult life was just kind of disappointing. But despite the exhaustion of trying to balance my regular life with being awake half the night, I was sort of enjoying myself. I could tell myself it was the horses, but it was also the magic and the excitement.

Fiona was eyeing me slyly.

"You bribed me with magic," I accused even as I smiled.

"Like a witch in a story book," she replied with unusual cheer.

10

Chapter 10

I was almost late for work Monday trying to text Casey while I brushed my teeth and hunted down my shoes. The news had reported two additional small tremors in the city that apparently baffled seismologists. Neither was enough to do more than knock a picture frame off the wall, but Casey swore he'd felt a whiff of magic off the second one. There wasn't really anything for us to go investigate, but my mind was still trying to piece together sinkholes, rapid-growth forests, and earthquakes into some sort of magical mosaic as I resigned myself to spending the next eight hours inside a fluorescent-lit, industrial-carpeted version of hell.

I was fumbling for my keycard outside the doors of Stevens and McKinley when Kara sprung out from behind one of the concrete columns supporting the roof overhang, startling me badly enough I almost fell backward down the stairs. Given my fighting reflexes these days, she was also lucky I didn't attempt to Chuck Norris her. She blocked my path inside, the distress on her face at odds with the sunny yellow cardigan she wore with black and white striped pants.

"Drew!" she hissed. "I've been waiting out here all morning for you."

"I get here at eight, Kara," I pointed out. "It's seven fifty-five."

"Well, you know what I mean." She pushed her bouncy hair back from her face. "I wanted to catch you before you went inside. Drew, Tanner is going to fire you."

That wasn't really a surprise, as I'd been frequently absent and permanently lethargic over the last few weeks. What was a surprise was how relieved I felt. I wasn't going to have to work at this shit job anymore. I could never justify *quitting*, but hey, if they wanted to fire me, what could I do about it?

"Why are you grinning?" Kara wailed. "Drew, you *lunatic*. What am I going to do here without you?"

"We'll still see each other," I consoled her as I stepped past her and went inside to face my fate.

She clip-clopped after me in her pointy-toe heels. "No, we won't. You're the most unsocial person I know. You'll absolutely disappear."

She wasn't wrong, but I wasn't forced to come up with a reply because as soon as I'd set my things down on my desk at exactly 8 o'clock, Tanner appeared on the other side of it, looming ominously. I really, really had to fight not to giggle.

"Andrea, my office, please," he ordered gruffly.

Kara continued to give me a look of despair.

"What do you want me to do, fight with him?" I started for Tanner's office.

"Yes!" she hissed, following me. "You're actually good at your job! Tell him some medical bullshit or something, and he'll let you stay."

I stepped through the office doorway, leaving Kara and her protests behind.

"Close the door and sit down," Tanner said gruffly.

I did, noticing that he was sweating. I would assume firing people was stressful, but I hadn't expected Tanner to be capable of normal human emotions.

"Andrea, I think you know why I've called you in here," he began.

I feigned polite interest but didn't say anything.

"Your work attendance has been unacceptable lately," he continued. "Our company can't function efficiently if the employees don't show up every day. We're a team, and all team members need to be—"

"I'm entitled to my sick time," I pointed out. I wasn't going to listen to him ramble for half an hour if I was going to leave without a job anyway. "My absences were all within the parameters of company policy. I was never gone more than three days without a doctor's note, and I did bring you a doctor's note for the last absence since it was so close to the first. It's not my fault that I got the flu, which normally takes longer than three days to get over, Tanner; nor is it my fault I had to get stitches. Sometimes life happens. And frankly, the sick day policy in this country is abysmal. I can't imagine anyone in Europe having to justify being *sick*. It's a part of the human condition."

Tanner just gazed at me in dead-eyed amazement while I ranted. "Well, this isn't Europe, Andrea. If we just let people be out sick any time they wanted without repercussions, everyone would just be sick all the time, and no one would work. Sometimes you have to suck it up a little. I know you're young, but at some point you have to tough it out and get the work done anyway, whether you have the sniffles or not. I've had to work sick before because if I don't, my job doesn't get done."

"When you came in with that hacking cough last February, you gave it to everyone else here," I pointed out. I hadn't even been there, and I'd still heard about it, people had been so resentful. "You lost productivity in the end because people did have to take days off because you made them sick bringing your germs to work. Carol got pneumonia from it."

Tanner's face was getting red. "Are you finished?"

"No. If the job can't handle you being out for a few days, it's poorly organized. You should always have someone trained and a backup plan in place to handle your being out of work unexpectedly. That's simple business planning."

"Unlike you, my work isn't easily done by others," he said with deadly calm. I was surprised he was holding it together this well. "And you will be easily replaced, Andrea."

"No, you'll spend weeks on the hiring and interviewing process while my coworkers struggle to manage while they're short a person. And then you'll spend months training whoever you hired, still not at full capacity. About the time you get there, someone else will quit from the stress, and you'll have to start the process all over again." I smiled serenely at him. "All because it offended you that I dared to be sick for a total of six days despite my excellent work output."

He'd really had enough of me now. "Andrea, you're fired."

"I would like that it writing, please," I informed him cheerfully.

"What, you want me to write 'You're fired' on a piece of paper for you?"

"No, I want you to type out when and why I was fired on company letterhead, print it out, and sign it," I explained. "You are firing me for taking too many sick days while still within company policy."

"You've been behaving like the walking dead while you're here too," he pointed out.

"Because I'm sick and trying to work anyway, just like you wanted. Because our sick policy doesn't allow for me to take the time off I need to rest and get well. I'll have that letter before I go, thanks."

He stared at me, blood vessel in his forehead throbbing. I stared back, smiling like a loon. He turned to his computer monitor, paused to give me a murderous glare, and started typing in that peck-peck-peck way old men who had missed the secretary generation by a hair do. I fixed a polite expression on my face and waited. The printer groaned to life, and Tanner snatched the paper it produced and scrawled his name at the bottom. He handed it over, and I scrutinized it carefully.

The letter said I was being terminated from my position for being absent on the dates listed and for poor attitude on dates listed between. I had proof I'd called in appropriately for all of those dates, a copy of the doctor's note, and the employee handbook. I couldn't actually get him to say he'd fired me for being sick, but it was close enough.

"Thanks, Tanner." I stood to leave. "My mom's a workplace lawyer. She'll appreciate this."

If he had been red before, he was purple now.

I opened the door and stepped out into the cooler air of the hallway. Kara was still lurking nearby, but I wasn't sure if she'd been able to hear our conversation through the door. Her eyes fixed on the piece of paper in my hand, but before she could speak, the building shuddered with enough force that I landed on my hands and knees.

The office was loud with people shrieking and the sound of things falling. I tried to get up, just in time for another shudder to dump me back on the floor.

"Earthquake!" Kara squeaked, trying to regain her feet in her impractical shoes.

I managed to stand on my second try and helped her up, and we ran toward the exit door like everyone else was doing. There was a lot of unreasonable pushing and shoving for grown people who should have been behaving more logically in an emergency. David and Eddie were escorting tiny, elderly Carol to safety at least, shielding her from being trampled by the chicken littles.

The sky wasn't actually falling when we poured outside, but there was definitely something wrong with it. A streak like fire cut through the blue haze, burning red so brightly it was visible even in the light of day, flickers of black, green, and orange swirling through it. The street was full of people expelled from the nearby buildings, all huddled together in fright as they stared upward. Drivers had pulled over as the ground shook and were climbing cautiously from their vehicles as if unsure if they were safer inside or out. The quakes had shifted some cars around in the parking lot and cracked the sidewalk, but there didn't appear to be any serious structural damage.

A third earthquake, stronger than the first two, roiled through, sending most of us to the ground. This time there was an accompanying boom as walls cracked and ceilings began to cave. This wasn't an earthquake-prone area, and the buildings weren't built to handle it. Car alarms joined in with the screaming as the asphalt of the street split and heaved. Telephone poles collapsed, dragging their wires down with them. I knelt in the flowerbed in front of the office, watching the sky.

It was sort of like watching a volcano erupt, though with light instead of magma. More bursts of red and orange spurted up from some source I couldn't see. It was mesmerizing in its terror, a sight that would have spelled the end of times to some ancient race. Maybe it was the end of times for us. I stood, trying to see where it began and ended or if the streak went on forever.

As I watched, the fire roiling in the sky swirled tighter and tighter like it was gathering itself together into something more solid. Then with a boom like a military jet, the churning mass of colors shot apart, dispersed so thoroughly that there didn't appear to be anything left of it. That might have been a relief, but the force of the final quake had shaken the ground hard enough to collapse one of the nearby warehouses and open a sinkhole in the parking lot that swallowed three cars. Smoke had started to come out of the cracks in the street, then the smoke became licking flames of red, green, and black like those that had slashed through the sky. Instead of continuing to burn, the flames wiggled out of the pavement like eels and evaporated before they'd made it more than a few feet. The world stilled again.

I was nearly deaf from the explosion, but past the ringing in my ears, I could hear the car alarms, the fire alarms, the screaming, and the police sirens in the distance. I looked around for Kara and saw her huddled wide-eyed against the concrete wall lining the upper riser of the flower bed, her face a mask of terror.

"Are you all right?" I asked her, or I tried to. I wasn't sure if I was making any noise.

She just stared at me and didn't answer. She'd lost one of her shoes.

I left her there and began looking around, too stunned to really grasp the magnitude of what had happened. It didn't look like anyone from our office had been injured beyond bumps and bruises because we'd been outside where fewer things were falling, but the street was half-destroyed. I cautiously approached the sinkhole and stared into it. It wasn't deep, the back ends of the cars were still poking out, but a tingly feeling of warmth was wafting from it. Now more curious than afraid, I walked down to the street to look into the crack there. It was far, far deeper, and I couldn't see the bottom. It felt like something was staring back at me, something that made the fine hairs on my arms stand up and my breath catch. It was like that brief moment when I'd been dead and some great abyss had been looking at me out of the darkness.

"Drew!"

Kara's voice pulled me back away from the edge, and I went to see if I could help. People were trying to call family members and finding the cell towers were down. Eddie emerged from the office with an armload of purses, passing them out so the owners could find their car keys and leave. We were starting to strategize how to untangle the parking lot when Kara gulped and pointed at something.

I turned to look where she was staring.

A horse with a coat like melted gold stood in the street, the red-haired Rider on her back contemplating the deep crevice that went through it. Fiona, and by the way Kara was staring at her, she was visible as more than just a woman on a palomino. I left Kara and jogged down to where Fiona was studying the street without a flicker of expression on her face.

"Fiona! What's happening?"

She turned her electric blue gaze on me. "The rifts have opened."

* * *

One of the bags Eddie had heroically retrieved from the office was mine, and in less than a minute I had my boots out of my truck and was sprinting back toward Fiona.

Kara had come to stand at the edge of the parking lot to stare at Fiona, who was patiently ignoring her, now holding her one remaining shoe. She turned as I passed her. "Drew, what's happening?" She looked so lost.

"I don't know. I'm going to go find out."

Fiona took her left boot out of the stirrup and held her arm out, elbow crooked. I used the stirrup and her arm to swing myself up behind her.

Kara watched with sad eyes that said the world didn't make sense to her anymore.

"Go home, Kara," I told her, feeling bad for abandoning her. "You'll be safer there."

Fiona gave Orlaith her head, and we were off, the mare's ivory hooves striking against the asphalt. We hit Rider speed within a few strides, and while the faces around me blurred, I was pretty sure they were gaping at us.

"Why isn't the Rider magic working?" I tried to yell into Fiona's ear.

"Too much interference," she said in a completely normal tone.

"What did you mean by 'the rifts are open'? They opened for a really strong surge?"

"No, they opened completely. I'll explain later. Quit shouting in my ear."

The world was in an upheaval, but Fiona, as ever, was unruffled.

I turned my attention to the city as we galloped by. Streets were riddled with cracks and sinkholes, power lines lay snapping on the ground, buildings were cracked and crumbling. Hardly anyone was trying to drive now because while many roads were still passable, the city had became gridlocked as cars couldn't turn back when they did reach an obstacle. I could hear sirens, but Fiona's route took us away from them. I tilted my head to look up at the sky for some trace of the fire that had burned there, but the heavens were clear and blue again.

We reached Fiona's property, and she dropped Orlaith to a walk. Luis's Subaru came rolling up after us. He cranked the window down and leaned out.

"I can't get a hold of anyone. There's no cell service in the entire city."

"Bennett and Trish will know to make their own way here," Fiona replied. "We'll have to go collect everyone else. Drew, let's get all the horses saddled."

"I still don't understand what's happening," I protested.

"I'd rather go through all this just once," Fiona said. "Let's just find everybody first."

She went to cool Orlaith down, and Luis and I started saddling every horse in the stable. Before we'd finished, Trish rolled up looking harried.

"I thought I'd never get here! The power is out all over the city, and no one knows how to treat a broken traffic light like a four-way anymore. Anyone's house damaged?" she asked worriedly.

I hadn't even thought about my apartment and that it might not be standing when I got back. I should call my parents, except there was no way to do that. I probably shouldn't ride up to their house on a baby blue pony unless I was planning on doing a lot of explaining about my secret life.

"I had trees down, but the house and the shop are okay," Luis said. "What about you?"

"Everything in the greenhouse doubled in size and broke the glass, but damage to the house is minor," Trish confirmed.

"We'll split into pairs," Fiona said, deterring any further anxieties about houses, families, and jobs. "Drew and I will pick up August, Valerie, and Kevin. Luis and Trish, you pick up Helen and possibly Bennett. I expect he's already making his way here, but he might be stuck on the road. We'll meet back here."

We took the saddled, riderless horses with us. Fiona insisted they would just run along with us, which I hoped was true because a couple of oddly-colored horses running loose through the city was an additional panic Asterville did not need right now. We went first toward the business district where Kevin worked, banking on him being at his office at this time of day. If he wasn't there, we'd trace his most likely route toward his house. We set out at a ground-covering trot—the horses were going to have a long day ahead of them, and their strength wasn't limitless.

We crossed paths with Kevin miles from the financial district, jogging with the easy stride of an endurance athlete in his crisp business attire minus the suit jacket he'd abandoned somewhere, his narrow braids bouncing against his back. He hadn't been able to get his car out of the parking lot. He put one slick-soled leather shoe that probably cost half my rent into the stirrup and swung onto his horse's back.

"I need to go check on my children," he said without preamble.

"Go," Fiona replied. "Meet us at the barn."

She and I continued on to find Valerie and August.

The university was absolute bedlam, cars that probably belonged to worried parents trying to get onto campus and being turned away by campus security, and cars belonging to students trying to get out but unable to get past the gridlock. We had to jump the decorative hedges by one of the entrances to get onto the grounds. The dorm buildings were tall, old behemoths, and I could tell at least one of them had crumbled. My heart squeezed painfully as I tried to remember which one Valerie lived in. A sorority house this year, I remembered. She'd been excited to be a junior. All the students were standing outside huddling together in the green spaces until the buildings were deemed safe enough to go inside.

"Maybe I should walk around and look for her on foot," I suggested. "Valerie isn't going to appreciate being seen with us." People could definitely see that there was something strange about our horses, and there had been some pointing and staring, but so far the citizenry were just too wound up in the destruction of the city and fear for family members they couldn't contact to worry about us. They would probably look more closely if we rode straight up to Valerie, and she would never forgive the blow to her social life.

Fiona gave me a flat-eyed stare that said exactly what she thought about that suggestion.

I closed my eyes and took a deep breath to try to gather the strength needed to argue with Fiona, which would be like arguing with a granite cliff face. Then because that still seemed too hard, I just jumped down from Charon's back and sprinted toward the students gathered in the quad. Fiona probably wouldn't chase me.

About thirty seconds into my search I was lamenting how short Valerie was, because I was never going to be able to see her over all these people. It didn't help that they all looked alike and were dressed in the same college student-chic attire from the bookstore. Blond bobs were a dime a dozen around here. After a few false alarms, I found her standing in front of a white-columned sorority building with a sizable crack in its facade, her arms crossed over her field hockey jacket. She looked to be standing in a group of her sisters, so I slowed down and tried to look normal before I called her name.

Valerie turned to look at me, faint eyebrows drawing slowly together as she tried to determine why I was on her college campus and what horror I was bringing with me.

"Hey, your Aunt Fiona sent me to come get you," I told her as her friends eyed me with the haunted expressions of people who'd hit their limit for horror and slipped into numbness. "We couldn't get the car on campus."

Valerie slowly uncrossed her arms, then without a parting word to her friends, marched resolutely toward me. She still didn't say anything as I led the way back to where I'd left Fiona.

"Are you okay?" I asked her. "Were any of your friends hurt?"

"I don't know yet," she said shortly. "What's happening?"

"Fiona said the rifts are open, but she won't talk about it anymore until we're all together."

Fiona hadn't moved from where I'd abandoned her, and she did not look pleased. I knew she wouldn't bother to say anything though because it was an inefficient use of time in a crisis. Valerie took her pink helmet from where I'd buckled it to her saddle, put it on, and climbed onto her horse's back. She didn't ask any questions or protest being dragged away from her life, just pressed her lips together until they disappeared.

"Let's find August," Fiona said.

August worked freelance from his house, but neither he nor his truck were there when we arrived. He'd taped a note that just said "barn" to his back door, which we took to mean he was attempting to join us. Valerie was the one that spotted the red monster he drove hauling down a median to get around some stopped cars. He waved cheerfully when he saw us and rolled the window down.

"I don't want to abandon the truck," he said. "I'll meet you there.

Anyone hurt?"

"Not that we know of," Fiona said. "Good luck."

We had an iffy moment when Spyder refused to go with us until August got out and talked to him, and even then Fiona had to lead him by the bridle.

Some exhaustive time later, we arrived back at the barn. It felt like days had passed since a streak of flames had blazed across the sky and earthquakes had ravaged the city, but it had only been that morning.

"Okay, now what, Fiona?" I asked her guardedly. I'd been too focused to have a lot of questions while we had a task to complete, but now I was uncertain about what was going on. She must have been gathering us all for a reason beyond making sure we were okay.

Fiona was gazing out at the horizon like she was expecting something. I could almost see her shake off whatever was on her mind as she turned her attention back to me and Valerie. "Now we make a plan."

* * *

In a surreal act of normalcy, we made sandwiches and sat around Fiona's airy farmhouse kitchen while her generator hummed outside to wait for everyone. Luis and Trish returned shortly after we did with Helen, but they hadn't been able to find Bennett and had decided to bank on him being on his way here. August eventually pulled his truck up the driveway, by the look of it having driven off the pavement most of the way. Fiona didn't want to start until Kevin arrived, seeming to feel confident that he would, but I could tell she was getting restless because she kept putting things away before people were finished with them. I kept a hand over my glass so she wouldn't spirit it into the dishwasher. We entertained/tortured ourselves by trying the phones and internet over and over again.

CHAPTER 10

Fiona went to the window before the rest of us even heard the hoof beats that signaled Kevin's arrival. Luis went to help him with Zephyr, and the anxiety in the house ratcheted up another notch as the anticipated conversation neared.

"Kids okay?" Trish asked Kevin anxiously as he slipped through the kitchen door.

"At home with their mother," he confirmed, collapsing all six-foot-something of his athletic physique into an armchair. Unlike most of our families, Kevin's wife was fully informed about his Rider activities, so she would at least understand where he'd gone. "What's happening, Fiona? Is this the surge getting stronger?"

"It's not a surge," Fiona said grimly. She stood behind the kitchen bar like it was a battlement at a castle. "The rifts have opened completely, or at least our rift has. I have no way of contacting our companions abroad at this time. I'm not sure how best to explain it, but wherever the rifts lead to, whatever is on the other side, it has entered our world now."

Luis propped his elbows on his knees as he leaned forward. "How does that differ from the usual other than sheer volume?"

Fiona went to the fridge and took out a plastic bottle, then took a bowl from a cabinet. She stabbed a few holes in the bottle with her knife and held it over the bowl. Little trickles of water streamed out. "This is magic trickling through the rifts into our world, the bowl." She unscrewed the cap from the bottle, and the rest of the water gushed into the bowl in a few seconds. "That is what just happened. All the magic that was contained within the rifts is now in the bowl. The bottle is empty, and there's no putting the water back in there." She put the bowl and bottle in the sink and turned back to us. "Whatever held that magic in whatever dimension or other world or pocket of space is gone. It would be a better analogy to turn the bottle inside out because I'm not even sure the rift is there anymore. We have never known its true nature, so perhaps we've colored our views with our terminology. The point is, a huge influx of magic has entered our world like never before."

"Where is it going to go?" Helen asked, hazel eyes moving worriedly behind her glasses.

Fiona shook her head. "It isn't. It is here to stay."

I thought back to the streak of fire in the sky and the split in the road emitting flames that disappeared like vapors. All that had been magic. "So it's in what—our environment? Our air? Does it interact with us?"

"The magic that has been seeping through the rifts for centuries has given power to or at least been accessible to those who could learn to work it and has been the source of arcane phenomena throughout history. I can only imagine this magic will be just the same only a magnitude stronger. There was so much around us today that Rider concealment magic had little effect on humans nearby like it was being drowned out. I don't know if the magic will stay localized, or if it will slowly thin and spread evenly around the world. Perhaps those who were near the rift when it opened will find they can work magic after the exposure."

"I'm going to be Spider-man," August said with what I felt was really, really inappropriate enthusiasm. When I turned to glare at him though, he was looking down anxiously at his chip bag. Either he was sad it was empty, or he was worried.

"What are *we* supposed to do?" Valerie wanted to know. Her hands were balled so tightly her knuckles were white.

"That is what we must decide," Fiona replied. "If the tethered life energies increased so dramatically during the surge, I can only fathom what will happen to them now. That that remains our responsibility is unquestionable. If magic continues to cause other anomalies as with the surge, we are likely the only ones who understand what is happening and the only ones capable of doing anything about it. Our city, and possibly our world, has entered a time of great fear and uncertainty. We can choose to help if it is within our abilities."

"It's already worse than I first feared," Bennett said tiredly as he came through the kitchen door. "The emergency radio still works intermittently, and the reports coming in suggest the entire city is without electricity or phone service. The roads are nearly impassible. I saw vines consuming the buildings of a neighborhood I passed, growing as fast as water spreading downhill." He looked helpless and sad for a moment. "I also saw a handful of life energies beside the bodies of car crash victims on the interstate. I couldn't get close to them with the police present. I imagine as soon as phone lines are up again, the reports of odd magical events will come pouring in. I think a state of emergency will be declared as soon as they can find someone to declare it." He dropped into a chair. "Have you been able to reach everyone yet?"

"Our nine in town are accounted for now that you're here," Fiona confirmed. "I can't reach Della and Sean. One of us may have to ride out to check on them. I imagine we will not hear from Gideon for some time."

"I don't want to do this anymore," Valerie said abruptly. "The rest of you can go play heroes and save the world if you want to. I want to go home. I don't even know if my parents are alive or if they're looking for me."

Fiona contemplated Valerie's mutinous expression for a long moment while the rest of us looked away in awkward silence. "That's okay, Valerie," she said very gently. I wasn't surprised she wasn't arguing, but I was a little surprised she was being kind. "One of us will escort you to your parents' house and bring your horse back."

"I'll take her," Trish offered. "They live in Henderson, right? We should get going now. It's a long round-trip."

"I can't go riding up to my parents' house on a magic horse," Valerie said, frustrated. "They don't know I have magical powers over dead things."

"Technically, you have magical powers over *life*," August pointed out prosaically. "Perspective."

"I just need to get back to campus and get my Jeep," Valerie said through clenched teeth. "I can drive myself."

"You might want to wait until morning if you're driving," Bennett suggested. "The roads are terrible, and you might not see the cracks in the dark."

"The Jeep has four-wheel-drive," she said flatly. "I'm going now." She left, letting the door bang behind her.

Trish shrugged and followed.

Fiona waited a patient moment for everyone to process Valerie's departure before she spoke again. "First things, who still has family they need to go check on? Let's get that done today while it's still daylight if possible."

"My family lives on the other side of the country," Helen said. "They can't reach me, but they should be well outside this at least."

Luis turned his hands up in a helpless gesture. "I hope that's true. It would probably take me a full day to ride out to my kids and grandkids. The streets might be clear enough to drive if I wait until morning. I'll stay for now."

Fiona looked at me. "Drew?"

"I should go check on my parents," I admitted. "But I'm afraid if I go there, I won't be able to leave again."

"Let's see where our night takes us then," Fiona decided. "We can swing you by there or let you leave a note on your apartment door."

"What do you plan?" Bennett asked, propping his ankle on one knee and lacing his hands around the other.

"Just reconnaissance," Fiona mulled. "Let's first find out what is happening."

"How are we set here at the barn?"

"We have plenty of supplies for a few days and gas for the generator," she said. "After that, we'll have to resort to the old-fashioned methods of candles and wood fires." She smiled a little at that.

"You think it will take that long to get things up and running again?" I asked. I was a veteran camper, so it wasn't like I minded doing without modern conveniences, but apartments just weren't set up for roughing it. I had canned food and bottled water, but I didn't have a fireplace for heat, and a non-flushing toilet situation would get unpleasant quickly.

"Yes, and the supply chains that dictate our modern lives will be a long time derailed. Do you think you will be expected back at work?"

"Well, no, since they fired me mere minutes before the rift split open, I guess not," I told her. I almost had to suppress a giggle at that. "My schedule is wide open."

Fiona looked politely surprised. "Well, at least you'll have plenty of time to ride."

11

Chapter 11

Dusk was nearing when Fiona led us out to examine the state of the city. The sporadic radio was reporting the devastation of the area, but it could tell us nothing of what influence the magic had had on the undead. We went first to the sprawling cemetery where we had encountered the Hazelwood Coven, wending our way through a less dense part of the city. There were only a handful of golden threads floating above headstones instead of the plethora I'd feared, but Fiona stood looking out sourly at the rows of graves.

"We've already done most of this cemetery at some point in the last two weeks," Trish observed. "I don't think there was anyone left to have their life energy lit up by the rift."

"No," Fiona said slowly. "I think any that were left were probably filled with such an influx of magic that they broke free."

"So they're, what, wandering around not attached to anything?" The incredulity in Helen's voice didn't quite mask the horror.

"Zombies," August said gravely. "And so it begins."

"Well, at least one of them is attached to its body," Luis said grimly, pointing. "Or somebody dug that guy up."

We rode closer to circle around the churned dirt of a freshly dug grave. Bits of the casket stuck out, broken.

"How did it get through the concrete?" I asked, perplexed. Did magically reanimated bodies have to do with our kind of magic?

"Super-strong zombies," August suggested.

"Let's finish up here and move on," Fiona said. "I have a feeling the real trouble is elsewhere."

We moved on from the cemetery, Fiona navigating toward something only she could sense. When we reached the commercial part of the city, it became clear that, as bad as I had thought the destruction was earlier that day, it was far worse. Asterville wasn't big enough to have high-rises, but the four or five-story office buildings with their glass fronts hadn't weathered the earthquakes well. The city was dark with no electricity to power the streetlights and no ambient light from business signs and windows. The cars that had been gridlocked during the day were abandoned now, many damaged by collisions with other cars and the destroyed street. Looters had already swooped in to take advantage of the situation to steal parts from cars. August rustled a pair of would-be thieves out from under a Buick by slapping the side of the car with the rope he always carried around his saddle horn and chasing them down the street while he made banshee noises. I'm sure getting chased by a howling man on a horse glowing reddish-black and silver was a uniquely terrifying experience.

As we neared the center of the city, the abandoned cars had been pushed off the road enough to create a center lane, probably for emergency vehicles. The hospital where I'd been only a few days ago, where Cole worked, was in chaos. A corner of the top two floors had been sheered off, but it was clearly still in use despite its questionable structural integrity because there was no other choice. Ambulances not bothering with the sirens queued outside the entrance to be unloaded, their silence somehow ominous. A spotlight, presumably powered by a generator, lit the scene starkly in the surrounding darkness. The staff who exited the ER doors to transport the patients had the weary, robotic movements of people who were so tired they were functioning purely on training. Barricades had been put up to keep out the crowds of anxious people trying to get into the hospital to look for missing loved ones, and they shouted desperate requests to the medical staff, who had to ignore them with hunched shoulders.

Off to the other side of the covered entrance to the ER was another cordoned-off area, this one lined with rows of black bags. They no longer had anywhere inside the hospital to put the dead. It had occurred to me that so many destroyed buildings and vehicles meant injuries and even deaths, but the scale of the fatalities was beyond what my mind could have imagined. I realized belatedly how fortunate I'd been to not witness the worst of the devastation. I had watched everyone near me flee to the safety of the outdoors at the first quake, and I hadn't seen much besides dented cars, downed power lines, and giant cracks in the asphalt as we'd ridden through the streets earlier. Emergency services wouldn't have even begun to reach the majority of the people who had been hurt or killed at that point. God knew how many more people were out there waiting for help.

There was a second crowd of people milling around the hospital, darting around the hospital staff and twining among the worried searchers. Those anxiously waiting for news of family members seemed to feel the gray, ghost-like things sliding among them because they shifted away from the touch, but everyone in such a tight, anxious crowd expected to be jostled.

"Well," Luis said very, very softly. "What do we do now?"

"We have to do something," Bennett decided. "We can't let them just wander around."

"We also can't just ride down there on horses swinging knives at something no one else can see," Helen pointed out. "We'll look like aggressive lunatics."

Fiona steadied Orlaith, who had begun to paw at the ground with one ivory hoof. "I have a feeling our presence will be very stirring to the dead. Perhaps we can lure them elsewhere." She turned her horse to circle the back of the hospital, and we followed.

The rest of us waited a ways back in the shadows while Fiona rode closer to the corner where the dead congregated. There was no Rider magic making us unseen anymore, but with the presence of the spotlight, most of the crowd would be night-blind to anything beyond its reach. They certainly noticed Fiona as she rode back and forth as close as she could get to the cordoned-off area, but Orlaith wasn't an unusual color for a horse, as long as you didn't see her amethyst eyes, so people were more confused about why a horse was there at all than alarmed. The watery mirages of the recently dead were sluggish, but they did eventually start to pay attention to Fiona, their bodies turning back and forth in rhythm with Orlaith's pacing.

"What are you doing?" one of the orderlies helping unload the ambulance demanded.

"Looking for someone," Fiona replied, not taking her eyes off her task. The orderly started to speak again, and she made a shooing motion at him. He looked confused for a second, then went back to whatever he'd been doing as if he'd never noticed her.

The life energies, most of which didn't appear to be attached to the bodies, slowly began to drift toward Fiona, and she guided Orlaith further back to lead them away. They followed her uncertainly like she was the Pied Piper of the dead. When she'd left the harsh glow of the spotlight behind, she had about twenty floating hesitantly after her like they didn't really have the capacity for deciding where to go but were being drawn by forces they didn't recognize. A few more lingered back by the body bags.

Whether it was the growing distance from their bodies or the increasing proximity to the entire Rider group, a change was beginning to come over the dead as they followed Fiona. They started to look more alert, more aware as they drifted along. She was trying to lure them far enough away from the people outside the hospital that we would be safely out of sight, but it didn't look like she was going to make it. Luis tried to help her corral them further away, but playing wrangler appeared to be the wrong choice. The life energies were nearly as solid as Asa had been now, and they had gained enough instinctive wariness to be afraid of us. They fled.

Fiona cursed in some ancient language as the dead dispersed like a flock of startled birds into the darkness. "Get them!"

I kicked Charon forward without much thought as to *how* I was going to "get them." The lives were fast, but Rider horses were too, and I'd spent years sticking to the saddle like glue over some hairy cross-country jumps. I picked a target and zeroed in. When I caught up with it, I realized I was going to have a hard time cutting through it with just my short little knife while we were both moving. I should have followed up with Fiona about that sword. But the knife didn't matter, I reminded myself. It was my intent to make the thing happen that made it so. I extended my hand, still gripping the knife, and waved my entire arm through the gray thing so I would have as much contact with it as possible. I willed it to disperse, and it did in an explosion of energy that rattled my teeth.

I slowed Charon, surprised by how much effort that had taken. I felt like I'd tried to bench press a car with my mind. There was no time for that though. I took stock of my surroundings, noting I'd ridden far enough away from everyone that I could only see August, who was using his rope as his weapon of choice. I spied another untethered life and launched Charon at it to do the whole thing again. The second took longer to chase down but less time to disperse now that I had a better understanding of what I was doing. I searched for another target and couldn't see anything.

I was two streets over from the hospital now, the night so dark the cars and buildings were only shadows. I was almost amazed I'd managed to ride here, and I hoped Charon could see better than I could. I knew I had passed Fiona at some point because her golden sword glowing like a torch in her hand, but I didn't see anyone now. We had been scattered pretty thoroughly in our chase. I couldn't see any stray life energies either, so I concentrated on the feeling of wrongness that accompanied them and followed that instead, back in the direction of the hospital.

There was a clatter of hooves down a side street, then a cry of pain. I turned Charon toward it in time to see Helen land on her butt in the road, Scout veering in the opposite direction. I started to go toward her, but she waved me away and pointed. "I'm fine! Get it!"

I spied the human-shaped mass of energy she'd been pursuing and gave chase, hoping I could catch up with it before it reached the hospital again. Charon managed to corner it against a building, and I studied it while trying to figure out how to get close enough to touch it without it slipping past me. It was a woman, an older lady with one of those tightly-curled hairstyles favored by her generation. There was nothing of the sweet, old lady in her expression though; whatever was looking back at me was just hunger and an instinct to flee danger.

"Hello," I soothed, reaching out a hand toward her as I shifted Charon to block her with his body. "I know you're scared—"

The woman lunged toward me with her mouth open and tried to latch onto my arm like a Rottweiler. She was only semi-corporeal, so I could feel her trying to bite me, but she couldn't really keep her grip. She gave up the biting as ineffective and took off, successfully dodging around the corner faster than I could signal Charon to follow in my unbalanced state.

"Shit. I know!" I added when Charon snorted in disgust. "It's my fault."

The woman barreled back toward the hospital, and I chased after her. I could hear hooves on the asphalt that signaled someone coming to join me, but I didn't look back. The hospital with its ambulances, spotlight, and crowd of desperate searchers came into view again. An ambulance was pulling out of the parking area, and I just barely managed to divert Charon out of its way. I could see the driver staring at me through the window, gobsmacked.

There was a scream from somebody in the crowd, and I thought it must be a reaction to me playing chicken with the ambulance, but when I looked up, another of the magic-saturated life energies had entangled itself into the crowd of living people and appeared to be struggling with someone. They were visible to even non-magic users now when they were this solid and active. I was about to turn my attention toward it instead when I realized my original target was heading in that direction, probably hoping to join in the fray.

I galloped after her, successfully catching up with her this time. I stabbed her with my knife, plunging my arm through her nearly up to my elbow. There were more screams, and I hoped no one was too emotionally traumatized by watching me appear to kill what looked like a ghost. I looked up to go after the one causing mayhem in the crowd, but Bennett was already there.

Persephone, breath steaming in the cold night air like a phantom horse, picked her way daintily through the panicking people without crushing so much as a toe as Bennett tried to cut a path toward the rogue life energy. Most of the crowd had the sense to get out of the horse's way, though they were still screaming and pushing each other. Bennett had what looked like one of those narrow cane swords in one hand, and he thrust it into the gray being with the elegance of a fencing master, neatly missing the living human who was still entangled with it. The life energy dispersed at once. Bennett leaned down like he might be asking the man if he was okay, though I couldn't hear from where I was.

I turned as hooves approached to see the rest of the Riders coming toward me. Bennett saw them too, and he left the confused and frightened people to join us.

"Are you okay?" I asked Helen, who was picking some road grit back out of her palm. "What happened back there?"

She made a face. "I'm fine. Scout just tried to jump something I didn't see in the dark. Some of us didn't grow up with the horses like you did."

"Are there any left?" I asked. "I don't feel any nearby."

"They are either gone or very far away," Fiona confirmed. "There is too much wrongness throughout the city to be able to feel these specifically. We should away."

I glanced at the crowd, who were staring at the group of people on strange horses. If we'd started out trying to be subtle, we'd failed miserably. Some of the medical staff had crossed the barricade to check on the fallen man, though he was on his feet now.

Without further discussion, Fiona trotted away briskly into the dark, everyone falling in line behind her. We could always outrun anyone who decided to chase us. I started to follow, then turned Charon back to the ER entrance.

"Have you seen Dr. McBride tonight?" I asked the two people in blue scrubs who were on this side of the barricade.

They both stared at me.

"Dr. McBride?" I repeated more urgently. Charon tossed his head, impatient to rejoin the herd.

One of the men shook his head. "I haven't seen him tonight."

"Thanks." Not unusual, I assured myself even as I felt prickles of anxiety. I'm sure the inside of the hospital was chaos, and Cole was only an intern. They just hadn't seen him. I turned Charon loose, and he cantered to catch up with the rest of the Riders.

* * *

We continued to ride around the city trailing after Fiona's instincts, but even she seemed to be growing frustrated. It was like trying to smell brownies in a room where someone had just sprayed an entire can of air freshener.

"So I'm not understanding what's happening here," Kevin said as we walked. "The life energy that we separate from the body when it remains tethered after death—it's just energy, right? 'The spark of life.' How is this magic turning those harmless, ego-less clouds of energy into these things?"

"The longer the energy is unrestrained by a form, the more it desires to create one around itself," Fiona said. "It will start to draw things to itself. Matter. Emotions. It was accustomed to being *used* for something, and it is still in the same shape of the last thing it inhabited because it never dispersed, like a cookie cutter. Most of the time, if left to absorb the magic around it long enough, it would try to draw those things from the most familiar source, its former body."

"Zombies," August said helpfully.

"They don't usually get that far," Fiona continued. "It is rare enough that the life energy remains tethered to the body at all. These dead are only reacting the way they are because of the huge influx of magic that has entered the world. Otherwise it would have taken years, perhaps decades, for a life energy to have absorbed enough magic and matter to acquire a form at all. Of course," she added, "those we just fought would definitely have resurrected the bodies in those body bags if we hadn't been there. They just hadn't quite woken up enough to do it."

My mind churned with images of the dead walking and questions about the dangers they posed to the still-living. I also couldn't get the desperation on the faces of the people outside the hospital out of my head, the sound of their shouts as they called for people they couldn't find, wondering if one of the black bags on the ground held someone they loved. What if one of those black bags held someone *I* loved? I had naively expected property damage, but the deaths had staggered me.

"I think I might want to go check on my parents now," I said softly when we had stopped to stand listlessly at an intersection.

"I'll ride with you," Fiona said without argument. She wasn't going to let anyone go anywhere alone after what we'd seen at the hospital. "Bennett, can you get everyone back to the barn? I think we've done all we can for the night. Anyone who wants to stay at the house is welcome to. We can regroup in the morning."

"I'll get everyone home," Bennett promised.

Fiona and I started toward the suburb where my parents lived in silence, the horses' heads hanging a bit. After about ten minutes I stopped.

"You know what? This is stupid. The horses are exhausted, and so are we. Let's just go back to the barn."

Fiona rode past me and kept going until I gave up and nudged Charon after her. She was going to my parents', with or without me, apparently.

The city was so quiet without the usual traffic; so dark without the light pollution. I heard a few cars go by, but few people were willing to brave the roads if they didn't have to. We started through the swath of treed land east of the city center from which the newer subdivisions had been carved as Asterville burgeoned outward from the mid-sized town it had been pre-Interstate, and we may as well have been in a forest somewhere in Montana. The sky was pretty without all the city lights. At least there was something the magic hadn't been able to touch.

The horses balked suddenly as something rustled in the trees around us like a flock of birds being startled into flight. A shadow passed over me against the moonlight, and I looked up. A herd of deer was soaring over our heads like Santa's reindeer, long, slender legs pawing at the air as if looking for purchase and wings like a large bird's beating in a frantic rhythm. A few of them managed to continue awkwardly upward, but some of them were fighting to maintain altitude, and one outright plummeted in a sickening free fall.

I gasped and kicked Charon toward where it had fallen. I found it in a clearing, its head bent back at an impossible angle. Wings of white and pale brown feathers grew from behind its shoulder blades. I heard Fiona join me, but she didn't say anything while I knelt to touch the deer with a trembling hand.

"It's dead," I whispered.

"Yes," Fiona said, not ungently. "It wasn't born knowing how to fly, and it wasn't ready for such an abrupt evolutionary upgrade."

I tried to arrange the deer's broken body into a more restful position, like it was merely asleep. "Will we have to do something about the others?" I asked hesitantly. "Because they aren't supposed to be like this?"

"No, Drew," Fiona said. "They are what they are now. If they survive long enough to master their new wings, they might pass them down to their offspring." She even managed a small smile. "And then we live in a world with flying deer."

I gave the deer another pat to say goodbye, and it jumped under my hand, startling me. I fell back against Charon's legs, and the deer jumped upright, standing with its delicate legs splayed and chewing its cud anxiously.

"Fiona, is it still dead?" I asked in a whisper.

"No, I don't think so." She sounded contemplative.

"I didn't mean to do it."

"It's all right, Drew. There's going to be a lot of weird stuff happening over the next few days. It might have just absorbed so much magic into its body that when you aligned its spine again, it healed fast enough for it to start breathing again."

The deer wandered off a few steps and just stood there. I gave Fiona a helpless look.

"Leave it alone," she advised. "It will either be okay, or it won't. Let's go"

The ride was long, the city sprawl not made for horse travel anymore. I had been awake since yesterday morning, and it was past midnight now, but I mostly felt bad for Charon, who had been trotting all over the city all night. At last the neighborhood came into view, the houses dark, but mostly standing.

"I'll wait here," Fiona said.

I left Charon with her and walked the rest of the way to the brick house with its tasteful ecru shutters and knocked. Both cars were in the driveway. There was a wreath of fall foliage on the front door, and if the porch light had been on, I could have pretended I was just coming for Sunday dinner.

There was shuffling behind the door as someone was probably trying to see through the peephole. "It's Drew!" I called.

The door flew open, and my father stood there, a baseball bat in one hand and a stunned expression on his face. My mother stood behind him, half-hiding behind the entryway wall in case I was a burglar.

"Andrea!" My father seized me in a gruff hug, almost bonking me in the head with the bat. My mom pulled me away from him so she could squeeze the air out of me.

"You're okay!" she wailed. "Where have you been?"

"I'm fine," I said. "It's just hard to get anywhere right now. How is the house?"

"We don't have power, but it's still standing," Dad said. He peered past me out the door. "How did you get here?"

I gestured to where Fiona waited in the distance, the horses barely visible in the dark.

"I went to Fiona's, and we rode over here on horses. It's impossible to drive. I'm going to stay there with her a few days until the electricity is back up," I explained. "She has a generator, and she needs help with the horses."

My parents leaned cautiously through the doorway to squint at Fiona. They both waved. After a pause, Fiona waved back, reluctantly agreeing to impersonate a human for a minute.

"I don't know, Andrea," my mom said hesitantly. "You should stay here with us. God only know what's going to happen in the next few days. I think they're sending in the national guard."

"I'll be safe at Fiona's," I persisted firmly. If I agreed to stay here with them, they'd never let me back out of the house again. "You two have each other here," I pointed out more gently. "Fiona lives by herself, and no one should probably be alone right now."

I could see that reasoning was working on them, as they pictured poor Fiona, all alone with her horses in this time of crisis. I was glad she couldn't hear us. And that they couldn't see her as more than a silhouette from here. She was about as helpless as an Army Ranger.

"I just wanted to make sure you were okay," I continued. "I guess you'll probably stay in the house for a few days?"

"Yes," my dad confirmed. "We have a full week of emergency supplies, and we're coordinating a neighborhood watch with the neighbors."

God bless my parents and their persistent by-the-book attitude. I don't know how they got stuck with such a wildcard child.

"That's great." I hugged them both. "I've got to go. I don't want to keep Fiona waiting. I'm sure she's exhausted."

They lingered in the doorway, watching me until I reached Fiona again and climbed onto Charon's back.

"Everyone okay?" Fiona asked patiently as we began the long ride back toward her house.

"Yeah, thanks for riding out here with me." She had been completely understanding of everyone's need to check on family, if not very empathetic. She wasn't the kind to get wound up in anyone else's emotions. I wondered if she'd just gotten tired of it after all these years.

"Do you ever miss your family?" I asked her.

"Not really," she replied.

"Okay." Not a night for personal topics, I guessed.

We rode back to the barn in silence. I was ready to put the day's problems to bed. We'd worry about tomorrow's problems tomorrow.

12

Chapter 12

I woke disoriented in my spot on the living room couch, trying to remember where I was. Sunlight streamed in through the curtains no one had bothered to close in the exhaustion of the previous evening. I was pretty sure it wasn't the sun that had woken me though, and I couldn't remember what had. I dragged myself into the kitchen and gulped down two glasses of water. I looked out the window while I waited for my brain to catch up. The horses were all turned out in the pasture; we'd fed them before we went to sleep. The clock on the radio said it was 7 am. I'd barely been asleep, and after being awake for nearly a full day, I would have expected to still be out cold.

I could swear someone had called me. I walked a circle around the bottom floor of the house, listening. No one else was stirring. Fiona would be in her bedroom on the ground floor, and everyone else had distributed themselves among the three remaining bedrooms upstairs. I was wide awake though, so I pulled on the boots I'd left by the kitchen door and wandered outside. Everything looked so normal, I thought I might be sleepwalking. Nothing was normal anymore.

I leaned against the fence and stared at Valerie's horse. Would she be sad if Valerie didn't come back? I rocked my foot on the fence rail, back and forth. Back and forth. Back—

"Drew!"

The sound was entirely in my head, but it had the volume of an air horn. I blinked, and I was looking up at the sky. I'd ended up on the ground somehow, but I didn't remember falling. I sat up, the sound of my name echoing through my head.

The voice was Cole's.

I was on my feet in a second, ready to run, then realized I wasn't sure why. The panic that had overtaken me didn't even like it was mine. How had I *heard* Cole? Was I dreaming about him because I was worried? I hadn't been asleep though; I was sure of it.

I dug my phone out of my pocket, but the call wouldn't go through. The cell towers were still down. Fiona had a landline, but Cole didn't. I had to find him though, the urge pressing down on me until it was my only thought. I didn't have my truck, and it was way too far to manage on foot. I eyed Fiona's truck—she'd forgive me eventually. Would I be able to get it through the streets? I wasn't sure I should risk it.

I looked at Valerie's horse, who had been watching my freak-out with interest. "Look, I know I'm not Valerie, but you're the only horse that didn't get ridden all night. Are you up for this?"

I opened the gate without bothering to go get a halter, and Sereia walked willingly toward the barn without waiting for me. I had her saddled faster than a professional pit crew could change a tire even as my hands trembled with adrenaline. The only way off the property was down the driveway, and I kept to the grass as far from the house as possible to muffle her hoof beats. I felt imaginary eyes on me as I passed the house, expecting someone to call out to me at any moment, but the house stayed quiet. I let Sereia trot for a few impatient minutes when we reached the street, then urged her into a fast-run.

I paid attention to the city only as much as was necessary to navigate. There were people in yellow vests moving through the streets checking the empty cars and leaving plastic streamers on the door handles, and a crew of utility workers tried to make sense of an electrical grid that no longer existed. I ignored them all and rode wherever the fastest path led, with no attempt at avoiding anyone. Valerie was going to beat me with a hockey stick when she found out I took her horse. I hoped she was safe at her parents'.

Cole lived in an old brownstone that had been converted into apartments; his was on the second floor. The whole building looked like one side of it had sunk into the ground, leaving it tilted at a perilous angle. I left Sereia on the grass in front of the building, trusting her not to wander off, and hauled at the door that led to the staircase. It was jammed from the frame being off-level, but I kicked it a few times, and it finally splintered enough to break the tension. I pounded up the stairs without paying attention to the way they creaked under my weight and grabbed the doorknob to his apartment. By some miracle, it wasn't locked.

"Cole?"

The entire apartment was slanted toward the hole that engulfed the bottom of the building; the contents thrown about like a hurricane had swept through. There was a crack in the ceiling that looked like it would give way any second. I heard a groan. I fought my way through the detritus of Cole's apartment to his bedroom, having to crawl over the dresser that had slid in front of the door. This side of the apartment had taken the worst of the damage, and chunks of the ceiling and walls had collapsed.

I found Cole lying on the far side of the bed, a pile of rubble burying his right leg. He looked unconscious, his face streaked with sweat and brick dust. There was blood on his head, but whatever wound it had come from had stopped actively bleeding.

"Cole," I whispered, settling next to him as gently as I could so I wouldn't cause anything else to fall. I pressed my fingers to his neck. He was breathing, but he was so pale. "Cole," I said a little more forcefully.

His eyes flickered open. "Drew."

"I'm going to get you out of here," I assured him. God, had he been here an entire day? I examined the rubble, trying to figure out how to shift it. I grabbed the first piece I thought I could move and inched it over as carefully as possible.

"Drew," Cole said again.

"I'm here," I said, rolling the chunk of brick to the floor. "Just going to take a minute."

"Drew." His voice was barely more than a whisper. "If you take everything off my leg, it's going to kill me."

I froze. "Cole, don't say that. Why?"

"Blood flow has been cut off too long," he murmured. "Need medical intervention before you move it. I tried to call…" He drifted off, eyes closed against the pain.

I glanced at the cell phone lying next to his hand. He had called, but it hadn't been with that phone. "There's no cell service in the entire city. No electricity." I seized another chunk of brick.

"Go get help," Cole muttered.

"I can't. There isn't anyone to come help us. Half the city is destroyed, and emergency services are barely functioning. It's just you and me." Because I had stupidly rushed out in a panic without telling anyone. I could have left a note on the chalkboard in the barn.

Cole groaned as I moved another piece of rubble.

"You're a doctor," I told him, "and I went to vet school. Tell me what you would do if you were treating yourself as a patient right now. Walk me through what to do, and I'll do it."

"The blood is trapped in my foot," he whispered, half-delirious. "It will try to flow again when you move all that rock." As he talked, his leg began to glow with a faint yellow light. "My kidneys are going to shut down."

"Yeah?" I said, watching the glow carefully. "Think about fixing your leg. Think about putting all that blood back where it's supposed to be."

"What?"

"Please, Cole. Picture yourself as the surgeon in the operating room. Fix your leg."

"Compartment syndrome leads to crush syndrome," he said. "Sodium bicarbonate to neutralize the alkaline. Should have done a fasciotomy right away, but I couldn't reach a knife."

He was babbling, but it was working. The golden glow was growing around his leg, which I could already tell was less swollen as I moved more rubble. I did it slowly, so he'd have time to keep up.

"Drew?"

I leaned over to put my hand on his chest for a moment to comfort him and instead felt a jolt of energy go through me. Cole's eyes popped open again as he felt it too. His whole body warmed and throbbed with the golden light now, and I could see it fixing his injuries, cleansing his blood of the toxins that would have killed him. Alarm grew on his face as he realized something was happening but couldn't understand it.

"Concentrate, Cole," I told him. "Think about how you would treat compart—whatever in the ER."

But his pretty gray eyes rolled up, and he passed out cold.

I had moved most of the crap pinning his leg down at that point, so I quit being dainty about it and hauled the rest of the brick out of the way. Either Cole had done enough to keep himself alive, or he hadn't. It was too late to second-guess my plan to move him. His leg, though no longer swollen against the ripped fabric of his joggers, was clearly broken, though fortunately the bone wasn't protruding through his skin. I hadn't told him to fix that because I hadn't known, but I realized now that was for the best anyway. He could heal from a broken leg but not from the system shock of a crush injury. I found his pool stick by happenstance and secured the two unscrewed halves of it to either side of his leg with random clothes I pulled off his floor.

Okay, now I just needed to get him downstairs. I moved the dresser blocking the bedroom doorway so I wouldn't have to drag him over it, then rolled him onto his comforter so I could slide him. I had to stop to clear the path a few times, but I managed to get him to the door and out to the landing. The stairs were going to be hardest part. Cole wasn't a big guy, but he was still bigger than me, and he was dead weight while he was unconscious. If I tried to drag him down on the blanket, I was really going to hurt him. I pulled the comforter out from under him and tossed it down the stairwell. Then I wrapped my arms around his chest under his arms so his head was against my shoulder and started down the stairs backward. I realized belatedly that the foot of his broken leg was bouncing on every step, but I couldn't put him down again at that point, so I had to keep going.

I paused at the switchback to catch my breath, but I realized quickly there was no point in stopping. I couldn't let go of Cole, so the faster I got him to the bottom, the faster the screaming muscles in my arms would get some relief. I laid him down on the blanket again at the bottom and checked his breathing while I tried to get my limbs to stop trembling. He was even paler than he had been before; I was probably really hurting him by moving him so much, even if he wasn't conscious to feel it. I had to get him to the hospital. I grabbed the blanket-sled and eased him outside.

Valerie's horse was still standing where I'd left her. She turned her ears toward me and Cole, then approached to see what I was doing. I eyed the distance between Cole on the ground and Sereia's back. I could get him up there, but it was going to be unpleasant. I prayed he'd stay unconscious. When I thought I had regained enough strength, I grabbed him under the arms again, hauled him upright, and slumped him over the horse's back, grateful Arabians were short. Then I squatted to wrap my arms around his knees instead before he could slip down and shoved him upward. He ended up belly-down over her back as I intended. Cole groaned piteously, and I knew I'd really hurt him that time.

"I'm sorry, I'm so sorry," I whispered. "I'm really trying here." I was still panting from the exertion of lifting him, but I started to lead Sereia toward the hospital, keeping one hand awkwardly behind me to steady Cole.

Cole's apartment was only a short drive from the hospital because he worked there, but it would take hours to walk there like this. I eyed Sereia, wondering if she could carry us both. Arabians were little, but they were pretty mighty. Still, Cole and I together would definitely exceed the recommended weight a small horse could handle. I decided to try it, and if she acted uncomfortable, I'd just get back off. Cole was lying across the saddle, and I had to stand in the stirrups while I tried to drag him back across my thighs without accidentally dumping him on the ground, but I eventually got my butt in the seat.

"Okay, let's try a trot," I told Sereia.

She took off willingly enough, and I relaxed a little as she didn't seem to be struggling. Then she shot forward, launching into a fast-run. I grabbed Cole with both hands so fast I almost dropped the reins. I managed to hold onto him somehow as she galloped through the streets, tossing her head like she was having a great time. It was about all I could do to try to steer without letting either of us fall off as the streets blurred by.

"Slooow," I pleaded as the hospital parking lot came into view. I couldn't really move my body to cue her to stop. The parking lot was still barricaded, and I was terrified she would try to jump the sawhorses. We would really need a hospital then after we crashed into the asphalt.

But Sereia slowed gracefully as the hospital staff around the ER entrance turned to stare at us. I recognized springy red hair.

"Dr. Smithers!"

The woman stopped gaping at me as her emergency training kicked in, and she jogged to me.

"It's Cole," I said, because she probably couldn't tell with him lying face down. Others had already followed to help lift him down from my lap. "His leg got crushed," I panted. "He was trapped a long time. I don't know what else is wrong with him." I watched them lay him on a stretcher and start to check his vitals. I felt oddly more panicked now that his care was no longer in my control, though the medical staff were the people he needed right then. "Is he going to be okay?" I asked in a very small voice.

"I hope so, Drew," Dr. Smithers said very gently. "You did a good job to bring him here. We'll take good care of him now."

I watched as they rolled Cole through the emergency room doors to join the hundreds of other patients crowded within the walls. I looked at the cordoned-off section where the body bags still lay in rows. Where Cole would have been if I hadn't found him. Where other people might be soon if no one found them. I hadn't even looked to see if anyone else had been trapped in the other apartments of Cole's building. There was an ambulance idling in the bay, and I turned Sereia toward it. Maybe I could get someone to go check on Cole's neighbors.

* * *

I expected the scolding of a lifetime when I dragged back into the barn, but Fiona just studied the weariness on my face and the brick dust that streaked my clothes. There was blood from Cole's head smeared on my shoulder. She didn't say anything at all. I could see Bennett pacing behind the big picture window in the kitchen, and I had a feeling she'd forbidden him to say anything to me.

"Cole was hurt," I said, an embarrassing tremor in my voice. I swung slowly to the ground, every muscle in my body aching. "I had to go find him."

"Where is he now?" Fiona asked calmly.

"I took him to the hospital." I started to run the stirrups up and loosen the girth on the saddle. I was a heartbeat away from just bursting into tears.

Fiona stepped between me and Sereia and took her bridle. "Go upstairs, find a bed, and sleep in it. Go," she repeated firmly when I didn't move.

I went inside, not looking at any of the people lurking, and went upstairs. I had slept maybe two or three hours in the past thirty-six, and I don't think I'd eaten anything since yesterday's lunch. The strain of lifting and holding someone who was heavier than I was had caught up to me without the dampening effect of adrenaline, and I could barely lift my feet to clear the steps. I picked a room and peeled off my shoes and dirty outer clothing before I crawled into the bed, not caring who had last used it. I gave up on the no-crying thing and sobbed away the exhaustion and stress of the last few hours for a few minutes until I was settled enough to sleep.

I woke later to something cold being pressed against my face. I opened one swollen eye to see Fiona sitting next to me, holding a cold glass of water against my forehead. Her expression was mildly curious.

"Fiona," I rasped, not moving so I wouldn't get water spilled all over me. "You know you're kind of weird?"

She lifted the glass so I could sit up, then handed it to me so I could drink it. I gulped the water down like I'd been suntanning in a desert. She waited patiently.

"Drew," she said, "how did you know Cole was hurt?"

"Well, I sort of heard him," I admitted.

"Heard him how?"

"He called me." I don't think I could have explained that to anyone else, but Fiona would believe me. "I heard him shout my name."

"In your head?"

"I guess so. I just knew that he needed me."

She ruminated on this but didn't doubt me. "What happened when you found him?"

I told her how I'd found Cole trapped in his bedroom and how his leg had begun to heal when I'd encouraged him to think about how he would treat those injuries as a doctor. She listened thoughtfully, looking out the window instead of at me.

"It sounds like you saved his life, Drew," she told me when I'd finished.

"I couldn't have if he hadn't healed himself," I said. "Or if he hadn't called for me. Did the rift explosion make Cole do magic? Or could he always do it, and he just didn't know until he was under pressure?"

"I'm not sure," Fiona replied. "It is not unusual for someone's first act of magic to be an instinctive response to danger or high emotion that disregards all established rules, and the density of the magic present would have lent that act an unusual strength. Cole had an established connection with you, another magic user, that might have made you more likely to hear his summons. There will probably be many people who have gained an unexpected skill in the next few weeks."

"I'm sorry I took Valerie's horse," I said guiltily. "I thought hers was the least tired, and I just sort of panicked. She's going to kill me."

Fiona stood. "She won't. Everyone has gone home to check on their houses and families for a little while. Luis will take you to pick up your truck if you want or just back to your apartment to pack some clothes if you want to come back here. We have at least a little electricity for the time being."

"I'd better get my truck," I sighed.

After she left, I got dressed in the grimy clothes I'd taken off and went downstairs. Everyone had already gone except Luis, and we climbed into his Subaru in exhausted silence.

"How is your friend?" he asked me quietly.

"I'm not sure," I said softly. "He was hurt pretty badly." I leaned my head against the window while he drove so I wouldn't have to look at the destruction in the city for a little while.

The vandals had reached the parking lot of Stevens and McKinley, leaving holes smashed in windows and cars teetering on stacks of bricks and wood scraps where their tires used to be. I wondered who the hell these people thought they were going to sell the car parts to—back to the people they stole them from? My truck, being ancient and my tires half-bald, had been spared. It was easy to see there was nothing inside, and it had probably been assumed that no one who drove a vehicle this old had any money anyway. Luis waited to make sure the truck started and I was safely on my way before he waved and drove off.

A driving lane had been cleared pretty much the entire way back to my apartment, though I did have to pull over a few times when someone was coming in the opposite direction. Everyone seemed unexpectedly patient about this. We all exchanged grim little nods as we passed each other, expressions saying, "This is a horrible tragedy, but we're all here together."

My apartment complex was still standing in all its squat, shabby glory. Maybe being square and concrete had protected the austere little buildings from the quakes. I went into the lobby building first to check for any notices from the management. Someone had made a big chart out of colored tape on the wall for people to mark themselves safe. I studied the empty squares with a sadness that had no energy behind it, then tore off a piece of green tape to put in my apartment's square to say I had come back. I trudged back to my building, reading the signs people had left on their doors to say where they'd gone or that they were okay. Someone had written "Empty 2:45" on mine so someone must have checked. The door was still locked, so it had probably been the super. I rubbed the chalk off the door before I went inside.

My apartment still had no power, which meant no lights and no water. I didn't even try to open the fridge—I'd face that horror later. I dug my camping gear out of the hall closet to see what I could make do with. Twenty minutes later I had my camping shower set up inside the real shower and filled with water heated over my propane camping stove. I expected it to be a disappointment compared to the real thing I was longing for, but after the last two days it was the best shower I'd ever had, even if I had to collect the water from the bottom of the tub again to get my thick hair wet all the way through. Once clean and dressed in fleece leggings and a sweater against the chill in the apartment, I climbed into bed and tried to push away the horrors of the world for a little while.

13

Chapter 13

I thought about ignoring the pounding on my door that had woken me, but I finally dragged myself up and answered it.

Fiona stood in the hallway, looking as she usually did both unfailingly at home and inexplicably out of place in modern breeches and riding boots and an ankle-brushing cloak that could have come from the costume department of a medieval period drama. I had the insane, sleep-addled thought that she would look exactly like that if she were dining at Windsor Castle or trekking through the hills in some far-gone past when wolves still ruled Ireland. She was wearing her sword hanging openly from her belt now. I guess she didn't feel like she had to hide it anymore.

Seeing her made me think she must have come to get me so we could go out and tackle some fresh threat to the city. It was nighttime outside the uncovered window now; the only light coming from the battery-powered lamp I shouldn't have left turned on while I slept. I should have already been back over to the barn. Had I missed a phone call? I remembered the phones weren't working anymore.

"Are we going back out again?" I asked her, trying to buck up and not sound so pitiful. I pictured hoards of the not-dead swarming city hall or something.

"We," Fiona said calmly, "are going to go get you a horse, Drew."

"To get a—" I froze, brain spinning on the last fumes of energy I possessed. "To get a horse? Now?"

"Yes, now," she confirmed with no change in tone. "Get dressed."

I turned a slow circle in my living room. "Get dressed."

Fiona surveyed me critically. "I'll make you some coffee. You can go back to sleep in the truck." She walked into my galley kitchen like she had been there a hundred times and found the cabinet with the coffee grounds on the first try.

"What about all the"—I gestured vaguely—"wild stuff happening? Shouldn't we be taking care of that?"

"'That' isn't going away any time soon," she replied practically, pouring bottled water into the pot over the camp stove and lighting it. "It's not going to stir everything up for a few weeks and then fade away again. The old way of life is gone; we'll find a new normal eventually."

"That's so pragmatic," I said faintly.

She looked at me sternly. "I drew water from a well as a child and fixed the plumbing in the barn last summer by watching videos on the internet. People adapt. Put boots on. And get a jacket."

I started looking for my shoes. "Because I don't have a *cloak*?"

"You are really silly when you're tired," Fiona observed. By the time I'd found my boots, one in the bathroom and one in my bedroom for some reason, she'd located a travel mug and poured my coffee into it. "Let's go." She grabbed my keys from the floor where I'd apparently dropped them and pushed me gently out the door, locking it behind us.

Fiona's truck, unlike mine, was a big, new, powerful beast she used to pull the horse trailer. I hauled myself up into the cushy leather passenger seat and turned the butt-warmer on. The diesel engine rumbled as she pulled out into the street.

The city had been placed under curfew, and given the tumultuous state of the roads, I was surprised we were driving instead of riding. To that point, I was surprised Fiona had even made it to my apartment without getting stopped and told to turn around. We seemed to have the streets to ourselves as we wound through back roads no longer lit by streetlights.

"What are we going to do if someone stops us?" I asked as I sipped the coffee she'd made me. It was strong enough I was a little concerned for my stomach lining. "Can you magic the truck into not being seen?"

"I can't hide the truck, but I can make people ignore us if we get pulled over," she said absently. "The cops are too busy elsewhere anyway to cover back roads right now."

"Where are we going?" I asked.

"Regatta Hills," she said, naming a town about an hour away. It was a rural area with lots of pastures and horse farms, so that made sense. She slowed as the road ahead of us disappeared into a dark crevice. "Damn it." She rocked the truck into reverse and shot backward, heedless of how dark it was outside.

We backtracked until Fiona found another winding road that hadn't been damaged so badly, and she dropped the truck into 4x4 to climb through the ditch. She didn't blink an eyelash as mud splattered the shiny paint of her truck. We had to turn back or off-road a few more times where the road had been broken or covered with mud by the earthquakes, and it took us twice as long to get there as it would normally have. Fiona seemed unperturbed by all of this and drove on in steady silence.

When she stopped, I could see a barn in the distance, no more than a shadow against the moonlight. She cut the truck engine off, and we sat in silence for a moment.

"Where are we?" I asked at last.

"I train horses out here sometimes," she said, eyes fixed on the barn.

"Susan lost her prized Dutch Warmblood mare two years ago. She was an amazing jumper back in her prime." Fiona's voice was fond, a tone reserved solely for horses. "A seventeen-hand bay, sweet as a kitten in the stable and a firecracker on the cross-country course."

I swallowed. "So we're here to steal Susan's dead horse?"

"Yes."

"Won't Susan mind?"

Fiona considered. "Susan would absolutely love the idea of her elderly mare getting reborn as a magical horse galloping around the night like the Wild Hunt. She would, however, want that magical horse for herself, and I don't know how I'd explain to her that she couldn't have her. So we aren't going to tell Susan." She opened the truck door.

I got out and hurried around the hood of the truck so Fiona could hear me without raising my voice. "Is two years long enough? I mean, she might still be—" The coffee in my stomach roiled at the thought.

Fiona took two shovels from the bed of the truck and handed me one, then lifted out a big plastic tub. "If it's not, we'll figure it out. Let's be quick." She started out across the expanse of field, heading away from the barn toward the back corner of a pasture.

I jogged to keep up. "If you knew this horse was out here, why are you just now telling me about her?"

"I decided you were ready," she said simply.

"What, I finally passed some test to deserve a horse?" That was a pettiness I didn't really expect from her.

She glanced at me sideways. "I didn't really know you were that interested until I caught you trying to dig that horse up at Hillside. You had been so reluctant about your Rider skills before. And we've been a little busy since then. I do try to keep an eye on good potential horses, and I normally wouldn't have said this one was ready yet, but I think we'll have to go for it anyway."

"Sorry I snapped," I said grudgingly.

"It's fine, Drew. My feelings aren't so sensitive. I should have just told you I had a horse picked out for you already. I'm sorry."

We'd reached the back corner of the pasture, and Fiona stopped to lean on her shovel while she surveyed the simple granite stone that had been placed there as a marker. I could see faint lights in the distance now that must have been the house where Susan lived, though I couldn't hear a generator from this distance. It was so dark and quiet out there that I don't think it would have mattered if we'd been shouting and shining flashlights everywhere; no one would have seen us.

"At least we know exactly where she is," I said. "That will save time."

"It will," Fiona said. She bent to lift a clump of sod from the ground and gestured at the hole left behind. "I stuck a few plastic pipes into her grave a while back, and I pour water down them every now and then to speed decomposition. I have to keep the pipes covered with the sod just in case Susan sees them when she comes out here, but they still let some air in. What won't save us time is having to cut away the sod so we can put it back when we're done."

I repressed a groan. I could do this. Fiona was going out of her way to help me, and I wouldn't complain. "How do we do that?"

She demonstrated by cutting into the ground to the depth of the grass roots with the shovel until she'd made a square the size of a place mat. Then she stuck the shovel under the square and popped it out. She put it to the side, out of the way of our digging.

"You're not going to get them all out so neatly, so don't fret over it. We just need to put as much grass back as possible. Hopefully with the world gone mad, Susan won't feel the need to pay her horse's grave a visit."

And then we were digging. The sod felt like it took weeks, but once it was gone, things improved a little. The dirt had been dug before, albeit not recently, and it wasn't as hard-packed as the surrounding ground would have been. Fiona produced a tarp from the plastic bin, and we tossed the dirt onto it so we wouldn't leave so much behind when we back-filled. I was feeling a little dizzy and disoriented with exhaustion after a few hours, but Fiona just kept digging steadily away like a machine, so I didn't stop either. I hit something solid and froze, shoulders somewhere up around my ears.

Fiona knelt to brush some dirt away. "Pelvis. Dig carefully now. We've found her."

More bones began to appear after that. Fiona's tending had aided the decomposition so they weren't fleshy, but they weren't exactly clean either. At that point, I was too tired to gag over it. We laid the bones out in the grass in their rough anatomical layout as we went to make sure we found them all. By the time we placed the last few bones on the grass, we both were covered in dirt and sweat. There was dirt in my boots, on the inside of my shirt collar where I'd tried to use it to wipe my face, and I'm pretty sure in my bra. Dawn was breaking over the tree cover.

I glanced anxiously at the house.

"Count them to be sure, Drew," Fiona said, unconcerned. "And we'll fill the hole back in."

I counted the bones into the tub, barely able to get them to fit, and Fiona started to shovel the dirt back in. I joined her, and it was thoroughly light outside by the time we started piecing the sod back together.

"It's really going to ruin your working relationship with Susan if she looks out her window over her morning coffee," I panted.

"She's sixty-eight, and I don't think she can see that far," Fiona replied. She started chopping expertly at the rough joins between the sod squares with her shovel to disguise them. "We can outrun her if she comes out here. And if she does recognize me, if I can speak to her fast enough, I can confuse her long enough to make her forget where we were standing. This should be about finished though."

We stood back to survey our handiwork. The missing mass from the horse was made up for by the extra air that our digging the dirt had introduced, but the ground would start to sink a little eventually. If you were standing right over the grave, you could definitely tell something was disturbed, but it looked a lot better than I'd expected. Hopefully what little was left of the growing season would knit it together again. Fiona and I shouldered our shovels and each took one side of the plastic bin. The walk back across the pasture felt like a death march with all the weight, and it was all I could do not to ask to stop and rest. It was truly morning now, and I wasn't about to get caught after we'd come so far.

When we reached the truck, Fiona bungee-corded the bin closed, and we slid it into the back seat of the truck instead of the bed. I melted into the seat as soon as I closed the truck door.

"Thank you, Fiona," I murmured, really meaning it.

She wasn't big on expressions of emotion, so she directed her smile at the steering wheel. "You're welcome, Drew."

14

Chapter 14

Fiona dropped me back at my apartment to pick up my truck, taking the bones of my future horse home with her. I used up most of my remaining water to shower, but I wanted to stop at the hospital to check on Cole, and I didn't think they'd let me in if I was this filthy.

The hospital was still busy, but the air of panic was gone. There was a large truck outside, refrigerator unit humming loudly, and the body bags were being carried inside. A tent had been set up to help those seeking missing loved ones, and they formed a weary line now in front of the table instead of a frantic hoard. I found Cole's whereabouts by just walking through the hospital and asking every person in a white coat I passed where Dr. McBride was until someone pointed me to the ICU. No one tried to stop me. There weren't any spare people for traffic control today.

Cole was lying in one of three beds that had been crammed into the hospital room. The hospital was so overwhelmed with patients, they were running out of space. He was asleep, face ashen and still, but he looked better than he had after being dragged belly-down across the city on a horse. The medical treatment was already helping. I didn't want to wake him, so I climbed into the bed with him and lay down with my head near his shoulder, careful not to jostle him, to wait. I was dozing a bit when someone moving around the bed drew me back toward consciousness.

"How is he?" I asked Dr. Smithers.

She was giving me the classic side-eye, and I wondered if it was because I was in Cole's bed with him or because of what she'd witnessed when I'd ridden up with him. "He's a lot better than he should be," she said as she pressed a stethoscope to his chest. "He had significant injuries to both his leg and his internal organs, but it was like he'd already started to heal." She was looking at me for an explanation, and I wasn't sure if I should provide one. I thought she'd believe me, but maybe Cole had the right to tell her himself.

Our talking must have woken Cole because he stirred. "Drew," he said softly, his eyes barely open. "I thought it was you."

"Hey," I said softly back. "How are you feeling?"

Cole's eyes drifted around the room, unfocused. "I remember you were there. I was hurt and laying there for what felt like days. And then you came and started taking the bricks off my leg even though I told you not to." He frowned. "You shouldn't have done that."

"You shouldn't have," Dr. Smithers agreed. She took a deep breath, her expression sad. "But I understand why you did; there probably weren't any good options. He might have died while you sat there waiting for help." She made a brisk annotation on the clipboard she was using instead of the usual computer station. "You can come pick him up in a day or two if the swelling on his leg reduces enough to apply a cast."

That seemed pretty soon given the rough shape he was in, but they probably needed the bed. His parents and brother lived hours away, and his apartment was no longer livable, so I was probably all he had to take care of him until he could call someone else to come get him.

How I was going to take care of him, I had no clue, but I had two days to figure it out. Cole was already nearly asleep again, so I kissed his cheek and left for Fiona's.

More progress had been made with clearing the abandoned vehicles, but long stretches of road had been blocked off for damage, and there weren't detour signs up yet to direct drivers to clear routes. The gas stations I passed all had signs out front saying they were closed or out of gas. I had a quarter of a tank left, but it wouldn't last long. At its advanced age, the truck was a boat.

The line of cars parked off Fiona's driveway said most of the Riders had returned, and I let myself into the house through the kitchen door.

"Hey, Drew," August offered from where he lounged on the living room rug tinkering with something electronic. "How is your boyfriend?"

"Cole is doing better, thank you. And he is not my boyfriend," I told him as I dropped onto the couch and put my feet on the polished coffee table where they certainly didn't belong. Fiona wasn't much for personal touches, but everything in her house was clean and in perfect condition. I suspected that was because she was never in the house unless she was sleeping.

"That's the spirit," August agreed.

"What is that?" I asked, pointing to the helicopter-meets-Roomba thing he was working on.

"A drone," he said. "I thought we could use it for scouting, if the camera can pick up the dead/not dead things. We've really got to come up with a name for them. It's cumbersome."

"Yeah, we do. Where did you find a drone?"

"Oh, I have a few. I'm a licensed pilot." He was fidgeting with the remote now, and the drone rose two feet in the air, buzzing angrily.

Of course he was. I wasn't sure why I asked. "Where is everyone else?" I was really wondering where my horse bones were and if I could go look at them.

"Kevin and Helen are in the barn, and Fiona and Bennett are doing something in the garden. Luis and Trish went to ride out to Della and Sean. That makes us down two people, but Fiona didn't want Luis to go alone. Valerie," August continued as he made the drone circle the ceiling fan, "has disappeared to places unknown."

I heard the kitchen door open and immediately dropped my feet to the floor, but it was only Kevin and Helen.

"Is that thing working?" Kevin wanted to know.

Helen's corgi, Ruby, shot through the door at her heels, barked at us twice, then lay down on the cool tile floor, guard dog duties complete.

"It is as long as the batteries last," August replied, landing the drone and turning it back off. "After that?" He shrugged.

"I don't think the electricity will be back any time soon," Helen sighed, pulling out a barstool to sit. She and Kevin looked like Fiona had been making them do barn chores. "There's sewage backing up on my street now, so I'm staying over here. I don't know what we're going to do when we run out of gas though."

"Is anyone sending any help to the city?" I asked. "I heard the national guard was coming." The hospital had been a good place to overhear gossip.

Kevin shrugged. "No help coming. The disaster was a lot more widespread than we first realized. Much of the country seems to have been affected, though perhaps not as badly as here. Towns that had less infrastructure had less infrastructure to lose. The bridge on the highway to where Luis's daughter lives got knocked out, but most of the town itself is fine. Fiona is pretty well set up here. She's on a well, not city water, and she has a few solar panels. That'll probably be enough to keep the fridge running and water pumping, but no long showers or lights on in every room."

"Fiona is having the time of her life," Helen said sourly, pulling the claw clip out of her hair so she could pick the shavings from the shoulder-length stands. "She's ready to cook over her outdoor fire and read by candlelight. I'm surprised she doesn't have a herd of goats to slaughter and hang in the smokehouse. You don't happen to have any dry shampoo, do you?"

"No, sorry. Speaking of food, is there any?" I asked. "I don't remember the last time I ate."

"There's leftover pasta," Kevin said, jerking a thumb at the fridge.

I got myself a bowl, and then because someone had unplugged the microwave to stop anyone from using it, I ate it cold.

Fiona and Bennett came in a moment later, Bennett carrying the map from his house. They were both frowning like they'd been deep in discussion, but they didn't continue talking in front of us.

"So what's the plan?" I asked, taking my bowl to the kitchen table.

"I've been thinking about how we might tackle the city," Bennett said, rolling out his map on the table. "I'm wondering if it's worth working it in sections as we have been doing, or if we should take a more reactive approach and respond as incidents arise. There's less need for secrecy now, so there's no need to work at night, at least until people have to go back to work."

"How would we know there's an incident?" Helen wanted to know. "We barely know what's happening in the city. I never thought I'd miss the internet so much."

"So we are making an action plan against these things?" Kevin asked.

Bennett shrugged like the question surprised him. "I feel we must. If the life energies of the dead are wandering the city, we must find them."

"We know you have children to care for, Kevin," Fiona interjected. "No one expects you to prioritize anything above your family's care. Those of us who don't have further obligations will handle this."

Kevin looked grim. "I have a feeling clearing the nasties out of the city is going to be necessary to my family's care at some point."

"We don't explicitly know that they are dangerous," Bennett said.

"One of them bit Drew," Helen pointed out.

"I mean, not very successfully," I reasoned.

"It had ill-intentions," she insisted.

"Are we going to call them nasties?" August asked. "Drew and I think they need a name."

"I'm not calling them nasties," I said.

"Ghouls?" he suggested.

"Ghouls eat flesh. I'm not sure we want to start that association."

"Fine—if it has a body: zombie. No body: *The Untethered*?"

"Sure," I agreed. I turned back to Fiona and Bennett. "I'm up for fighting some untethered. What's the plan? We go out and patrol cemeteries?"

"That would be our usual starting point," Bennett confirmed. "However after the events of the hospital, it appears that the 'untethered,' as you are calling them, could be wandering hither and yon by now. We might station someone at the hospital, but the rest of us need a way to track down the strays."

"It is not so hard," Fiona said dismissively. "It is how our counterparts in less populated places handle the duties. We are all quite spoiled. I am more concerned about what other magical surprises await our attention beyond the dead."

"None of us are equipped to deal with such things, save yourself," Bennett pointed out. "Perhaps we should stick with what is within our abilities."

"We may be all the city has," Fiona said, sounded oddly bemused despite Bennett's resistance. "Unless our local coven is en route to handle that pool of tar that opened up in the amphitheater parking lot."

"A pool of tar? Sounds harrowing. We are definitely not handling that."

We all turned to look at the door, which had been left open, and I almost did a double-take. "Casey?"

Casey worked up a smile as he leaned against the door frame. "What's up, Barrymore?" He was wearing navy work pants and a gray t-shirt with a red insignia on the chest. Asterville Fire Department, I realized. Casey was a firefighter. By the shadows under his eyes, he'd been caught up in the disaster response. He'd shaved the stubble, though he was already losing that battle again, and there were red marks on his cheeks where a mask had been pressed against his face. He looked tired.

Fiona was staring at him like she might call down lighting to strike him dead. "How did you get in here?" She looked at me. "Did he come in your car?"

I shook my head, confused. "No. I didn't bring him."

"That's an amazing ward you have around this place," Casey said conversationally. "Every time I tried to walk up the driveway, I kept forgetting why I'd come and where I was going. It took me a few tries to figure it out." He pulled up the sleeve of his t-shirt and showed Fiona where he'd written "Keep Walking" on his forearm in black marker. "I did though. It's only about fifteen feet deep."

I had never considered that Fiona might have the entire property warded, which in retrospect seemed stupid. Of course she did. I was further surprised that Casey had managed to thwart her safety measures so simply. Fiona looked even more surprised than I was, though distinctly less amused.

"How did you know to come here at all?" she asked, her voice deadly calm.

If Casey knew he was sailing in dangerous waters, he was choosing to feign nonchalance. "I followed Drew from the hospital."

I felt my face redden at that for some reason. "Oh. Sorry," I said guiltily to Fiona.

"That's not your fault, Andrea," Fiona said, never taking her eyes off Casey.

"Yes, it is," Bennett said stoutly. "She may not have led him here on purpose, but she invited him into our business. He's following her around because she's his entrance into what we're doing."

"I didn't realize what we were doing was such a secret," I said, irritated.

"That is *not* why he is following Drew around," August declared with a smirk that left no question what he was suggesting. Casey and I both shot him dirty looks that he deflected with a tranquil smile.

"Look," Casey said, more serious now, "I'm not here to learn all your super-secret Bone Rider shit." He glanced briefly at Bennett. "I am here to discuss what's going on with the magic right now. That *is* something I need to know, and no one in my coven knows anything about it. There are other more experienced covens we could contact, but we can't contact anyone right now because communication is back in the stone age. You're the only other magic group nearby I know about, and you know more than I do, so I came here."

Fiona studied him for a long moment to make him sweat, her chin tilted up at an angle that suggested he should consider himself at her mercy. It was a bluff though. She was angry about the invasion of her personal sanctuary, but she was far too practical to actually turn him away. Despite her dismissal of the local coven as dabblers unworthy of her notice, she wasn't against magical cooperation in a general sense the way Bennett seemed to be.

"Fine," she said at last. "You may join us."

"Great," Casey said. He pulled out a chair at the kitchen table and sat next to me. "So I'm guessing this is not a normal thing to happen in a surge because history books would definitely have recorded a disaster of this scale, even if they didn't know it was magically caused."

"No," Fiona said. "This is no longer a surge. The rifts have broken open entirely, and all magic that was held within has now spilled into the world."

"So what happens now? It gets sucked back in eventually? It wears off? We're stuck with it?" He was eyeing my goat cheese rotini, and I pulled the bowl closer.

"It's probably here to stay," Fiona confirmed. "Have you encountered any magical phenomena since the rift split?"

"I've seen plenty of things that don't make sense in the last few days, including what might have been a zombie," Casey said, leaning his head on his fist now. "I can feel magic everywhere and can't pinpoint any of it. I haven't really had time to look."

"Anyone else in your coven?" Kevin asked. "Kevin Ellison, by the way."

Casey offered his hand across the table, and they did the man-shake to prove neither of them was a wuss. "Casey Redvers. And I haven't had time to try to track everyone down." He was looking at my bowl again, and I sighed and pushed it toward him. He took it and started eating with my fork like he didn't give a rat's ass about my germs. Helen took pity on him and got up to get the rest of the leftover pasta out of the fridge for him. "Thank you," he said quietly as she brought it and a fork that hadn't been in my mouth to him. "I've been eating MREs for every meal, and I swear they were all veggie omelets for some reason."

"There's been an extreme increase in the number and behavior of the tethered life energies," Fiona told him. "Non-magical people seem able to see them when they reach a certain strength, or perhaps it's the magic in the environment now. Are you seeing an influx of ghosts?"

Casey stopped chewing like he'd lost his appetite. It was a few seconds before he could answer. "God, they're everywhere. It's horrible. They're hanging around the hospital and around collapsed buildings. That's how I've been finding dead people half the time. Their ghosts stand there and point at their bodies like they're waiting for me sometimes." He stared down at his bowl, the horror of the last few days in his eyes. I put my hand on his wrist, but he didn't react.

Everyone else found somewhere else to look for a minute, lost in the contemplation of the city's death toll. Fiona let Casey have time to collect himself before she spoke again. "Do the ghosts seem troublesome in nature? Are they communicative beyond the pointing?"

He shook his head. "No. Ghosts are rarely aggressive, and they aren't good at it even if they try. Most of them will go on by themselves."

"The same cannot be said for our half of the dead," Fiona demurred.

"Any idea how that works? Why I see ghosts and you see whatever it is you see?"

"The *untethered*," August explained. He really seemed to like the term.

"Bennett?" Fiona said, nodding to him.

Bennett put on his teacher-voice and explained how he believed the ghosts were related to the personality and memory of the person, whereas the life energy, tethered or untethered, was the electricity that powered the body. He had embellished upon his theory somewhat since we'd first discussed it, and I was sure he was longing for the peace to study it properly.

Casey seemed to be following. "So what does magic do to the tethered lives that makes them become"—he glanced at August—"untethered?"

"It energizes them enough to make them attempt to seek substance to recreate their previous form," Fiona replied. "If it succeeds in re-entering the body, it is not true life because it is no longer connected to the other half, the soul or ego. More commonly, it becomes a being of increasing energy that August has decided to call the 'untethered.'

Normally that would take years or decades; with the magical explosion, it seems to take hours."

"So we've got a bunch of the walking dead in the city?" Casey asked.

"If we don't now, we will soon," Fiona answered as if stating a simple fact.

"Is the magic doing anything to the living? Some of our coven members developed minor talents with the surge."

"Yes, we know of at least one case of a person who couldn't previously do magic appearing to have gained the ability after the explosion." Fiona studied me in a way I didn't like. "And we've seen animals that were fundamentally altered by the magic as well. Drew was there for both incidents."

"Yes," I agreed. "I saw them both."

"You were involved both times," Fiona corrected. "I'm mostly curious about what happened when you were with Cole."

"I told him to think about how he would treat himself if he was his own patient, and while he talked about it and thought about it, his leg started to heal. And his internal injuries too, I guess," I added.

"But it sounds like he improved more rapidly when you put your hand on his chest."

I didn't like where this was going. "Maybe he just started to get the knack for it. Or he found my presence reassuring."

"Hmm. I think you had something to do with it. You were touching the deer too."

"You said I didn't resurrect that deer!" I said, aghast.

"I don't think you did, because you didn't do anything active that I could see," she answered. "But I think you were conducting magic somehow that lent power to its own processes."

"Deer?" Casey inquired.

"Deer with wings," I whispered, like that was the important part.

"I could lasso…" August trailed off, his arm making circles in the air with a phantom rope as he thought.

I ignored him. "Conducting magic?"

"Yes, I was hoping we'd find a way to test your ability," Fiona said. "And Casey's arrival has presented us with the perfect opportunity." Her expression suggested she was considering using Casey to practice vivisection or test the ability of the body to withstand torture.

"I'm sure I'm happy to help in any way I can," Casey said charmingly, but he bumped my knee with his under the table.

"Good. Andrea, let's see if you can conduct some magic to Casey like you did to Cole."

I rubbed my suddenly sweaty hands on my jeans. "Why Casey?"

"Because he can already work magic, but not the same magic you can do. He'll be able to tell us if he feels it."

"You're just mad he defeated your fancy magic with a Sharpie," August told her. Fiona shot him a look that should have frozen the blood in his veins, and he only shrugged.

"Anything in the name of the pursuit of knowledge," Casey agreed solemnly, but he looked uneasy. "What do you want me to do?"

"Do you have a spell you can maintain continually?" Fiona asked. "A small working, preferably visible."

He thought, then held out his hand, palm up. A little flame appeared above it, burning without touching his hand. "Okay."

I raised my arms in a confused gesture. "Now what?"

Fiona crossed her arms and leaned back against the bar. "Try to do what you did to Cole."

"I wasn't aware I did anything to Cole," I pointed out.

"Perhaps it's unconscious. Try touching him."

I held out my hand for Casey's.

He smiled like he was enjoying my suffering. "Why don't you put your hand gently on my chest?"

"Why don't I punch you not-gently in the nose?" I suggested through gritted teeth.

"Thumb outside your fist, Drew," August said idly as he perused the contents of Fiona's pantry.

Casey put his hand in mine.

I could definitely feel something, but I wasn't sure what. It felt more like the magic I'd felt when I'd touched him at the spring, so maybe I was just feeling Casey's magic. "I don't think this is doing anything."

"Try giving him some magic," Fiona prompted. "Think of whatever metaphor helps you mentally picture that happening. You know how to sense magic."

I looked at Casey's hand instead of at the flame and tried to send a little magic down my arm and up his like water through a siphon. My arm burned.

"Not *your* magic, Drew," Fiona interrupted. "Not from you; pull it from the atmosphere."

I glared. "You didn't specify."

"I thought that was obvious," she muttered. "Try again."

"Hurry up," Casey said. "This is kind of exhausting."

I pictured condensation gathering on a pot lid instead and tried to give Casey what I collected. The flame in his hand flared until we all jumped back, then disappeared. The smoke detector blared briefly, then decided it was a false alarm.

"Like that?" I asked.

"Eh," Fiona said.

"She wasn't aware she was doing anything before," Bennett pointed out. "She'll probably have to wait until she does it again on accident to pay attention to how she's doing it."

"I still don't understand what you think I'm doing," I said.

"Remains to be seen," Fiona mulled. "Be careful about touching people, Andrea."

I was about to demand further explanation for that nonsense when something nearby crackled with static, making me jump. Casey pulled something black from his belt—a radio.

"Mr. Redvers has a radio," Bennett observed with obvious excitement. "Does it work?"

Casey gave him a cautious look. "Yeah, the signal is really crap, but mostly."

"Could you get hold of another one?" Bennett asked intently.

"They're fire department property," Casey said. "Why?"

The radio gurgled again, this time some of the words audible. "Available emergency teams respond—sewage treatment plant."

"Well, that's my cue," Casey sighed, wearily unfolding himself from his chair. "I have to go. Redvers responding," he said into the radio.

"We'll see you there," Fiona said, already on her way out the door.

15

Chapter 15

I followed Casey out to the driveway as everyone else trooped toward the barn. There was an old Blazer parked halfway off the street.

"Where's the Chevelle?"

Casey looked at me like I was crazy. "In the garage. It's not coming out until the streets are fixed." He looked over my shoulder at the barn. "So you're going to go do the horse thing?"

"Yeah, I guess so." I felt awkward now. I should just tell him goodbye and go saddle Charon. "I'm not sure what Fiona was trying to accomplish back there." He'd been a good sport to put up with it.

"I think Fiona probably has her own agenda," Casey replied darkly.

I didn't know what that meant, but I didn't particular like it. Or disagree with it. It wasn't so much that Fiona was inscrutable on purpose as she didn't think other people might need to know what was going on, including people who were directly involved. "Are you okay?" I asked Casey. "I mean, that's a stupid question. Of course you aren't, I just—"

"I understand you," he said quietly, still not looking at me. "I'll be fine. Listen, do you really think you can do anything about this treatment plant thing? It doesn't sound like dead people."

I shrugged. "Me personally? No. But I can never tell what Fiona can do. Maybe she's just curious."

"Hmm. I guess I'll see you there then."

"We'll probably beat you," I told him as we turned to go in separate directions. "Horses will get there faster."

"We'll see," Casey said as he opened the driver's side door. He took out one of those magnetic lights cops in old TV shows used to stick to their car roofs.

"Hey, you aren't a cop," I protested.

"I'm emergency services," he replied smugly as the light started to flash red. "Loser buys dinner."

"Fine!"

We did just barely beat Casey there, but in his defense, he hadn't known Rider horses could fast-ride. I felt a tinge of smugness at winning as I waved from the top of the hill we'd ridden over, then realized if the bet had been dinner, I'd apparently agreed to go to dinner with him. Okay, a problem for another time.

The present problem was the sewage treatment plant, which looked like it had been transported to a primordial swamp. When the dispatcher had requested emergency responders, I had pictured a malfunction of the facility's equipment. We hadn't had power for three days, and I don't know what sort of generators they had here. The thought of what would happen to a city the size of Asterville without working plumbing was pretty unpleasant to ponder. I knew there were normally several pools that were used for different stages of the treatment process, but the plant building now seemed to be sitting in the middle of a lake like a castle surrounded by an overfilled moat. I might have thought it had flooded from the strain, but there were mature trees in full leaf and ropy green vines growing out of the murky water. They must have sprung up shortly after the rifts opened.

A police car and a red pickup with the Asterville Fire Department symbol on the door were both parked a few yards from where the street disappeared into the water, their respective occupants standing by their vehicles. I don't know what they thought they could do about it, and I guess they didn't either. This was more of an environmental disaster, unless there were still people somewhere that needed rescuing.

"So what are we supposed to do about that?" Helen asked warily. "Cut it down?"

"No, I don't think that will help," Fiona decided.

"It's the sewer plant though," Kevin pointed out. "We're really going to need that."

Casey had parked behind the other vehicles and was talking to the other responders, all of them with their arms crossed and their body language tense as if they weren't sure what to do. They could see us from there, but we were just nosy people on horses from this distance, not entirely unexpected.

"I can't help but think this is distracting us from pursuing our own duties," Bennett said delicately. "This looks like a problem for a construction crew with heavy equipment." He had questioned more than once on the way there why we were bothering to ride all the way out here to look at a sewage treatment plant. Fiona had replied the first time that she wanted to know what was going on and then ignored his subsequent attempts to discuss the topic. I'd guess Bennett was getting really frustrated that despite his extensive management efforts, if Fiona decided to do something, we all always defaulted to her plan.

"I want a closer look," Fiona announced.

"I doubt the police want us involved," Bennett remarked.

Fiona ignored him and nudged Orlaith down the hill toward the plant and its new swamp. "Come if you want," she suggested to no one in particular.

I followed her, hoping fervently there was no horrific smell and trying to remember if diphtheria was airborne.

The cop and firefighters did a double-take as we approached, but the swamp held my attention. Green and purple algae flourished along its surface, and I could hear the croaking and chirping of frogs and insects now. There were birds among the trees, and little shadows moved in serpentine patterns under the water, air bubbles rising from the depths. The swamp was already home to new life, its own growing ecosystem. It looked like it had been there for decades, vines already wrapped around the main building. I could see the back of a car floating in the distance.

"Hey, it's not safe for you to be here," the cop protested.

Fiona ignored him as she studied the water's edge, careful to keep Orlaith's hooves from touching the muck.

Casey took a few steps closer to us so we could hear him. "Anything you can do about this?"

"What do you *want* to do about it?" Fiona inquired. "It actually looks quite pleasant."

"Do you know these people?" one of the other firefighters asked Casey. "And why is your pony blue?"

"We dye him for children's parties," I explained. "It's just a shampoo."

Fiona made a huffing noise that might have been a chuckle.

"We kind of need the sewage plant," Casey reminded her just as Kevin had. "It's pretty integral to the safety of our city."

"Ma'am, we're going to need you to clear out of here," the cop insisted.

"Go away," Fiona told him coolly.

He looked faintly puzzled for a moment, swaying where he stood, then turned and walked off a few yards to stand staring in the opposite direction.

Casey's face contorted in outrage. "Fiona, you can't go around enchanting the police force."

"Apparently, I can." She looked at the swamp. "I can't tell what organism has moved into this spot, but you can understand why it sought such a perfect environment. This place was full of water and microorganisms and the things that feed them. A good injection of magic, and life flourished within. It might be easier to just build a new treatment plant than to try to kill whatever is in here and drain it."

"I don't think that's an option," Casey said grimly.

Something moved under the surface of the swamp, sending out little ripples as it passed. Something about the water displacement made me think it was something larger than I would have guessed would live in such a small place. We all watched it in silence, subdued.

"I think it would be best that no one touch this water," Fiona said quietly. "I say that without impudence this time, Casey Redvers. We don't know what grows within these waters, and we don't have the means to deter it yet."

Both Casey and his fellow firefighters considered her warning and the swamp.

"Lunatic parts about magic aside," one of the firefighters said, shooting a side-eye look at Fiona that she returned in spades, "the horse lady is right that we shouldn't touch it. We need hazmat gear to go around human waste, which is probably what half this pond is. And we probably need heavy equipment to dig a ditch to even drain it down until we can see the place again and start having it repaired, and I don't think we're going to be able to find a backhoe for weeks."

August came loping down the hill toward us. "Any plans?" he asked. "I got tired of waiting."

"No," Fiona said. "We can leave."

"Can I use the drone first? I brought it all this way."

Fiona shrugged minutely.

August lifted the drone from its case behind his saddle and balanced it on his head so he'd have both hands free to mess with the remote. Bennett and Kevin began to ride toward us as it now appeared we were doing something. Helen elected to remain far away from the sewage pools-turned-swamp because she was smarter than we were.

The drone ascended with a gentle hum, then flew forward toward the center of the swamp above the trees.

"I don't even know what's happening anymore," the first firefighter sighed. "If there's nothing we can do here, we really need to move on. The city is one big emergency right now."

"Fiona, can you return the cop to normal, *please*?" Casey requested, not quite keeping the exasperation from his voice.

"He could probably use the break for his blood pressure," she replied. "Talking to him will snap him out of it. He'll be fine."

Casey trudged off to revive the cop.

"What do you see?" I asked August, who was squinting at the tiny screen.

"There's lots of things living in the water," he said. "I can't tell how big they are because I'm not sure how deep they are. There's—oh." He fiddled with the controls, and the drone disappeared over the trees to the other side of the swamp behind the building. "There's half of what looks like a deer carcass at the edge of the water. Either something that's living in it is eating deer or...the water is eating the deer."

The firemen both swore.

Casey returned with the policeman, who now only looked puzzled about what everyone else was doing. "What?"

"Erm," August said, doing some more control-maneuvering. "Going deeper."

"What exactly is the kid doing?" the cop asked.

"I think there's something—" August began absently. "Yeah, there's something moving this way, like a school of little fish." He pulled back on the joystick, and the drone topped the trees again and buzzed back toward us. It hovered a few feet over the water for a minute while August squinted at the screen. "What is—"

Something long and dark snapped up through the water and grabbed the drone, pulling it down toward the water. August screamed in rage, arms moving wildly as he desperately tried to fly the drone to safety.

"What the hell?" Kevin said sharply in a tone that made me tear my gaze from the drone to look where he was pointing.

An army of frogs was beginning to emerge from the edge of the swamp, possibly disturbed by whatever had caught August's drone. There seemed to be only a few of them at first because they camouflaged so well with the landscape, but when they started to move, there were suddenly hundreds of them, and instead of hopping like frogs, they *skittered* like some enormous insects. In a second they had swamped our feet like a wave.

"Get in the truck!" Casey shouted, and the responders all split for their vehicles.

Horses do not like things running around their hooves. They are prey animals, and no amount of domestication or training could completely override their instincts to run from danger. Zephyr took off for safety without waiting for any input from Kevin, and Charon tried to do the same before I managed to circle him a few yards away. August had put his reins in his teeth and was just trying to keep Spyder somewhere in the vicinity of the swamp while he attempted to steer the drone back to him. Spyder was stomping frogs like a tap dancer, so that was quite a feat. Fiona and Bennett were the only ones who managed to keep control of their horses, Fiona mostly by blasting the frogs with sweeps of fire that kept them away from Orlaith's legs. The firefighters hadn't made it to their cars before the frogs engulfed them, and they were trying to peel them off their legs and stomping with their heavy work boots. Bennett was trying to help them drive the frogs away, but he didn't have anything to hit them with. Finally he took out his cane sword and started jabbing at the frogs. It took me a few seconds to realize he wasn't stabbing them, but using the sword the same way I used my knife to separate life energies from dead bodies.

Charon refused to ride back into the deluge, so I left him behind and ran back on foot. The frogs tried to climb my legs as soon as I waded into the chaos, and I grabbed one to pry it back off. It had some sort of hard, flexible carapace around its body and extra legs that were shaped like a frog's but jointed like a crab's. It also started to burn my hand when I touched it, so I threw it before I got a better look.

Casey had realized Fiona's fire was deterring the frogs from approaching her, so he began using fire too, sending little darts of flame toward them. He had good aim, but he was hitting them one at a time, which wasn't doing much against the mob. There were dead frogs and their squished guts everywhere. I pulled some more frogs off my legs, gagging at how sticky they were, then tried to do as Bennett was. I could have just stabbed the frogs, I guess, but I didn't think my aim would be that good (plus it was gross), so I pointed my knife at one like I was severing the life energy. It fell over dead. Well, that worked, but it wasn't working any faster than Casey shooting fire darts at them one at a time. I turned in a direction where I wouldn't be facing any people and made a sweeping motion with the knife, this time taking out a whole swath of creepy frogs.

"Andrea! Stop doing that," Fiona shouted at me. She was herding a whole expanse of frogs back into the swamp, but they were fast, and she was having to turn Orlaith rapidly back and forth to keep shooting fire at each side.

I pulled a few more frogs off and considered running back to wherever Charon was. Maybe they would only go so far from the swamp. I didn't want to abandon Casey and the firefighters though. One of them had fallen on the ground, and the other was trying to help him back up. A swarm of frogs didn't seem like they should be so hard to fight, but they burned the skin, and I could swear they were still multiplying despite Fiona guarding the water's edge. The police officer had chosen the tactic of just getting into his car frogs and all and catching them to push them back out a cracked window one at a time.

I didn't have any magic other than Rider magic, the extent of which was severing tethers and "don't see me," which didn't seem to work anymore. Fiona had told me to stop killing the frogs, so I gave "don't see me" another try. I concentrated all my attention on making myself unseen, which was difficult because I had to ignore the frogs climbing on me, one of which had reached my shoulder. I spied Charon in the distance, Helen having caught him, and tried to pull magic from him. He wasn't really my horse, but it seemed to be working. No new frogs were attaching themselves to me, and I slowly pulled the remaining ones off, wincing as my hands started to blister.

Still concentrating so hard there was a tight band around my forehead, I waded carefully through the swarm toward the nearest firefighter and grabbed his arm. He almost elbowed me in the face in surprise. "Be still," I hissed. "Trust me." I willed the frogs not to see either of us.

Being still when things were crawling on you was almost impossible, and he was trying so hard he was shaking with the effort, but I was able to pull the frogs off him when they stopped jumping. I tugged him toward the truck, moving painfully slowly. "Get in!"

When the door shut behind him, I went back for the other firefighter since Casey seemed to be holding his own okay. Bennett had grasped what I was doing and drew Persephone closer. I could feel his magic join mine, and I reached out a hand for Casey to join us too. The hoard began to calm around the four us, and we tried to shift around to huddle together toward the cars. The cop had un-amphibianed his cruiser, and he shifted it into gear and began to drive back and forth over the frogs, his face grim behind the windshield.

Another car came barreling down the road to skid to a stop behind Casey's Blazer. Before anyone could shout a warning, both front doors opened, and a man and a woman popped out.

"Get back in your car!" Bennett shouted, but the pair ran past us all toward the swamp like they knew exactly where they were going.

The woman stopped a few yards from the water and planted her feet. She held her arms out in front of her, hands perpendicular to the ground. She began to speak and a current of air swirled around her. Then she threw her arm down in a slashing motion, and the current of energy followed, striking the ground near the swamp. Frogs splattered everywhere.

I would have assumed by her actions that the woman was on our side, but Fiona immediately shifted her focus to the strangers and sent a wall of *something* toward the woman that knocked her on her butt, so fast I couldn't really see it, only the air it displaced as it moved. The man, who had stayed a few yards back, staggered but stayed on his feet. He raised his arms like he was preparing to fight back.

"Drew!" Casey said urgently.

I hadn't been paying attention, and the frogs had noticed us again.

"I've got to help Fiona," Bennett said and abandoned us.

"Argh," Casey muttered, kicking a frog. "What happened?"

My head was splitting, and I nearly checked my nose for blood before remembering my hands were gross. "I'm not strong enough to do it alone. It's really exhausting."

There was the rumble of an engine turning over, and the pickup I'd put the first firefighter into eased up as close to us as it could get. The driver side window rolled down, and the man squeezed the handle of a fire extinguisher in the direction of our feet. The white foam seemed to incapacitate the frogs, and we all scrambled for the back door. I was going to turn around and try to make it back to Charon, but Casey shoved me into the backseat too. Only a few frogs managed to follow us inside, and we caught them to shove them out the window, hissing and cursing as they burned our hands.

I half-stood, trying to see through the windshield. Clods of dirt and frog guts flew as Fiona and the woman deflected spells toward the ground, while Bennett and the woman's companion tried to keep the frogs back from their teammates. I could see the rest of the Riders gathered far enough away to avoid attracting the frogs' attention. The cop had gotten the cruiser stuck and was shouting into his radio, the sound coming through the firefighters' radio as nothing but static.

"Drive me to my horse," I urged.

"I don't think there's anything you can do," Casey said. "You might as well stay in the car."

"What the actual fuck is happening?" the driver demanded.

"Hazardous waste mutant frogs," the other firefighter said. He had blisters on his neck and his arm from where they'd touched him.

"That doesn't explain why there are women out there reenacting Gandalf versus Saruman or"—he twisted around to try to look at the backseat—"why Redvers can shoot fire darts from his hands."

"Okay, you want an explanation?" I demanded. "Magic is real. Brave new world. Drive me to my horse."

Without another word, the driver put the truck in gear and hauled off in a big circle around where the fighting was taking place and toward the Riders. When the truck stopped, I had to climb over Casey to get out because he wouldn't move.

"Do you know what's going on?" I asked the gathered Riders as I stumbled toward Charon. I was covered in frog guts, my hands felt like I'd tried to grab a pan out of the oven without mitts, and I'd definitely been in better moods than this one.

"Fiona seems to have objected to the interference of these newcomers," Kevin said. He leaned to look at Casey through the truck window. "Are these your coven?"

Casey shook his head.

"That thing ate my drone," August complained.

"Gee, August," I told him, my voice deadly calm, "I'm so sorry. I hope you can download the footage. I'm going to go help Fiona." I took Charon's reins from Helen.

Casey bolted out of the truck. "Absolutely not. Drew! You can't go back there; you're going to get hurt."

I ignored him. "Can I have that fire extinguisher?" I asked the firefighter in the driver's seat. He shrugged and handed it over. "Thanks."

"So what exactly are you going to do, Drew?" Kevin asked cautiously. "What do you want *us* to do?"

"Can you try to make me unseen? It was working a little bit earlier."

"Got it," Kevin confirmed. "We'll stay as close as the frogs allow, but Zephyr won't go any closer."

He said "we," and August nodded, but I could tell Helen wasn't really keen on the idea.

I kicked Charon toward the mage battle, and Kevin and August fell in behind and on either side of me as I barreled toward the pair of strangers. After a moment's hesitation, Helen joined the rear of our parade. The Rider magic must have been working on the people as well as the frogs because they didn't turn at our approach. That or they couldn't spare the attention from Fiona's attacks. Fiona, however, had noticed our arrival, and frustration crossed her face as she had to stop throwing magic in that direction lest she hit us by mistake. Our diamond-shaped wedge cut through the carnage until I was right behind the woman.

The woman saw her opening now that Fiona had withdrawn, and she readied to launch a new attack. I squeezed the handle of the fire extinguisher and covered her in a cloud of white foam which at least startled her enough to make her freeze in shock. I hoped fire depressant wasn't full of carcinogens. The foam had just surprised her, not incapacitated her, so I hit her with the empty canister too, and she toppled over with a *woof*. I turned to gauge how to take her companion down too, but Fiona had already sniped him, and Bennett was rushing to collect him.

"Andrea!" Fiona called, clearly annoyed as she galloped up toward us. She spat some harsh sound at the woman, who was trying to get up again, and the woman went motionless. "Get her away from the frogs."

* * *

The red truck rumbled down to join us, a trio of suspicious firemen looking at us through the glass. August and I lifted the fallen man and woman into the bed of the truck while everyone else tried to maintain the frog-free zone. The cop bolted from his stranded cruiser and jumped into the bed too, and we turned the whole caravan around to go up the hill again, away from the swamp.

"What the hell did you do to these people?" the cop demanded when we'd stopped. He was cradling the handle of his taser like it was a security blanket.

Both of the strangers were already struggling to sit up, their expressions a mix of woozy and angry and their movements jerky. We all waited around the truck, a dirty, exhausted group who didn't have much of an idea of what was going on. In the distance below us, the frogs had begun to recede from the carnage back into the swamp. Fiona had Orlaith pacing back and forth, wisps of pale golden magic rising from both of them like steam. That gut-feeling that she was something far more powerful than she looked was stronger than usual as if using so much magic had heightened it, and everyone except Casey was avoiding looking at her.

"The paralysis is temporary," Fiona said tersely. "I cannot speak for the fire extinguisher."

She was really, really not happy with me.

The woman had managed to pull herself upright, and I could see her face now. She was covered in foam and frog guts, but there was something familiar about her.

"Hey, I know her." I glanced at the man. "Both of them, actually."

"Where from?" Bennett asked.

"She was on the news. She's a member of a local coven, and her name is Alice Phillips."

Alice rolled her eyes at me. Her hair wasn't green anymore, which I realized had played a larger role in my not recognizing her than I would have guessed. She didn't look like a flower child wacko at all now—she was wearing dark slacks and a dark blue blouse with the sort of practical dress shoes that wouldn't come off if you had to run. Her now-chestnut hair had probably been pulled back in a bun, but half of it had come loose in the fight. She looked professional, unmemorable even. She had regained some control of her face too and was making an effort to appear impassive.

"And the man?"

He had been harder to place because I hadn't seem him as closely, but unlike Alice, he hadn't changed in appearance since I'd first encountered him. "He was investigating the park where the forest grew up overnight."

Vague alarm passed over the man's face, but he resumed a neutral expression quickly.

"They aren't members of a local coven," Fiona stated flatly. "Speak, if you will."

The two exchanged looks as they silently tried to decide what information to divulge.

"We are investigators," the woman said at last. "We investigate incidents of a potentially magical nature. If an enchanted object starts to hypnotize people, we track it down and destroy it. If an inexperienced magic-worker loses control of her spell, we can help mitigate the damage. If a coven decides to take over their entire city by bespelling the local government, we intervene."

"Are you part of the government?" Kevin asked.

Alice shook her head, causing some frog guts in her hair to slap her face. She grimaced and wiped them away. Bennett gallantly offered her a cloth handkerchief, which she accepted. "No. There are a few in the government who know about us and will call us in unofficially if someone realizes something magical is taking place, but we are an independent agency."

"What, like vigilantes?" Helen inquired. "How do you determine what magic is and isn't allowed?"

"We're largely supported by a collective of covens throughout the country," the man explained. Like the woman, he wore unremarkable business wear, just someone who would disappear in a crowd. "They vote on acceptable parameters and help support us in our work."

The Riders all turned to look at Casey curiously.

He turned his hands up. "I know nothing about it."

"Your coven is not a member," Alice said dismissively. "When the Hazelwood Coven reaches a certain level of proficiency and longevity, someone will likely contact you with an invitation." Her eyes scanned over the rest of us, six people on magical horses, and she frowned. "I do not know who the rest of you are."

"How do you know who *I* am," Casey demanded, "if my coven isn't a member?"

"We still investigate magical incidents wherever they take place, and that requires a knowledge of local magic-workers." She still sounded dismissive, but she didn't look at Casey either.

"What business have you here?" Fiona asked, her voice low with anger held in check. I wasn't sure why she was mad, but it worried me.

"We came to investigate the magic phenomenon in this place," Alice replied. "And we found people under attack by the magical happening." She frowned. "And then you attacked *us*."

"You interfered before making an attempt to learn," Fiona said sharply. "You attacked with force against something you did not know. I only stopped your actions. You are unhurt."

Other than me hitting her with the fire extinguisher.

"Fine," the man countered. "What is it you think is happening here?" He waved away his companion's huff of protest and gave Fiona one of those very patient looks adults give children while waiting for them to explain why they colored on the walls.

"The influx of magic from the opening of the rifts has magically altered this place," Fiona explained as if he were very stupid.

"Yes, and you decided to try to kill whatever was living in that swamp?"

Fiona stopped Orlaith in place. She looked offended. "No. I was merely holding them at bay while the rest of the group moved to safety. I would not recommend tangling with whatever has taken up residence there." She lowered her eyelids slyly. "It is you who attacked the frogs to kill them."

"They were attacking you," the man pointed out. "You might be grateful."

"I did not need your help," Fiona sneered.

"Yes, who *are* you?" the woman asked, eyes intent on Fiona. When Fiona didn't answer, she looked around at the rest of us one by one, and we remained silent too.

One of the firemen cleared his throat. "For the record, Hunter and I are not weird magic users of any kind. We're just firefighters."

The cop rubbed his face with both hands. "So you two claim to be magical problem solvers. I'm not even going to go through the entire argument about magic right now. I just don't have it in me, and I'm pretty sure we all just saw a bunch of frog/crab hybrids come out of a swamp where our sewage processing plant used to be. Maybe they're mutants created by nuclear waste. Maybe we're having hallucinations from breathing swamp gas." He cut a hand through the air. "Don't care. It's been a hell of a few days. *Can you fix it?*"

The investigators exchanging glances.

"That isn't necessarily within our—"

The cop waved that down with disgust. "So you have contacts with the government? If you aren't here to fix the problem, are you planning on advising local law enforcement about what is going on, so at least we'll know what we're up against and how to fight it?"

"We haven't been authorized to do that," the man said very carefully.

The cop's face was red. I'd guess trying to navigate a city under distress had exhausted his patience. "Authorized by who?"

"By the witches they answer to," Fiona cut in. "Their chief objective is to maintain the secrecy of magic to protect magic users, who traditionally have been hunted and disparaged for their craft." She turned to the pair of investigators. "You might as well give that up. The magic has entered our world in such force that there will be no escaping from it, no hiding from it. The world will simply have to adapt to its new reality."

"Can *you* do something about it?" the cop tried, despair coloring his voice now.

Fiona managed to cut back on the scary for a moment. "Perhaps not in the way you hope, but we can try to help as we are able. You have magic users in the city who are not members of any organization who may come to your aid, but I fear most of them have few skills."

Alice was looking oddly relieved. Maybe she was happy Fiona was willing to shoulder the burden of Asterville's magical crises so she wouldn't have to. Something else bothered me though.

"If you can't do anything to help and you're so intent on maintaining secrecy," I asked her, "then why did you put on a costume and go on the news?"

August was twirling his rope in lazy circles over his head, looking up at it instead of at us. "She was trying to warn *us*, Drew. She can't get involved, but we can."

Alice looked down at the truck bed so she wouldn't meet anyone's eye.

"Okay, well, I have to go back to the precinct and somehow convince my superiors that we have weird magic frogs and no working sewer system in the city." The cop sighed. "You boys mind giving me a ride?"

"We've got a tow strap," Hunter said. "We'll pull your cruiser out." He eyed the investigators. "You want a lift back to your car?"

"Yes, please," the man said politely.

"Case?"

"I'll follow you to the station," Casey said. "We need to talk first." The look he shot the Riders suggested the conversation was not meant for our ears. I didn't blame him. He'd had to unexpectedly divulge something personal about his life he clearly had meant to keep to himself to his colleagues, and it wasn't just that he liked *Desperate Housewives* or he was a Browns fan. It would likely irrevocably change the way they saw him, but as Fiona said, the world itself had been irrevocably changed.

We watched until the truck dropped everyone off at their respective vehicles to make sure there was no frog resurgence. The investigators' car drove away, and the truck towed the police cruiser out of the muck.

Casey got into his Blazer, and all three vehicles convoyed away.

"Now that they're gone," Bennett said, overly-patient, "is there anything *else* you want to do with this cursed swamp?"

Fiona studied the murky water with its vibrant green plant life for a long moment. "No, I don't think so. It would require such force to clear, and I'm not sure anything beneath would be salvageable. In any case, that is a longer term project that would need careful planning, and I don't think we should devote the resources to it. Let's go home."

"What about this working with the cops thing?" Kevin asked as we rode.

"They'll contact us, I'm sure." She sounded certain, but I guess she wasn't going to elaborate on what she expected us to do. I hoped it went a little better than the frogs.

* * *

It was some cruel twist of the universe that the nastiest I'd ever been in my life would be when hot, running water wasn't readily available. In the last few days, I had gotten covered in brick dust from Cole's apartment, dirt from the horse's grave, and now frog innards and slime. When we got back to Fiona's, she wouldn't let me come into the house in my current state. The plumbing in the house was old, she demurred; she didn't want the frog guts to clog the pipes. She sent me to rinse myself off in the wash bay of the barn instead, reminding me to use the water sparingly. That particularly stung because it was very nearly October, and the water from the hose was cold. I washed off, clothes and all, while I cursed and shivered, then got dressed in the clean clothes Helen (guiltily free of frog) brought me from my bag.

When I came inside, there was a little girl with pink bobbles adorning her ponytails lying on the living room rug while she colored in a princess coloring book. August was sprawled on the floor next to

Cami, dutifully coloring in a pumpkin. Sheri, Kevin's wife, rounded the corner from the smaller den, their younger child on her hip.

"Are you staying over here with us?" I asked Sheri as I huddled in front of the fireplace, a massive stone affair that was original to the house.

She settled the two-year-old onto Kevin's lap. Addy had half her hair in braids and the other half in a little puff ball like she'd gotten too wiggly for Sheri to finish styling it. Her face bore the trademark pout of an aggrieved toddler. "Yes, things were getting pretty rough at home without power. I figured I'd at least come do some housekeeping for you all while you're working."

"She made us burritos," August said with great reverence.

"Get a plate, Drew," Sheri instructed, hand on her hip. I didn't see Sheri all that often, but she always struck me as Kevin's perfect match. They were both such vigorous go-getters that they could probably tag-team solving world hunger and cleaning up the Great Pacific Garbage Patch all on date night, but Sheri tended to take the uncontrollable in stride a little better than Kevin did.

I grabbed a burrito on the paper plates Sheri had left out and returned to my spot in front of the fireplace. The house was chilly with no heat turned on, but no one was going to challenge me for the prime location after I had to hose-shower in the barn. Someone had hung a battery-powered camping lamp from the ceiling fan light fixture, so I guessed we were reducing our electricity usage further now that the cooking was done.

Fiona appeared from somewhere in the shadowy depths of the house, and her eyes fixed on me and the melted cheese stuck to my chin. "A *fire extinguisher*." Her tone didn't convey any criticism, just bewilderment.

I swallowed before I'd even finished chewing. "Well, I had to do something, Fiona, and no one else was doing anything. It was the only weapon I had."

"I didn't need help, Drew," Fiona said, forehead beginning to wrinkle in confusion. "I was waiting for you all to move to safety, and when you finally did, you all came *back*."

"We didn't exactly know that, Fiona," Kevin pointed out levelly. "It looked to us like you and Bennett were under attack. How stupid would we have been if we just stood there while you needed us? And I guess we would have if Drew hadn't figured out we could activate some concealment magic if we worked together." He looked down at Addy, bouncing her in the methodical, absent way parents did. "I regret that I didn't attempt to help sooner."

Fiona contemplated this in silence. "I appreciate your intent," she said slowly, "but I don't understand why you all thought that I was incapable of defending myself against a pair of witches."

"Um, because we don't know much about magic, and it looked pretty intense from the outside?" Helen suggested. She pushed her glasses up onto her head when Fiona turned to her, taking the tried and true if-I-can't-see-you-you-can't-see-me approach.

"I see. I suppose I did not consider you would think me in danger." Fiona paused. "I didn't want to reveal to the strangers the extent of my skill. I was only buying time for you to get away."

"If you don't communicate the plan to us," Kevin said patiently, "we can't do things according to the plan. We can't just read your mind."

"I don't normally explain my plans to you." Fiona's tone was guarded. She was really making an effort to be reasonable, but we were annoying the shit out of her.

"Luis usually does it for you," August explained, not looking up from his coloring. "He's the people-person who passes out the orders to the troops while you do the lone wolf thing."

Fiona gazed at August for a long moment. Then she blinked a few times and decided to move past it. "The Ellisons have the largest bedroom upstairs with the attached bath. The rest of you can divide the other two bedrooms as you wish until Luis and Trish get back. Or you can sleep in the living room where it's warmest." She disappeared through to the kitchen.

Kevin, Helen, and I exchanged looks.

Bennett descended the stairs, holding up the emergency radio. "There's a broadcast about to start. The radio has some charge left, but someone might have to take a turn cranking the handle to power it if it starts to die."

"I can do it," Helen offered, taking the radio from him to rest it on the table. "It'll be good for my biceps." She fiddled with the dials, and the radio buzzed with static.

"...emergency radio broadcast," a man's somber voice intoned. "This broadcast will occur every three hours. Please share the contents of this broadcast with your neighbors who may not have access to a radio. A curfew is in effect from dusk until dawn at this time. The police and national guard request all citizens stay in their homes as much as possible to keep roads clear for first responders. An emergency shelter has been opened at Asterville Central High School. Space is limited and relief workers request only those in great need utilize this resource. The city requests citizens to make arrangements with neighbors to share shelter and resources as a community. Due to the high demands on hospital staff, the hospital requests all non-emergency issues be treated at home. Brookview Medical Center is also open for non-emergency medical care."

The broadcaster launched into a factual, deliberate explanation of how to create an emergency toilet, collect and treat rainwater, and stay warm in a house with no heat. It was all good advice, the most absolutely basic kind for people who didn't realize you shouldn't start fires in an unventilated room, but the sobering reality was if the people listening didn't already have water stocked up somewhere, they were in for a hard time. It wasn't too cold to go without heat, most people had food in the cabinets, even if it was just crackers and cereal, and a bucket situation for the toilet was gross, but you could figure it out if you had to. But most people didn't plan for week-long interruptions to vital services. They didn't have water purification tablets or kitty litter or candles stocked up. When the crackers and the half-case of bottled water ran out, things were going to get ugly.

The broadcast finished with a solemn report that there were currently no gas stations with available fuel and that all shelf-stable grocery products from the local stores had been commandeered by the national guard and would be available for distribution by emergency workers at the high school on a per-household basis. There was a list of streets closed followed by a list of buildings and services that were destroyed, including the sewage processing plant. There was no timeline on the restoration of electricity or water.

"This disaster has affected numerous cities in our country, putting greater strain on relief services," the man said soberly. "Citizens are asked to display the fortitude and compassion for others that make this nation great at this time. We will all pull through this disaster together. This broadcast will be repeated in three hours."

We listened to the static in subdued silence for a long moment.

"Well, that was grim," I noted, wrapping my arms around myself again, this time for comfort instead of warmth. I'd been focused on the big things, but there were so many people to worry about—my parents, Kara, relatives in other states, Cole's parents, my elderly coworker, Carol. We all had families and friends that would just be trying to make it through the next few days.

Bennett pushed his glasses up so he could rub his face tiredly. "They aren't listing the death toll yet, but I imagine that's coming."

"They don't want to alarm the populace with how bad the situation really is," Fiona said. She had come to lean on the wall between the kitchen and the living room with her arms crossed over her chest.

"It's panic control to give people simple, actionable directions. What people will eventually realize is that they are being given instructions on how to keep themselves alive because no help is coming."

"They didn't say anything about magic or otherwise strange happenings," I remarked.

"No." Fiona stared off into the distance, face troubled. "They won't until it becomes impossible to ignore. Controlling panic is paramount right now. They haven't even provided a way for people to report such incidents yet because they have no ability to respond."

Helen pulled the afghan she was wearing like a shawl closer. "Who even knows what is happening quietly with no witnesses right now."

"Well, we'll face it one day at a time," Sheri declared firmly, scooping Cami up. "Let's get the kids ready for bed, Kevin."

Helen and I claimed one bedroom, which left August and Bennett as the odd couple in the other. Before I climbed into my twin bed, I went to close the blinds and paused to look out at the moonlit pastures below. There was a light on in the barn, which surprised me only because we were conserving power. There was always a light on in the barn under normal circumstances. The light went out, and a cloaked figure led a horse from the barn, turning back to slide the door shut.

I recognized Orlaith by the golden sheen of her coat, so the cloaked figure must be Fiona. She swung up onto Orlaith's back and started down the driveway. Where was she going so late—to look for more untethered? Did she think the rest of us needed rest too much to take anyone with her?

"Lights out?" Helen queried, hand poised over the switch.

"Yeah," I said, turning away from the window. "Go ahead."

16

Chapter 16

After some digging through the pantry, Sheri unearthed a giant canister of steel-cut oats, and she and Kevin cooked a cauldron-sized pot of oatmeal for breakfast the next morning while Helen and her corgi chased the kids around the house. Fiona, to my complete unsurprise, was startlingly well set up for doomsday, but there couldn't be enough food in the house where she normally lived alone to feed all of us for long. We were going to have to venture out for supplies soon or manage to make our own homes habitable again. Fiona didn't come back inside until the food was ready, probably to avoid the shrieking children and dog.

"I am curious about the extent of the area this explosion may have affected," Bennett commented as he ran his finger down the page of a Rand McNally. "I want to travel to the estimated outskirts of our usual territory to see if these new mobile untethered are flooding neighboring towns or the forests. That will have to wait until Luis and Trish return of course, but I'd like to know if there are things outside the city we should be attending to."

"I don't want you to go out by yourself," Fiona said. "Asterville was likely affected the most strongly. There is only so much we can worry about at once."

"I might be safer to just take the car and drive a loop," he reasoned, more to himself than Fiona as he traced a likely route. "Just see what I can feel as I go."

Fiona didn't argue with him.

"What do we need to get done today?" Helen asked.

"We should continue to hunt for these new untethered," Fiona replied. "We will focus on the most populated areas of the city where they have the potential to frighten people for the time being. But housekeeping obligations first. Check on your homes and families if you need to."

"We should take the opportunity to gather supplies from our own homes while we're there," Bennett noted absently. "I'm sure we all have some things to contribute to our mutual comfort here."

"I'll get us some gas," August said, offering no clarity on how he was planning on doing that. Probably best we didn't know.

My phone still had no signal. I lifted the handset of Fiona's landline phone from the cradle, and it blared a harsh tone into my ear. Maybe we should invest in some carrier pigeons or something. "Do we have enough to get me to the hospital? I have to go get Cole today or tomorrow, and there's no way for me to call the hospital and find out if he's ready to go."

"Just take a horse, Drew," Fiona said. "We should save the gas for the generator if we can help it. There is as yet no way to get more."

"If he's well enough to leave, I want to take him with me. I don't think throwing him over a horse will go down so well if he's conscious." It had been bad enough when he wasn't.

"There's a cart in the back of the hay shed," Fiona said, absently stirring her oatmeal. "Charon knows how to pull it."

"I don't know how to drive a cart." Which she knew.

"You'll figure it out."

Of course I could. The little two-wheeled cart was light enough that I could pull it up to the barn easily, but getting Charon attached to it was a lot harder. The harness had about eighty-three different straps, and Fiona watched me struggle with them for a long time without offering to help.

I finally looked at her over Charon's multi-colored mane. "I know you're mad about the fire extinguisher, but time is a bit of the essence here."

She looked away, and I thought she was ignoring me for a moment. Then she let out a breath and turned back to me. If I didn't know better, I would have thought she was embarrassed.

"I'm not mad about the fire extinguisher, Drew. I'm mad you had to defend yourself with a metal canister because I failed to teach you any other skills you could have used. The wrap strap goes around the cart shaft." She fixed all the buckles and straps in about ninety seconds flat. "Where are you planning on taking Cole if they release him?"

I shrugged. "Back to my apartment for now, if he hasn't decided somewhere else he'd rather go. I'll have to stay there to take care of him."

"That's not going to be very practical. Just bring him back here. Your apartment is hardly livable, and he'll have Sheri for company, at least."

She was right about that, but I wouldn't have presumed to invite a bunch of people to her house. If anyone knew the setup she had here, everyone within twenty square miles would be trying to move onto the property. "There's twenty people already living in your house, Fiona, and you don't even know Cole."

"Oh, well," she said indifferently and walked away so I couldn't argue with her anymore.

Driving the pony cart wasn't that hard once I just let Charon do whatever he wanted. I lifted a rein when I wanted to make a turn since he (probably) didn't know how to get where we were going, but he didn't need any additional input from me. We had to stick to the road more instead of galloping over green spaces and parking lots, so the trip took a lot longer at a brisk eight miles an hour. The cart rattled and bumped over the destroyed pavement, but the few other cars present shared the road admirably. They probably understood the "out of gas" issue.

I pulled the cart up under the emergency room drive because I could see people through the automatic doors here. A nurse in green scrubs came out and surveyed me placidly for spurting wounds.

"I'm here to pick up Dr. McBride," I told him. "He was on the ICU floor with a broken leg. I can't leave the pony to go get him, but if you can wheel him down, I'll take him home. Free up a bed."

"Go 'round to the main entrance, and I'll send him to you," the nurse replied.

God bless the medical staff and their nerves of steel.

About ten minutes later, Cole arrived in a wheelchair pushed by a volunteer, his face pale. He was wearing scrubs and tennis shoes that had probably come out of his own locker. Well, one tennis shoe. The other leg was encased in an orange cast. He stared at Charon.

"Ready to go?" I attempted some cheerfulness to counteract the fear seeing him in this condition had spiked through me.

Cole looked dazed. "Is that pony blue? Where are we going?"

"Blue roan. We're going back to Fiona's," I told him, applying the brake so the cart wouldn't move while the volunteer and I eased Cole from the chair to the cart seat. "She's a friend of mine who owns this pony. We'll make arrangements to take you somewhere after that."

"My apartment is gone," Cole said.

He was really struggling. "I know, Cole. We'll take care of that later. One thing at a time. Thank you," I told the volunteer.

"You got someone to get him out of the cart when you get there?"

the man asked.

"Yep, plenty of help where we're going." I removed the brake and clucked to Charon. "Go home, Charon."

"Is he taking me to the land of the dead?" Cole asked in a deadpan voice.

I twisted to look into his face, concerned, but he'd lost the dazed, listless expression now. He was joking.

"Yeah, but he likes to be paid in carrots, not coins."

Cole gazed out at the damaged city as we passed it in slow motion. This would be the first time he'd seen anything of it, and I didn't know what news he'd picked up on at the hospital. I'd seen a lot of the city, and I was still amazed at the fickle nature of the destruction.

"Drew," he said at last. "What happened?"

I glanced over at him. Maybe he'd been too delirious to comprehend the disaster. "There was a major earthquake that destroyed the roads and knocked the power out all over the city." And made a bunch of dead things roam.

"No, I mean at the apartment. With me." His hands curled into fists in his lap.

This wasn't going to be a fun conversation, though I'd already decided we needed to have it. Cole had a low tolerance for things being out of order. "What do you remember?"

"I was dying on the floor of my apartment, and you came and got me. I don't know how you kept me alive on the way to the hospital." His voice was distant, perplexed. "I should have died of those injuries. What did you do?"

Charon made the executive decision to cut across a green space, and I decided not to argue. "I didn't do it, Cole; you did. I told you to think about how you would treat your injuries as a doctor, and when you did, your leg started to heal. That's why you didn't die of crush syndrome."

Cole's eyes were half-closed as he watched me, his expression nonplussed. "You're saying I magically healed myself."

"Yes, you did," I confirmed. "I watched you do it."

Cole twitched in his seat. "Drew, I can't do magic. And since when do you even think magic is real?"

"I've known about it for a while now," I told him. There was no point hiding anything from him now that he had apparently joined the ranks of the magic users. "I'm afraid I got that initiation a few months back, so I get that it sounds unbelievable. You might as well know now though. The whole fire-in-the-sky thing when the earthquakes happened? That was magic too. There's always been a little bit here, but when that earthquake hit, magic went everywhere. Looks like you caught a bit of it, Cole. Very fortunately," I added in a whisper as my throat tried to close up. "And I am so sorry I didn't find you faster."

He looked away. "Drew, you're assigning miracles to explain the unexplainable. Maybe I just survived until you drove me to the hospital."

I was glad he didn't remember that tumultuous horseback ride. I jabbed him gently with my elbow until he had to look at me. I showed him my hand, which was still red from handling the mutant frogs. "I burned my hand. Heal it for me."

Cole looked weary. "I'm prescribing some cool water."

"No, *will* it to heal. Picture it happening." I stopped Charon and looked at Cole. "Try, please." He probably shouldn't try to work magic while he was this weak, but we needed to get this settled now. The longer he protested, the less willing he was going to be to believe me.

"What, if I just believe, it'll work?" He sounded irritated, but when it became clear I wasn't going to move the cart until he at least faked something, he reluctantly took my burned hand into his and stared at it.

The redness visibly faded, not completely healed, but like it was two days further along. It hadn't stung much anyway, but I could barely feel it at all now.

Cole dropped my hand. "You did that."

I clucked at Charon to go, and he took off at an impatient canter. "Nope. My magic, somewhat to my dismay, mostly involves dead things. Don't keep trying to do that without resting though—I'm sure you use energy while you're doing it, and you might hurt yourself if you over-do it. That's probably why you passed out earlier."

Cole sighed and angled himself away from me. "I don't want to talk about this anymore."

"That's fine. We'll have plenty of time when you're ready."

We were both quiet the rest of the trip. Remembering being in this situation not that long ago myself, I knew the news was going to settle by degrees.

"Now I know why people invented cars," Cole muttered when we turned up Fiona's driveway. "That would have been a twenty-minute drive."

The jostling from the cart must have been killing his leg the entire trip. I shouldn't have let my stubbornness toward Fiona stop me from pleading with someone to borrow their car.

"He can go a lot faster, but I'm not sure the cart could." I would have risked it if it was only my neck on the line. I pulled the cart up right outside the kitchen door, and it swung open as Kevin and August came out.

"Hi, I'm Kevin, and this is August," Kevin told him. Kevin had a pretty solid way of making you feel like he had everything under control, so Cole might be temporarily lulled about the situation. "Let's get you inside."

Cole looked at them, then back at me. "I'm still not entirely sure where I am," he murmured as they each took an arm and hauled him up.

"I'll be inside after I take care of Charon," I promised.

* * *

Cole was in Fiona's recliner with his legs propped on the extended footrest when I came in, and his guarded expression said he was very uncomfortable at the attention he was receiving. He'd had a traumatic few days, and now he was sitting in a room full of strangers. *Strange* strangers at that. I scooched him over and climbed into the recliner with him.

"Okay?" I whispered

"Yeah," he said softly.

"They didn't give you any crutches or anything?" Helen asked him, hands on her hips. They must have been quizzing him on his medical care.

"Nothing left to give out," Cole said tiredly.

"I'm sure I have a cane you can use back at the house," Bennett said.

"What about pain medication?" Helen demanded, indignant on his behalf.

Cole closed his eyes. "Rationing it," he sighed.

I smoothed his hair down. We really should put him to bed somewhere, but all the bedrooms except Fiona's were up a flight of stairs.

"People are coming," August called from the den.

The front door opened and closed again as someone went out.

"Drew, who are all these people again?" Cole whispered.

"Remember how we just talked about magic being real?"

He leaned his head back and closed his eyes again. Yeah, not ready for that conversation.

The door opened again, and Fiona entered, this time followed by Casey, the cop from our frog debacle, a second cop, and another man in an Asterville Fire Department windbreaker. A faintly quizzical look crossed Casey's face as he saw Cole, but he kept walking. Fiona stopped in front of the fireplace and made a stiff gesture for the guests to sit. Kevin solved some of the ensuing awkwardness of *where* they were meant to sit by arriving promptly from the kitchen with a chair in each hand. Casey went to grab two more, and after a minute we were all sitting around the living room in tense silence. The cops and firefighters were eyeing the Riders, and the Riders were eyeing them back. I wasn't sure what Casey had told them so far, but they must have made introductions outside because he didn't offer to now. Fiona continued to stand so her enemies (and friends) would feel uncomfortable.

When no one said anything, the cop with the extra bling on his uniform decided he might as well start things off. He rubbed his hands briskly against the knees of his work pants. "I'm Sergeant Conrad with the APD, and this is Lieutenant Pierce, head of the fire department." He nodded toward the older man in the AFD jacket. "Neither of us is here in any official capacity, but we were informed by Officer Kilpatrick and Firefighter Redvers about the events that took place at the sewage treatment plant." His expression had gone a bit reluctant. "Normally I would be inclined to think they were exaggerating or had possibly inhaled dangerous fumes, but all four witnesses are claiming the same thing. Unfortunately, no one higher up is willing to pursue this, and we technically have been told not to as well. We don't have the manpower to investigate these claims right now beyond establishing that the sewage plant is no longer usable."

"We still want to know what's going on," Lieutenant Pierce added, sounding more open to the idea. "We'll take what help we can get, but we can't officially liaison with you. I can't say a story about a swamp full of mutant frogs went over well."

"Do you think a video of a swamp of mutant frogs would?" August interjected conversationally from where he lounged on the floor focused on his laptop. I don't know what he had against chairs, but he never seemed to be in one. "I caught a little bit of it."

"You were able to retrieve the footage from the drone?" Bennett said curiously. "Well done, August."

"You have video footage of the incident?" Sergeant Conrad asked, leaning forward with his elbows on his knees and drawing his thick eyebrows together.

"Some of it," August corrected. "That thing in the swamp ate my drone before it was over." He rolled up to his knees, balancing the laptop in one hand, and half-crawled to the coffee table to put the laptop in front of Conrad and Pierce. "Sorry the screen is so small, but Fiona doesn't own a TV, and I left my projector at home." He hit play, and they leaned forward to watch.

I couldn't see much of the screen from the recliner, but I could make out the basic shape of the tree-covered swamp as the drone flew over it. The drone had two cameras, and August had both feeds running side by side on the screen. I could see little figures that were probably us as August flew the drone back toward himself, then the perspective dropped abruptly as the drone was jerked down under the murky water. The drone managed to resurface a few times and succeeded in catching some surprisingly good footage of the Riders and firefighters running around on the edge of the swamp since the camera was only about a foot above the water. Featured front and center was Fiona, sweeping a stream of fire across the ground. The second camera had captured some bone-chilling images of a dark, tentacled thing, no less horrific for its obscurity. Then the drone was pulled under one last time, and the camera went dark.

"Water got the best of it at that point," August apologized. "It's not meant to be submerged."

"Well, that was certainly enlightening," Lieutenant Pierce noted. He made a few jabs at the computer screen to restart the video.

"Can I get a copy of that, son?" Conrad asked, stroking his standard-issue mustache.

"Sure, I think I've got a thumb drive around here somewhere," August agreed. I thought he was about to knee-crawl away again, but he deigned to stand up this time and wandered upstairs.

Sheri passed him on the way down and waved away Casey's offer of his chair in favor of sitting on Kevin's lap. "Kids are napping," she told him quietly.

"Okay," Sergeant Conrad said after the second viewing of the drone footage. "Okay. I don't have an explanation for any of this. Nuclear waste mutations, chemical warfare, CGI, whatever. So I'm open to whatever your explanation is if it might start us on the path to getting things back to normal, even if that explanation is magic. The sooner we understand what happened with that earthquake, the sooner we can fix things."

Fiona made that sort of slightly sympathetic face she'd taken to showing when anyone mentioned an end to the horrors or a return to our previous way of life, not so much as if she felt bad for anyone, but more like she thought they were being incredibly naive. It was marginally less terrifying than the stony expression she had been wearing, and the police and firefighters were understandably fooled into relaxing a little.

"There is no return to the way things were," she said simply. Not for the first time, I considered that she seemed to feel rather happy about it. "There is only the way forward."

"So these things," Lieutenant Pierce said very deliberately, "that are happening aren't going to *stop*? We have a blackberry vine that overran a whole neighborhood."

Fiona shrugged minutely as if she did not care one way or another. "They might continue unabated, or these incidents might disperse over a wider territory and thus be more manageable. If I had a better idea of what was happening in the rest of the country or the world, I might be able to predict that more accurately."

"Who are you anyway?" Lieutenant Pierce challenged. "How do you know this?"

"We went over that already," Casey interrupted. He had correctly guessed that if they started interrogating Fiona about her qualifications, she was going to boot them all out. "We can exchange credentials later. Let's go back to that part about the incidents not stopping and how we fix this because we cannot go on like this."

That insubordination didn't go over well with Pierce, but Casey ignored his glare in favor of looking fixedly at Fiona.

"The magic is here to stay," Fiona told him quietly. "But that doesn't mean the disaster is. The earthquake is what caused the majority of the damage, injuries, and deaths. What the city is going through right now is no different than the aftermath of any other severe natural disaster. Eventually the hospitals will catch up. Crews will begin to rebuild roads and restore power lines. Supply chains will either be restored or created anew. I realize as first responders the greatest burden lies on your shoulders, but the world will go on."

"According to my military contacts, these earthquakes hit in multiple places around the world," Sergeant Conrad said gravely. "There was at least one tsunami, and a big chunk of Australia's coastline fell into the sea. Even the best in the field have got no clue what kind of tectonic plate activity could cause so many to happen at the same time. That's privileged information, mind you—people hear that, they're going to panic that the continents are breaking apart. Supply chains may not be back for months. Repairs for this sort of damage will take years."

Fiona's smile was almost reassuring. "The Black Death killed a third of Europe, and yet we persist. The eruption of Mount Tambora brought a year with no summer, and yet we persist. Humans are surprisingly adaptable, though also remarkably whiny." She seemed a bit amused at that. "We'll persist through this too."

"A bunch of people died during both of those events," Officer Kilpatrick pointed out.

"I never said they didn't."

Sergeant Conrad waved a hand before Officer Kilpatrick, eyes bulging, could get in a retort to that. "Okay, so what sort of, um, 'magical' dangers are we up against then?"

"We've seen instances of magic mutating animals, the frogs included," Fiona mused.

Conrad flipped open a notebook. "Others?"

"Flying deer."

He sighed and looked at Kilpatrick. "I guess those kids weren't making things up after all."

"I guess not," Officer Kilpatrick agreed glumly.

"The deer don't appear to be dangerous," Fiona offered. "There's no reason for you to interfere with them until they do."

"All right. Any incidents of magic mutating people?"

"Hmm. Dr. McBride over there appears to have developed some healing abilities, the extent of which remains untested."

Cole had been so still through the entire meeting that I would have thought he was asleep if I couldn't see his barely-open eyes moving to follow the conversation. His eyes popped open now, and he stared at Fiona, who was watching him with pleasant interest.

"Leave me out of this," he breathed. "I am not part of whatever this is."

Fiona nodded to him politely, prepared to drop the subject.

August returned with a USB drive and set about messing with the computer. "It's cool, bro. We've all be there before."

Cole sighed.

"Okay, this young man's...whatever aside," Conrad said, "should we expect people to be shooting laser beams from their eyes and getting super strength?"

"Not likely," Fiona said. "People have to learn to work magic. If someone ended up with comic-book type powers like that, they'd probably be so overwhelmed they wouldn't survive their first attempt to use it."

She didn't seem to find this as horrifying as everyone else did. Cole was staring at her again, and I patted his leg.

Sergeant Conrad cleared his throat. "All right. So Redvers told us a little bit about what your group does. Can you actually do anything about the weird things that are happening, like the frogs?"

The kitchen door opened, and everyone turned automatically to look in the direction of the noise. I was expecting Luis and Trish, but a crisp white sneaker appeared through the doorway, followed by a leg in a pair of wide-legged jeans. Valerie swung the door the rest of the way open with enough force to make the curtain over the window bounce. She took in the crowded room and glared. Her baby blue eyes fixed on me snuggled up to Cole.

"What is Cole doing here?" she demanded.

"Because he's hurt, Valerie," I told her, unbothered by the aggression. I felt strangely happy to see all five-foot-two of her barely contained rage. It had felt weird with her gone.

"What are *you* doing here?" Kevin asked her in a tone that wasn't exactly accusatory, but was definitely bordering on crisp.

"Leave it," Fiona interrupted before Valerie could snipe back with what I'm sure was an acidic retort. "Are your parents all right, Valerie?"

Valerie ignored her, but a sheen of something like anxiety clouded her eyes for a moment. "You can't get back together with Cole."

"I'm not," I assured her as Cole huffed like I'd mortally injured him. "He just doesn't have anyone to take care of him right now."

"Whose kid sister is this?" Casey asked.

"Dude," August whispered. "Not smart."

"And who are you?" Valerie demanded, turning her gaze on Casey.

"You'd know if you'd been here," Kevin said.

"Kevin," Sheri warned softly.

Casey replaced his stunned expression quickly with a charming smile. He stood and offered Valerie his hand. "I'm Casey. Nice to meet you."

Valerie floated past him and went to sit on the floor next to the recliner in one of the few places not already occupied by a body. The Riders, cops, and firemen had watched this show go down like it was a tennis match, and they were all still staring at her while she feigned oblivion.

"I missed you," I told her.

She didn't look at me, but the corner of her mouth twitched.

"We're glad you're back safely, Valerie," Bennett told her in his usual gracious manner. "We'll get you up to speed later. For now, if we can return to our previous conversation. As you said, if Mr. Redvers told you what the Riders do, you understand that most of our work involves the dead."

"Yes," Conrad said uneasily.

"And he has explained to you how active the dead are becoming?"

Sergeant Conrad shot Casey a confused look, but Casey was already shaking his head.

"I don't really understand what's going on with that well enough to explain it to anyone else."

"We encountered a very active group outside the hospital the night of the earthquake," Bennett continued. "The life energy was drawn from the dead outside the hospital doors. They gained considerable strength in a matter of minutes and demonstrated a rudimentary capacity to both flee perceived danger and fight when cornered. Lay people were capable of seeing them at that point. It would normally take months, years more likely, for that to happen under normal circumstances, but the magic influx is so great it took only hours at most."

Officer Kilpatrick put his face in his hands. "Fucking zombies. Great."

"We actually call them the 'untethered,'" August offered. He looked thoughtful. "Though I suspect there might be actual zombies out there as well."

"Are they dangerous?" Conrad asked.

"They don't have mass to utilize when interacting with the world," Bennett explained, "but I am afraid we must assume so. One of them tried to bite Andrea which shows a capacity for aggression, if not an actual ability. I suspect the older they are, the stronger they become."

"But you can definitely do something about those," Sergeant Conrad stated.

"Yes," Fiona said firmly. "We can. It is our job."

"And the other stuff?"

She shrugged. "We'll try. There are others more practiced in different spheres that might arrive to help. It is early days yet." She looked at Casey. "What of your coven?"

He shook his head. "I've only heard from two people, and I haven't had time to try to track anyone else down. I had to choose the firefighter thing or the magic thing, and it was a clear decision."

"And those other people, the investigators, aren't going to help us," Officer Kilpatrick said.

"Not openly," Fiona agreed. "Though I suspect they will rally others to help us instead behind the scenes."

"Look, like I said, we're technically not allowed to coordinate or share anything with you," Sergeant Conrad said. "Officer Kilpatrick is going to write up his radio as destroyed in the line of duty. What code are we using for the suspected supernatural, Kilpatrick?"

"10-103W," Office Kilpatrick replied. "'W' for weird, I guess."

"Officially, I'm telling you lot of horse-owning civilians to stay away. Stay home and obey the curfew. Unofficially, we'll try to tell our people not to interfere with your work." Conrad looked like he was longing for a lounge chair on a beach somewhere, or maybe just a nap. He had my sympathies there. "But we can't do that without explaining a lot of things that would just draw attention. Try to be discreet."

"We've been MIA for long enough now," Pierce said, standing. "We need to get back to our jobs. We'll try to keep people out of your way," he told the rest of us, "but assume they don't know what you're up to. We'll communicate with you through Redvers, since he has an established, preexisting relationship with you that can be explained if scrutinized." He put his hat on and started for the front door, the rest of the party following.

Casey sneaked a look at me as he left, and I thought about following him out to talk, but I wasn't sure if that would get him in further trouble with his boss. Or if he really wanted to talk to me.

"So is that what we're going to do?" I asked when they'd gone. "Try to do something about weird magical stuff like the sewage plant?" We hadn't really accomplished anything there but general mayhem.

"It is unlikely we can step in and solve anything they believe to be magical," Fiona said. "But we have at least alerted them to the reality they are facing so they can plan more appropriately for the safety of the city. And having spoken to us, they are more likely to stay out of our way as we work so we won't have to sneak around them."

We all watched her silently. So that had been her intent in meeting the responders at an emergency call all along. A vein began to pulse in Bennett's forehead.

August picked up the abandoned radio and examined it.

"The radio is a nice addition," Fiona observed, oblivious to our reactions. "That might help us track down locations where the untethered are harassing humans more quickly. Or help us avoid places where the police are congregating in numbers. Well, do we want to start patrolling on the map you made, Bennett?"

She disappeared into the kitchen where the map had been thumbtacked to a wall.

"I miss Luis," Kevin muttered.

17

Chapter 17

We didn't manage to start on Bennett's grid before the first call came over the radio.

"10-103W," August announced. He'd taken charge of monitoring the transmissions. "It's weird time."

We'd moved Cole to the couch where he was lying with his leg propped on a pillow. Cami had brought him a stuffed bear, which lay nestled between his neck and the couch cushion. He watched us scramble around to get ready, long eyelashes casting shadows on his pale face.

"You're going to go look for whatever they're talking about on the radio."

I knelt next to him. "Yes. Sheri will still be here if you need anything."

"What if it's dangerous?"

"If it's dangerous, we can hardly do nothing while people who don't know what's going on try to handle it. We've got to do what we can."

"And I'm going to just lay here like a lump." God, he was really unhappy.

"Cole, you've got a broken leg," I pointed out. "You need to rest and heal."

He sighed and fixed his gaze on the ceiling.

"Come on, Drew!" August called.

I squeezed Cole's arm and ran out the door.

Valerie had followed everyone to the barn, but she was just standing by the tack room with her hands balled up at her sides now, her horse's halter over her shoulder.

"Rest now and come with us tomorrow, Valerie," Fiona advised her as she walked past.

Valerie looked unexpectedly lost. "I'm just not *cut out* for this stuff. If I wanted to do dangerous hero shit, I'd join the marines." Despite the aggressive words, she was clearly struggling with indecision.

"No one will think the worse of you if you stay here," I told her. It wasn't like she'd signed a contract to fight strange magical creatures. She was just a college student.

Kevin grunted.

"No one except Kevin, whose opinion you don't care about anyway," I amended.

She kicked a post with almost comical anger. "*I'll* think worse of me." She stomped out of the barn.

Kevin watched her go, incredulous. "Does she just scream her way through every decision she makes in life?"

"Yeah, I think so." I didn't think that was so uncommon; Valerie was just more external about her screaming than most of us.

"Hmm." Kevin's expression was still frustrated. "You all baby her too much putting up with her temper tantrums. She's a brat who has you all trained to be afraid of making her mad. She ran out on us, then came back like nothing happened."

"Yeah, Kevin, I know," I sighed. "But getting mad about it won't help anything. She'll learn when she learns. Come on—we've got to go."

The first radio call turned out to be three untethered—our job, no sweat. There were cops on the scene already, but we ignored them and divided up to chase down the unquiet dead. The police didn't argue with us or even acknowledge our presence. They turned their attention to managing the civilians who were screaming over the ghosts and their aftermath, and we drove the aforementioned "ghosts" away to handle them out of sight.

"Are they getting harder to separate?" Valerie asked when we regrouped. She'd caught one of the untethered, but it had escaped her again. She looked uncharacteristically frazzled.

"Yes," Fiona said. "The more time they have to absorb magic, the stronger and more aware they grow. And they are picking up on the atmosphere of fear in the city now."

"Why are they moving in packs?" Kevin wanted to know.

No one knew.

"This radio is great," August marveled. "We'll have them all tracked down in no time."

"We'll clear the city perhaps," Fiona said, "but I'm certain they're spreading out over the country."

What? "Do they normally pop up away from the rift? I thought that's why we worked here."

"That is why we work here. We rectify incomplete deaths quickly so they don't escalate into these untethered beings or zombies and wander the earth." She looked around. "The magic has now likely spread far beyond the rift, and so has its effects. We are no longer patrolling an epicenter. We just happen to live in Asterville."

It took all of us to manage Asterville during a surge. What the hell were we supposed to do now if the undead were popping up all around the country where no Riders lived? Why *weren't* we doing anything about it already?

"One thing at a time, Drew," Fiona said patiently.

It's a lot easier to be patient if you aren't watching your way of life crumble around you.

The radio had kept up a steady buzz of information through the day about fires, robberies, and fights. Its now familiar static ended my existentialism for a moment.

"10-103W herd of cows rampaging through the Meadowlake subdivision," a woman reported. "Cows appear to be sick."

"Weird sick cows?" I asked.

"Mutated?" Kevin suggested.

"What?" Valerie asked in alarm. We still hadn't told her about the frogs, and I'd vowed it wasn't going to be me who finally did.

"Let's go find out," Fiona replied.

There were still plenty of semi-rural sections of Asterville outside the city center, and while subdivisions and new roads chipped away at the former pasture land, some farmers were holding their ground. We found the cows dispersed over a subdivision not far from the high school. The police officer who had called in the sighting stood on her cruiser watching while one of the Holsteins headbutted the door. Another was trying to climb the trunk. She had her gun in one hand, and she fired a few rapid shots into the cow ramming the door. The cow didn't react other than gaining a few ventilation holes.

The cows were not mutated. They were definitely dead.

August let out a "yee-haw" that nearly startled the cop into falling off the car and took off toward the cows. The ones closest to the cruiser took one look at Spyder and decided it was time to move on like good little doggies. August tipped an imaginary hat to the cop, who did not look amused.

"What happened?" Fiona asked tersely as the rest of us reached the car.

The police officer was young, her blonde hair pulled back in a short ponytail beneath her hat. She looked like a herd of dead cows was just the cherry on top of her shit-Sundae of a day. "The farmer said they all died a few days ago. They were all lying around their pond, so he thinks it was poison. And today they decided to stop being dead."

"They're still dead," Fiona said, attention already elsewhere. "We'll take care of them, but they're probably going to scatter."

"How? They won't die again. Can you herd them back to their pasture?"

"We'll take care of them," Fiona repeated. "You handle crowd control."

The cop's eyes narrowed. "Now listen here. I don't take orders from you."

"Take advice then," Fiona suggested. "Stay out of our way."

"Subtle, Fiona," Bennett murmured, voice strained.

Predictably, she ignored him. "Get the cows," she ordered the rest of us.

The cows did scatter as we chased them, but since unlike the untethered, the zombies were encumbered by the flesh they'd chosen to reinhabit, they couldn't move all that fast. They also stank to high-fucking-heaven, and little bits of them were falling off as they ran. When Charon pulled parallel with a bolting Holstein, I stabbed my knife into its neck and willed the life energy to separate. I expected it to dissolve in a brief cloud of sparkling matter, and when it didn't, I realized to my absolute horror I'd just actually stabbed a cow. There was no blood because it was already dead, but it was gross just the same. While I was parallelized with shock, the cow took off with my knife still in its neck.

Great, now I'd stabbed a cow, it was still moving, and it had my knife.

I galloped after it, trying to get level with it again. Charon was definitely faster than an awkwardly-moving cow, but he was reluctant to get close, and I had to keep an eye on the curbs, potholes, and mailboxes since his reaction to encountering one of those things would probably just be to slam to a stop. I managed to grab the knife hilt again and put more force behind the order to disperse this time. The cow stopped mid-stride and fell over, the life energy gone from the body. It took my knife with it again since Charon kept running, and I had to let it go.

I circled him back and dismounted to retrieve it. I'd thought roadkill duty was bad. At least those dead animals hadn't been running from me. As I stood, I looked up to see a family of four watching me from their living room window, mouths open. Perfect, I'd just traumatized some kids. Why didn't their parents move them away from the window?

"It's fine!" I shouted. "Being taken care of! Stay inside."

I climbed back into the saddle and went to look for more cows. I gave up using the knife since it just seemed to be getting in the way and just put my hand on the cow's neck. August and Bennett were working as an efficient team, with August roping the cow and Bennett stabbing it with his cane sword. Fiona had probably gone to the perimeter to catch those farthest away. The cop was driving through the streets using her intercom to tell the citizens to stay indoors.

Valerie caught up with me on someone's manicured lawn. "I don't know what to do! I don't have a weapon."

"Just try to herd them back toward us," I suggested. "They'll run from your horse."

"Six over here on Magnolia Street," the policewoman's distorted voice announced.

"Come on," I said, moving toward the noise.

Kevin was already on Magnolia, where the cows had crashed through a privacy fence and one had fallen into a pool already covered for the winter. Kevin was trying to catch it as it wallowed in the pool tarp.

"Valerie, just guard the end of the road," I told her. "Don't let them past you."

A man stepped out of his house with a shotgun in one hand, his determined gaze fixed on the herd of rotting Holsteins in the street.

"Don't try it!" I called.

He ignored me, but I caught the cop's attention at least.

"Do not shoot the cow," she bellowed over the car's intercom.

The shotgun blast made Charon shy so hard I ended up somewhere on his neck instead of in the saddle. The cow was unaffected.

The cop's screaming moved from the intercom to in person as she strode from the car like she was about to beat some asses and wrenched the shotgun away from the flummoxed man. Two of the remaining cows ducked their heads and made a run for the people on foot.

"Shit." I tried to put Charon between them, but he was still feeling spooky from the gunshot.

The cows bowled over both gun owner and policewoman, sending them sprawling, and I went after them. Valerie tried to block them with her horse, but neither she nor her mare were experienced with cutting cows, and she only managed to stop one of them.

"Just hold it here!" I cornered the cow between our two horses and managed to get my hand on it. It collapsed.

I went back for the other three. A woman, probably his wife, had come out to help the trampled man back into the house. He looked a little worse for wear, but the cop was upright and trying to fend off another cow that had fixed on them. She shot it with her taser, which to my amazement, froze it in place. Maybe the electricity kept the muscles from moving. I reached my hand toward the cow, then realized I'd get tased too. I made eye contact with the cop to see that she understood my plan.

"Now!"

She stopped tasing, I grabbed the cow, and a few seconds later, it fell over.

Kevin cantered up, Zephyr's eyes rolling. They both looked stressed.

A very angry man was jogging down the street after him, fist in the air. "There's a *dead cow* in my pool! You can't just leave it there!"

Why didn't people have the good sense to just stay inside?

Helen had appeared at the opposite side of the street and was trying to guard it. If she and Valerie could keep them on the street until I could catch them, we'd be set.

"Look, they fixate on moving things," I shouted above the arguing. "Get inside!"

Kevin and I went for the remaining cows while the cop returned to her cruiser and began screaming at people to get and stay indoors.

"One went that way," I told Kevin when we were done, pointing in Valerie's direction. "I'm after it."

He nodded, and he and Helen went the opposite way.

"I hate this with every fiber of my being," Valerie told me, aggrieved.

We rode past a cow with its head severed completely off. That had to be Fiona. No one else had a sword.

"Yeah, it is really gross."

Valerie huffed angrily at me. "Drew! You are absolutely loving this."

I scoffed and turned to argue with her. I did not enjoy stabbing dead cows. "I'm not loving it, it's just…"

"Fun," she sniffed. "You are having fun."

I kind of was.

A cow stampeded by on the cross street up ahead, followed by a horse and Rider. It took me a split second to realize the horse wasn't one I recognized. What?

I nudged Charon in that direction, and Valerie followed because she'd just decided to stick with me.

The horse circling the dead cow had a pearly coat that shimmered with flashes of color. The Rider's back was to us, and I tried to place her. Petite, collarbone-length black hair in a ponytail, bright yellow coat. She turned and, spying us watching, waved.

"Della?" I called.

"Hi!" she trotted over, smiling like she hadn't just downed a zombie cow. I had only met Della once before, when she'd been visiting the Asterville Riders. She looked to be in her forties, though with older Riders, you couldn't tell, and she had a chipper optimism that probably drove Fiona nuts. She was like Valerie in that she was tiny and had a sweet baby face, but where Valerie looked cute and was mean, Della looked cute and was completely nice, though she could kill you a lot faster and more precisely than Valerie could.

"We came to join you," she told us.

"You and Sean both?"

"Yep! We figured we might as well come back here with Trish and Luis until the cell towers are back up. We'll coordinate better as a group."

There was a piercing whistle in the distance.

"Oops, guess we aren't done yet," Della said cheerfully and took off toward the sound.

Valerie and I followed. There were dead cows littered everywhere, but I didn't see any more ambulatory ones until we caught up with the rest of the Riders. The last handful of cows had reached the strip of shops on the other side of the subdivision. I wasn't sure if the stores and restaurants were open or not, but people had congregated there in search of supplies, and the introduction of a few rotting, angry cows didn't go over well.

Luis and Fiona were attempting to stop them, but there were parked cars and flailing people in the way, and the horses had to dodge those too to even get to the cows. One cow climbed over a sedan, and another slammed through the glass storefront of a coffee shop and disappeared inside.

"I'll get the coffee shop," I volunteered.

"Good," Della answered. "Everyone else circle!"

I left Charon outside so he wouldn't get cut on the broken glass and went into the coffee shop on foot. I realized a few steps later, I'd made a giant mistake when the cow, having wrecked everything it could find, came barreling back out. Yeah, I was going to get trampled.

A rope shot past my face, and the cow was jerked sideways.

"Get 'em, Drew!" August howled as Spyder danced backward to keep the tension on the rope.

I darted in and put my hand on the cow's neck, getting clocked in the chin for my trouble before it keeled over. I pulled the rope back off for August and ran back out to the parking lot.

I got there just in time to see a severed cow's head go flying through the air to smack the windshield of a police SUV.

* * *

The police were ungraciously incensed at our intervention with the cows. There was an entire neighborhood littered with dead bovines and their various body parts, but Kevin pointed out very politely (because Fiona's face was getting that look like she was about to share her less delicate thoughts) that killing already dead cows was not a crime. The police chief whose vehicle Fiona had inadvertently (one assumes) thrown the severed cow head onto had shot back that the cows could not possibly have been already dead. Fiona suggested he consult with the farmer on that score. The chief spurted something about destruction of property, to which Kevin charmingly informed him the dead cows had been the ones to damage the storefront, cars, and fences. The police could perhaps charge the farmer with the damage for having loose livestock, but as Kevin said very loudly so the gathered audience could hear, that would be very cruel to the poor farmer whose cows were already poisoned.

The crowd booed, the cops decided they didn't have time for an insurrection, and they ordered us all to leave. There was another tense moment when they wanted Fiona to surrender her sword since it was a deadly weapon, and she calmly informed them it was a stage prop. Since her "stage prop" had decapitated an entire cow, no one really bought that. When the beefy-faced cop further insisted, she shrank the sword back down to a knife and put it in the sheath on her belt.

"What sword?"

"Haven't you got something else to do?" someone in the crowd jeered. "There's people stealing catalytic converters from the grocery store parking lot."

"You didn't do anything about the damn cows! Why are you mad they did?"

A bag of french roast burst open against the police car, making them all duck.

The cops gave it up. These people had no electricity, they couldn't reach friends and family, some of their houses were destroyed, and no one knew when life was going to go back to normal. If they didn't want a riot, the cops were going to have to let us go.

We left, trotting back through the streets toward Fiona's house. Della and her burly-shouldered husband, Sean, exchanged greetings with everyone as we went. We caught Luis and Trish up on everything that had happened while they were gone. No one asked why or when Valerie had returned so everyone was going to graciously ignore the fact that she had stomped out. Or the fact that she looked on the verge of tears was earning her some sympathy.

"It's good that we are all gathered now," Fiona said, in her usual after-battle pleasant mood. "You would not want to miss the creation of Andrea's horse."

I was suddenly the focus of a lot of attention.

Trish beamed at me. "Congratulations, Drew!"

"Thanks," I said shyly. "Do we really have time for that, Fiona?" I asked uncertainly. "With everything that's going on?" It didn't seem right to be taking a break from battling the horrors to indulge in something I so selfishly wanted.

"Yes," Fiona said simply. "I've already started the process, so we won't wait no matter what happens. Tomorrow night."

Cole was still on the couch when we all trooped in, though he was propped up with some pillows now. He looked alarmed at the number of people who came pouring through the kitchen door. All eleven of us were here now, everyone except Gideon, still in South America.

"Hey, how are you?" I asked him, kneeling on the rug next to him. His eyes were a lot clearer now, and he wasn't so wan. There were Barbie stickers all over his cast.

"I'm fine. Sheri fed me about six times. What did you go do?"

"Fought some zombie cows," I told him.

I expected him to go into denial-mode again, but he just looked at me.

"I'm sorry things are so weird, Cole," I told him.

"It's not your fault, Drew," he said quietly.

"I'll take you to my parents' tomorrow." I'd decided that would probably be the best place for him to recover. "They have space for you, and they'd love to fuss over you until the phones are working again, and you can decide what you want to do."

Cole didn't answer.

I looked up to notice everyone else had chosen to loiter as far from me and Cole as possible to give us privacy even though we were in the middle of the living room. I went to wash my hands, and everyone resumed affecting casual attitudes again when I returned.

Sheri had made potato soup since she'd thought that would be easy to heat at whatever odd time we returned and Fiona had a restaurant's worth of potatoes in her pantry.

"We should probably start planting these potatoes instead of eating them," Fiona observed. "I've just never had the time to garden."

"Who does?" Helen said. "Except Trish."

Trish smiled. "I mostly grow flowers, but it looks like I might need to switch to vegetables for a while."

"Sheri, you don't have to keep feeding us," Helen told her, faintly guilty. "You aren't our housewife."

"Oh, I don't mind," Sheri assured her, to August's obvious relief.

"She's bored," Kevin said. "She can never not be busy. She'll start re-wallpapering the house or something if she's here long enough."

Sheri stuck her tongue out at him.

We had a surprisingly tame night for once. We kept the radio close to answer any calls that seemed like they needed our help, but things seemed to have calmed a bit. Or more likely people were in their houses for the curfew, and there was no one to notice the odd things happening outside. The fire department responded to a small fire set by someone using a gas grill too close to a house, and cops were called to rescue people inside a car that had fallen into a crack in the pavement. The urgent dangers were fading to be replaced by the slower, more insidious dangers of no clean water, limited food, and no plumbing. The radio broadcast said the national guard was helicoptering in crates of food soon.

We played cards in the lamp light, and Bennett performed a surprisingly adroit hand shadow show for Cami and Addy that had them screaming with laughter. Valerie braided my hair in two french braids and grumbled about why did I have so much hair if I never did anything nice with it? When the kids were in bed for the night, Della and Sean told us about the things they'd seen in their area. Cole listened to everyone in silence but didn't speak unless someone asked him a question. They assumed he was in too much pain to be social, and they left him alone. I was pretty sure he was logging everything said and charting it somewhere on a big mental whiteboard—horse skeletons, cauldrons, mutant frogs, zombies. I had brought Cole into our midst, and I hadn't asked anyone to play coy around him, but I couldn't resist watching him from the corner of my eye as they talked. He was certainly gaining a new view of me.

When August retold Fiona's beheading of the cow for a horrified Sheri's benefit, I reminded Fiona she'd said I should get a sword. "So do I order one online from one of those reenactment stores or what? Steal it from a museum?"

She smiled. "I'll lend you one." She disappeared to her bedroom and returned with a long sword in one hand, steel with a silver pommel instead of golden like her own.

She held it out to me, and I stood to take it from her carefully. There was no room to swing it in a room full of people, so I struck a dramatic pose instead, careful not to stab the ceiling fan. It was heavy but well-balanced.

Fiona returned to her chair, still amused. "I wouldn't suggest you actually attempt to use that on horseback. You'll cut your own arm off. We'll have to add swordsmanship to your lessons."

"Very 'Lady of the Lake,'" Della observed.

I knew Fiona was just humoring me by letting me play with the sword, but I liked holding it more than I expected. As I turned it over in my hands, I glanced down to see August, who was lying on his stomach with his face a few inches above an open book, watching me from the corner of his eye. August was one of those perpetually dreamy people who never seemed to be paying attention even when they were, but there was something sharp, watchful in his gaze now that almost felt like someone other than August was looking back at me. Then he turned back to his book and continued reading.

Shaking off the uneasiness, I laughed with the jokes that were still being exchanged, we passed the sword around for everyone to hold, then I put it on top of the kitchen cabinets where Cami and Addy couldn't reach it.

With the house now this crowded, we just made beds on the floor where we could. The wood-burning fireplace made the living room the warmest spot, so a lot of us stayed there. Cole still had the couch since he couldn't climb the stairs, and Sheri and I made it up properly with sheets and bedding for him. I lay on the floor next to him where I could hear him breathing, thinking it was a long time since we'd slept that close.

* * *

Over breakfast the next morning, Fiona laid out our new plan for the day. "I don't want to keep the entire team working all day, every day. You'll all be exhausted. Bennett is minding the cauldron today and leaving to do some reconnaissance on the roads around the city tomorrow. The other ten of us will split into two teams to work half-day shifts."

"Not day and night?" Sean asked as he lurked protectively around the french press. It took so many batches of coffee to get us all sufficiently caffeinated in the morning that there were starting to be squabbles when someone got a second cup before someone else got their first. Sean was much too nice a guy to actually argue with someone over coffee, but he didn't need to since his linebacker bulk kept anyone from reaching the counter behind him anyway.

"Not yet," Fiona said. "Hopefully it won't come to that."

"What are we going to do when we all have to go back to work?" Kevin brooded. He deftly caught the apple slice Addy had thrown and put in back on the tray of her portable highchair.

Fiona didn't answer, but I had the feeling she didn't think we were any time soon.

"I hate that this is starting to feel normal," Helen remarked, pushing her glasses up so she could bury her face in her hands.

"Drew is having the time of her fucking life," Valerie grumbled.

"Valerie, don't curse," Bennett chided.

"Who is on what team?" I asked, ignoring Valerie. I was not having the time of my life. My regular life just wasn't as disrupted as Valerie's. She had school and sports and friends she was missing out on. My life consisted mostly of a job I hated and no longer had. A return to "normal" for me would mean eating ramen while I sent out resumes. I wasn't in the mood to try to explain that to her though. And to be honest, while I wasn't enjoying the destruction of our city and the uncertainty of our future, I liked trying to help fix things. I couldn't remember the last time I'd felt like I was doing something worthwhile. Maybe if this ever was all over, I should look into a career doing, I don't know, something helpful. Something adventurous.

I realized Fiona had been talking, and I hadn't listened to the answer to my own question.

"I'll write that down for you, Drew, since you've been fascinated by that carton of milk for the last minute," she told me. She had been sorting through a dozen or so little wooden circles that looked like they'd come from a board game while we talked. "Here, everyone take one of these."

I examined mine. "What are these?"

"They are rudimentary emergency signals," she said. "We still don't have phones. I can't believe I miss texting."

I couldn't believe she did either.

August flipped his and caught it like a coin. "Flare or find?"

"Find," she said as if this made sense. "If you break one, others should be able to find you and assist. The accuracy of the navigation is poor though. Finding spells are usually complicated and require the essence of the thing being found. I used Rider magic as the focus instead."

"How do they navigate?" I asked. They just looked like wood with symbols she had drawn on them.

"If one is broken, the symbols on the others should glow when facing its direction. They are only useful for an emergency situation," she grumbled like she hadn't just enchanted some wood scraps to find people. "I'll have to make something better since these will only work once, but we needed something quickly for now."

"I might need some more firewood for the cauldron, if one of you young whippersnappers wants to chop some," Bennett announced, pushing away from the table. "I'm afraid my old back isn't up to it."

I pocketed my token. "Can I go look?"

"No," Fiona said. "There's nothing to look at. Get ready to leave."

I was on the morning shift with Fiona, Luis, Valerie, and August. We focused our attention on the less populated south side of the county to chase down stray untethered in the more rural areas. Most of the human lives seemed to have stuck around the city, either because their bodies were there or because they were drawn to the activity of the living. The animal population hadn't been entirely spared by the carnage, and their life energies were sticking around the fields and forests as stubbornly as the humans', though more of them stayed tethered. We found an entire mangled flock of geese that must have fallen from the sky, and it turned out untethered geese were just as nasty as live ones.

"This is so sad," Valerie mourned as she looked at the dead winged deer whose tethered life energy August had just dispersed, its feathers bent from its fall.

Fiona glanced over at her, puzzled, then looked at Luis. From their silent communication, I figured they'd planned what they thought would be a lower-stress morning away from the city center under the reasoning that it would be easier on Valerie since she was still struggling to come to terms with what was going on. They had miscalculated how distressing dead animals would be for her. They were upsetting to me too, but after the cows, I was finding regular tethered animal life energies easier to deal with. I still sorrowed for the animal itself, but at least I felt like I was saving it from becoming a zombie. I had witnessed enough of the travesty that was death gone wrong over the last few days to understand why we had to do what we did, and I could focus now on righting the wrong instead of angrily grieving that something had died before its time. I was humbly grateful I hadn't been made to face the reality of the human dead bodies yet.

"Let's move on to the cemeteries on this side," Fiona suggested quickly. "I want to remove the wards."

The cemeteries were mostly quiet now, though there were several graves that had been disturbed, the coffins lying in broken shards among the churned dirt. Everything that was going to happen here had happened. Fiona examined the cemeteries and took down her wards while the rest of us tooled around to peer into the empty graves. There was no reason to keep the alarms active if she didn't have time to respond to them, and there were few life energies left anchored in cemeteries now for the mysterious cloaked man to manipulate anyway. Maybe he was chasing untethered around the city like we were.

We had brought the radio with us so we could respond to any 10-103W codes, but Fiona didn't want us to get involved in anything that wasn't untethered today. Part of me was impatient that we were taking things so slowly instead of tackling problems, but I understood. It wasn't like there was a finite number of issues out there and once we'd finished them, we'd be done. Wearing people out would just make them more likely to give up, and she was taking the tactic of protecting the team over getting more done, though I'd hazard if she were alone, she would have been working night and day quite happily.

Cole had made it to the table with the aid of the cane Bennett had brought him when we trooped back in for lunch.

"I'll take you to Mom and Dad's as soon as we finish eating," I promised. I felt guilty for making him sit here all morning.

Cole just looked at me for a long moment. "Actually, could you just take me back to the hospital?"

"Why? What's wrong?" I demanded, alarmed.

"What's wrong is everyone else is doing something to help out in this crisis, and I'm just sitting here," he replied. "I'm a doctor. Take me back to the hospital."

"Cole, you have a broken leg. You can't even stand up."

He lifted a shoulder. "I'll do paperwork. I can do sutures while I'm sitting down."

"You're still hurt and in pain," I reminded him. "If the hospital didn't need the bed, you'd still be there as a patient. Mom and Dad can take care of you for a few days, and they'll take you to the hospital after that if you want."

Cole looked at August. "August will take me."

"Dude, I fully would," August agreed, reaching for the mayonnaise, "but to be honest, I'm scared of Drew."

Cole looked at Kevin. "Kevin?"

Kevin sighed. "I'm with Drew. You need to rest."

The expression on Cole's face just grew more mutinous. "Fiona!"

I looked at him in disbelief. "She is not going to be on your side."

Fiona appeared from the living room. "He's an adult. Let him make his own stupid decisions. Besides, he spent the entire time we were gone yesterday healing his leg."

"Cole! You're going to hurt yourself worse."

"It's pretty intuitive to stop when you start to feel dizzy," Cole replied.

"You should stop well before that," Fiona said and left again.

I crossed my arms. "You cannot go up there and start trying to heal people."

"I won't," he told me, sounding sincere. "I'm not going to practice magical medicine on anyone else. I just can't sit on a couch all day waiting for the world to fix itself."

I was falling for his argument. Where was Valerie when I needed her? I took a deep breath. "Cole, if I leave you at the hospital, I won't have any way of knowing if you need me to come get you again. You're just going to be stuck there."

"I know."

"Fine," I said at last. "Fine! I'll take you to the damn hospital."

August volunteered to drive us, having apparently "found" some gas for his truck. I wouldn't let Cole go inside until one of the doctors came out and agreed he could sit in a chair and handle paperwork or consultations. I was really hoping they weren't desperate enough to take him, but they were.

"They have food for us in the cafeteria," Cole said from the wheelchair they'd brought out. "And we have beds. I don't have to leave. I'll be fine."

"Be careful," I told him reluctantly because there wasn't anything else to say.

"He'll be okay, Drew," August said as we drove back toward Fiona's. "I know you want to hide him somewhere safe, but he wants to help just like you do."

"I know." I was perfectly aware of that, I just wanted to sulk. "I'm not hurt though, and he is."

"If you were, we'd be tying you to the furniture," August replied. "If you were completely missing a leg, you'd still be out there."

"Yeah, but Cole's not like—" I broke off. I had always been the stubborn, impulsive one in our relationship. I guess I'd kind of thought of Cole as passive, which wasn't really fair to him. He was compassionate and dedicated, just in a much quieter way than I was.

"Emergencies do strange things to us all."

I glanced at August, remembering that weird little look from the night before, but his attention was on the road.

He must have felt my gaze, because he turned to smile at me as we pulled up to a stop sign. "Tonight's the big night, Drew. Let's go meet your horse."

18

Chapter 18

The sky was filled with stars and the air with the smell of meat cooking over a fire as we gathered in Fiona's garden. It wasn't the party we would normally have had, but I didn't miss it. Bennett lit the tiki torches, and Luis manned the grill while Sean and Trish laid out table wear and hamburger fixings. Helen had elected to cook her baked beans in the kitchen instead of outside, and, in an unusual display of humor, Fiona had jokingly called her a spoilsport. I had expected some rationing of the food supplies and firewood, but Fiona had pulled all kinds of meat out of the deep freezer without hesitation. Everyone who had gone home to check on their houses had brought back bags of chips, veggies from the crisper, and even a few half-cases of beer. An end-of-the-world party, leaving the past behind in style.

It was almost too cold to be outside, but I don't think anyone minded. The men gathered around the grill to do the usual grilling technique critique like they were planning an assault on Okinawa, then the burgers and ribs were passed out and the beers cracked open.

"Are you excited?" Trish asked me as I took a seat at the giant picnic table Luis had built for Fiona.

"So excited," I agreed. Anxious might have been the more accurate word. I had a plate full of food, and my stomach was so tight, I didn't think I could eat a bite of it. I looked over at the cauldron, which had been uncovered for the occasion. The liquid Fiona and Bennett had filled it with shimmered slightly with the heat of the fire stoked beneath it.

Trish patted my arm like she understood.

"You look nice," August told me, his attention to all appearances on the mustard he was squirting.

"Thanks." No one else had really dressed up since they hadn't packed party clothes, but I'd picked out a dress for this occasion a long time ago, and it had been tucked into the bin that held my horse-making stash. It was a knee-length, midnight blue cocktail dress, and I'd picked it because of the silvery sparkle across the bodice and bell-shaped skirt. The dress coordinated with the other treasures in the bin, but it wasn't really compatible with the weather. I was determined to wear it anyway, and Fiona had eventually gotten tired of watching me shiver and thrown a cloak over me. I thought the cloak went okay with the outfit. Maybe she'd let me borrow it again.

"I'm surprised you own a dress and heels," Valerie said. She was still in jeans and a cropped sweater since she hadn't packed a dress, but she must have packed her makeup bag and her hair stuff because she looked like she'd just left a salon. Valerie could have done fashionable in a mud field. She'd managed to eat ribs without messing up her lipstick. "I don't think I've ever seen you out of jeans and boots."

"Well, they didn't let me dress like that at work, so I do own exactly two pairs of slacks," I told her. My idea of office wear was whatever technically didn't violate the dress code enough to make someone bother to reprimand me.

Cami ran squealing by with a flaming marshmallow on a stick in one hand. Kevin followed in hot pursuit, arms outstretched.

"Camille!"

"So how did your Jeep get all dinged up, Valerie?" August asked her like he was mentioning the weather.

Valerie's eyes narrowed. "The road was rough." She still hadn't said a word about what had happened while she was gone, but there was a big dent in the Jeep's fender, and the spare tire was gone.

"You should get a winch," he advised. "Very helpful when you get stuck. I'll install it for you."

Out of respect for my special night, Valerie elected to just ignore him.

When the fire had burned low, and Sheri had taken the kids inside to bed, Fiona summoned us to the cauldron. "It's time."

We all moved solemnly toward the patio where the uncovered cauldron waited, steam drifting away into the cold night air. I shed the cloak and took my place next to it, and the Riders gathered around the edge. There was no light here but the tiki torches, and for a moment gazing at the sober faces looking back at me across the water, we were no different than our ancestors who had made the first horses in this same cauldron hundreds of years ago. Hoodies and sweater vests and sneakers aside, we were warriors and knights, sworn to guard the separation of life and death, diligently protecting the world from something they didn't even know threatened them.

I knelt next to the cauldron. I could see the bones of my horse arranged in the bottom through the murky liquid, full of potential and patiently waiting to be brought to life again. I took the lid off the plastic tub that held my treasures, then looked up at Fiona.

"Go ahead, Drew," she said quietly.

I had pictured this moment so many times that it felt surreal to be happening. I lifted each item from the tub one at a time, methodical and focused as the nerves vanished to some far corner of my mind. The bolt of dark blue Italian silk slithered into the cauldron yard by yard, the water sending it swirling with an unseen current. The powdered lapis lazuli pigment made lighter streaks against the dark blue until it dissolved. The dark, shiny chunks of obsidian sank into the depths and disappeared, but the polished labradorite and the raw emerald and amethyst chips hung suspended in little bursts of color. The water was churning more vigorously now, and the black raven feathers I scattered were pulled under by the current though they were light enough to float. The water was so dark I could see nothing through it anymore. I could feel the magic rising like steam, and I breathed it in, letting it fill me. I took the silver bracelet my grandmother had given me from my wrist and let it fall. It vanished without a sound. I wasn't sure what the magic would do with something so small (or how I would explain its absence), but it was the most sentimental thing I had, so it seemed like it belonged.

The surface of the water rippled, dark as ink with flashes of color when it moved. There was an unnatural hush as the Riders waited around the cauldron, an anticipation strengthened as it was shared. Cold, silvery Rider magic settled over us, stronger than I'd ever felt it. Without taking my eyes from the cauldron, I extended my arm behind me toward Fiona. My hand burned as she cut the heel of my palm.

"Pull her out, Andrea."

I put my hand into the water, letting my blood and my own magic mix with the Rider magic. I leaned forward so far I felt someone grab for the back of my dress. My arm was in nearly to the shoulder before I felt something—a velvety soft muzzle. I knew instinctively that it would follow my hand as I withdrew it. I slowly pulled my arm out of the cauldron, watching the water stir with something dark and solid rising to the surface.

As my hand left the water, a dark horse rose to stand within the confines of the cauldron, her coat a sleek midnight blue flashing with iridescent streaks of purple, green, and lighter blue as the light moved across it. The horse turned her neck to put her nose in my outstretched hand again and huffed. Her eyes were as blue as the lapis lazuli, and she had a snip of silver on her nose.

"Vesper," I breathed. "You are mine, and I am yours, for as long as we live, fighting against the darkness together."

* * *

It had crossed my mind that there might be some logistical difficulties to getting a horse out of a giant cauldron, but I assumed Fiona would know what to do because she always did. I didn't need to worry—Vesper just jumped in a move few normal horses could have managed. I had my arms around her neck as soon as she landed, not caring that her wet coat was soaking my dress. There were appreciative murmurs from the rest of the Riders, and I finally stepped back to introduce her to the team, who all came to pat her neck and congratulate me.

Fiona wouldn't let me ride her, which I knew I'd realize later when I was less excited was the right decision, but I was disappointed in the moment. I took Vesper to the stall I'd prepared in the barn and brushed some of the water from her coat, which was as silky as the fabric while still somehow feeling like horse hair. The raven feathers had added a softness to her mane and a curious double-vision effect that meant I saw feathers at one angle and hair at another. She was the most beautiful thing I'd ever seen. Vesper nibbled the hay in her feeder and seemed to be content with her new home. I don't think I would have taken my new existence so well. I leaned against the stall wall and slid down until I was sitting in the shavings. There was no way I was leaving. I'd just sleep here tonight.

The door rattled, and I looked up to see Valerie leaning over it. "Here, I brought you clothes." She tossed me an armful of fabric that landed in my lap. "I knew you weren't going to be able to leave. Change out of your wet dress."

"Thanks, Val," I told her, actually touched. It occurred to me that Valerie was the last person before me to create a horse, so she probably most acutely remembered the feeling. She sniffed, probably because she didn't like being called "Val," but she didn't say anything. It was only her here, so I kicked off the heels and began fighting with the zipper on the back of the dress. Valerie made a noise that communicated how much I physically pained her and leaned over the door to help me. I pulled a sweatshirt on and shimmied out of the dress, tossing it over the door before I pulled on my socks and jeans.

"Thanks, Valerie," I said again.

"Uh huh. I'll throw this in with my dry cleaning," she said, gingerly picking up my dress in a pincher grip.

"You don't have to do that," I told her. I wasn't about to break the news to her that dry cleaning probably wasn't going to be available any time soon. "It's just wet; it'll be all right when it dries."

"No," she sighed. "I know you won't have it cleaned, and I'll just lie awake at night thinking about it." She sighed again and left, taking my dress with her.

Fiona appeared in her stead and looked first at Vesper, then down at me. "She's beautiful."

"She is," I agreed, a ridiculous grin breaking out on my face again.

Fiona passed a rolled-up sleeping bag over the door to me. "I'm not going to bother to tell you to come inside and get some sleep. Goodnight, Drew."

"Goodnight," I replied.

I crawled into the sleeping bag and lay there looking up at Vesper, my prayer at night.

19

Chapter 19

I flipped the shaving-covered blanket off my face the next morning to see a pair of hooves as dark and shiny as black glass a few feet from my face.

Vesper lowered her head to look back at me curiously, dropping the hay she was chewing on me. Well, she was real. Her eyes shifted with deep shades of blue, as I stroked her dark forelock.

"Hey, you want to go out for a ride?"

She pricked her ears. It was probably just at my voice, not because she understood me, but I decided to take it as confirmation anyway.

It was barely light out, and there was no one else in the barn yet. I crept into the tack room for some gear I thought would fit her and scampered back to her stall. In the mundane daylight, Vesper looked like the Dutch Warmblood she really was, tall and athletic with a long, arching neck and low hocks for jumping power. Only her coat, rippling iridescent blues, purples, and greens beneath the silky navy base coloring, gave her away as a supernatural creature. She came willingly as I led her outside, not concerned about where we were going and eager for anything. She stood with the practiced patience of a school horse by the mounting block, and I took her to the arena to warm up.

I'm not sure what my expectations of a "newly-born" horse were, if training needed to be started over from the beginning. Vesper wasn't the same horse Susan had buried two years ago. If she had come out of that cauldron remembering nothing, I should be starting like I was gentling a yearling, not riding, but something about the way she had reacted to being saddled told me she remembered this whole routine. After a few turns around the arena, I was pretty sure why the original mare had been Susan's prized eventing horse. She was perfect.

I didn't realize until I dismounted to shift around some jumps that I had gained an audience. There were people sitting outside the barn, including Fiona in her fancy camping chair, and people loitering outside the house like they were trying to be subtle. They hadn't come to the arena so they wouldn't disturb me, but they were all watching me. When they realized they'd been seen, they drifted closer. I had years of competition experience at ignoring a crowd, but I got a little shy at having them watch. I took Vesper over the low jumps I'd set up a few times before I turned her toward the rail where everyone was standing now.

Fiona rubbed Vesper's forehead gently. "She's a good girl. I think she was insulted by how easy the jumps were."

"Do you think she remembers?" I asked.

"She remembers what she's capable of," Fiona replied. "Cool her down, then go feed and turn her out. You'll wear her out."

I did as she said, then stood at the pasture fence until I got told to come inside for breakfast.

"Can you feel her magic yet?" Sean asked. The kitchen table was full, and we'd spilled over into the living room to eat. "Sometimes it takes a few days to settle."

"Yes, I can feel it." I could feel it the second she rose from the cauldron. I'd felt Rider horse magic before with Charon, who was old enough to have a lot of it, but I hadn't realized how different actually being connected to it would feel. Before it was like I was standing in the rain with a bucket catching whatever came my way. Having my own horse was like someone had handed me the hose. "Has Bennett left yet?"

"Yes," Luis said. "Well, maybe. He was going home first before he went on his little tour. I don't think he'll get very far before he realizes the roads aren't drivable. You know how he is though." He shrugged. "He can't stand not knowing something."

"He has a scientific mind," Helen demurred politely on Bennett's behalf.

He did, and I'm sure Helen shared his desire for further data to catalog and analyze until the problem felt measurable and manageable. I was curious too about how far the effects of the magic explosion had spread, but I wasn't sure the information Bennett was trying to gather would be as useful as he thought. Luis was probably right that he'd end up driving around until he ran out of road, then sheepishly returning. We'd have to make that scouting trip on horseback in a week or two when things had settled down.

I was on the afternoon shift this time, so I used the morning to entertain Cami and Addy by playing stick horses around the riding arena. Having to do the jumps when you were being the horse instead of the rider was rough. When the kids had been thoroughly tuckered-out, Fiona had me do my "feel the magic" practice by sending me to find various magical workings she had around the property. I could feel the ward across her driveway now like it was a headache. It really put the dinky ones around the cemeteries to shame. She had spells everywhere, and I pretty quickly began to wish I couldn't feel them anymore.

A car door slamming shut made me look up to see Casey's Blazer parked on the street and Casey on his way up the driveway. I wondered if he was still tricking Fiona's ward, or if she had made an allowance for him.

"What are you doing here?" I asked him when he reached me.

"I have a few hours off work to rest, and I just wanted to leave the damn station house for a while," Casey said. "If I have to listen to Kenny laugh at his own farts one more time, he's going to have a sliding pole accident." He shrugged. "My house doesn't have power or food, and this one does. Besides, you can update me on what's happening, and I can covertly update Pierce. What are you doing out here?"

"Fiona is teaching me magic," I told him.

"The kind of magic she does?" He canted his head to the side cautiously as though this meant something.

My turn to shrug. "I guess so. Are there a lot of different kinds?"

Casey rolled his neck like this was difficult to explain. "Most people use spells of some sort—words, mixtures of ingredients, gestures, rituals—just anything symbolic to focus the magic where they want it to go. It's not like those things are strictly necessary; the really skilled can make up spells ad hoc. But they are still making up spells based on existing spells, altering them or building on them. What Fiona does—" He broke off to shake his head. "When I saw her by the swamp, it's like she just bends *energy* or something. She doesn't look like she's funneling or shaping it through anything but herself. I can't even tell where she's getting it."

The explanation surprised me, but the reality of it didn't. Trust Fiona to always, always be doing something a weird way. "And that's unusual?"

"She could be making spells up on the spot," he conceded reluctantly. "You know no one in my coven is very experienced, so maybe I've just never seen anyone as talented as Fiona. Maybe she casts spells so accurately it looks quicker than thought."

Maybe. We both looked at each other in polite disbelief.

"Drew," Casey said after a moment of quiet, "I know we've been over the whole rift surge and explosion thing. But did anyone ever determine *why* it happened? Why the rift just burst open like that?"

I considered. Surges were just natural, random occurrences, so we had all been treating this explosion as the same, just an unpredictable natural disaster like a volcano eruption. "We don't really know what the rifts are or why they leak magic into the world, so we don't know what forces can affect them. Maybe something geographical caused them to weaken. Maybe it was just time."

He still looked unsettled. "So you don't think anyone *caused* the explosion on purpose?"

"On purpose?" That stunned me. "That just seems like something impossible for a single person to do."

"A powerful coven, maybe?" Casey frowned. "But there is definitely one person who seems really pleased that this whole thing happened."

He was definitely talking about Fiona. "It's in her nature to just accept things the way they are," I told him. "If aliens landed on the planet tomorrow, she'd just make a plan to deal with that too. She wouldn't bother to get upset or scared like the rest of us. And I just don't think it's possible for any one person to have blown open the rifts like that."

Casey wasn't convinced, but he wasn't going to argue with me about it. "Did you ever find out who stabbed you?"

I blinked, a little surprised. Trying to figure out who had been tampering with life energy in the cemeteries had dropped to low priority after the rift explosion. I hadn't really shared any of those details with Casey though, just the attack. "No, no idea."

He nodded. "I was wondering about those investigators."

Ah, he thought they might have been involved. It wasn't a bad theory. They had come to investigate magical happenings, and the graveyard activity had caught their eye. That would explain the actions of the cloaked man with his bottle and net. "I doubt they would confess to it, but we should mention it to Fiona. She'd want to know if they were messing around in her territory."

"And that they stabbed you," Casey reminded me, disbelieving.

"Yeah, that too." Fiona probably thought I'd brought that part on myself.

"Lunch!" someone shouted from the house.

"Think they'll feed me?" Casey asked.

"Maybe some scraps if you ask nicely. Come on."

* * *

No one really questioned Casey's presence (except Valerie, who glared daggers at him all through lunch), and we left him napping on the floor of the den when we went out that afternoon. He said he'd probably be gone when we got back. I took a peek at him before we left, and he was already out cold, one arm slung above his head, his work boots dropped haphazardly on the floor next to his feet. It was sort of endearing. I was getting kind of fond of Casey. I wished I'd gotten more time with the glib, relaxed version of him I'd met before the world dissolved into chaos. Maybe I'd get to meet that Casey again one day.

Fiona urged me to continue riding Charon, saying I needed more time to bond with Vesper before I took her out to do work and that I should introduce her to Rider work gradually. I decided riding her would be the best way to bond with her and that actually doing Rider work with her would probably be the best way to introduce her to it. It's not like we were anticipating a slow spell, after all. Fiona called me reckless and incapable of exercising logic, but she was holding her hand in front of her mouth so I couldn't see her smiling by the time she finished her lecture, and she didn't actually try to stop me. It occurred to me that Fiona probably tolerated it when I did impulsive things not because she appreciated my courage but because she found me amusing.

Out of deference for my foolish decision, Fiona took me, Luis, Kevin, and Helen first out to patrol through the southeastern side of the city where neighborhoods were more sparse, houses sat on acreage, and fields lay planted with winter crops to give me a chance to test Vesper in a quieter environment. She probably hadn't been ridden on the street or out on trails before, but she was a cross-country horse, so she took the landscape in stride. She did have a moment of shock when we encountered a field of cows, and she stood with her neck rigid and ears pricked while she neighed at them repeatedly, demanding to know what these strange horses were. When they ignored her, she eventually gave it up.

"Best to watch her around animals," Fiona noted.

She was probably right. I never worried about Charon because he'd seen and done it all, but however brave and agile Vesper was, it would be years before she had that sort of real-world conditioning. She would not have reacted well to a herd of zombie cows.

A quiet day in the countryside wasn't in the cards though. The radio summoned us back to the business district and the surrounding subdivisions before we'd been out an hour. They still couldn't actually request our presence, but the cops had just started describing the untethered over the radio when they saw them as if for dispatch's benefit, knowing we would show up.

Cows, cars, and city streets aside, the untethered were the real test. Luis and Fiona cornered the first one we encountered with their horses, and I brought Vesper close enough to observe it, letting her take a good look while it wasn't moving. She side-stepped to get it in view of her left eye, sniffed the air carefully, then lunged at it, neck snaking forward to bite it. It wasn't solid enough to get caught in her teeth, and it fled, the instinctive fear they seemed to have driving it away.

"Well, she isn't scared of them," Luis noted. "That's a good start."

"She senses that the dead oppose the magic which created her," Fiona said as she turned an irritated Orlaith in a tight circle to make her stop pawing the ground. The older horses hadn't decided what they thought about the new girl just yet. "You have to show her that she can trust you to remove that source of irritation for her."

Showing Vesper how we could make the untethered go away proved a challenge. She was used to responding to sudden changes in direction at high speeds, even if the unfamiliar pavement wasn't the grass she was used to, so she obeyed my cues without hesitation. The difficulty lay in convincing her that she didn't need to attack the untethered when we reached them. I would draw level with one, only to have her turn her body to trample it at the last minute, putting it out of my reach.

"Drew, wherever did you have your medieval warhorse trained?" Fiona inquired, clearly amused at my expense.

I tried to feign some dignity as I hunted for the stirrup I'd lost in the last attempt. "Your sarcasm is unbecoming, Fiona."

Kevin and Helen had both been watching my struggle with Vesper with a sort of indulgent patience that said they were probably recalling their own early rides with their new horses.

"Were your horses like this?"

Helen patted Scout's copper-colored neck. "Our horses all learned on tethered life energies. Scout was scared to approach them at first, but they weren't moving like this."

"Zephyr may have tried to trample a few," Kevin admitted sheepishly. "He stomped all over a dead possum once." He shuddered at the memory.

"I'm afraid you have a bit of a higher learner curve," Luis told me.

"And we don't have time to indulge you while you learn either," Fiona said, eyes roving around the streets. "I feel many life energies in this area. Let's get them taken care of. Drew, just keep trying. She will understand after you catch a few."

The radio calls stayed mostly in the same section of the city so we didn't have to cover a lot of ground. The untethered were abundant enough here that I had plenty of targets to practice on. After the fifth or sixth try, I finally managed to disperse one we'd caught up to without Vesper spinning toward it, and she started to catch on that I would take care of the untethered if she would just keep moving in a straight line. I did wonder why the untethered seemed to be congregating here, but I reasoned it might be a sampling bias. The police presence was heavier here, and they were the source of the radio reports.

Now that I was able to get some work done, I noted that the untethered were strong ones too, difficult to disperse. If they had broken free from their bodies at the time of the earthquake, it made sense that they had strengthened nearly a week later, but it made me concerned for those we hadn't found yet. What would they be like in another week, or a month? We spent hours chasing them down, but when nightfall approached, Fiona turned us back toward the house.

"We could hunt them around the clock, and it still might take weeks to find every last one," she said. "There's no point in risking our own safety when the situation isn't an emergency. If the untethered begin to disturb the living, we will address that as it arises."

I assumed by "our" safety she meant mine, Kevin's, and Helen's, but I was grateful. Chasing down untethered was tiring, both physically with the riding and mentally with the magic worked. It took so much effort to get the life energy to disperse now that I felt like I'd used some invisible muscle that was left aching and exhausted from overwork.

My real muscles were being pushed to the limit too. Vesper was a much bigger and more athletic horse than Charon, and my whole body was sore from keeping up with her. I would give a hundred bucks to soak in a hot bath right now.

"The business district is barely inhabited right now," Luis murmured when we were all sitting around listlessly by the fire after dinner, his cheek propped against his fist and his eyes half-closed. "Why are they going there?"

We were all too tired to do much tonight and hoping someone would cave and go to bed so the rest of us could follow.

"Maybe they don't want to be around people," Helen said.

"I don't think that's it." Della's sleepy, muffled voice came from somewhere around Sean's shoulder. "I don't even think they're conscious of regular people. They want magic."

"There might be some magical concentration building in that area," Fiona theorized. "Something like the sewage plant sucking it in. That could attract them."

The way she talked about magic made me think of it as molecules suspended in the air. Nitrogen, oxygen, argon, and little magic to refresh the lungs. I'd ask her to explain more later when I had a spare brain wave to comprehend it.

"The radio broadcast is about to start," Sean said, looking at his watch. "Do we want to listen?"

"Too depressing," August sighed.

"I'll listen to it," Kevin said. "Just to make sure there's nothing we need to know. No point in all of us suffering through it."

When he stood to carry the radio outside, everyone took that as their cue to stumble off to bed.

"I've got the police radio," August announced as he followed Kevin.

I took the air mattress on the living room floor, but I had a hard time sleeping. I must have finally dozed off because August was kneeling next to my bed, shaking me.

"We've got to go back out, Drew. There's a big fire in the city."

I sat up. There were footsteps thumping down the stairs and anxious murmured voices as people appeared from the shadows of the dark house. "A fire? What does that have to do with us?"

"I don't know," August said. "But they called for us directly over the radio."

20

Chapter 20

"There," Fiona said, staring at the red glow lighting the horizon in the distance. Something was burning, something big enough to light the sky up.

There was a hunt for flashlights and waterproof gear as a low rumble of thunder sounded in the distance. Rain was about the only trouble the disaster-struck city had been spared over the last few days, but it looked like our luck was about to run out. Maybe it would quench whatever fire was burning.

The horses stirred anxiously as we saddled them for the second time that day, made uneasy by the weather and picking up on our apprehension. Fiona brought me a set of boots for Vesper's hooves to help her with the pavement, and I fastened her into them quickly. She danced a few steps in her stall and eyed me boldly, letting me know she was ready for wherever we were going. I stroked her raven-feather mane and felt a new calm ease my nerves.

As we prepared to leave, Fiona paused to let Charon out of his stall as she passed, stopping him only to slip a halter over his head before letting him go.

"Who's taking Charon?" I asked, slightly guilty that I wasn't now that I had my own horse. I didn't want poor Charon, devil that he was, to feel abandoned.

"He'll just come with us," Fiona said, leading Orlaith away.

Charon eyed me like he was daring me to argue, his muzzle in the air. Then he trotted out of the barn on his glossy little hooves. If Fiona didn't think he would terrorize the city, there must be a reason.

Slow, fat drops of rain were beginning to fall as we left the house behind. I could feel the snap of the ward around the property as we passed through it, like walking through a cobweb of elastic. With no street lights and no moon, I couldn't see much past Vesper's ears. Fiona muttered softly to herself in a voice that stirred the wind, and a flickering light like a torch appeared in the air in front of her horse, the flames burning nothing. Like the Israelites, we followed the pillar of fire into the night.

Running on pavement is always dangerous for horses; wet pavement even more so. Rider magic glowed silvery-blue around the horses' legs as they hit unearthly speed to protect them. Sometimes they were just horses, but sometimes they really weren't in a way that sent a chill of delight through me, like a child falling into a storybook and learning both unicorns and demons were real. The city had reached a level of quiet more intense than even the first nights after the earthquake. Fiona directed us toward the glow of the fire in the distance. As we neared, the smoke grew heavier in the air, even through the rain.

The fire was in the business district of the city, offices and warehouses burning. They would be unoccupied buildings, at least, instead of homes. The ghostly city finally began to show signs of life as we reached the surrounding streets. The people living in the nearest subdivisions had seen the fires and decided to evacuate, a prudent decision given the far-diminished manpower of the city's emergency responders. People streamed away from the fire in cars if they had them, packed with everything they could fit inside, or on foot if they didn't, crying children tossed over their shoulders. Someone passed us on a bike pulling one of those little two-wheeled carts they make for kids, the vivid yellow and red out of place in the grim parade. Every face was bleak. It said a lot that we were ten people on horses standing under a floating torch and people were tactfully choosing to ignore us.

"Hey, horse people!" a guy pulling a beach wagon with a blanket-wrapped toddler and a beagle in it called to us. "The ghosts are over there."

We all looked at him, then in the direction he had pointed. We were getting a bit of a reputation, it seemed.

Fiona went wordlessly in the direction the man had indicated, and two streets later, we understood why they had called for us over the radio.

The untethered were flowing through the streets, drifting like half-filled balloons blown in a breeze. They were solid enough to see, but they were still translucent enough to get lost in the darkness as they moved. It really was like being surrounded by ghosts. The rain that had been just hesitant sprinkling before had increased to a more determined drizzle, and the pavement was shiny with water. It was dark except for the glow of the fire in the distance and the flicker of the flame overhead.

"Should we..." Trish began, then trailed off.

I could only see a slice of Fiona's face, but I knew her posture enough to know something was wrong. "No, stay here a moment."

She nudged Orlaith forward toward one of the passing untethered, and her sword appeared in her hand. She swung the sword down and away from her horse's shoulder. The untethered wavered in place for a moment, clearly sliced through, but it didn't disappear. It began to float on again in the same direction it had been heading, the two separate pieces starting to lose contact with each other as they went.

It was too dark to really make out any features, but the untethered was obviously human in shape, and the sight of it severed in two and still trying to move was chilling. I heard someone I was pretty sure was Helen whimper behind me.

Fiona gave Della a questioning look. Della shook her head slowly, her mouth open in shock.

"Give it another go," Sean urged. "Maybe enough dispersion from the whole will weaken its cohesion."

Fiona darted toward the untethered again and cleaved the top half, which was bobbing slowly above the ground, proving the untethered didn't really walk so much as they just floated where they intended to go. When the now-three pieces of the life energy continued to hang around, flickering feebly, Fiona punched her sword into its midst and held it there, concentrating.

With a burst that hurt my teeth, the untethered dissolved into a cloud of life energy that hung briefly in the air like tiny golden motes of sparkling dust before fading or being swept away.

"Did it work?" Kevin asked.

"I don't..." Fiona studied the place where the untethered had been. She looked uncertain.

I had been frightened by some of the unnatural things we'd faced over the last week, and I was unnerved by the horde of untethered slithering through the darkness now, but adrenaline had mostly overridden any fear reaction until the danger had passed. Now that fear was beginning to crystallize in some dark, cold spot deep inside me. If Fiona was uncertain, there was something very, very wrong taking place.

Fiona looked up and tossed her head, regaining control of herself. "I believe it was rendered harmless, but no, that did not feel as it should. Still, we might be able to lessen the burden, and we must continue as best we can. Spread out to the adjacent streets, but stay within sight of each other. We'll work parallel. No one wander far from the group."

With the floating torch extinguished, the eerie red glow of the distant fire was amplified against the sky, and we continued slowly up the dark street, trying to sever each untethered without startling the others into fleeing. They weren't currently agitated, and if we approached them quietly and at least got a hand on them, we could hold them before they attempted to bolt. But it was instinctive for them to avoid our magic, and once we touched them, we had a limited window to subdue them before they escaped us or grew aggressive. They were so hard to separate that it was like throwing a rope around a sleeping bull only to have it wake up and start thrashing. Some of them we could manage individually, but some of them took two people. Valerie and I teamed up to combine our efforts.

"Shit," she whispered as we walked next to a bobbing untethered we couldn't seem to disperse, both of us breathless and sweating with the effort. "What the hell?" We had to break into a trot to keep up with it as it pulled in vain against us.

I raised my head to look around for someone stronger, ready to admit we needed help. Sean saw me and trotted over to lend a hand. Under the sharp edge of his hand axe, the untethered dispersed at last.

"Try combining your magic together instead of just both attacking the same one at the same time," Sean told us. "It will amplify the result."

The staccato of hooves on pavement drew our attention as Kevin pounded by in pursuit of a fleeing untethered. He must have startled it, or it was strong enough to have escaped him. Sean followed to help him chase it down.

"What was he talking about?" Valerie asked, frustrated.

"I *think* I know. I'll show you on the next one."

I scanned for our next target, and my senses were drawn by the usual feeling of wrongness, very strong this time, toward an alley between two buildings. There was a figure lurking there in the shadows, and it took me a moment to understand that it couldn't be an untethered. The rain went right through the untethered because they weren't solid, but it was bouncing off this human-shape. A person? It made a jerky movement that was so outside the way any person could move that I abandoned that possibility immediately. I found the flashlight I'd put in my jacket pocket and pointed it at the thing.

It was a corpse, standing upright in the tattered remains of a burial suit, fragments of skin stretched across the bones of his face. The wrongness of lingering life energy burned within him. I'd found one of the zombies that had torn open the graves. Trying to keep it in my sight, I looked around for help. Despite Fiona's admonishment to stay close, we were getting more spread out now. The newer parts of the city zoned for office buildings and warehouses were designed with cars in mind, big parking lots and wide streets between buildings. No one was near enough to summon without shouting except Valerie.

She stared at what lay in the beam of my flashlight. "Drew, I don't think you should touch that."

"Go find Sean," I told her, and she turned her horse to go.

I approached the zombie-thing cautiously. Okay, this was just like the cows. Disgusting, but manageable. Unlike the untethered, its head moved to track my approach, and a chill went down my back. I nudged Vesper up to it sideways and reached for it, hating the way my hand trembled. I did not want to touch a dead person. He had been dead so long I wasn't sure what was holding his body together except magic, but I couldn't escape the knowledge that he'd once been a loved human being. His suit was soaked through, but dirt and other gross stuff still clung to it. Just do it, I told myself, gripping my knife in my sweaty hand until it hurt. The undead watched me from eyeless sockets, then turned with an unexpected speed and lurched away down the alley. I chased it reluctantly, still not sure what to do.

We emerged the next street over with me still not having worked up the nerve to stab or grab it. I could see both Fiona and August on this side though, and I tried to drive the zombie toward them.

Fiona noticed the zombie and came cantering up, her sword raised. I stopped and stayed out of her way. I knew she was going to slice through it, but the sight of the sword cleaving its brittle, half-decayed body still made me have to lay my head against Vesper's neck for a minute.

"It didn't feel anything, Drew," Fiona told me. "It does not live."

"I know," I mumbled into Vesper's mane. "That was just gross."

A scream from behind us had Fiona galloping past me faster than I could sit up. I turned Vesper to follow.

There were more zombies in the street now, and both they and the untethered present seemed to have grown agitated. One of the dead bodies had caught Valerie's leg, its toes dragging on the pavement as her horse galloped by. I wasn't sure if it was trying to hurt her, or if it just didn't have the capacity to let go. She couldn't free herself because it was taking everything she had to stay in the saddle of her panicking horse.

"Hold still!" Fiona called to her, nudging Orlaith after her.

The remaining zombies congregating in the street fixed on me and August as he rode up behind me.

"Be still," August said quietly.

I was, but I could tell Vesper wasn't going to let the strange things approach her without bolting. She was already starting a sideways jig. "What, are they drawn to movement?"

"I don't know." His voice was contemplative, but he didn't sound afraid.

Kevin and Helen came riding in from the opposite direction, probably drawn by the sound of Valerie's scream. Kevin had a length of pipe he'd picked up somewhere in one hand, and when the nearest zombie lurched in his direction, he swung the pipe at it like it was a baseball bat.

Every dead thing in the street rioted.

"Well," August said, "not the greatest." He nudged Spyder forward into street, rope already twirling over his head.

Kevin's impressive swing had crumpled one side of the zombie's body, but it had done nothing about the life energy. It was trying to clamp onto Zephyr's leg, and Zephyr was protesting immensely. Another was reaching for Helen, who was backed up against a wall, Scout's ears pinned back in terror.

There was nothing else to do but dive in too. I wished I'd brought that sword with me; I was certain I would *not* have cut off my own arm. I tried to stab one zombie and didn't succeed in doing more than cutting its desiccated flesh. I needed a second person. I looked at August, but he was almost to Kevin, a broken skeleton in tattered cloth lying on the asphalt in his wake.

I pushed Vesper forward, trying to reach Helen, but the dead things were beginning to surround me. One latched its decrepit hand around my ankle, pulling with strength but no intelligence. I kicked it hard enough to make it release me, but while I was occupied with that, another grabbed the rein of Vesper's bridle, pulling on her mouth. I slammed it with everything I had to make it let go before it hurt her, going lightheaded from the force I'd sunk into felling the zombie

The thing let go of the bridle as it collapsed, but it was too late. Vesper decided she'd had enough. She kicked out, successfully clipping a zombie in the head hard enough to knock it over, then made a sharp spin on her hindquarters and bolted. I was already leaning to the side from reaching for the zombie, and that was all it took to corkscrew me right out of the saddle. I landed on top of the zombie, which was both disgusting and painful. It was still fighting me, so I fought back, screaming through my gritted teeth as I willed the life energy inside it to disperse. The skeleton disintegrated in my hands as the energy left it, leaving me headache-y and nauseated. Another came right after it, and I scrambled to my feet. I still didn't know what exactly they wanted to do to us, if they could do anything, but it's human instinct to fear something that tries to grab onto you.

I was on foot now, but I still had my knife. Maybe if I damaged the body badly enough, that would slow them down too much to chase me. I kicked the next one in the side of the knee like I'd learned in my one semester of self-defense class in college and heard the bone snap. I plunged my knife into its shoulder and pushed until I started seeing little black dots in my vision. I could hear someone I thought was Trish calling me, but I couldn't look. I was so tired, I didn't think I'd manage the second one, but it crumbled unexpectedly to reveal Spyder's legs. I looked up at August, who was unhurriedly winding up his rope, then back toward whoever was calling me.

"Drew!" Trish urged. "Come stand between us." She and Helen had formed a wedge with their backs to the wall so the dead couldn't get behind them.

I started to obey before the sound of hooves drew my attention down the street.

Orlaith came galloping back down the street toward us, Fiona with her sword blazing in one hand. She took out a passing zombie, then whirled toward another. She was glowing golden again, a sure sign of her magic building. She stopped in the street a few yards away, Orlaith's sides heaving and steaming in the rain.

"August!" Fiona called like a summons through the darkness.

August looked steadily back at Fiona as if waiting for something. He didn't seem concerned about the dead bodies circling him. They weren't reaching for Spyder, and I realized now they were no longer reaching for me either while I was so close to him.

There was a note of apology in Fiona's voice I didn't understand. "August, I need your help."

The seriousness in her tone stunned me, and I tipped my head back to study August in confusion. He had only been with the Riders for a few years, and I didn't think he had a lot of magical skills. What exactly did Fiona expect him to do?

August must have known though, because he looked resentful, then resigned. He lowered his gaze for a moment, and when he raised his head again, the beachy-blond, laid-back frat boy had been replaced by a cold-eyed, world-weary viking. I don't think he'd changed anything but his posture and expression, but I suddenly got that same pit-of-your-stomach feeling I got from Fiona when it felt like she'd let her human-seeming slip for a moment. August left whatever he had been before behind and joined Fiona in her hunt, moving Spyder forward with preternatural speed and grace. The two of them tore down the street, burning through the hoard of zombies. Fiona swung her sword like a knight on the battlefield, while August's rope lashed itself around the dead bodies with perfect aim as he galloped by, fire and magic sizzling down the rope without burning it. I got the impression that August could have moved a lot faster if Spyder had been capable of it.

Now that I was no longer standing in August's invisible force field, I moved quickly to stand between Trish and Helen, but there was no need. The remaining undead had begun to flee instead of fight. Luis and Della had arrived, and they joined in to pick off the untethered that lingered as the zombies fell. The rest of us stayed out of the way. I couldn't see Valerie, but Fiona wouldn't have left her if she'd been hurt. She must have told her to stay put, and, unlike me, Valerie would actually do what she was told.

"Okay, Drew?" Kevin called.

I gave him a thumbs up. Fine, but on foot, which felt vulnerable. I had to find my horse.

"Stay here," Trish said firmly.

"Got to find Vesper," I replied and took off before anyone could stop me.

With the street cleared, I jogged in the direction Vesper had gone, hoping she wouldn't continue to run from the untethered. My hip hurt terribly from impacting the pavement, but I sure wasn't going to look at it tonight. Everyone knew injuries weren't real until you saw them. The sky still had that eerie red tint to it, and I was starting to smell smoke. I must be getting closer to the fire.

I found Vesper on a side street where she'd stopped, probably uncertain about where to go. The other Riders must not have passed her, or she would have joined the safety of the herd. I checked her over, and she was trembling but unhurt.

"Don't feel bad," I told her. "They scared me too."

I could see more untethered up ahead of us, and I followed in pursuit. As long as it wasn't dead bodies, I could manage. And all the dead bodies had been taken care of by an inscrutable magical terror in a woman's skin and her ponytailed sidekick. Seriously, what the hell was up with August? A question for tomorrow, I told myself.

I followed the untethered down a side street and heard shouts. I rode toward the sound, expecting to find civilians cornered by the dead. Instead I was met by a dense fog of smoke and ash. I'd reached the fire. I moved closer, trying to verify no one was shouting for help. A little further, and I saw the flashing lights of the ladder trucks through the haze, then the firefighters scattered around the five-lane street in front of a warehouse. Both the warehouse and what looked like every other building down the row was on fire.

The firefighters had hoses aimed toward the blaze, but it didn't seem like they were accomplishing much. The flashing lights from the trucks reflected off the black water on the streets and the walls of the buildings still standing in a hectic pattern. There were untethered here too, drifting around the emergency workers like jellyfish. A firefighter swung an axe at one that was entangling itself with a hose, and the axe passed right through it to spark against the asphalt.

I pushed Vesper toward it, and the force of her presence drove the untethered away from the firefighters. I edged close enough to stab it a few times, hoping I could catch it by surprise. I didn't, and it struggled back, pulsating with its inability to control its strength. I couldn't control mine either anymore, I was so tired. I took a deep breath and concentrated on my connection to Vesper and to the rest of the Riders. Rider magic grew stronger the more of us were gathered together, that shared power what allowed us to ride so fast or conceal ourselves when we were together, and I could reach for some of that strength now despite the short distance between us. I buried my knife into the untethered's body and willed the particles to separate from each other. It exploded in a cloud of mist.

I left the stunned firefighters behind to concentrate on their own work and chased down another untethered. This one fled from me, which under the circumstances I figured was the better outcome. The rapid tapping of little hooves caught my attention, and I turned to see Charon, eyes rolling, come barreling down the street toward a loitering group of untethered like he was planning on trampling them to dust. They prudently retreated as best their limited instinct could manage, moving away like the pony was an opposing magnet. He darted across the street to send a few more scattering, then continued to herd his fleeing untethered away, throwing in a crooked little buck for added sauce as he went.

I was wondering where he'd been all night. I guess Fiona had a reason for bringing him after all.

With the street cleared of undead threats for now, I looked for Casey. The firefighters were identical under all that gear, but I found Casey when I saw him put out the fire on a piece of debris that landed near his feet with a wave of his hand. He went back to sweeping with the hose. If he could extinguish fire with his magic, why wasn't he? He couldn't have heard me over the noise, but he sensed Vesper as we reached him, and he turned to look.

I leaned down so I could shout next to his head. "Why don't you use your magic?"

Casey unlatched the strap on the back of his helmet to loosen his mask. "I can't do a big enough section to be worth it. Get away from here. You're going to get smoke inhalation."

I looked up at the black smoke billowing from the warehouse in front of us. The firefighting efforts were so ineffective, they'd be better off just guarding the edge of the subdivision and letting the fire burn itself out. I dismounted instead and held out my hand to Casey, my other hand on Vesper's neck.

"Try it again," I shouted to him. I had given Cole strength once; maybe I could rally some for Casey too. That I didn't really know how I'd done that seemed less important now than I *try*.

I couldn't see much of his face through the mask, but his dark eyes held a world of frustration. If I thought it was ludicrous he couldn't use his magic to fight this situation, Casey found it infuriating.

"Try!"

Finally Casey wedged the hose against his side under his arm, seized my hand in his gloved one, and stared at the flames consuming the building. He didn't have a free hand to gesture with, so no physical aids to the conducting. I don't know how he was holding the hose except the water pressure was weaker than it should have been. I hadn't been able to shift much magic to Casey when Fiona had had me try before, but that didn't worry me now. I hadn't had Vesper then. I didn't have a connection to Casey like I did to her, but I knew what it felt like to share magic back and forth in a way I had not before, how not to become frightened into clamping down on the flow out of self-preservation. Logic and uncertainty would only interfere, so I let them both go. I hadn't trusted Casey enough before, but I trusted him now.

I could feel the magic in the air around me as surely as I could smell the smoke, and I tried to visualize pulling it in, inhaling it with every breath. I mentally reached for Casey and found him waiting. My attempt was tentative, wobbly, but Casey had a lot more experience at working magic, and the flow steadied between us. I let him take over, trusting him to manage it. He let the current go through him and out again toward the fire, both of us knowing instinctively that holding it in would fry us. The flames began to die like they'd been smothered, blinking out across the top of the building in a wave from left to right that followed Casey's gaze.

I watched the flames at first, concentrating completely on Casey and the electricity running through the two of us so I wouldn't lose it and hurt either of us. Then I stole a glance at his face, fixed in concentration behind his mask, eyes wide with the effort this was costing him. I realized he was glowing faintly in the darkness, and when I looked down, so was I.

Someone else had realized what we were doing, and the hose was pulled out of a Casey's hand where it had gone motionless. Something snapping around my head almost frightened me into losing my concentration, and I realized as something appeared in my vision that someone was trying to fit a pair of goggles over my face. I held still, and the goggles were followed by some sort of mask over my mouth and nose, probably one of those hi-tech medical masks because it got easier to breathe.

Casey tugged my hand as he moved further down the street, following the fire he was putting out. My world had narrowed down to keeping the stream flowing, and I could sense it wasn't going to last much longer. As usual, I was all enthusiasm and no training. The magic around us was getting thin, and I couldn't reach further for any more of it. I followed Casey, legs moving numbly, trusting him to lead.

There were still other people around us because someone was trying to cover me with something and struggling to do so without jostling me. I couldn't tell if the roaring in my ears was the fire or a warning from my own brain to stop.

"Casey," I croaked. "Got to stop now."

He couldn't possibly have heard me, but someone else repeated my words at a thunderous volume, and I squeezed his hand to let him know it was coming. He squeezed back, and I cut the flow, successfully stopping it both into and out of me in near tandem so I didn't fry any circuits. I let go of Casey's hand, and the asphalt smacked my knees.

Someone scooped me up, then tried to pry Vesper's reins from my hand. When I wouldn't let go, they just carried me with her presumably following behind. A few steps later I was settled down next to one of the firetrucks, and the mask and goggles were pulled off. My vision was clearing up now, and I wriggled around to be a bit more upright. Hunter, one of the firefighters from the frog incident, was kneeling next to me, and he squirted me in the face with a plastic water bottle, leaving me sputtering in a really undignified fashion. Vesper waited patiently at the end of my outstretched legs. Someone had threaded a wet cloth through the noseband of her bridle since they couldn't fit a mask over her muzzle and thrown a couple of fire blankets over her to protect her, a consideration that touched me to the core. I realized I was wearing a fire blanket too, tied on like a toga.

I looked for Casey, briefly panicked, but he was sitting next to me, drinking a bottle of water with his eyes closed.

"Stupid!" Hunter said. "Impressive, but stupid. Can you do it again?"

I shook my head. "Tired."

"Oh well." Hunter disappeared.

I let my head fall back against the truck and closed my eyes. Just one more minute and I'd get up.

Someone ruined my one more minute by sticking what I guessed was the world's driest emergency protein bar in my mouth. In less desperate times, maybe I could say something to the firefighters about their bedside manner. I tried to chew the protein bar, because I probably did need it, but it was like trying to swallow sawdust. Next to me, Casey looked like he was scraping up the strength to wade back into the firefight. He looked at Vesper.

"Where's the pony?"

"This is my horse!"

My sudden enthusiasm clearly startled him, but Casey nodded politely. "Very pretty!"

The falling drizzle suddenly intensified into a downpour. Shouting in the distance caught my attention, and I dragged myself to my feet and rounded the truck to look, Casey following close behind me. There was a woman striding down the middle of the street toward us, her bare arms raised above her head, startling white against the darkness. Above her black clouds roiled in time with her step. I twisted to take in the entirety of the sky around us—the storm was concentrating itself around the woman.

As we watched, she gestured violently like she was casting the clouds toward the burning buildings, and the torrent of rain followed. The street was drowned in a downpour that was almost blinding, but it was working. The flames were dying. I flipped my blanket-toga up over my head like a hood so I could see. In the middle of the deluge, the woman spun like a dervish, pulling the clouds tighter and tighter around the burning section of the city. In the distance I could see clear sky where she'd pulled the storm so far in.

"It's Alice!" I shouted to Casey over the deafening noise. "The investigator!" I clarified when he looked confused. She had shown up to help after all. I hoped she didn't get in trouble for it. I pulled one of Vesper's now-soaked blankets over her head in an attempt to stop the rain from blinding her. She wasn't a happy horse right now.

There was nothing we could do while Alice was working. The rain had reached hurricane levels of force, and it was almost impossible to move or hear anything. But there wasn't really a need for anyone to do anything now. The firefighters had realized the rainfall was extinguishing the flames, and they hunkered down to wait it out. They didn't have to wait long. Alice lasted another two or three minutes, then sat down hard in the middle of the road, clearly exhausted. The rain didn't stop right away, but the clouds had been nearly drained, and the deluge eased now that she wasn't pulling on them so forcefully. Two of the firefighters jogged out and chair-lifted her away to one of the trucks.

"Well, that was something else," I said. I didn't see any flames left, but the street was ankle-deep in water as the storm drains were overwhelmed.

"Yeah," Casey said, half-dazed. He turned to look at me. "Climb into the truck. You're shivering."

I was, but I wasn't about to hole up and relax. I started to fight with the knot on my blanket-toga. I was still wearing my raincoat under it, and by some miracle, I wasn't completely soaked, though my shoes were full of cold water. I pulled the blankets off Vesper, who *was* unfortunately completely soaked. "I'm going to catch up with the other Riders."

"Drew." Casey's voice was so tired that I almost felt guilty, like I was the reason somehow. I looked at him, and I could tell he was about to repeat the request for me to get into the truck where I'd be safe and he would know where I was, but he just stared out at the smoking ruins of the business district. When he looked at me again his face was resigned. "Be careful, Drew."

"I will," I promised.

Casey looked down, then up at me again through his eyelashes. "You won't. I barely know you, and I can already tell you just blunder recklessly into things."

"Well, then you should also know I'll figure it all out somehow," I replied brightly.

"Yeah, okay," he said softly. "Come back, please."

"I will," I repeated.

I climbed back into my now-soaked saddle, which squelched water under my weight in what was probably one of the most uncomfortable sensations I'd ever experienced. I gave Casey a farewell wave and started off through the flooded streets to find the rest of the Riders.

* * *

A few streets later, Vesper was still sloshing through pastern-deep water, but I hadn't found anyone. The darkness was enveloping away from the lights of the firetrucks. The rain had reduced to a mist again, but the sky hadn't cleared enough to let moonlight through yet. This part of the city had evacuated, and I might have been the only person left in the world it was so lonesome. Where was everyone? I could feel the wrongness around me, lurking but not aggressive. I took out my flashlight and clicked it on.

The street was full of untethered. That alone probably meant there were no Riders nearby. I studied the vague human-shaped outlines, pondering if I should attempt to take them out. I was recovering pretty quickly from the duet Casey and I had performed because the magic had mostly just gone through me, not been used by me, but I was still tired, and separating these extra-powered untethered took enormous effort. I let Vesper walk along with the untethered as they drifted down the street, trying to make our their blurry faces. Long french braid, business suit, cowboy hat, pigtails. A child. Ugh. Half a body floated past. Someone had cut into it, but they must have lost track of it before finishing the job.

We reached an intersection, the dead stoplights swinging in the wind overhead, and I saw more untethered join the crowd. I had thought they were moving away from me and Vesper, but when I drew her to a halt, they kept going. They were all moving steadily in the same direction. Where were they going? Was it on purpose? They were mindless, but they did react to stimuli. Maybe they could sense the concentration of Rider magic behind them and were moving away from it. I was certain now I was going the wrong direction, but I was curious.

A mile later, the number had continued to grow, and I could see them moving on parallel streets as I crossed intersections. They were definitely moving toward or away from something. I decided I wanted to know what. I looked back over my shoulder. The business district, what hadn't burned down, was nothing more than a faint outline now. "You just blunder recklessly into something," Casey had said. Yeah. He wasn't wrong. I decided to keep following the untethered. Fiona would find me. She had her ways.

The further I went, the more obvious it became the untethered were moving with purpose. Half an hour later, I was far outside the city proper, following their trail as they moved steadily toward their unknown destination. They were gaining speed as they moved, and Vesper was cantering to keep up now. Their route narrowed as they went now that there were no buildings to separate them. I wasn't sure what good finding out where they were going would do me, but I felt strongly that finding the source of the life energies' agitation would be the solution to stopping them.

The sky had cleared, and there was at least a little light to see, which helped more than my flashlight did. The big houses with their expansive yards passed by, then fields, then the treed land far outside the city, a little state park where people came to camp and walk on the hiking trails. Evidence of the rift explosion was present here too. The woods were littered with downed trees, and the branches above us were probably full of loose limbs that would fall at the next strong breeze. I was about to make up my mind to just return to the edge of the forest and summon Fiona from there when I noticed the untethered were disappearing somewhere instead of continuing their strange, forward path. I edged a little closer, carefully examining the ground with my flashlight.

There was a deep gash in the land I didn't think had been there before the earthquake. The ground had split, and the earth on one side had been shoved upward into a hill of mud jumbled with broken trees. The untethered floated around the ravine, bumping against the raised hillock like light-blinded insects until they found their way inside. Whatever they were being drawn toward was inside that dark crevice.

The memory of the yawning darkness the night of the car crash swelled around me until I couldn't breathe, the dim landscape around me beginning to vanish as if eaten by rolling shadows. I couldn't see, and I was about to be drawn into the void I had just barely escaped last winter.

Vesper snorted and began to paw the ground, her hoof striking a rock with a decisive noise. She turned a circle in place before I could react, and the darkness recoiled again. I leaned forward until I could lay my head against her neck. I was not dead. And hell, even if I was, I wasn't about to stay that way.

Time to investigate. Vesper moved like she'd read my mind, and we descended into the ravine.

It wasn't as deep as the darkness had suggested to my frightened mind, only about twelve feet or so, but it was full of uprooted plant life, giant chunks of dirt, and even the odd boulder or two, and it made a forty-five degree turn halfway down. I knew I should leave Vesper here so she wouldn't get hurt on the treacherous footing, but I had a real fear that she was my only source of bravery at that point. The flashlight found a narrow path at the bottom of the ravine as if something had already walked there.

I looked up and was certain I saw the flicker of a light around the bend of the ravine. Was someone else here, or was it just the reflection of my own flashlight? If someone was there, there would be no concealing my approach. And no way to quickly escape. The untethered continued to stream by me, toward whatever waited at the other end. They did not want to come anywhere near me or Vesper, but they were being drawn too strongly to avoid the danger. They might as well have been sleepwalkers.

I should just go back out and go around to the other end of the ravine where I could see, I reasoned. Vesper decided that was enough prevaricating and started forward. I wondered if the other Riders were as bullied by their horses as I was by Vesper and Charon. Vesper picked her way delicately through the rubble, neatly jumping a log that crossed her path without being asked. She paused at the bend as if giving me time to make up my mind. There was definitely a light reflecting dimly off the side of the ravine. I took a deep breath and dismounted so I could creep around the edge of the bend, crouching low to the ground like that might conceal me somehow.

There was a man standing in the bottom of the ravine with his back slightly toward me, a dark cloak swinging from his shoulders. The cloak was something fancier and cut more narrowly than the one Fiona wore, like an opera cape or an academic robe, and the hood hanging down the back showed a purple-striped lining. The man's head was bare, revealing graying brown hair cut in a short, nondescript men's style. It was the man from the cemetery, I was sure of it, even if the cloak was the only thing I had to go on. It couldn't be a coincidence.

The man had a lamp and a little gas stove like my camp stove set up on an oblong boulder like it was a table, the source of the light I had seen. Over the stove was a large bowl, wisps of steam rising from its surface. The semi-translucent bodies of the untethered wafted around him.

As I watched, barely breathing, the man reached out and pulled one of the untethered toward himself. He pushed the object in his other hand into the untethered as Fiona had done with her sword, willing it to separate. The untethered shook, its mouth gaping and limbs flailing like it wanted to get away but didn't have the cognitive ability to know how to do that. After a moment, it dissolved into a cloud of sparks, each infinitesimal molecule of energy pushed apart from the others.

That was the point where the energy of life was meant to return to the ecosystem of the world, to be born again in something new. But the energy of some of the stronger untethered back in the city had attempted to reform itself, refusing to forget the memory of its previous shape. This untethered had no chance to even do that because the man spun a miniature cyclone of air with a whip of his wrist that kept it from scattering. The whirlwind drew the tiny motes down into the pot on the camp stove.

What the hell was he doing?

The man turned as he lifted the pot by its handles and took a sip from its edge, and this time the sharp angle of his jaw and the aquiline nose were familiar. My breath caught as I rocked back against the side of the ravine to conceal myself.

Bennett.

What was he doing out here, and *why*? Did anyone else know? I didn't know what he was attempting with the life energies, but rationale told me it was outside of Rider duties. And if Bennett was the man from the cemetery—that fucker had *stabbed* me.

"I know you're over there," Bennett said quietly, the sound carrying toward me like we were the only two people in the world. "Either come out or go away."

I looked at Vesper for inspiration, and she pricked her ears at me. Well, I wasn't about to run away from him. I quickly fished Fiona's wooden medallion out of my pocket, snapped it in half, and put the pieces back. I stood and stepped out where he could see me.

"Ah, Andrea," he said. "You shouldn't be out here by yourself."

Trying to guess if I *was* alone. "What are you doing out here, Bennett?" I asked him in as level a tone as I could manage.

He was watching me very closely, his body language non-threatening but alert, hands loose, shoulders tight. He wasn't afraid of me or ashamed of anything he was doing. Or he was an excellent actor.

"I'm attempting to find a solution for these overactive life energies," he replied. "We need to know what differentiates them from the others so we know how to properly disperse them."

Half-truths were always more compelling than outright lies. "And you decided to do that out here by yourself." Where none of us would know.

"The magic is strong here," he replied. "The rift must be beneath us. Fiona can't have allowed you to wander this far by yourself. You should be getting back before she worries about you."

"You said you were driving around the outskirts of the rift territory," I said. Repeatedly refusing to confirm I was alone wasn't going to fool him, but I still wasn't going to admit it.

"I am," he answered patiently. "This is part of it. I'll drive some more of the county tomorrow. The roads are difficult to navigate." I saw the skin around his eyes tightened just a bit in the uneven glow of the lantern, and my instincts went on high alert.

"You were the one who warded the old graveyard," I said. "You were doing something with the life energy there before the rift ruptured. And you were doing something in the cemetery the night that *you stabbed me.*"

That finally seemed to fluster him a little bit. "I didn't mean to stab you, Andrea. I was just trying to push you away. You are a surprisingly strong girl, and I miscalculated."

"If you weren't doing anything wrong, why didn't you just say, 'Andrea, it's me'?"

"Well, I didn't know it was you," he insisted. "I just knew someone came flying out of the woods toward me."

I didn't believe that somehow, but I hadn't known it was him either. Bennett was no fighter, and it was possible he'd just panicked. That still didn't explain why he was being so secretive about whatever it was he was doing. "But what were you trying to accomplish? Why are you working on this by yourself?"

He drew his eyebrows together, getting annoyed at me now. "Andrea, not everything is your business. You are very new to the Riders, and there are things the older magic-workers of our group study that you are not a part of. When you are more experienced, you may become part of those things as well."

I could easily believe that was how Bennett thought. He came from a time when young people, especially girls, were quiet when older people told them to be. But that definitely wasn't how Fiona thought. Fiona, so old she had lived through plagues and wars and the rise and fall of empires, would not have refused to explain something to me if I asked her.

This was the time when I should have meekly agreed with Bennett and left to wait for Fiona and let her deal with it. I wasn't sure he would really let me leave since he couldn't doubt exactly where I was going if I did. But maybe he really believed I would buy that his actions were sanctioned or maybe he had a plan to explain this to Fiona later.

More likely if he got rid of me, he'd abscond somewhere. If I could keep him talking, Fiona would have time to reach us. I'm sure she could track him down later, but it would be easier if I delayed him. He was a scholar at heart—some part of him had to be bursting to talk of his genius ideas. "How did you get them to congregate like this? We could use that to lure them out of the city."

He nodded cautiously, not falling for my curiosity but willing to pretend to keep me pacified while he decided what to do with me. "They are drawn to the energy I have already collected here with the addition of a summoning spell that targets their essence."

For a man who repeatedly insisted none of the Riders but Fiona could do any real magic, he sure could do a lot of magic. "So now that you've figured out a way to call them to you, why aren't you dispersing them?"

Bennett's eyes were like black pools with the harsh lighting to his back. "We have the unique ability to sense and capture the very energy of life. There's so much that could be done with it, if we tried. Cures for illnesses. Youth for the aged. We only need to *try*. This great influx of magic is the perfect time to master it, and yet we waste our time pursuing the petty problems of one city instead of solving the great problems of mankind."

I looked around at the untethered, still gathered around us, though they wouldn't come too close to either of us without force. "Bennett, if you take the energy from one thing and give it to something else, won't that create an imbalance in the universe or something? Everything about this feels wrong."

I looked back at Bennett just in time to see him launch something at me. For a split-second, I thought it was the lamp from his stone table, and I raised my arm to shield my face. But what hit me was a spell, likely one meant to make me pass out because my ears rang and I felt suddenly very, very faint. I'm not sure why the spell didn't knock me out immediately, but it frustrated Bennett. He reared back like a baseball pitcher to launch another, and every cell in my sluggish body panicked as I fought to move. I was only still upright because my knees were locked and my shoulder had caught the wall. If I lost consciousness, God knew what he was going to do with me. When he threw the second spell at me, I screamed at it to stop with every fiber of my being.

If the air had been thick with magic in the business district, it was almost a mist here. I grabbed onto it like I had before, but there was nowhere to send it, and I didn't know how to shape it. Bennett's spell shattered in front of me like it had hit a glass wall. Whatever I was holding wasn't letting anything else pass, and I tightened my mental grip. The first spell that had hit me began to fade as well, and the feeling came back to my limbs. I straightened to face Bennett, who was growing red with frustration. He launched a hot ball of air at me that sizzled as it flew. I willed my shield to stop it too, my panic that it wouldn't pouring strength I couldn't control into it. The third spell felt different; he wasn't trying to make me sleep this time. He threw a fourth, then a fifth. The effort it was taking me to hold him off was already making me tremble with exhaustion. I had no training to temper what I was doing, and I knew I was hurting myself.

There was a soft neigh behind me, and I reached back mentally toward Vesper. I felt her magic connect to mine as if something had clicked perfectly into place. With her strength added to mine, I immediately felt less tired, stronger, more alert. I pushed that mist of magic I was holding in place toward Bennett to drive him back. I needed to think of an exit plan here. I couldn't outlast him, even with Vesper. I would eventually exhaust her too.

Bennett screamed something incoherent at me, and a wall of fire smashed against my shield. I could feel the heat even through my magical defenses. I needed to hit him with something offensive. I didn't know any spells, but I was holding this wall up without one. Maybe I could throw a rock or a gust of wind to knock him over. I made a thrusting motion toward him with one hand, thinking to shoot a force at him to knock him down.

A patch of red appeared on Bennett's shoulder, a knife sprouting from its center. For a long, stupid moment, I thought I'd done that somehow. Then the knife exploded into a full-sized broadsword. I looked up to see someone standing on the edge of the ravine above us: Fiona, glowing faintly in the darkness. She looked down at Bennett, the anger in her face fit to rival Nemesis in her winged glory. Bennett was staring down at the sword through his body, his mouth agape, one hand reaching for it feebly. He tipped over backward and landed with a soft thud. Fiona gave me a brief, appraising look, then disappeared again.

21

Chapter 21

Bennett wasn't dead. He was, in fact, so full of the life energy he had consumed that he not only didn't die, he healed quite quickly.

He confessed under what I imagine was the ultimate torture of Fiona simply asking him a question in a stern voice to everything he'd already admitted to me in more detail and with passionately-explained motives. I wasn't really surprised by that as he didn't seem to believe there was anything wrong with his actions other than that other people wouldn't approve. He was experimenting, and he stubbornly believed the knowledge he gained would have benefited us all.

I curled into the corner of the couch and watched the other Riders' faces instead of Fiona's as she gave her brisk, factual summary of her interrogation. Only Luis, Della, and Sean had been included in the discussion of Bennett's crime and punishment, so the rest of us had gathered to learn the outcome of their investigation. Expressions were cautious, wary of discovering more betrayal. Kevin wasn't bothering to hide his anger, his hands on his knees as he leaned forward in his chair like he might shoot to his feet. August apparently had declined to participate.

While they generally agreed, Luis explained in a slow, tempered voice that said he was hating every minute of this conversation, that while what Bennett had been attempting was far outside the Rider ethos, there wasn't a specific rule he'd broken anyone could point out in an official codified document. The old-timey Riders pledged an oath, but it was a short declaration to uphold the values and work of the Bone Riders, not a detailed set of rules. Whether someone had failed to uphold this oath was a determination made by fellow Riders Socratically. And as all decisions were made by group consensus, there were no established punishments codified anywhere either. They had decided to place Bennett under house arrest for the time being.

I listened until Kevin started shouting, then decided I needed some time to think. I gently shrugged away the protective arm Trish had wrapped around me and left for the barn. I appreciated Kevin's outrage since it was on my behalf, but I had known as soon as I'd seen Luis's, Della's, and Sean's faces that whatever decision had been made, had been made by Fiona. There wasn't going to be any changing her mind.

About an hour later, Fiona joined me in Vesper's stall, but she let me sulk for a little while without speaking.

"Okay, why?" I asked at last.

"Because I do not have the authority to punish him more thoroughly yet," she replied. "There is little precedent for this situation; rarely have the Riders had need to exile a member. A condemnation of such magnitude cannot be done without the agreement of the most veteran Riders. At a time when we were few and saw ourselves as a single group, we could meet to form a consensus on such grievous matters, but we are not able to reach anyone outside our own group for now. Here, the only veteran Riders are August and myself, and I am loath to proceed without the judgment of Riders not from our own group. When we do this, I want it to be unarguable, no possibility of claiming unfairness."

I could get wanting a solid trial, but it wasn't like he was going to get his case thrown out for lack of due process. I also didn't see why these mythical "other" Riders had any input in what our group did; if we had formed separate groups now, we should judge our own problems internally. And Bennett was still dangerous. "You're letting him go on a technicality? Aren't there different provisions for times of emergency?"

She turned to look at me now. "I want him where I can see him, Andrea. I can't take his magic away. If I just cast him out, God knows what he's going to get up to with no one knowing. He isn't going to stop. I've been trying to gather evidence of his schemes for a while, and I will continue to do so as long as he stays in my line of sight. I want him under my authority so I have grounds to monitor his behavior." She let her head thump back against the boards of the stall, letting on how frustrated she was. "And I'm probably the only one who can handle him, so I have to keep him here."

"To what, scold him lightly if he gets caught doing something else?" I asked bitterly.

Fiona shook her head. "Eventually he'll either get a proper trial, or he'll do something so stupid I'll have to kill him, and no one will be able to challenge my decision to do so."

"So trying to kill me at that ravine doesn't count?"

She twisted her mouth in disgust. "Yes, if he'd had the decency to die then, it would have. Your life being in danger was reason enough. But I can't kill him in cold blood a second time. Now we have to wait."

I shredded a stalk of hay into tiny pieces. "That's stupid."

"Yes," she agreed. "And he isn't getting away scot-free, Drew. He's under house arrest, and I've placed some spells on him that limit his ability to work magic."

She'd said she'd been trying to gather evidence of his schemes. "Did you know what he was up to before?"

"I suspected he was doing something with the life energy, but I didn't know what, and I didn't have any evidence. I didn't want him to know I suspected him until I had enough proof."

"I guess I just charged in and messed that up."

"Oh, I don't know. You caught him in the act, and you summoned me to catch him too." She shrugged. "If nothing else, I saw a fight in which you were on the defensive, and he was on the offensive. I wish I'd witnessed him actually capturing the life energy. He may have gone rogue scientist, but he has a clever mind. I'd like to understand the implications of what he's done so I can monitor the consequences."

"Do you think anything will happen to him after drinking the life energy?"

"It made him stronger," Fiona pointed out. "Or standing directly on top of the rift did if it's still off-gassing a little. I'm watching him to see what happens to him, which is another reason to keep him close by, but he isn't foolish enough not to hide things from me."

"I'm not sure how I was able to fight him," I admitted. "I don't know how I did that or how I helped Casey, except that I tried to do those things."

"I don't want to disappoint you," she said almost dryly, "but your magical feats probably have less to do with your talent than with the concentration of magic in this place right now. If the magic dissipates the way I think it is going to, you'll be back to learning to do things the hard way. And as for how you held your own against Bennett, you've got a knack for reacting in an emergency. Self-preservation is a powerful instinct. You've learned enough magic to be able to feel it, and you pulled on what little you knew to hold that magic between yourself and Bennett. You did well under the circumstances, but we've got to get serious about training you now. That sort of reaction isn't consistent or guaranteed, and if you came up against a trained magic-worker, you likely wouldn't last long. Worse, if you keep doing that without knowing how to temper your power, you'll kill yourself."

A sobering thought, that.

"You showed good control over how much magic you were feeding Casey from the sound of it," she continued. "I'm sure he helped; he has talent, if not the training for it. But I really don't want you to try that again without oversight." She looked at me sideways. She wasn't going to give me an actual order here; it was up to me to recognize the danger to my own life.

"I won't unless I am afraid for my life," I promised.

"Good," she said, standing and brushing the shavings off her jeans. "We'll get started on that tomorrow. And don't worry too much about Bennett."

"Because he'll get what's coming to him?"

"Because he knows I'll kill him because I've already tried it once," she corrected with a smile and walked away.

My second visitor was Casey. He stood with his arms resting on the stall door for a long time, looking down at me where I was now lying on a horse blanket, having decided to sleep there, his expression unfathomable. We didn't speak. Finally, he let himself into Vesper's stall with the cautious look of a man unfamiliar with horses. When she didn't rush him for the door, he came to lie down on the horse blanket next to me, squeezing between me and the wall. I scooted over a little so we wouldn't be squashed together.

"There's beds in the house, you know."

"I know. Fiona told me what happened."

I let out a painful sigh. "Yeah."

"It's a pretty big betrayal," Casey said. "But it sounds like in the end the only harm done is a lost colleague."

"Yeah, if you might remember, he also stabbed me."

"You were pretty nonchalant about that at the time."

"That's before I knew it was Bennett."

"From August's harrowing description, it sounds like he got stabbed back way, way worse," Casey pointed out.

"I guess that's true," I conceded. "What did you come over here for, Sheri's cooking and our working plumbing?" Casey's presence at my back was pleasantly warm, and I was having a really hard time remembering not to roll over to him. He was being careful not to crowd me, but he was a big guy, and I hadn't left him much of a gap.

"I actually came over here to tell you two things. The first is that some relief trucks have rolled in with generators and supplies. They had to get off-road army vehicles to bridge the gaps in the road, but they've got water and gasoline. They'll be rationing the generators to the medically vulnerable first, but they brought crews of electricians in too, so you might have electricity again in a few days."

"Awesome. What about the sewer system?"

"They're coming up with a short term plan, but I think they're trying to bring more portable toilets in for now. You've got to go get a cholera vaccination when the hospital starts offering them. The next wave of this disaster is going to be disease."

Cholera. Wow, what century was this? "I'll do that. What was the other thing?"

"The police are ready to officially liaison with the Riders. The state government is arranging a meeting between police, emergency workers, and representatives of magic-workers including the Riders and some witches. I'm not sure what will come of it, but they have at least reached the point where they're willing to consider it."

Enough zombie cows, flying deer, ghosts, overgrown blackberry vines, and sudden tar pits would do that. "Do you know the witches?"

"No. They're from a coven a few hours south of us. The witches have collectively decided to come selectively out in the open." He didn't sound particularly thrilled about that.

"Collectively and selectively?" I echoed.

"They decided as a group to admit their presence to the world now that the existence of magic is pretty much undeniable," he explained. "The soldiers brought a lot of news with them. There have been several covens who decided to do what the Riders did and help out as best they could. As for selectively, they decided only covens who could reasonably defend themselves should admit their presence." His sigh stirred my hair. "It's going to get really nasty, Drew. People don't like witches, and this isn't going to change everyone's mind."

He was right. Even the people who were pleased we'd solved their problems for them were going to be revisiting the old "burn at the stake" thing once their lives started to return to normal as if we were just a reminder of how strange things could be.

"Are you going to be 'out'?"

Casey grunted. "Everyone at the fire department knows now. They haven't decided if they're going to make me play poster boy or tell me to keep it locked down yet. I'm guessing if they decide it has to be a secret, I'll be out of a job in a few months."

"A firefighter who can put out fires with a wave of his hand seems like an asset," I pointed out, insulted on his behalf.

"I can't make much of a difference that way unless I'm holding your hand, and I can hardly drag you around with me," he said. "How did you do that anyway?" he asked me after a few minutes of silence.

"Fiona says it was mostly the high concentration of magic in the area," I explained with a half-shrug. "Apparently pulling it in is something I can do under life-threatening stress and I need to stop doing it until I've had some supervised training because I could accidentally kill myself."

"That sounds like good advice. Do you think she'd teach me too?"

"Yes," Fiona said from somewhere by the barn door. "Both of you come inside and sleep in the house like intelligent people." The door shut behind her.

We were both quiet.

"So how long do you think she was there?" Casey asked.

"I just assume she's everywhere at this point."

Neither of us moved.

"So what's the deal with Cole?" Casey asked me in an overly-casual tone.

I wriggled around on the blanket to get more comfortable. "He insisted I take him back to the hospital so he could help people even though he has a broken leg and he needs to rest," I grumbled.

"Of course he did," Casey replied. "He's a doctor. But I meant what's up with *you* and Cole."

Uh huh. "I'm sure you used context clues to guess he's my ex-boyfriend."

"So why did you dump him?"

"I appreciate your assuming I won the breakup, but he broke up with me," I sighed, not particularly wanting to talk about this yet again. I didn't need one more person to have an opinion on my love life.

"Why?"

I rolled slightly until I could see Casey, my shoulder bumping against his chest. "What do you mean why?"

"Well, did you cheat on him with his brother? Run up his credit cards? Do you snore?"

My narrowed eyes were having no effect on him. "What's it to you?"

Casey picked up the end of my braid and brushed my nose with it, letting me know he was only teasing and I could ignore his prying. "Because it's hard to believe a guy that smart could be dumb enough to let a girl like you go."

I rolled away from him again. "Sometimes things just don't work out."

"Eh, but sometimes they do," Casey remarked. He sounded suspiciously pleased, and I didn't know why.

He dropped an arm over me loosely, and I decided not to tell him to move it. He didn't speak for a while, and I looked back at him to see that he'd fallen asleep. Leaving him by himself in Vesper's stall would be stupid, so I just went to sleep too.

* * *

As fun as the old hay lofts were for summertime lounging, hay is extremely flammable and can spontaneously combust under the right conditions, so most people who have to store a lot of it have a separate building. Fiona's "hay shed" was a cavernous steel structure thirty yards past the barn, and since Fiona had already bought hay for the winter, it was filled to its lofty roof.

I climbed the stack with a quick little prayer that it was packed tightly enough not to fall on me and crawled across the flat plateau at the top to where August was lying on his back, his hands tucked behind his head. I lay down next to him, our faces only two feet from the roof. He'd done an admirable job of avoiding all of us over the last few days.

I breathed in the sweet, grassy smell. "I used to like to do this when I was a kid."

He didn't answer right away, and his voice was soft when he finally spoke. "Me too."

"Della and Sean are about to head home if you want to say goodbye," I told him. As the magic that had erupted from the rift dispersed away from Asterville, the tide of new untethered had slowed and so had their growing strength. We weren't sure what the new baseline for the city would be, or what that spreading magic would mean for the rest of the country, but we would figure out a new plan for our new normal. "I'm going to go stay with my parents for a day or two, now that things have calmed down a little. My apartment still doesn't have power, so I'll probably be back when they start irritating me. I just wanted to see you before I left."

"You should spend some time with them," he agreed.

He still sounded so subdued that some little part of my heart ached for him, though I didn't even know why he was sad. I let the quiet stretch for a while.

"Okay, old man," I said gently. "What gives?"

He didn't look at me. "When your life just goes on forever, you find ways of coping with it," he said at last. "When I feel like I'm getting tired and life doesn't have any savor anymore, I like to start again to try something new."

So he was old.

"So you just build a new persona?"

"Nah, I'm always me. It's more like I just find something else I want to be interested in. When I lost my last horse, I was starting to think maybe this should just be the end of it. I could let myself age and die and be done with everything"

We both contemplated the weight of that for a while. I couldn't imagine the burden of my life stretching on and on like that and trying to determine if I was tired enough to let things go. That sort of sadness was so unlike the easygoing, untroubled August I knew that I had to swallowed back the tears threatening to close my throat.

"Some of the other Riders convinced me to come hang out with Fiona for a while," he continued. "You don't do a whole lot here, so I wouldn't be devoting my entire life to Rider work. I went to college and learned all the computer stuff and started some hobbies. It was nice. Made life fun again."

"I guess this whole rift explosion kind of ruined that for you." I would have hugged if he was the hugging type. "Sorry about that."

"Eh." He did his best to shrug while lying down.

"So how old are you, August?" Lying here now in his jeans and hoodie, he still looked no older than I was. No wrinkles, no gray hair, a young, athletic body. I wondered how your body decided at what point it would stop aging. Fiona looked to be in her forties.

He scoffed. "Never ask a Rider their age, Drew."

"Are you as old as Fiona?"

"Nah, not as old as Fiona. She's her own special case."

Interesting to know. I rolled onto my side and propped my head on my elbow so I could see him better. "So I guess she has her own way of coping with the aging thing."

"I think Fiona copes with the past by pretending no past exists," August replied in a carefully neutral tone. "There is today and occasionally tomorrow."

"The past is a foreign country," I quoted. "She knew about your past though, and she was letting you start over without telling anyone."

"Well, one of her better qualities is not feeling the need to push her own ethos onto other people. She understands, at least, how I feel, even if her solution to it isn't the same."

I plucked at a loose hay tie. "Casey thinks she's happy the rifts split open."

"Part of her probably is," August said without judgment. "She would love a world where she could finally work magic and be herself openly. I'm sure having to feign subservience and respect to people you could turn into ash bites at times. And I'm sure she gets bored. Not a lot of new challenges for her."

"Casey also thinks she was responsible for the rifts' explosion somehow."

August turned his head now to fix that too-sharp, too-knowing look on me again, and my breath involuntarily caught. I understood why he affected such calm now, dreamy eyes always gazing at something in the beyond. We would never have fallen for his "start over" if he looked at us like this.

"Oh, yes," he said. "If anyone did open the rifts on purpose, it was definitely Fiona." He tucked his hands behind his head again. "But hey, this might get fun."

About the Author

Cady Fletcher, former horsey kid and current archaeologist, enjoys traveling, reading on patios, and collecting animal bones in the woods. She doesn't reanimate them, just keeps them in the shed (she promises).

www.ingramcontent.com/pod-product-compliance
Lightning Source LLC
LaVergne TN
LVHW100516110826
845146LV00002B/664